Survival of the Fittest

KEVIN LOGAN

Survival of the Fittest

A Third Millennium Thriller

HarperCollinsPublishers

HarperCollins*Publishers*
77–85 Fulham Palace Road
Hammersmith, London W6 8JB
www.fireandwater.com

First published in Great Britain in 1999 by
HarperCollins*Publishers*

1 3 5 7 9 10 8 6 4 2

A catalogue record for this book
is available from the British Library

ISBN 000 274043 5

Printed and bound in Great Britain by
Caledonian International Book Manufacturing Ltd, Glasgow

To Linda –
my better half and research partner.
To Peter and Cathryn
and their future.

MY THANKS

Once upon a time the general consensus was that everything revolved around planet Earth. On its flat surface, the agreed antidote for sickness was bleeding patients with leeches. It was accepted that if a man could run, climb and swim like other creatures he would one day fly like the bird he envied.

In our fallible world, consensus may develop in any area of life simply on the accumulated say-so of generations. Ideas become accepted, not because they have been proved to be true, but because they have been repeated so many times that they must be true. We cannot conceive of life without them. That is, until another way is shown.

My gratitude goes to those who dare to go on thinking the unfashionable, the unthinkable, the unacceptable. It is for those who prefer personal evidence rather than general consensus; for the 'little boys' who refuse to accept that the king is indeed wearing new clothes; for those who see the nakedness of things which have not been demonstrated to be true.

I thank three such questioners for the scientific, moral and technical stimulus for this book. They are Professor Michael Denton (*Evolution – a Theory in Crisis*), Professor Phillip Johnson (*Darwin on Trial*) and Brian Leith (*The Descent of Darwin*). Professor Miriam Rothschild and her work on nematode worms, was also an inspiration. Karl Popper's philosophy of science has been hugely influential for many, especially when he asks whether evolution is, strictly speaking, scientific. Is it testable, as any scientific theory should be? So far the answer has been 'no'.

My gratitude extends to many more individuals to whom I owe so much for the research, the ideas, the corrections, the support and the encouragement. I especially thank my bishop, the Rt Rev. Alan Chesters of Blackburn (I'm an Anglican vicar when not posing as a novelist). The sentiments of this and my other books may not always coincide with his, but nevertheless his strong, believing and caring leadership has done more for me (and many others) than he will ever know. I thank God that he is the exact opposite of the first victim of our thriller. To all, and especially my family, my deepest gratitude.

Kevin Logan

1

The pinkness around the bishop's puffing jowls was a giveaway. Even the least observant bishop-watcher would have known that the Right Reverend George Henry Williams was close to eruption on his personal Richter scale.

The enforced march through dark woods and snaring undergrowth released snorts of steam and perspiration. Each one built up, rather than eased, the pressure within the heaving purple. The bishop would have blown much earlier, but for the appearance of the double-barrelled shotgun. It had done wonders for his self-control. However, a body had its limits, and the twin barrels prodding his well-cushioned rear at each hesitation were stoking rebellion.

From what he had seen so far, en route from Bishop's Court to this god-forsaken wood, the bishop believed he had the measure of his abductor. He could tackle him. No trouble. Just a question of timing. How could anybody take seriously a sad-faced clown topped with a day-glo orange wig and kitted out in a harlequin romper suit? Surely he, the Lord Bishop of Hoghton, must be the victim of some stupid student prank.

This, of course, was the judgement of optimism. The realistic compartment of Bishop Williams' substantial brain knew that rag-week stunts and firearms did not normally go together. And, besides, other possibilities hovered. Those angry – very angry – churchgoers last week, for instance. He had merely hinted that Jesus Christ was 'arguably the best magician who had ever miracled a few loaves of bread', and they'd gone berserk! Blown their tops! Perhaps one of them had caught that rather nasty transatlantic fundamentalist habit of shooting opponents.

There was also another, slightly more fearful, more immediate, query: why had they left the car in a remote lane behind WildWorld? And why were they now trekking ever nearer to its howls and roars? As this worry nagged, another sound seized the bishop's attention: a whimper of pain? He stole an over-the-shoulder look. Was that a limp? A disabled clown?! George Williams was not one of nature's external smilers but that part of his mind which probed for weakness in others did lighten a shade. A chink in an enemy – and most two-legged creatures fell into that category – always made his day.

The ever-nearing growls at that moment reached a fresh climax; an odd, untamed cacophony not heard on the Lancashire moors of northern England since they were cloaked in primeval forests. The bishop's patience threshold was now perilously close, and the jowls blazed bright red. Anxiety and exertion brought rapid breathing to a figure whose normal aerobics were no more than altar genuflections. The final explosion came with a sudden faceful of wire fence.

'Enough! Enough!'

The bishop recoiled in fury from the outer barrier of WildWorld Safari Park. The hand that bore his episcopal ring was clenched and raised high, and the attitude was not one of blessing. The other hand tenderly cradled his stinging nose.

'Listen, I'm getting tired of this hu—!'

The shotgun barrels buried deep into his ample midriff, jangling the silver cross of office to one side. His knees gently bent towards the earth.

'Bishop!' The word hissed out of the darkness. 'At this present moment, tiredness is not exactly your greatest problem. Take and cut.' Something was thrust towards him but the tears of exhaustion blurred the outline.

The last words, almost consecrational, made the prelate look up and wipe his eyes. Oddly, the voice was faintly familiar. The cadence was haunting. A face danced just beyond memory's fine focus. The shape of his abductor gave little away; not age, not temperament, and only shadowy proportions. The ludicrous thigh wings curving outward from the harlequin jodhpurs didn't exactly help. The eyes – George Williams always looked there first for hints of weakness – remained unblinking and cold. They were centred in white circles, each slashed from brow to cheek with black eye-liner. Even now, when reflected moonlight should have added at least a glint of life, there was only deadness. Unreadable, emotionless eyes. No weakness. No fear, yet creating fear.

'Take and cut.'

With the gun cradled in one arm, the abductor's free hand once again thrust forward what the bishop now identified as long-handled wire cutters. The prelate gasped noisily as he rose up, again setting himself to challenge. He had a certain pride in an inner arsenal which included a daunting indignation – rage, some said. It was usually reserved for those of lesser status than his diocesan self, like minor clerics who had stepped outside his grace. Wayward vicars were curtly reminded that their titles were, after all, merely shorthand for the bishop's vicarious underlings.

The Right Reverend Williams haughtily spurned the cutters, jutted forward his jaw, stretching most of his chins out of sight. He then gave his intercostal muscles permission to stage what was always an impressive preening of the chest.

'Uuff—!' was all he painfully managed as his embryonic pomposity was aborted by a ramming muzzle.

This time, the pectoral cross flicked outwards and upwards, hitting him sharply in the forehead as he bent to

3

the blow. The bishop fell heavily into the wire mesh of the fence, the impacts of gun and barrier depriving his lungs of oxygen. No longer a Lord Spiritual, the form now retched for survival.

The gunman abruptly pinned the heaving frame to the undergrowth, one knee pressed down on the neck and the other against an arm. The bishop hardly noticed the pinprick of a syringe followed by a leaden inpouring into the sacred rear. It was nothing compared to the craving for rush upon rush of great draughts of forest-flavoured air, even though tainted by the drifting tang of wild animals. Once lungs were at full throttle and life was assured, his eyes opened on strange bell-shaped legs and the dangling shotgun silhouetted against the full silvery-blue orb in a dark velvet sky. Now, there seemed time to relax. The idea of panic the moment before was suddenly quite amusing.

'How absurd,' the Bishop of Hoghton grinned crookedly. The moon suddenly turned into a sixpence, spinning and pirouetting around crowds of clouds. Within, an intoxicating pleasantness soothed the labyrinth of his Lordship's veins.

'Now,' the cutters rapped his forehead, 'take and cut.'

This time, the voice was almost gentle, even sad, as though breathed through dried-up, tragic memories. It seemed to pronounce that an issue of great import was nearing its end.

* * *

The metallic schlock-click of the artificial lung was no more. Only quiet. The instruments were dead. So too was Sammi.

Her skeletal face and frame were wizened and shrunken. Her one-time rose-fresh skin was shrivelled crepe. Once, she had been large. No. More accurately, titanically massive, and proud of it, for Sammi made mini-buses bow towards her as she hauled herself on board. Sean Connaughton leant against the bed in the intensive care unit of Hoghton Royal

Infirmary. His eyes were full and his chest lead-heavy with a sadness that made swallowing difficult. A slight smile came as he recalled the effects of Sammi on his own car springs.

He felt the quiet; stood in the shadows surrounding death.

'Be still,' he silently recalled a poem. 'Be still and know...'

'Know what?' The Reverend Sean Connaughton suddenly choked out the next line. 'Know that you're God?'

An eavesdropping angel might have filed it under blasphemy but not the man. Nor his Maker. It was blunt honesty. It came in the wake of a friend retching up three times her massive weight in as many years. Later would come the understanding. Now he wanted what was natural: somebody to blame.

He looked down at the still, slight figure. 'Your own silly, stupid fault!' Sean regretted the words almost before they sobbed out, and his thoughts carried on the monologue: 'She'd never listened ... swore she'd never shared needles...' Endless, big-eyed denials. Massive overt manipulation exerted only by those so heavily abused in childhood that they could not conceive of human relationships working in any other way. Futile, obvious lies.

'Of course she had used infected needles. She had! She h—'

Anger burst out. It was aimed at himself, at life, at the Creator; at Sammi herself. His eyes smarted, but no more than that. Tears might well up, but never to be shed. That was not the Connaughton way. Control. Calm. Fighting for calm. Hurts padlocked behind the mental security shutters. The existential today blotting out half-forgotten memories of yesterdays.

He forced the mind elsewhere, and looked at his watch – 1.45 a.m. Home by two. A note to the mother-in-law not to wake him. A lie-in on one of those rare bank holidays. Most of the last seventeen days had been one long wrestle with the final throes of AIDS and Sammi. Or so it had seemed. Of course, there had been the bustle of his lively parish and his enjoyably demanding family. There was also the bad-tempered news editor who came with the part-time reporting job Sean had taken on to help pay his wages and keep his church open. The crazy existence gave him little time to think. Soon, even Sammi would be interred in some half-forgotten mental vault.

'Hard work never killed anybody.' His mind suddenly echoed with the old northern adage. It justified his mad, kaleidoscopic existence. Not that he conned himself deliberately. Strive for integrity he might, but he was simply too human and weak to be absolutely honest with himself. He worked because if he did not, he would remember. And that he simply could not allow.

He negotiated the dogs and armed guards at casualty. Nowadays, it was the only access since those turn-of-the-millennium anniversary riots a handful of years back. The Third Millennium had promised so much. A new epoch. A caring, sharing age. Humanity in maturity. Yet so little had been delivered: only more of what humanity wanted less of. With the millennium just two years old, right-wing hatred had exploded against political ultra-correctness; foreigners had been stoned; gays had been hunted and lynched; the multi-starred flag of Europe ceremonially burnt.

Connaughton patted one of the German Shepherd dogs, wished the guard 'Good morning', and walked out into the warm May darkness, across orange sodium reflections on a wet hospital car park.

* * *

The wire finally cut, a bemused bishop was prodded through into the woods beyond. There was now no mistaking the night's noises. The big cats of WildWorld roared at the advancing crashes as the bishop clambered and lunged clumsily, sometimes with a laughing jig-hop. He was amused, especially by the voice behind. No longer was it embalmed with fear. Now, it was just plain silly.

'Do you pray?' asked the voice.

How absurd! He, a bishop! Of course he prayed. Maybe not to some myth on a throne of clouds. Not to a giant-fingered deity stirring fate and fortune. No. Nothing make-believe like that. Nevertheless he had a mystical, soothing, transcendental communion of inner meditation – with himself, the universe or something.

The bishop giggled as he stumbled against a second wire fence. Nice long theological words swam and failed to fall into the right order, so the cleric drooled, grinned and rested his forehead in a somnolent posture against the cool wire.

The clown with the gun moved away. Rust rasped against rust and a thin wire hawser snapped taut by the resting head of the bishop. He jerked away as a narrow guillotine door began to rise before him. The higher it grated, the closer some ill-defined anxiety seemed to float.

'Pray, bishop.' The voice was too flat to be beseeching. The bishop giggled all the more.

'Amen!'

The word was emphasized with the abductor's hefty foot on the bending sacred posterior. The bishop tumbled under the now fully risen door, and the grating began again. This time from two entirely opposite directions; one guillotine falling behind while another rose ahead.

It was only then that the fear swam – no, pounced! – clearly into view. A terrifying orchestra of vibrant, thoroughly dangerous-looking throats materialized before him.

'O God help me!' screamed the bishop, and he really sounded as though he meant the prayer. He had no time for an amen.

The clown gave one final wrench of a winding wheel to secure the shutter of the holding compound. He stood watching a large lioness. He recognized her as Jezebel. She was shaking the remaining life out of the now still figure, arched face upward and held by the neck.

He waited for the rush. Satisfaction. Achievement. Revenge. Nothing came. It had been quick: perhaps too quick. A massive head framed with dark mane appeared under the open shutter from whence the lioness and her cubs had emerged. Ahab posed briefly like some stuffed wall trophy, but then rushed to put his mate in her place. She killed. He devoured. She and the cubs could have what was left.

'Live by it ... perish by it.' The killer's voice was as lifeless as the corpse at which it was aimed.

He swung away and slumped backwards against the fence. The sinews of his jaw sagged with the weight of disappointment. His gloved hand parted the velcro front fastener of his tunic, and he withdrew a long brown envelope. He opened it to check the white paper contents, then licked and closed the flap before ramming it into the wire mesh above the shutter door.

No feeling. Just deadness. No relief. There had been none with the first victim either.

Maybe the next...

* * *

'Dad!'

At the end of his tether, Dad screeched to a halt.

'How many times do I have to tell you?' He swung round, snarling at the trio of noise-machines his ex had dumped on him shortly after 6.30 that morning. 'We're in a car and this is not the World Screaming Championships of two thousand and—'

'But—'

'No buts!' shrieked Father as though going for outright victory in the same contest. 'Not another squeak!'

He turned back to the wheel with a finality the kids feared. The three brothers knew they had reached the line over which they feared to go, unless one of them was feeling particularly suicidal. With Dad, words could be safely ignored; even outright orders. You could even laugh at him, without consequence. But when the anger exploded ... well, that was different. That was the boundary after which came certain and painful action. With Mum, the line always came with crisp first words, and you simply obeyed.

The car began to inch away from its emergency halt.

'Dad! Are you deaf or something?'

Dad snapped. He swung round and flailed with a wild fist at the origin of the noise – his eldest; always the lippy one. It sent the lad flying into the armrest of the back seat.

'Why,' Dad snarled, 'even the baboons we've just left wouldn't have squatted for that!'

Come to think of it, the driver suddenly thought, how could monkeys live in harmony while supposedly sophisticated Homo sapiens mangled and murdered each other? And how come there was more civilization in a baboon compound than in his car?

'Pleeease.' This time the voice sobbed in a submissive, wheedling way. The boy rubbed his chest and stubbed a finger on the inside of the side window. 'Over there, Dad.' Then a hint of righteous reproach was added as Father's eyes swivelled. 'You'll have to back up a bit now.'

Dad clenched futile fists in this war of wills. He couldn't remember winning even one battle. Again, he surrendered, and slowly reversed. A collective gasp filled the car.

About five metres away and lying against the inside of a fenced-off compound, was an oddly familiar object. It was gouged, and holed in one more place than it should have been. The lower jaw was missing altogether but it was still, unmistakably, a human skull.

Above it, caught in the fence, hung a ragged ribbon of purple.

2

The telephone meowed. The sleeping mind behind the closed eyes screamed without sound. Somebody had reset the telephone tones yet again. No doubt Michael, Number One (and only) son. A pre-pubescent Michael had enjoyed making daddy long-legs into daddy no-legs, and now, as pimples raged out of control, he had graduated to tormenting his real dad. He knew exactly how much that strangulated catcall was detested. Oh for the good old days when telephones simply rang. Sean Connaughton shot out a hand from beneath the duvet and pressed the answer button.

'I want you in this office five minutes ago!' boomed the rough demand.

The rest of Sean Connaughton emerged slowly, with resentful groans. The volume control had been turned to maximum. Dry, sandpaper eyes, red for want of sleep, blinked rapidly and he softly cursed himself for forgetting to set the answering machine. One eyelid was steadied at half mast to allow for a leer at the fingers on the old-fashioned alarm clock. It was perched deliberately on a large floppy leather Bible to deaden its sharp tick-tock into a tuk-tuk. A discarded clerical collar encircled both.

'Connaughton? Is that you?' The telephone voice was growing more irate. 'Hello!' A yawn was stifled, but not without some sound escaping.

'Good God, man, are you not up yet? Do you know it's almost midday?' Exaggeration as usual, thought Sean as the other eyelid opened and he noted the minute finger at 15 with the little one just leaving 10.

'Take that name in vain once again,' Connaughton groaned at the tiny image of his news editor on the bedside videophone screen, 'and I'll take it as an invitation to give you a twenty-minute sermon on just what God thinks of bad-tempered newspaper men.'

'Don't give me any of your holy claptrap.' The anger rose another notch. 'If I don't see your ugly face in front of my desk by half past ten, you and your church can starve with Ethiopia, and you'll be HIS-STO-RIE.'

Frank Winter's flat north of England tone rose into mid-American sing-song to dramatize the last three syllables. It really was an irritating habit. Frank thought it cool. Everybody else agreed that he sounded like a foolish throwback to the twentieth century.

'For heaven's sake, Frank,' pleaded the now fully awake Connaughton, 'be reasonable. I've been up half the night with—'

'No!' Winter's face snarled. 'Don't you dare! You bring that other job of yours into my business once again and you really are finished. Half past ten!'

'For your sake then, Frank. Why call me in? You know you can't take too much of me. Think of your ulcers.'

'Aye, and that's the very truth. Only ten minutes to go now.' More hyperbole.

'Two days a week!' stressed Connaughton staring at the screen. 'We've got an agreement. I'm not due in till Wednesday. Anyway, why me all of a sudden, Frank?' His voice rippled into a wicked chuckle. 'Why do you NEED your favourite religious fruit-and-nut case to dance attendance on you today?'

Silence.

'F-r-a-N-K?' Connaughton began the name low and slid

11

the tone upwards in a tease. Still silence. Winter's videophone face twitched with embarrassment. 'Speak to me, Frank.'

'You're, er...' A heavy sigh came down the line and the mini-mouth on the screen paused half open. Tiny though the screen was, Connaughton could see the news editor's eyes dart nervously from side to side. 'You're, erm...', and then a quick intake of breath and 'Oh, hell, yer needed.' The hurt in dragging out the last word was obvious.

'Hell, my dear friend...' and Connaughton smiled as Winter's rectangle of a moustache began to dance with displeasure, 'is when some inconsiderate news editor rings you up at—'

'Five minutes now – and then that-is-it!' Again the phoney sing-song.

Connaughton, despite lack of sleep, felt affection for this blunt Lancashire rottweiler. He had once met him in tow behind Ada, a shrew of a wife beyond taming, and had immediately understood why poor Frank needed so desperately to be the boss at work. He had no chance at home. Sympathy also bubbled up for a hard-pushed news editor who had demanded an extra top-flight addition to his overworked reporting team, only to end up with 'a part-time has-been who had gone religious'. It was crazy. Winter had said so. Often! Two jobs. Both of them vocations. Neither with nine-to-five parameters. How could you be called in two directions – one reporting the good news, the other touting the bad?

'I'm your god!' Winter had once snarled. 'Worship me with scoops and exclusives. No man can serve two masters.' Connaughton, in his more honest moments, knew Winter was right. But this wasn't one of them. This moment was straight from hell, and a weary, wayward reverend relished it.

'Let me get something straight. What you're saying, Frank, is that YOU ... NEED ... ME! Have I got that right, or would you like to repeat it?'

12

The bedroom filled with 'Frank noise', as Sean described it. The decibels of obscenity were turned down, the vicar-reporter watched his belt-and-braces boss foam with words mined straight from the Lancashire pits of his proud ancestry. Sean was grateful that the vicarage bedroom extensions were not linked up to the transmitting camera. A vision of his unkempt self in his next-to-nothing would have given him insufficient standing on Winter's editorial monitor.

'Whoa! there,' Connaughton eventually interrupted. 'Frank, let's be reasonable; two days a week and not a second longer. That's not only the agreement we've got, that's also as much as I dare. Otherwise, his Holiness at Bishop's House will have my guts for garters. As it is, I had a blazing row with him only last week and there's no way I can give you any more time now. Please, Frank, I really don't need this from you today.'

'Well now, aren't you the lucky one?' Frank leered. 'Your right reverend boss is the story, and I can guarantee that your knuckles will remain lily-white and completely unrapped. So get your butt off that bed and—'

'How can you be so sure?'

'Your boss has been trying out his Daniel routine,' the leer became a sneer and then a malicious grin, 'and he didn't quite make it. He was reported missing in the early hours, then they found a rather worse-for-wear skull, and the remains of a scarlet shirt in the lion's den at WildWorld! They identified the remains by his episcopal ring which some lion called Jezebel was licking.'

Connaughton was overwhelmed by conflicting reactions. Disbelief was immediately dismissed. Jokes were never Winter's forte, not with a disposition that matched his surname. In days to come, Sean Connaughton would never be able to remember which emotion came next. Relief at the end of a church disaster? Or sheer horror that anyone, even Bishop Williams, should come to such a terrifying end.

'Frank, you're sick!'

Winter asked, 'You still padre, or something, to that zoo?'

He referred to the pastoral chaplaincy that Sean exercised among WildWorld's three hundred staff by virtue of the park's main entrance being in his parish of St Thomas's, Hoghton.

'I'll be in by eleven,' Sean said by way of answer, already stumbling into his boxer shorts. 'No, on second thoughts, Frank, I'll go straight to WildWorld.' He cleared the phone.

'Sorry, luv.'

The shout came up the stairwell, and the oddness of the accent charmed him yet again as he rushed across the landing to the bathroom. It was more Lancashire than hotpot, yet spiced with a gorgeously fruity Florida twang.

'I was out back hanging the washing when the telephone rang.' It was the mother-in-L, as Sean affectionately called the formidable Ma Hannigan.

Despite the alarm and rush, Sean's mind switched from images of blood-dripping jaws at WildWorld to those of the plush lobbyists' lounge in Washington's House of Representatives, a quarter of the world and half a lifetime away.

'... and this is our most famous import from England, Nora, the wife of Congressman Hannigan.' A mutual friend had performed the introductions.

Nora Hannigan, a petite figure in a billowing southern ballgown, had fitted the part perfectly. But then she had opened her wide, smiling mouth and out had poured talk of black puddings in the most homely of Lancashire accents, and he had burst out laughing. Before he could apologize, she had responded likewise, and within minutes she was soaking up home news faster than he could deliver it. Did people still have webbed feet in rainy Manchester? How were United doing in the Cup? Did he know Hoghton? And what about Twistleton next door?

And then Sean had been introduced to daughter Karen, beautiful, incredible Karen who made his great American factfinding reporting tour pale into insignificance. From that meeting onwards, only Karen had mattered. Lovely Karen, and he could not stop saying her name. She was a southern belle, a lady in the classic mould of an age gone with the wind. She had the beauty of a Scarlett O'Hara, with the gentle temperament of Scarlett's best friend Melanie Hamilton. These days the brain cells refused to perform their Karen magic. She was fading. The image was diffused. And the pain wasn't as sharp, either.

'Sean, are you up?' and he returned to Lancashire, bishops and blood.

'Okay, Nora,' he called. 'I'm flying! Are you right for the kids today?'

'Sure,' that came with a pure south-eastern drawl. 'Michael's up and out in the park throwing sticks for the dog. His room's as foul as a gasman's mac!' That was pure Lancashire, and once on a roll, Nora had the knack of going until her seventy-something lungs tired or somebody interrupted. 'Kate's still stewin' in her bed. We forgot to recharge Herbie' – that was Kate's state-of-the-art go-anywhere electric disabled buggy – 'and she's been plugged into her laptop since breakfast still scouring the Internet for a new mother. As for me...'

Sean shaved to this comforting background noise while his mind juggled with WildWorld's recent dead bodies. He hoped that the present one might not be as gruesome as the first. Nor as problematic. There had been so many unanswered questions that he had kept it in his pending pad. Why should the town's education officer end up stomped to death in WildWorld's elephant house? Frank Winter had told him to ditch it and wait for the inquest.

'It'll be suicide.' Winter had waved it away. 'Police think so.' Sean had had his doubts. Still had.

'By the way, Sean...' Nora's call dragged his mind back, 'you will be back early tonight.' It was not a question. 'I'm going out.'

'Yep. That should be fine.'

Sean ceased mid-shaving stroke as the import of Nora's words sank in. Ma Hannigan going out? Stay-at-home/

telly-addict/feet-elevated/cup-of-tea-balanced-on-ample bosom-shelf Ma Hannigan going out again? She was developing the habits of a lodging teenybopper. She hadn't had a social life for years. Then, the Wednesday mornings had started. Friday afternoon tea dances followed. Now, it was Monday night...

'Nora,' he shouted down. 'You don't think it's time we had a little chat, do you? Hope you're behaving yourself.'

'You don't be so cheeky,' she remonstrated, starting up the stairs. 'You're never too old to have a clip round the ear, Sean Connaughton. And don't think a dog-collar sways me like it does with all those silly fillies of yours.' That was her collective for the church ladies' group. 'If I want to go out once every Preston Guild, then I don't see as it's any business of yours!'

She came to a halt astride the bathroom's threshold, hands on hips, with chin in the attack position, and Sean was glad he had remembered to slip on his boxer shorts.

'And you ought to get some of that weight off,' Nora added rather unfairly. 'Forty-something, going to seed and—' The rest was lost in an unvicar-like giggle as Ma Hannigan pinched his spare inch overlapping the elastic waist band. This in turn was drowned by a strangely staccato mechanical voice.

'Thou shalt not bear false witness against thy neighbour!' The deep voice of Charlton Heston boomed across the landing, followed by gurgling laughter from bedridden Katie, a precocious ten going on twenty.

Ma Hannigan and Sean responded with patient noises and both silently cursed Aunt Molly's acquisition of the latest software gadget for speech-challenged children.

To begin with, clever Kate – ComputaKate, she preferred – had had them all convulsed with her many voices. Her favourite was the voice of the new young King of England, whom Kate worshipped. But, too often, she returned to the old-fashioned Heston with his Moses and Ten

Commandments. So far, she had found use for most of them. Monotonously! Only the seventh was virgin territory, the concept of adultery still baffling her. So too, apparently, did the one about children obeying their parents.

'I'll be home for tea.' Sean had stopped giggling to wriggle free from Ma Hannigan's fat-pinching fingers. 'By the way, they've just found our infamous bishop dead.'

He left Nora on the landing imitating a cod in shock, and quickly donned his clerical gear to ensure a trouble-free passage into WildWorld. As he did so, he idly wondered about the callous juxtaposition between his giggle and the bishop's death notice. Shouldn't there have been just the slightest sadness? Perhaps a respectful pause for reverent silence? No. Honesty was the best policy. Crocodile tears would just melt the ninth commandment, bearing false witness. Still...

He popped in to give Katie her good morning kiss while fending off endless questions from Nora with half answers and suitable noises. Eventually, he made the front door, bellowed a last farewell to Katie, and, with his getaway assured, risked a last dig.

'Hope he's worth it, Mother-in-L!'

Her explosive expression turned a simple one-liner into an intrigue. What a curious reaction! Surely she wasn't really dating at her advanced age. And yet there had been an odd sparkle dancing around her eyes recently. Then there was last Sunday, watching her prepare tea when she thought nobody was around. She kept smiling to herself – and humming! Nora was not, and to his knowledge never had been, a hummer.

He drove off to WildWorld and a death that made him want to hum.

3

Most stomachs in the serried terraced streets of Lancashire were still coping with cornflakes when confronted with the gruesome news of their bishop's well-gnawed remains. Local television broke the news but a rushed-out lunchtime edition of the *Hoghton Evening Argus* was only minutes behind. Bold print was slashed across a fresh outer skin wrapped around the stale innards of yesterday's news.

Just after nine, in a rushed editorial conference, editor Henry Parrott had personally chosen BISHOP DEAD IN LION'S DEN as the banner. A compact and overly neat chief sub-editor, Albert Entwistle, had added the strapline *WildWorld claims second mystery victim*. He had then ordered one of his more computer-literate subs to design a special top-of-the-mast graphic trumpeting RECORD EARLY EDITION.

'Sell your own greatness!' ran his motto for the success of the *Argus* – and, by association, his own.

'At any cost?' queried those who thought that newsprint and truth should have a closer relationship than Enty's promotion sometimes permitted.

The presses in the building's bowels were being plated ready for the first run before news editor Frank Winter snatched a page proof from a passing messenger. With a certain grim satisfaction he bellowed, 'Rubbish! Horse Guards was a good half-hour earlier!'

All action froze for a split second in a haze of ageing fluo-rescents and fading primrose paint. It took a loud Entwistle curse to kick-start the tennis-court size editorial department back into life. Winter would normally have made a much bigger issue of his opposite number's blunder, but even he had wit enough to allow for some sensitivities.

Horse Guards was one of those euphemisms the British use when place names become the plasters over a nation's pains. Schoolchildren wiped out by a slithering, smothering slag heap was still simply Aberfan. Three hundred Yanks and Britons blown up in mid-air was Lockerbie. Crazed gunmen maiming and killing was Hungerford or Dunblane. Horse Guards was the exact moment when the turn-of-the-millennium razzmatazz collapsed into national mourning. It was one of those 'where-were-you?' moments. 'Where were you when Kennedy was shot?' 'Where were you when Horse Guards went up?'

Somehow, it seemed crude to ask, 'Where were you when terrorists blew up half the Royal Family, and dismembered the then Prime Minister plus half a Guards company? Where were you when the yellow grit of London's Horse Guards Parade turned blood-red halfway through the annual Trooping the Colour?' Even a tough old pro like Winter was aware that yet another anniversary of the horror loomed.

The *Argus* lost another five minutes while the top-of-the-page boast was erased and a fresh front plate struck.

The lead story on the bishop – very little 'flesh' to it, according to one sick sub wit – began in double-size 18pt let-ters, reducing to a still-oversize 14pt, and was set across broader-than-usual columns. These were wrapped around a full-colour library picture of the victim in his day-of-enthronement finery.

The inside front and back pages were a sombre monotone photomontage of the prelate at work: here, opening a reno-vated stretch of the Leeds–Liverpool Canal; there, flying crane-high over the restoration of Hoghton's terrorist-bombed Arndale into a Multiplex. Hard top had replaced mitre and a roll of architect's plans was his shepherd's crook. The *Argus*'s back page read like the meanderings of a bored sub-editor's late-afternoon stint on the obituary files. The turbulent bishop's controversies were rehashed without vitality: marrying gay and lesbian priests; challenging fundamentalists to 'get real' about evolution and stop rewriting modern science; his mockery of miracles; his hint that if God wasn't exactly dead, he wasn't at all well.

'A religious transvestite,' the obituarist briefly sparkled. 'The bishop was a humanist who cross-dressed in religious skirts.'

All of which was ancient news. Hardly sufficient to distract a fickle public from the ever-hot, ever-present television cameras, some of which were already craning over Wild-World's perimeter fencing. By comparison, the *Argus* was unsophisticated, and unadorned by the blood and gore the British public had come to know, love and expect.

It was for this reason that Frank Winter had buried his pride and telephoned Connaughton. The vicar was his one hope of stealing the inside colour from the snapping opposition.

* * *

'Who's in charge?'

The query shot through Connaughton's neurones with such force that he eased off the accelerator. Normally, only fast driving and flashing visions of tangled flesh and metal brought such caution. This time, it was almost as though somebody had spoken out loud. It was a momentary, easily reversed reflex. Professionalism squashed inner distractions, and he refocused on circumnavigating an impatient four-lane queue of family-filled cars steaming at WildWorld's gridlocked entrance.

This was not a taxing problem. He was on his own patch; priest-in-charge of all he surveyed, with its esoteric nooks, crannies and byways. Further, it was his old childhood stamping ground of crinkled ankle socks and scuffed knees; of idle holidays netting silver sticklebacks and scooping frogspawn from a pond that was now a burger bar by WildWorld's main gate.

Sean had snatched at St Thomas's Church of England parish when offered. Not only was it a return to his roots, it was here that his apathetic atheism had been beheaded into theism. That had happened in the desperate aftermath of Karen's death. But more than that. It was a coming home to the wild hills and moors of a hundred hues of greens and browns after the boredom of coastal flatlands he had endured since leaving college four years before.

To his local knowledge was added his safari park chaplaincy role, which made him privy to various staff entrances – together with their codes and keys – around the twenty-eight miles of giraffe-high wire. Pulling into one such entrance, he mentally rehearsed the three pairs of digits that he would enter.

'Who's pushing your buttons?'

Again, the nudge was almost audible. This time images flashed across his mental screen. They centred around a metal pinball with a human face, ricocheting around a life of obstacles ... from vicarage, to car, to work, to church, to car, to family, to parishioners, to car, to newspaper office, to God. Even to God.

Connaughton hauled hard on the handbrake lever of his ancient black taxi cab, the only vehicle he had found that could take his disabled daughter's buggy. He lowered his window and stretched to the keypad at the outer gates. Moments later, he was repeating the process at the inner fence, and waiting for iron gates to yield. The corner of an eye noted yesterday's hastily discarded dog-collar peeping from the glove compartment.

'A fallen halo...?'

The priest in him automatically identified the origin of the spiritual promptings, and the journalist within answered, 'Later'. He caught sight of himself in his rear view mirror, and the dishonesty behind the neutral expression. He accelerated away into WildWorld.

*   *   *

'... and my big beauties once had 'em on the breakfast menu.' Les Moore raised his rasping Lancashire accent above the noise of his protesting charges – twenty-nine Asiatic lions.

'Who was on what menu?' Detective Sergeant Molly Hannigan shouted back, almost immediately regretting the encouragement.

'Them there first Christians, my dear,' grinned the lion-keeper.

'Well, I'll be safe then!' Hannigan countered quietly in a lilting Florida accent. More loudly, she added, 'Now, quit your Billy Graham act or I'll book you for wasting police time. Answer my question.'

Lionman Les risked one more stab. He nodded towards a blue plastic body bag with its few chewed remains, still awaiting a police surgeon's diagnosis that they were beyond resuscitation. 'Yon bishop's burning in 'ell right now, lass,' he chuckled to lessen the harshness of the words, 'an' all you can think of is police time?'

'Excuse me...?' It was her American feminine shorthand for 'Just who do you think you're talking to, mister?' She gave a dismissive flick of the head and there was a flurry of shoulder-length dark titian hair to rival Ahab's mane. Les carried on grinning, and Detective Sergeant Hannigan cursed herself for rising to his bait.

'Mr Moore?' Molly Hannigan returned to business, 'the question?'

'Well, as yer askin'...' Les growled in his flat Northern vowels, 'we've 'ad about half a dozen customers throwing 'emselves at' lions since we opened three year back. Normally, my lovely lasses are too well fed to do 'owt but maul 'em a bit. So, I suppose, in answer to your question, I'd have to say – yes, it's always possible that the bish climbed over into my lions' den. 'Course, it's normally in t' daytime that the funny folk climb over, yuh know,' the sergeant nodded encouragement, 'and my beauties are then far too busy guarding their human catch to eat it. Too many prying eyes. Be a different matter at night, 'course. Like last night. Yon scarlet heretic was a right good nosh up for 'em, an' my Ahab's got a gut ache—'

'Do you really think it's possible—' The sergeant tried in vain to win back control but Les Moore pressed on.

'Aye, we gets all sorts and conditions here, lass. Some thinks they've special powers over wild beasts. They just steps out of their cars, cool as cucumbers and as daft as brushes with no bristles. T'other sort are the religious mania types. Thinking they're martyrs for—'

'Mr Moore.' The interruption came firmly this time. 'Is it likely, in your opinion, that the bishop could have got his two hundred pounds over that fence?'

'Well...' drawled Les, his brain for once trying to catch up with his mouth, 'to be honest – no.'

'So?' Hannigan encouraged.

'Well, yer know already our security lads have found th'oles in th'outer wire. Well, there's no 'oles 'ere. But I'll tell you this, lass,' and Les began leading her to the compound fence, 'my liftin' wheels aren't set right. Least, not the way I always leave 'em when I knocks off work each night.'

By this time they had reached the guillotine doors of the enclosure, and Les's grin faded into pursed lips over a protruding, disapproving chin. His eyebrows knitted in puzzled hesitation. He wanted to say more but there was a skirmish within.

'Well...?' Hannigan used Les's own word by way of encouragement.

'Well, sergeant, I'm, er, not a detective, you understand...' She nodded in silent agreement. 'But I reckons as 'ow somebody put him in, and then did him in.' The lionman emphasized his conclusion by slitting a thumb across his throat.

'I mean, these...' and he walked along the fence to steering-wheel size circles of cast iron at waist height. 'Yer see, operatin' me lifting gear. Well, it's 'ard on the wrists at the best of times, but to turn the wheels through the wire with your fingers? No way. And to lower the outer shutter once you're in ... well...' His voice trailed off and a knowing shrug of the shoulders replaced the rest of the sentence.

Detective Sergeant Hannigan could have kissed him.

'YES!' she gasped under her breath, and she felt like punching the air with a bunched-up fist. Instead, she contented herself with a sideways look in the direction of her self-important boss, Francis Spencer, the last of an endangered species of pompous chief inspectors. He was, at that precise moment, facing an irate safari boss, Giles St John, at the car entrance to the lions' compound.

She slowly smiled.

'Got him!'

* * *

Only three dozen black rhinos remained on a globe of greed and concrete. Now, the armour-plated rear end of one of them blocked the narrow macadam strip that laced its way over the flank of a brooding moorland hill en route to the lion enclosure. Connaughton decided that caution and a quiet, stationary car was the best strategy.

Pushed by deadlines he may be, but it was a toss-up between the wrath of the rhino and that of Frank Winter. Not much to choose between the two on a good day. However, a moment of patience would not go amiss. Sean's

24

instinct, born of months pastoring a highly mobile staff in the forty-nine square miles of WildWorld, whispered caution.

Something was not quite right with the dangerous end of the one-tonner. He – most definitely a well-endowed and pugnacious he – was becoming more irritated with each attempted nibble. A wayward front horn of compacted and hardened hair thwarted each lunge for tender grass shoots. This ill-formed protrusion – a long, squared, tapering stump – grew forward and slightly downwards, instead of upwards with a backward curve. The result was that the solid outcrop remained unbowed, despite the mass behind it, and the rhinoceros could not quite get mouth and grass to meet. Connaughton made a mental note to inform the safari vet or St John. Meanwhile, he gently reached down to switch off his engine to wait in silence.

It was then that the in-car phone shrilled, its volume turned abnormally high to counter the grind of east Lancashire's traffic. The monstrous head lifted, turned, and the feet gave a remarkably agile jig to bring a tossing tusk to within two metres of fragile automobile metal. The hand that shot down to the ignition key also accidentally flicked on the phone. The rhino was further assailed by a vaguely mechanical Shirley Temple-ish voice, coyly squeaking with excitement over an urgently revving starter motor.

'Hello, my sweet Daddy, I've got another definite possible for you.'

'Katie, my dear,' Connaughton heard his own voice an octave higher than usual, 'just give me a minute.'

As the charging head dipped below the bonnet line, the gear-lever was rammed into reverse and the accelerator pedal jammed flat to the floor. The ensuing impact was somewhat minimized by this manoeuvre. It also mercifully skewed the car to face away from the now off-balance tank of flesh and horn leaving a clear road ahead.

'What's happening, Daddy?' The voice conjured a picture of golden curls bobbing round a face of childish innocence.

The reality, unfortunately these days, was by no means as angelic. Not since the car accident. Not since Karen and—

'Not to worry, love.' Connaughton slammed down a mental trapdoor on unwelcome memories, and he was relieved that his voice had returned to earth. 'Just a bit of heavy traffic.' He thankfully noted through his wing-mirror that his black cab, despite a freshly refashioned front fender, was proving an adequate match for a frustrated black rhino.

'By the way, little clever Katie Connaughton,' and the voice grew fatherly stern, 'don't I need an apology from you after last night? Goodness knows what your Aunty Molly made of it all!'

There was a longer than usual delay, and Sean guessed that young Kate was not only programming in her reply but was also choosing another voice from her computer library of thousands.

'Aw, gee,' James Cagney crackled, 'I really didn't mean it, you dirty rat.' It was followed by the infectious giggle used in *Yankee Doodle Dandy*, from where the software had probably borrowed its sounds.

'You know, honey,' continued the wide Bronx twang, 'this newest computer lady I've picked out for you is a definite possible, and she'd make a great ma.'

'Okay, honey, yourself,' mimicked back Connaughton, 'Who are you trying to get me married off to now?'

Another short delay. They had discussed getting the latest mind-control computer used by fighter pilots for Kate but her fingers were so fast over the keyboard that she hardly needed it. Sean reassured himself that the rhino was at a safe distance, while simultaneously cringing inwardly as he recalled how Kate had proposed to her Aunty Molly.

'Everybody else has a mom,' Kate had wheedled in her best tearful Temple. 'I've only got a Gran-Gran and an aunt.' Two authentic sobs had formed the punctuation at this point. 'I might lose an aunt but if you became my mom, Aunty Molly, I really wouldn't mind.'

An awkward silence had filled the room, and Kate had keyed on...

''Course, you'd have to sleep with my dopey old dad' – Ma Hannigan had gasped at the audacity – 'but I'd make up for that by being the bestest little girl that any stepmother could have.'

Sean and Molly had exchanged looks designed to humour the situation, yet their eyes unaccountably lingered together. Embarrassment had eventually caused them to break away, and Aunt Molly had broken an awkward silence saying that she would like to think about such a great privilege. A huffy Ma Hannigan had promptly packed 'too-clever-for-her-own-good Katherine Connaughton' off to bed.

Kate's present telephone call and her latest discovery of 'a new possible mum' from the Internet Dating Bank showed that she had taken Aunty Molly's words as just the sort of thing grown-ups say when they want to avoid an outright 'no'.

'This one's not as ancient as you,' said the Californian tones of Phil Presley, the hostess of the transatlantic hit show *The Blind Dating Game*. 'She is thirty-five, with her own real hair. The colour, I mean. Light straw. She lives over the Pennines in little old Yorkshire. She's got a quaint cottage and a lovely Irish red setter. And here's the best, Dad. She goes to church for high days and holidays, so she'd be a great vicar's wife.'

'Kate,' Sean interrupted, 'if the lady's just a Christmas Christian, vicarage life would drive her batty.'

The lion enclosure came into view and he passed an elephant in must, dribbling the contents of its bladder in hope of attracting a mate. It wasn't a feeling he shared at that moment.

'Kate, can we postpone finding me a new wife until tonight, and then I will definitely give your possible-definite the once over. Honest!'

'Only if you let me read you a bedtime story, Daddy?' said Orson Welles. Sean sometimes marvelled at the speed of his prodigal computer nerd. 'Gran-Gran's going to see her – ping!'

ComputaKate suddenly had Dad's full and undivided attention. Grazing wildebeest and skittish gazelles suddenly blurred as the mind focused on the last sentence. And more precisely, what was hidden behind the ping?

'Do you know something I don't, Madam Katie?'

'No!' grated the voice of a Dalek, after a moment.

'Sure?'

'Exterminate! Exterminate! Exterminate!'

'Katie...?' but the line was dead and a baby giraffe was perilously unsteady on its new stilts a hundred metres ahead. Gran-Gran's evening assignation would have to wait.

* * *

'Chief inspector, for every twelve point five minutes you keep me shut I lose £2,000.'

Accountant-like words sounded bizarre coming from a bronzed and rugged Giles St John, all the more because he emphasized the words by wringing his felt hunter's hat between burly hands. It looked like he wanted to do the same to the chief inspector's neck.

'Listen, there are hundreds of bank holiday cars queuing. At the back entrance I've got Country Rights protestors picketing for more pathways across my Water Buffalo Valley. I've got the Save Wildlife Liberation Front at the main entrance. An investigative television crew are about to descend hellbent on slaughtering my livelihood. Did you know, chief inspector, that without the likes of us there'd be no wildlife left on this rotting planet? Wouldn't you think somebody would be queuing to praise us?'

The chief inspector smiled weakly.

'... and further, did you know that Africa would be elephantless and every last one of India's tigers would all be in China's medicine pouches without our selective breeding and restocking policy?'

Chief Inspector Spencer interrupted lamely, 'We are trying our best, Mr St John—'

'Meanwhile, in the forecourt, I've got the cloud cuckoo land New Age fundamentalists who think animals shouldn't even be kept as pets, let alone in a safari park. Last night, some religious moron dressed in scarlet risks poisoning my lions by feeding himself to them. And now, on top of all this, you now turn one of the best days of the year into a disaster which—'

'Really.' The chief inspector's chins wobbled in sympathy and flabby hands patted the air before Giles St John in a forlorn quietening gesture. 'We're being as fast as possible, sir, and will keep you no longer than is absolutely necessary.'

'Officer,' growled St John, clearly unconvinced, 'the queues at the front now stretch back to the motorway turn-off. Dozens have given up already. My solicitor says I can sue you for—'

'Ah, Detective Sergeant Hannigan.' Francis Spencer was delighted with his subordinate's timely approach. 'I was just telling—'

'Excuse me, sir,' interrupted the sergeant. 'Could I just have a quick word with—'

'Sergeant!' Spencer's jowls hardened. To be trodden down by a member of the public had to be tolerated. But to be interrupted by a mere underling was too much; especially a female one, good-looking or not. 'Sergeant, we're finished here.'

'But, if I could just have one—'

'Detective Sergeant Hannigan, you may have been a lieutenant on the other side of the Great Pond with Miami Vice, or whatever, and they might not have operated on the revolutionary principle that subordinates take and carry out orders, but here, in this tiny sceptred isle of ours, we do things slightly differently. Please tell me that you are not yet again about to regale me with your foul-play theories?'

'But there's new information to hand, sir.' Hannigan spoke each word tightly and slowly. An awkward stand-off ensued.

A wiser superior would have used the pause to sigh and walk aside a few paces. Even to ask the odd question. But not Spencer.

'Suicide, sergeant!' smirked Spencer. 'Same as that education officer in the elephant house. Just look after that bloody body bag of bones until the police surgeon arrives, and let's get Mr St John back into business.'

He turned back to the safari boss intending a quip about 'not being able to get the staff these days', and saw Connaughton's car coming towards them. His cab was chugging away from an indignant and chasing mother giraffe.

'Sergeant?' Spencer felt a better line coming on and pointed beyond the safari boss.

'Now, if your bishop had been topped, here would be your prime suspect.'

4

'**M**orning, padre.'
 Spencer's greeting was in sharp contrast to his jibe
at a mere sergeant. His fawning to the Cloth oozed from a
nominal High Church upbringing and a brief stint in the
Territorial Army. The origins of his boot-licking character,
however, lay not so much in nurture as in a natural craving
for self-elevation. 'Trust we find you in good health on this
fine bank holiday morning?'

Francis Spencer was also one of life's each-wayers; a gam-
bler who put nothing on the nose of conviction, and everything on all the other choices. He'd never seen any God, but
just in case it wouldn't hurt to be friendly to Connaughton;
an easy-term instalment on his religious insurance policy. Be
nice to churchmen and their boss might smile on you. It was
cheaper than loving your neighbour and giving up Sunday
morning lie-ins. That aside, there was also a residual, albeit
grudging, respect for Connaughton's reporting of police-
related matters, and hadn't he won some national provincial
journalist of the year award back in whenever-it-was? The
finer details eluded the police chief.

'From the presence of your clerical collar, padre,' he gestured with an oily smile, 'I take it that this is a pastoral rather
than a press visit.'

'Not quite, chief inspector.' Connaughton, no more

immune to people power play than any other human being, rested content in this face-to-face, knowing that life's circumstances had gifted him the upper hand. Even so, the next less-than-respectful line left him floundering.

'In that case, it is pressman rather than padre,' Spencer huffed, still with respect, 'and I'm afraid I'll have to ask you to leave.'

It was St John who came to Connaughton's rescue. 'Have I got this right, chief inspector' – and the voice was not affable – 'not content with ruining me physically, you're now depriving the condemned man of his last spiritual rights?'

Opposed on two fronts, Chief Inspector Spencer exhibited the main reason why he had never made superintendent, and why his superiors had attempted to downgrade him after his rank had been phased out. He dithered with a fluster of 'ums' and 'ers', before finally opting for 'Yes, well, I suppose we have really finished here so, er, perhaps...' and turning away he shouted, 'Sergeant, what the devil's keeping that police surgeon?'

Turning back to the safari boss with 'Not be long now, sir,' he walked off to avoid a further climbdown before Connaughton.

The two remaining figures smiled conspiratorially, comfortable in each other's presence. Connaughton enjoyed the argumentative bluster of this craggy former big-game hunter. Behind the gruffness, he knew St John to be an introvert who found people too tiring, much preferring the company of his wild, uncomplicated charges. Connaughton was an honoured exception. St John had a sneaking admiration for any human who could cope with the tragedies life tossed into the normal cauldron of relationships in a medium size company such as his. Connaughton, somehow, gave the impression of embracing every last sad victim of marriage breakdown, death, sickness and a dozen other crises. Not that he actually did, of course. An all-encompassing pastoral skill just gave that impression.

Their occasional drink-fuelled late-night sessions were fiery attempts to solve the riddles of the universe. What or who preceded the Big Bang, if in fact there was one? If it was a 'what' that caused the bang, who or what came before that? One argued for a universal designer and a super-intelligence behind the intelligence of Einstein and his ilk. He suggested it wasn't intelligent to expect intelligence to emerge from a dead primordial blob in some stagnant pond. And, in any case, who was the first mover and the present sustainer? Just who set up the laws that kept the world going round? The other argued for Mother Nature repeating herself with multiple universes until one chanced on the recipe for life. Human intelligence, in this case, was merely a chemical reaction in an electrically powered ape. Neither so much as hinted at their long list of doubts. Both were adamant that the other was hopelessly wrong.

They coasted through midnight in search of why humans worshipped soccer teams, film idols and gods of varying hues. And also, just where did that irritating inner 'ought' of humanity come from? St John had trekked Africa from Cairo to the Cape without finding a tribe that didn't worship, or possess an ethical code to tell its people what they ought, and ought not, to do. If all humans worshipped and had a conscience, where did it all come from? Why hadn't he, St John, been able to swap one woman for another – which he did with some regularity – and not feel that he ought to behave better than the animals he kept?

'Simple human conditioning,' he had argued. 'Over thousands of years of civilization.' Connaughton had counter-suggested that humans could just as easily have been designed to be moral, with an inbuilt need to worship the intelligence who had designed them. And when they didn't worship their Creator, they searched the universe for something else to adore. Endless questions and a thousand conundrums beneath starry nights magnified through the bull's-eye bottoms of pint-glass telescopes.

With the departure of the chief inspector, Sean casually mentioned the frustrations of the rhino, handicapped by its crooked horn. 'Just to add spice to all your other woes,' he grinned, and strolled off to report on whatever the incident in the lion's den would turn out to be.

He was mildly surprised at the absence of blue and white police cordon tape. Why no forensic boys dusting, photographing and bagging bits of evidence? Why only two local officers?

'We were just about to call on you, sir!'

The mocking arched eyebrow and a slight upward quirk to the corner of Molly Hannigan's wide unadorned mouth, made Connaughton smile with pleasure.

'No, don't tell me, officer,' he said, holding up a silencing hand as she withdrew her notebook. 'Let me guess. You've at last seen the light. You've fallen madly, passionately and truly in love with your Maker, and you felt you just had to go and see your vicar. Now, am I a prophet, or what?'

'You're a what!' The sergeant's eyes rolled heavenward, but only in resignation. 'Considering your highly critical view of the deceased, can you tell me where you were between the hours of midnight and six this morning, sir?'

A grin was the only reply she got.

'This is no laughing matter, sir.' Molly curtly played out her hand. 'After all, this wouldn't be the first time you'd broken the law, would it?'

'Ho-ooh, nasty, sergeant, nasty!' chuckled Connaughton, 'She stoops to conquer – so low she hits below the belt.' She had referred to the time when, in the first flush of his conversion, he had squatted in trees to prevent their removal for yet another idiotic motorway.

'Now,' added a sadistic Molly, 'what's an honest copper to think when a vicar with a criminal history and one who is always denouncing his bishop in the media as a heretic, suddenly turns up to view the body? Could it not be a case of the guilty party returning to the scene of his crime?'

'Very funny, Molly,' and Connaughton tried to deflect the banter, 'any idea how he came to be here? I expected a bit more of a police presence than—'

'Sergeant!' the sharp voice of the chief inspector interrupted. 'We are here to work, if you could possibly drag yourself away from your brother.'

'In-law, sir.'

'What?' Spencer's subordinates did not qualify for 'pardon'.

'Brother-in-law, sir.'

'Whatever,' muttered Spencer dismissively. 'Any joy yet on that police surgeon?'

'He's been on his way for half an hour, sir. Got stuck in the traffic outside, and a uniform has gone to the rescue.' Spencer's lips moved silently in the padre's presence.

'Unless I'm very much mistaken' – Connaughton caught Spencer's attention – 'the absence of your scenes-of-crime boys tells me that you're treating this as an odd death. Right? You can't see any signs of foul play. You'll be interviewing the family and friends later but it looks like suicide. You think a murder theory is as dead as the body itself. Have I got that about right?'

He was hoping for a straight 'yes' or 'no'. Maybe even a brief formal response for the copy Frank Winter would soon be demanding. 'No comment' always sounded as though a reporter hadn't done his job properly.

'You know better than that,' and Spencer began to walk away leaving Connaughton no better off than the journalists outside. 'And don't try grilling your sister-in-law, either.'

Sean heard but did not obey.

'Foul or fair play, Molly?' Her return look was a hesitant shrug as she watched her superior still watching her over his shoulder.

'Come on, Molly,' he coaxed, ungallantly using his sister-in-law to incite Spencer. 'How many times have you heard me go on about this bishop? An evangelist never slits his throat in the middle of his appeal. Tell me one visionary who topped himself when only half the world was converted to his quaint notions?'

'Padre!' Spencer barked. 'If you really must stay, stick to your pastoring!'

'Why do you think he's committed suicide?' The journalist in Connaughton now surfaced in full inquiry mode as he walked towards the chief inspector. 'I'd stake my life on the fact that the Bishop of Hoghton didn't take his.'

Spencer nibbled the bait at last. 'Okay! Nobody quoting, and nobody quoted. Maybe, just maybe, he was about to be outed in the latest gays' list?'

'He'd have fought it,' countered Sean. 'Anyway, he was straighter than a church aisle.'

'Then he'd just been told that he had three months to live ... or there'd been a domestic tragedy ... perhaps his mistress had eloped with the archdeacon ... mental illness and a love affair with big cats. Do you want me to go on?'

Sean shook his head. 'I saw him two days ago at church synod. He told me I was a throwback to Noah's Ark, if it ever existed. I told him he was in danger of not making it into God's Ark. He was firing on all cylinders; on fire for the conversion of England to his own odd god. This was no heretic about to give the Church an easy time with DIY martyrdom. This was a fiery character determined to tell every soul that there was probably no such thing as a soul, and, if one did exist, there would be no logical way of proving it. Chief inspector, this Daniel was put into this den!'

'Sir?' Hannigan saw another chance. 'The lion keeper was telling me about the wheels which lifted the shutters and the difficulty of—'

'Enough!' Spencer was seething. 'Let me say this one more time, sergeant. And I will say it slowly, so that even your brother, or whatever, can grasp it.' Connaughton was now well and truly off his pedestal. Merely a sergeant's relative. 'Hard evidence! That's what we need these days before calling out scenes-of-crime. You're not the one who answers for the thousands of pounds needed to turn out a team. You don't have to weigh up what that means in a society with twenty thousand suicides a year. Priorities, sergeant. Priorities. The only reason you and I are here, rather than a couple of uniforms, is because the victim is a bishop. Without real evidence, it's another suicide. Is that perfectly clear?'

'What!' blurted Connaughton. 'Like the elephant man last month?'

The inspector's chin stuck out, totally ignoring the last interjection. 'And if one word of this appears in your rag, Connaughton, I'll make sure you never get another scrap of news for the rest of your natural.'

* * *

On the way out, Connaughton called at the lionman's hut.

'God bless you, my child,' hailed Les, raising his right hand in a papal-style salute while extending his wedding-ring finger for Connaughton to kiss. Sean instead punched him hard on his barrelled chest and received a massive bear hug of friendship in return. In personality, they were as different as lions and lapcats. Les was an evangelist who always went for the spiritual throat; Sean a pastor, preferring the persuasive purr. Les, a rough diamond with a prison-to-pulpit conversion story, would tell anyone who gave him a half chance how God met him in his jail cell. Connaughton, more often than not, had to be pushed into telling of a Shepherd who guided him through the dark valley of death after the loss of his wife to a hit-and-run driver.

'Did your sister-in-law tell you about me liftin' wheels?' asked Les. 'Come an' 'ave a look.'

Sean would rather have left to fax through his story, but curiosity and the company made him tarry.

'See!' stressed Les, prodding his fingers through the wire and trying to turn the wheels with his stubby fingers. 'You 'ave a go.' Sean did and, though his slim pianist fingers got more of a grip, he was only able to edge round the wheel a centimetre.

'Well,' Les began to summarize, 'we've either got somebody with incredibly long fingers and the strength of Samson, or somebody who shoved the bishop in and then wound down the doors from the outside.'

Sean did not respond.

'Right?' encouraged Les. 'You're not convinced?'

'What if it was the bishop,' Sean turned devil's advocate, 'and, once in, he then used a couple of sticks to poke the wheel round?'

Sean could almost hear Les's brain tick behind his animated face. At last, he exploded, 'No! No! Look. The bish isn't the type. Anyway, where's the sticks?'

Both began searching through assorted crisp bags, Coke cans and even the odd soft toy.

'Incredible what people'll toss out of their cars,' huffed Les, sifting debris by one of the guillotine shutters. 'They're not even supposed to open their windows in the lion enclosure, let alone throw things out. I mean, look at this,' and he waved the remains of what had been a long, narrow brown envelope, which had obviously had the Ahab treatment. As he did so, the shredded contents showered like white confetti.

'Stupid! Can't see any sticks, can you?'

* * *

Connaughton sent two stories via his in-car computer.

The first would certainly be the lead, with adds and blends from other reporters. Some of the lads would have the background on WildWorld – its safety record, its protests and controversies. There would be a panel on previous mental-case entrants into wildcat compounds. Other scribes would be adding responses to the bishop's death, from friend and foe alike. No doubt, one quote might have come from himself had he not been involved in reporting.

Sean's second item was a two-hundred-word suggested editorial entitled THIS WAS NO SUICIDE! It was risky, he knew, and perhaps too strong for chief sub Entwistle. Anyway, both would keep Winter quiet. And for a long time, Sean hoped.

Yet another day away from his parish and people! His reporter wages might keep the wolves from his flock, but what was the use if they also kept away the shepherd? For the first time since waking that morning he thought of Sammi and the shell of her remains. Madness! What was a vicar doing chasing stories; ignoring even the recent dead? Pastoral needs filled his vicarage diary. Those must now be his priority. Those and Sammi's funeral.

The mobile shrilled as Connaughton made his way out of WildWorld.

'Hello, Sean?' It was the soft voice of the assistant bishop of the diocese. The suffragan Bishop of Twistleton, he was informed, had now become the acting diocesan Bishop of Hoghton, and 'would you be good enough to call at Bishop's House this evening'.

'Yes, of course, erm, bishop.' Sean almost used the first name. Not only was the bishop slightly younger than he, but they had both been at the same college; he a 'geriatric' student in his late thirties, while the bishop, before enthronement, had been his doctrine tutor. Would their friendship survive, he wondered? The invitation had not been unfriendly. More importantly, would the new bishop also be telling him to quit reporting or be fired?

'Connaughton,' the late bishop had fumed days before, 'finish with that infernal rag, close down the parish as you have been told to do – or get out of my diocese!'

A divided Sean had left without Bishop Williams extracting a commitment one way or the other. And conflict had raged within. At his ordination, he had promised to work under his bishop. Why then was he now disobeying him? Four years before, Sean had been licensed to St Thomas's as priest-in-charge and his orders had been clear: be a caretaker and help the parish to merge with others. He later discovered that the 'others' were five believe-anything churches all of which were in the care, and pocket, of Bishop Williams.

What was he to do? The collections at St Thomas's nowhere near covered his stipend, yet there was great potential, surrounded as it was by young families on three large housing estates: eight thousand souls going their own way, being their own gods and in danger of paving their way to the wrong eternal destination. Could he really stand before the end-of-time court and plead the Nuremberg defence 'I was only following orders!'

The answer, Sean had decided, was an emphatic 'NO!' He had subsequently called on his old editor, Henry Parrott, a regular at a neighbouring church, and asked for his old reporting job back on a part-time basis. His wage would cover half the parish expenses, and then all that would be needed was a miracle. He figured he was in the right business for that.

But now there was a new bishop. A believing one. New decisions to make. What would the new acting bishop make of it all?

The question left little room for mundane matters – such as Gran-Gran Nora and his promise to be home early.

Connaughton reckoned that before seeing his new bishop he had time for a couple of sick visits and a quick snack in the nurses' canteen at Hoghton Infirmary. On the way, he picked up a copy of a late-edition *Argus*. He smiled, noting that Entwistle had judged his second piece too radical for an official leader. It had been relegated to Page Three and placed firmly under his own byline. He tossed the paper to one side and his mind turned to the sick – and his new bishop.

5

The quadraphonics in Molly Hannigan's ancient cherry-red Jaguar XJS tolled the first four notes of Beethoven's Fifth above the whine of air.

''Tis I,' she mimicked the voice of a posh English lady. It was her favourite voice-recognition signature to activate the on-off switch for the car phone. She snuggled further into the beige upholstery – real leather rather than Third Millennium sham – awaiting the caller's identity.

She tucked in wisps of hair blown loose from her scarf by the warm May slipstream and wondered if a new Jag might help. She could afford it with what her father had left her, and these odd technical glitches were increasing. Apart from this, and annoying chief inspectors, life was, she felt, beginning to run in her favour. At long last. Especially with a couple of days' break stretching before her. She purred in harmony with her cruising Jag, and allowed herself a touch of innocent kitsch, imagining herself the sporty heroine in one of those magazine short stories in her Well Women's waiting room. Twice the age of them she might be. Her body may have started to slip slightly in hidden places. Nevertheless, even practical, pragmatic professionals needed the gentle massage of romance every once in a while.

''Tis I,' she sang out again as the Beethoven code sounded a second time. Still nothing. She tapped the dashboard above the speakers for no logical reason and, when that didn't work, she yelled in an unheroine-like voice.

''Tis I, you stupid piece of junk.' Simultaneously she thumped the manual override switch.

'Now really, my child.' Connaughton's voice had a mock parsonical cadence. 'Is that any way to speak to your vicar?'

Molly smiled, and readied herself to give as good as she expected.

'Kidding aside, Molly,' her brother-in-law rushed on, 'are you still free tonight...?'

Words suddenly deserted her. What could he possibly have in mind, she wondered. A meal perhaps? A relaxing country drive? Even a glass of wine in a candlelit pub?

'... only, I'm in one heck of a jam.'

She might have known! It wasn't her he was calling, merely his kids' favourite baby-sitter.

'So?'

Sean ignored the frosty syllable. 'Your mother'll kill me if somebody isn't there for Kate in fifteen minutes. Michael's in but she still doesn't think my strapping thirteen-year-old is ready to take on any more responsibility than himself. I suppose after last month's court case, she has a point. Meanwhile, I've had a three-line whip call to the bishop's house and I can't make it home till late.'

Silence followed.

'Molly?' Still no response. The little-boy-lost voice took over. 'Do me this one big favour.'

'Nope!' replied Molly, but she said it too lightly and without resolution.

'Thanks. I owe you.' Connaughton sounded relieved, and carried on, 'By the way, do you know what your mum's up to these days? She's behaving like—'

'And you, Sean Connaughton,' Molly spat out the YOU with the force of one of her native Florida hurricanes, 'are behaving with about as much sensitivity as a thick-skinned, hard-scaled everglade 'gator with the tact of a sounder of wild razorback hogs.'

42

The blast of exotic mixed metaphors shocked him into silence, even if precise understanding escaped him. 'Where on earth did that come from?' he wondered, and in true male fashion speculated about his sister-in-law's hormones. Perhaps one of his funny little stories might be helpful at this point. 'You'll never believe...' But the tirade wasn't over.

'You would know exactly what my mother was doing,' spat Molly, 'if you gave just one ounce of the energy to your family that you devote to your precious church. You might even have time to consider other people's existences besides your own selfish self, and that God of yours!'

With that, Molly flicked off the phone and found that she was doing a ton in a sixty-kilometre-an-hour zone. She eased back to execute a U-turn, and then wondered herself from where such venom had erupted. She headed for the vicarage and an evening which she knew she would enjoy, despite her words.

In fact, the mid-forties of Molly Hannigan were proving that life can start again. And again. And again. She figured she was on her third career, and she was determined that nothing would stop this one.

The first one was born out of the gauche naïveté of those agonizing teen years. Simply, she aspired to be the wife of the beautiful English journalist who had stepped right out of the middle-spread of *Teens & Twenties* and on to their Atlantic veranda in St Augustine. He was, this lustrous knight explained, on assignment in America, tracking down Lancashire folk in preparation for his 'silly season' summer column entitled 'Far and Away Connaughton'. Could he interview one of the most famous of all ex-Lancastrians, Mrs Nora Hannigan, whom he had met the previous week in Washington?

And then, after mother had finished with him, this Sean had chatted about cloud physics, suspended ice crystals, precipitation, and Molly could have listened to the rich voice for hours. Perhaps, he suggested, she would be kind enough to direct him to Florida's Lightning Alley. He had a week's holiday due and wanted to spend it chasing anvil-shaped clouds and photographing bolts from the heavens. Molly would have taken him by the hand and guided him personally and lovingly every step of the way down to Key West and then back up again to Jacksonville. She would have taken him to dreamy nights in West Palm Beach – her favourite – exotic Miami meals and exciting spins on Daytona. But all she could manage, as she told her bedroom mirror later, were 'stupid idiotic girlish giggles'. She berated her image for still not having 'got it together at nineteen'. And, of course, it had left Big Sis Karen with a free run and little competition, and the poor journalist did not know what had hit him. Thunder and lightning were suddenly set aside once Sean learned that Karen was home, and Molly had eventually ended up a maid to the bride, and gave up hope of ever capturing Sean Connaughton.

That was until Karen's funeral – and she still asked for forgiveness. From whom, she wasn't too clear. Even now, after eight years, she cringed at her eagerness to step into her dead sister's prematurely vacated shoes. Her self-confessed callousness was only assuaged by unbelievable frustration when the idiot Sean went and got religion, of all things!

So much for the first plan for the rest of her life. Of course, she had long ago recovered from it. Oh yes. Merely a teenage phase with a later echo. Her dusty psychology notes explained it all away, and anyway what was love but a mere cocktail of chemical and electrical reactions? All completely and neatly rationalized. Not a shred of feeling worthy of note.

It was then that the second career assumed pre-eminence – to make captain in the Florida State Police Department and, in the process, smash through the increasing syndrome of domestic violence. Beneath the towering palmettos and swooping mockingbirds, and hidden away behind rainbow swathes of orange blossom, mimosa, and myriad forms of orchid, lay the canker of domestic ugliness. And it mattered not what the type of home, whether in the sub-tropical south and down to the Keys or up on the Panhandle. It made little difference whether among the predominant whites or the minority blacks, Seminoles or Asian Indians.

Newly commissioned Officer Hannigan, proud to bear the state seal and motto 'In God We Trust', was nightly staggered by the breakdown of trust in homes. Equally appalling to her was the apathy of a careless society which shrugged away its hidden disfigurement of domestic violence as 'just something between man and wife'.

Molly, now an ocean away from this aborted second career, looked back with mixed feelings. It had by no means been a complete failure. It just seemed so. There was a sourness of surrender.

It had started well, fast-tracking through the Miami Police Academy and university with a basic, but high-scoring psychology degree. She had made lieutenant way ahead of some of the men. Then she was hurt for the first time: shot while arresting a liquor store thief. The bullet stopped her only briefly yet killed her career stone dead, or so it had seemed. Being a woman heading for captain was hard enough. Being a woman who had also seen her shrink was considered a risk too far by the powers on high. Male colleagues could get the shakes and accept trauma counselling all without prejudice. But a woman? Emotional? In tears! Well...! And this happened despite what her record described as 'otherwise a brilliant success in spearheading the police part of Florida's experimental domestic violence courts'. These were also the glowing terms used by superiors whenever they introduced her to worldwide visitors who came to view her model.

The international feting had been cut short one morning when Hannigan was rushed once again into a Miami emergency room, this time having been stabbed in one of her own courts. A husband, 'not one of my top admirers', Molly had said later, objected to the restrictions placed on his wife-beating hobby. His hunter's knife had entered upwards under the left rib cage, slicing easily through the diaphragm and puncturing the base of the heart's right ventricle.

She'd been aware of Ma Hannigan at her side through the touch-and-go night when nobody would offer even fifty-fifty. One junior doctor, she later learned, had felt sorry for Ma Hannigan and 'because your husband did a great job for us in Washington when he was alive' had eventually and grudgingly allowed a seventy per cent chance of recovery. People prayed. Ma Hannigan had. Even a semi-conscious Molly had found her unthought-out atheism inadequate on the threshold of death. She had started to join in the prayers – silently! She had got better – 'what a coincidence!' – and wondered vaguely about the efficacy or otherwise of talking to this God. During one recovery setback, she had made a pact with the Divine, whoever He, She or It was: 'I'll keep a few of your commandments and maybe even go to church occasionally if you get me back on my feet and try just a little bit harder to keep me and metal from meeting so much.'

Slowly, the star patient of Miami General progressed and received her reward: a bravery medal and demotion to just another forgotten stabbing statistic in a long, boring column. The world rushed on to another crisis.

But not her.

Ideas of a third career, minus guns and knives, were forming. Her body was growing weary of impacts from various dangerous metals. If it wasn't blades and bullets, then it was a crazed machete-waving wife wanting to chop off odd conjugal bits from her erring husband. On that occasion, Molly had got in the way, collecting a dozen stitches, with reams of official paperwork to justify herself. Fears of facing something similar fuelled nightly panics and terror-dreams. There had to be more to life than the fear of going to sleep, and in such fertile thoughts blossomed the seeds of alternatives. Chief among them was that Old Country idyll of Ma Hannigan's fond and misty memories.

Rolling green lands with skylines of strong chimneys, and valleys and flanks of lowland hills populated by the quaint cobble-clacking, clog-wearing Twistleton folk in shawls and cloth caps. It sounded secure and close to heaven. Here, amid soot-stained stone houses and dark satanic mills ranging the banks of brooks, twistles and lazy rivers, the dome-hatted policemen were the respected carers of quiet town life and needed to carry nothing more dangerous than a small, polished length of lignum vitae.

'More an ornament than a weapon,' Ma Hannigan had smiled in reminiscence.

Perhaps Molly had not accepted every nuance of her mother's Mills and Boon postcard of the old place, but she instinctively felt that a 3,000-mile stretch of water between her and her painful past would not be entirely without merit. Time out would also help. Perhaps she might also extend her psychology degree at the leading Glasgow University. She might herself even become a PC 49, the one her mother was always going on about in their childhood bedtime stories. And why not? She held dual nationality through her GI bride ma. She had much to offer in forensic and legal skills, and it would be lovely to be near Karen again, even if she had pinched every boy Molly had ever fancied.

Her arrival was a triumph stretched over ten glorious gossipy days and culminating in the worst weekend of her life. It was a tragedy that left her wondering whether she had really escaped all that much. It was that Sunday morning that Karen had been killed in a hit-and-run. They never did find the culprit. It had happened only yards from Molly's side, as her big sister set off with the two kids to the morning service at the nearby church.

On her way to church! What sort of a God allowed that?

Molly's pact with the divine had been rescinded from that point onwards. And more fool Sean Connaughton, who not only reached out to God, but 'fell in love' with him. Weird!

Nuns did that. Maybe even monks. Fancy a grown man talking such garbage!

* * *

Three men stood outside WildWorld in the gathering evening gloom. The last holidayers were drifting away with armfuls of cuddly hippos and monkey puppets on string. Two of the men were in animated discussion while the third watched, unseen, from nearby shrubbery.

'If the key grip swings low at this point, Brian,' one of the two gesticulated to the other, 'the camera can come up close to a half profile on the right side of my face with the safari entrance slightly diffused over my left shoulder.'

Brian Mather smiled outwardly and seethed within. Dr David Henderson, high and mighty and full of himself, was at it again. Treating him as little more than a stage hand. He, Brian Mather, ASC, ACE, the prime mover behind the BBC's flagship wildlife series scheduled for the coming season. He with an awards cabinet bigger than this prima donna naturalist's ego.

'Of course, you're the director, Brian,' and this stoked Mather's fury further for he doubted whether Henderson had ever been interested enough during his meteoric rise to stop and look up the meaning of director. 'Can you see it, Brian? Can you grasp what I mean in this evening twilight?'

Now he was being treated like a dim-witted imbecile.

'Look, let me show you. I'll start on my piece to camera. Let's see,' and he rifled through loose sheets clipped to his script board, 'yes, here we are, cue camera, and I start...

> *The Killing-for-Kicks controversy still rages this summer after Lancashire's moorland WildWorld declared its intent to open up a real-life safari in which tourists will swap cameras for guns with real-life bullets. Next year...'*

At this point Henderson swung round to point to WildWorld's entrance fast disappearing into the gloom and shouted back, 'Brian, you then zoom over my shoulder to that "Fun & Thrills for all the Family" slogan arched over the turnstiles, and I carry on...

Next year, will family fun really involve hunting, tracking and butchering these magnificent creatures...?'

It was his caring and humbly inquiring style that made Henderson compulsive watching and made even average television viewers want to spring from their armchairs and do something about his subjects. Mather could glimpse it now, even though it was a rehearsal. Despite being a trodden-on, taken-for-granted and belittled director, Mather could sometimes only stand and admire. It never lasted for long. It was little more than showbiz hype. The presenter persona suddenly snapped back into frenetic know-all Henderson, jumping round like a kangaroo on speed with arms akimbo.

'Then after the line "butchering these magnificent creatures", we cut to library pictures.'

Henderson struck the pose of the genius at work with elegant fingers to forehead. 'Let's see now ... hmm ... what can we tug the heartstrings with?' It was rhetorical. Not even directors were wise to stop the star reaching his crescendo of creativity.

'Yessss, I have it. First, a glorious, full-maned lion, maybe that handsome, rather mournful one we framed last year in the Ngorongoro Crater in Tanzania. Then perhaps a few vulnerable gazelles. Hey, Brian, didn't we shoot some footage on the black buck carnage in South Africa? Remember? All those butchered Bambi shots. What do you think?'

'You want my opinion?' asked the director flatly.

'Brian, Brian, hey, come on now,' and Henderson cradled his creative potter's hands in Mather's direction as if wanting to mould him too. 'We're a team, aren't we?' Henderson gushed and charmed but went on without awaiting confirmation. 'Look, we'll have this Giles St John and that Twistleton MP partner of his – what's his name, Richards? That's it, Stanley Richards – we'll have them both hung, drawn and quartered with the audience baying for blood before this episode is half over, and...'

Mather had stopped listening and just looked at his tormentor with blank eyes. There was so much beauty his camera had wanted to feed to millions locked away in their concrete and plastic prisons. If only he could have been left to get on with it...

The third man watching all this hovered in the shadows, the other two remaining ignorant of their secret audience. The dark figure was still. Lifeless eyes stared at the animated wildlife guru of television without flinching. Gently and absent-mindedly, the figure picked at specks of white paint and mascara that he could still feel in the crevasses fanning out from either side of each sad eye.

Henderson was launching into another rhapsody, when the third man abruptly turned and walked away, limping slightly.

* * *

'Hi, Ma. It's me.'

Molly let herself into the vicarage. She was conscious of being a few minutes late. There was no answer.

'Hi, Kate ... Michael?' Not even the dog. All that could be found was a short, terse note in Gran-Gran's capitals on her kitchen work top.

'SEAN. GONE FOR WALK. WILL SEE YOU WHEN I GET HOME!'

A warning more than a message.

* * *

Sean's mobile went just as he stepped out of his car in the bishop's drive. He counted three rings, hoping it would stop. When it did not he activated it with an introduction.

'Good to talk to you, Reverend Connaughton.' The voice was muffled and low. 'You really are quite clever.' No trace of sarcasm. Just matter-of-fact.

'Hello, can I help you?'

'No, but I can help you.'

'Look, I know this might sound a bit rude, but I wonder if I could telephone you back later, only I'm—'

'Won't be necessary,' sighed the breathy voice, more cultured than not, and with a slight accent that escaped identification. 'Your Page Three piece this evening...? Quite right. The bishop was killed. I did it. The education man on April Fool's Day was also mine. Expect a third victim soon. Oh, and do watch out for the post tomorrow.'

The line went dead and Connaughton felt helpless as he called 'Hello! hello?'

* * *

Molly had her feet up on the lounge coffee table watching the early evening news and waiting for anything on the bishop's death. There had been more youth riots in London. This time the Asians were fighting back and burning a giant Union Jack. Second lead had featured the resignations of two parliamentary ministers, both male and both insisting vigorously that they were not the sort to bother with paedophile sex rings. The morning news pages had provided evidence to the contrary. All of which meant that the bishop and his demise had been relegated to below the halfway adverts. The story still had not been reached when the vicarage mobile telephone rang.

'We were right!' Sean's excited voice almost deafened Molly.

'You're in trouble, Sean Connaughton,' she said, ignoring her brother-in-law's opening, 'and if I were you—'

'Molly, the killer's just telephoned me.' Sean's voice, now serious, made her listen. 'He's not only claiming the bishop but also that April 1st death. He says there'll be another victim soon.'

'Anything else?' Molly was immediately a detective sergeant. 'Age? Accent? Was it definitely a male? Educated or uneducated?' By this time, she was on her feet and by the front door, ready for a quick departure. Connaughton answered her specific queries and added, 'He's sending something in the post. What about Spencer? Will you tell him?'

'No,' came the quick reply. 'He's got too much invested in his suicide theory. Wait for the post. Then, hopefully, we'll have some hard evidence for the chief inspector's undivided attention. Without it, he'll simply dismiss what we have as a hoax. Okay?'

'Fine. Look, I'll see you soon.' Connaughton ended with, 'I'm just about to step on to the bishop's carpet.'

As Molly signed off, her nephew's labrador cleared the vicarage gate, followed rapidly by its owner, and didn't Michael look well compared to the walking vegetable of only a month before! She smiled towards him. He was back on methadone, and hopefully the drug-carrying charge had taught him a mighty lesson.

A moment later, Katie appeared in top wheelchair gear, her artificial voice convinced it was a Formula One engine. Molly craned her neck to look up the road and see where Ma Hannigan was and whether or not she was alone.

She was not, and Molly's emotions were mixed.

6

The old oak door of the new acting Bishop of Hoghton's detached house swung open. The exquisite smile Sean remembered so well from college days was just as wide and as warm.

He could have kissed her with relief. Instead, he settled for the offered hug of old friendship and wondered what to expect next. If severity and sacking were not on the agenda, then what was?

He followed the bishop inside. As they exchanged catch-up news she seemed more subdued than in college days. The smile was muted, though occasionally catching at the corners of her mouth, and Connaughton idly thought that he would not be noticing these nuances if the new bishop had been just another male in purple. But then, political correctness had never been his strong suit, and he quite enjoyed the feminine lines of his boss's artwork.

The diminished smile did, however, have a marked asexual effect on her appearance, leaving the set-jawed sternness and confident presence which, together with a sharp intellect, had made Julia Durham the obvious choice as England's first female bishop. The brief, pleasant exchange of news ended abruptly after the first rattle of coffee cups, and the Right Reverend Julia Durham's voice became brisk.

'As you might expect,' she began, 'Canterbury's been in

touch with us since the news broke, and you don't need me to tell you the impact this death – suicide or whatever – is going to have on the Church.'

'Not suicide, bishop.'

'It's still Julia,' she corrected with a smile, adding, 'Yes, I've already read your *Argus* piece about the improbability of—'

'No, Julia,' Sean interrupted quietly, 'I mean there's been a new development.' He then gave a near-verbatim account of the two telephone conversations he had just had outside her front door.

'I see.' Julia paused to ensure that she did. It also gave her an extra moment to mentally cross-check the new information with her previously made plans.

'Sean, you're here because I need help.' The face seemed to sag heavily with responsibility. 'The archbishop has landed me with this giant diocese. It's going to take every ounce of ingenuity I possess just to maintain what we have, and I am going to need constant updates on this situation. Sean, we worked well together in college, and I need an extra pair of eyes and ears.'

The bishop paused for response but only got rueful smile. 'You won't have had time to look up my file.'

The bishop answered by picking up a manila foolscap wallet from a nearby desk. She withdrew a sheet and began to read,

> *Connaughton is a contrarian by nature. Not a team player; a loose cannon and sometimes perverse. Likes to plough his own furrow though I suspect that if somebody else, especially those from above, agreed with the direction of the furrow, he would start ploughing in the opposite direction, just to be awkward. Loves to be odd man out; the contrary one.*

Sean remembered that part of the dead bishop's assessment of himself almost word for word, and the way the prelate had enjoyed reading it out loud. This had been the prologue to the quit-or-be-sacked ultimatum of a few days before.

'And you're not just the slightest bit worried about that, Julia?'

The reply came with the appearance of a second file. Again Julia Durham read aloud,

> By nature, Connaughton likes to be liked, and sometimes too much. On the other hand, he loves to love and has learned well the truths of 1 Corinthians 13, believing that love bears all things, believes all things and trusts all things. This is the source of his profound and vast reservoir for service. Admittedly, this naïve biblical kind of loving would be a great weakness were it not tempered by an equal liking for truth. When this is at stake, Connaughton can be contrary, and infuriatingly so. This balance of grace and truth, when harnessed will, I am confident, successfully grow churches. One thing I add, you will need to watch his inconsistent management of time. He continually attempts to perfect the miracle of squeezing a week's work into each day. He is a driven personality, possibly to do with his wife's death, and this may well be his undoing, if he is not careful.

Julia tossed both files back on to the desk. 'You're the ears and eyes I need.' Her firmness did not invite debate. 'Don't let me down, Sean.'

Each looked at the other in a waiting, expectant silence. The bishop's pause urged confirmation. The priest's ... well, he frankly found the whole thing rather bizarre after years wrestling with diocesan powers and a doubting bishop.

'I have a parish.' It sounded a lame way to claim thinking time. 'No you haven't!' And seeing Connaughton's immediate apprehension, she quickly added, 'We've got a good man ready to step out of retirement for as long as this takes. You're free to be a journalist to your heart's content, so long as I'm the main editor you report back to. Agreed?'

'Agreed.' he smiled in resignation. 'One extra pair of eyes and ears at your service, ma'am.' Julia rose to signal an end. Sean followed suit, but risked another question.

'How did we end up with this mess?'

'George Williams, you mean?'

'Yes,' and the irritation of years suddenly burst forth. 'We had it made, coming out of the nineties. The heretics had been retired, doubting bishops dethroned. The God-is-dead theologians were safely reinterred in the vaults of academia. The top jobs had gone to strong believing men, and we'd almost convinced the nation that the Church did actually believe in something after all. Then this godless disaster is enthroned and—'

'Not now.' Bishop Julia held up an apologetic hand. 'Explanations are luxuries that will have to wait. There is an answer, but right now I have an emergency meeting of the old bishop's council in ten minutes, and I need the time.'

Connaughton found himself gracefully ushered on to the illuminated tarmac drive of the bishop's house, while her attention turned to the arriving dark-suited diocesan dignitaries. Some, mainly the deceased bishop's yes-men, nodded icily at him when they failed to avoid eye contact. Not for the first time in high clerical company, Sean wondered just what the Almighty had up his sleeve to turn an eternity of theological misfits into heaven.

He climbed into his cab and accelerated away into a cloudless night with relief. Sean was halfway home when the inner nudging voice came again.

'Now?'

Why not? Ma Hannigan would be waiting at home. She'd still be up. Another hour to her bedtime. The decision was made. He turned into a layby, switched off the lights and pulled out a Bible and prayer book from the glove compartment. A million diamonds in the dark velvet beyond his windscreen inspired worship, but he knew that wasn't the real reason why he delayed his journey. He was scared of facing Ma Hannigan. He wondered how God coped with him and seven billion others with their seven billion gods.

* * *

Safari boss Giles St John walked past endless giant wall murals in stark primary colours. The Friends of Curzon House Holding Hospital had commissioned them to brighten up the clinical half-mile-long spinal corridor. Hi-tech wards branched off every few yards and some anonymous committee had chosen names of growth and new life for each of them – Holly, Laburnum, Oak, Cherry, Ash, Beech. Curzon was the limbo into which modern science consigned its living dead; those whom it refused to, or could not, let go. They were the persistent vegetative state victims of road accidents, or muggings or the times mother science herself had blundered. Occasionally, St John passed retreating relatives whose faces sagged with mourning, years before it was due.

St John turned into Evergreen Ward and made for the far cubicle.

'How is she, Stan?' he asked without hope as his oldest friend looked up.

'Same,' and the Honourable Crompton Stanley Richards, MP for Twistleton, smiled warmly. These days he found that he needed to comfort the few who still came to visit.

They both looked down in silence at the still-pretty and slight form that was Sheila Richards. They sat mesmerized for a moment by the gentle rise and fall of the sheet that covered her ventilated form.

'A sleeping beauty. Almost as though she'll open her eyes any—' and St John caught his breath, realizing he had said something similar during a previous visit. Stupid, stinging tears were suddenly there; chest muscles smothered a rising ache, and he turned away.

'It's okay, Giles,' Richards winced as stiffened joints protested about movement after sitting so long. With compassion he reaffirmed, 'Really, it's all right,' and he walked stiffly past his friend, patting his shoulder and beckoning him towards the relatives' lounge. St John followed and stood gazing out of the window at the gathering gloom, and the rubble and weeds crowding the shabby outer walls. The Friends of Curzon had obviously channelled limited funds internally, knowing their patients were beyond the pleasures of outside landscaping.

'I'm afraid I have to add to your lot, Stan.' St John eventually turned from the window. 'They've arrived already. Television cameras, the lot. We've even qualified for the attention of Dr Nature Henderson himself. Are you going to be able to cope?'

'Giles,' the MP sighed with exasperated patience as though they had been through this a dozen times before – which they had – 'we've been expecting this ever since I finalized the project six months ago.'

'What? Pilloried by the media?' St John rapped his knuckles against the window sill, 'Not to mention the loss of votes this summer in the General Election; possibly no job, no more of your beloved Parliament, perhaps your knighthood in jeopardy—'

'Giles, enough!' A harshness had come to Richards' voice. 'The bed's made. We lie in it, and that's that.'

'Something is wrong!' St John thought he had detected some unidentified nuance in his friend's quick anger. 'Has something happened?' No response. 'You've heard something? The investiture? They've put it off, haven't they? They're reneging! Giles, this is going to lose you every—'

'Nothing!' Richards said emphatically. 'This is going to lose me absolutely nothing whatsoever. This TV episode is a

hiccup; a minor irritation. In fact, I shouldn't be too surprised if the whole thing fizzles out long before it gets to the
small screen.' He stretched out and gave his friend a playful
pat on the chin. 'Oh, and by the way, Saturday? The knighthood thing? It's still on. Sir Stan it shall be.'

'If you say so.' Then St John half-heartedly, but hopefully,
added, 'Sure you won't change your mind about some company at the palace?'

'Sorry, Giles, old son,' and Richards smiled at his friend's
drooping expression, 'not after the last three aborted occasions. Hush-hush. No publicity until afterwards. No pomp
and ceremony. No friends or relatives. Just a quick dubbing
before His Majesty pops down the Mall for his birthday
Trooping the Colour.'

'But on your own? It's idiotic!'

'Giles, it makes sense, and you know it.' Richards patted
the flushed cheek of his friend and added, 'If the truth be
known, they're a little exasperated about Sheila's health rul-
ing the young king's engagements. It's either this quickie ceremony or sometime, somewhere else next year.'

St John's disappointment dissipated only slowly. Even on
the drive home, he felt like returning to reargue his case. At
least there was one good thing. Exactly what, the safari boss
was unsure. There was a contentedness in Richards. Perhaps
a new resolution? Maybe. A year of depression, bitterness
and anger. And now, of a sudden... What? Trying to puzzle
out this pleasant change in his friend left St John precious
little time to rehearse what he would say to camera the following day.

* * *

Michael Connaughton held the syringe in one hand and the
belt from his trousers in the other. Aunty Molly had gone
and everybody was in bed except his father, and only God
knew where he was these days. He thought back over the

hard days now coming to an end, albeit for only a night. He had been clean for twenty-six days, thirteen hours and...

'Oh whatever!' he croaked in a voice still twanging in the mid-throes of puberty.

The decision was taken. Just one more injection. Then, perhaps chasing the dragon in the early hours – sniffing the wisps of smoke rising from reheated heroin on silver foil. After that, sleep and quits. No more. No money, certainly not from the paltry part-timer's pounds from WildWorld. No gang. They had gone with the police swoop and the court case. No more freebies from the chemist raids, and no muggings, and no more purse snatches.

'The last trip of a lifetime,' and he grinned, savouring the moment, eagerly anticipating the coming rush.

He withdrew the small self-seal plastic packet slipped to him by Fritzy while out walking with Gran and her new friend. Kate had almost caught them. She had zoomed round a bend so fast, but they had covered the transfer with play wrestling, the old gang supplier and he, and the bag had ended up in the inside breast pocket of his leather jacket. A good mate was Fritzy. Fancy him thinking he might like a bag 'just for old time's sake'.

Michael set out on his bedside table the old syringe he had found some days before, buried at the back of a neglected toy drawer, a favourite hiding place of old. Alongside it, he placed the small spoon he had pocketed during supper, plus the matches borrowed from the emergency candle kit in the electric meter cupboard. The vinegar had turned out to be the biggest risk of all. Gran had actually caught him, evidence in hand, by a kitchen cupboard. But she was easy. A year of gang life had done wonders for his imagination, and she seemed more than eager to accept his casual explanation about school experiments and acetic acid, and return to her friend in the sitting room.

Now, Michael squeezed a trickle of water from his wetted face cloth on to the spoon, added droplets of vinegar and emptied in, ever so carefully, exactly half the contents of Fritzy's bag. Patience began to ebb and he flared six matches bunched together to speed-heat the spoon's mixture to bubbling point. Quite suddenly, the repulsive odour of frying heroin filled his nostrils. The nausea rose up and the retching began, worse than he had remembered.

Balancing the spoon on the table, Michael waited the few seconds it took to cool before drawing it into the syringe and fastening the belt tightly around his left arm. Slapping the skin in search of a rich blue-purple vein, he suddenly remembered Scrapie, the old gang leader. Every externally available vein in his limbs had collapsed so that he had to force his mates to take turns with the painful injections into his neck. Not so for him, though. Slowly, a ribbon of purple rose under the skin and Michael inserted the needle. Belt tight, arm's circulation at a standstill, he pulled back the plunger to extract a few drops of blood to confirm that he had struck the vein. Michael then heard his father's car on the gravel of the drive, and he quickly pushed the plunger down to the hilt. Belt still tight, he swept the makings out of sight behind the bedside table using his tourniqueted arm. He flicked off the bedroom light and, with a little difficulty, slid between the bedclothes. Only then did he release the dam and feel the rush, and the rising, racing exhilaration taking over the back of his throat.

Only slowly, and much later, would the regret seep in.

7

'Parcel from a killer, indeed!'

Ma Hannigan slapped butter on toast as she eavesdropped on a familiar *Argus* voice, clearly irate at having to address an answering machine.

She glanced up to the ceiling with furious thoughts focused beyond it and muttered, 'He's got to get past me first!' The knife once again plunged into the heart of the butter dish.

'A Sean Connaughton skivvy!' she scowled at the next consignment of toast. 'That's me!' Each half-grilled round was then flipped and assailed with a disgruntled litany. 'Vicar's maid...! Vicarage receptionist...! A grandma too busy being ma to spoil her grandkids...! Listening to grumpy news editors with bad telephone attitudes...!'

Her semi-burnt audience, white side up, gazed back blankly.

'... and then, when I want an hour off for good behaviour, what do I get?' The four unresponsive rounds were thrust into another kind of grilling, and Ma Hannigan answered herself, 'Nothing! Absolutely, blooming—'

The monologue ended abuptly as she gathered the skirts of her dressing gown and marched out of the kitchen to the foot of the stairs.

'Sean Connaughton!' She tried hard to sound severe and it would have worked had she had her teeth in. 'This is your

62

alarm call and, believe me, you have every cause to be alarmed!'

An inattentive groan from above was her only reward, and she was about to flounce back to the kitchen when the importance of the telephone message tugged at her conscience.

'And there's a message from Old Walrus Face.' Such was her assessment of Frank Winter, despite the last Christmas office do when it was generally agreed that she had drawn out of him hitherto unsuspected human tendencies. 'He says there's a big envelope addressed to you at the *Argus* and signed by A. Killer.'

The groans became more alert. Thudding feet certified that the message had been received and understood.

It was then that Ma Hannigan came to a decision. Today was the day. She would tell him while the mood held. The inventor of the menopause never designed grannies to be mothers. Enough was most definitely enough.

A sense of the ridiculous, Ma Hannigan reckoned, was what elevated humanity above the rest of the animal kingdom. No ape truly laughed at itself. Not many goldfish held conferences on the absurdity of bowl existence or wet nursing their grandchildren. Only she and seven billion other souls had that privilege. Only she and the old dears in the butcher's queue philosophized about the necessity of being able to grin and bear it, as they tried to outdo each other for the week's worst tragedy – always tragedy, 'for there's nowt much to laugh at besides, is there?' They laughed when there was too much sorrow. They cried when their cups of joy overflowed. Nora had done both on a journey away from working-class asperity to the political heights of Washington and then back home to a Lancashire vicarage sink – 'as a vicarage skivvy!'

Overhead, large feet lurched from bedroom to bathroom. She placed the burnt offerings for her priest-in-law on the breakfast table: black-edged, cold and crisp.

'Serve him right!' she huffed.

The scene sparked a memory into life, and Nora was immediately in a different age and in another kitchen. It was a dark and draughty one in a weaver's cottage in Ramstwistle, a few hills away from where she now stood. Her mum was perched on a low, three-legged stool before glowing coals, toasting doorstep-thick wedges of bread on a three-pronged wire fork. She, a diminutive, pigtailed Nora Lumb, hopped beside her, ready for the next charred slice, wanting to coat it with bacon dripping for her waiting dad. Funny how these ancient recollections were more vivid now, in 'the evening of one's life', as those TV funeral ads drooled. There were times when Nora couldn't quite recall what had happened the day before – but sixty years ago! No problem.

Nestling in a tarry of nostalgia were those breathtaking rainbow ribbons, one to each pigtail; so rare two years into a world war. She was wearing them for Joe next door; handsome in a gnomish sort of way. He was a short, cheeky chappy in his butcher's apron of blue stripes on white, sat astride his gleaming black delivery bike. It was his first job and though he was three years older than she, they had a secret understanding. It was engraved within a heart – their initials intertwined in ancient wood in the clough where the first wild rams were said to have quenched their thirst in the twistle, or stream. Underneath, Joe's multi-purpose scout knife had solemnly picked out 'IWFY' – 'I'll Wait For You'.

Stripes in white faded to grey-blue as the uniform changed. Joe Trezise, having deliberately mislaid his birth certificate and lied about his age 'to get in before the fun ended', was now a gunner in the RAF.

And then the painfully shy Joel entered the picture.

'Like a film star from 'ollywood', Nora's schoolfriends used to coo. Joel came back with daredevil, go-anywhere Joe on weekend leave from the American airforce base at Burtonwood, near Warrington. He came, and never seemed to go away again. And there they were; in the Manchester Ritz, opposite Oxford Road railway station, the three of them, taking turns at dancing and laughing and living because you never knew when the next buzz bomb would stop droning and fall out of the sky.

Thoughts of Joe and Joel had a melting effect on Nora, and she was suddenly back in the vicarage kitchen and reaching for the plate of stone-cold toast. She dropped the pieces in the bin and reloaded the grill with fresh bread, and even as she did it, her mind was again sliding out of the present.

And now, there she was with a long face next to Joe's excited one. His posting had come through; to an aerodrome on the south coast, and Joe had got American Joel to promise that he would look after 'his Nora'.

And he had.

A quiet gentleman of the Deep South was Joel, tall and distinguished with a pleasant baby face, and a good ten years older than she. Somehow, that made him safe. At least that's what Mam and Dad had happily decided. And Joel was marvellous for nylons. Nora never had to stain her legs with streaky gravy browning, nor pencil in make-believe seams. Always, Nora saved a pair for the occasional weekend homecomings of Flight Sergeant Joe ('Three stripes are just for show,' he'd grinned self-consciously but with pride, 'so that the Huns treat us better if we're ever shot down'). She always shuddered at the hateful stripes.

A tail-end Charlie, Joel had called Joe. Then, on the forty-seventh tour of duty – far too many, they later admitted – Joe was hit over Dresden. Ack-ack had burst the perspex bubble around him and his gun. In one cruel night he had lost his job, his mates, the lower part of his left leg and, worst of all, his courtesy stripes. It had been a bitter and angry Joe who had eventually limped home to Nora.

And Joel had been marvellous; over from Burtonwood as often as his bomber pilot ops allowed; though with wings and legs still intact he was the last person to pull Joe from the depths. Nora, sixteen in that spring of '45, felt a lifetime older, especially when Joe took the tram 'to t'other side of

Manchester' to live with his uncle and work in his butcher's shop.

'I can't look after myself,' he'd cried that day, 'so 'ow can I look after thee, lass?'

And he had gone.

She had looked for him everywhere. And Joel was there, as usual. Rock solid. He had even borrowed a jeep to search for Joe's butcher's shop. And then it was VE Day, and they had celebrated at the Ritz in the hope that Joe might turn up. They had danced till dawn, feeling oddly guilty in each other's arms. VJ Day arrived and then there was no patience for guilt. Time was too precious, for they had reached an understanding, and demobilization and Joel's imminent return to his 'flowery Florida state' loomed.

That taut confrontation with Dad was as though it had happened yesterday. Father and Joel Hannigan face to face, calmly at first and then with intensifying heat. Chapel-reared Dad had finally and flatly pronounced with Lancashire obstinacy, 'No daughter of mine's running off t' 'merica with a Yank, especially one who's old enough to be ... er ... well, old enough to know bloody better!'

He had muttered on about loose women and foreign soldiers, and Mam had tried to shush Dad, but Dad wasn't for shushing, and the demob boat wasn't for waiting. She had cried so that Joel's Liverpool boat blurred long before it reached the horizon beyond New Brighton. It was to take another two years of crying, and a return visit of a rather prosperous looking Joel in respectable civvies, before Dad finally relented.

* * *

Heavy footsteps taking the stairs two at a time turned a glowing, laughing young Nora Lumb back into a fractious old Ma Hannigan.

'So,' she said, slithering the word menacingly towards a quickly advancing son-in-law, 'and where were you last night?'

'Gran, you're not going to believe this,' Sean unwisely began addressing the wrong subject, 'we've the makings of a serial killer, right here in Hoghton. Can you believe that?'

'I could suggest his next victim?'

'Hmm?' Sean feigned cool surprise. 'Molly arrived all right last night, didn't she?' and his attempted innocence only compounded his guilt.

'Sean Connaughton, this household drudge is giving you a month's notice.' Nora, short and dumpy and having to look up to her six feet of son-in-law, folded her arms across her outsize bosom. 'I trust that you will find that acceptable, reverend sir.'

Sean smiled uneasily. This was not his mother-in-law's usual form of humour. He was not immediately sure which line he needed to take to extricate himself so that he could go quickly to hunt a bishop killer.

'You're upset, aren't you?' He seemed amazed at his own insight. 'Look, I promise—'

'Too late.' Ma Hannigan started a slow smile, and actually felt relieved that her news was almost broken. 'One month, and then you grill your own toast.'

Sean decided to humour this weird, unfathomable mood. 'And is one allowed to ask what happens in a month's time?'

'Yes!' Ma Hannigan was brusque. 'You're going to marry me!'

* * *

'Your Holiness?' Frank Winter's thick sarcasm tried to penetrate. 'If we might just proceed?' Still, Connaughton sat oblivious of the surrounding editorial conference in progress.

He had known immediately on waking to the less-than-dulcet tones of Ma Hannigan that he had only one priority: to secure and, if possible, make sense of what the killer would send him, if indeed sense could be had from a multiple murderer's mail. But then, Ma Hannigan had shaded his black and white day. He now felt somewhat confused as he sat before the still-sealed, ten by eight buff envelope on the editor's desk while around him the higher-ups – the heads of editorial, circulation and advertising – heatedly debated at what stage the police should be called in. Before, after or even while it was opened.

Sean's mind was still back in the kitchen. He now realized from give-away clues like the flying toast, that there could have been a more sensitive way of dealing with his mother-in-L. Perhaps his reply had been a tad over-jocular ...

'Isn't there something against marrying your wife's mother in the Prayer Book's Table of Kindred and Affinity?'

At this point he had had to duck to avoid a lethal slice. Yet, the whole subject had been a family joke ever since a young Kate had burst into tears one Saturday morning when Daddy had announced that he was off to church to marry such-and-such a lady. Katie, too young to understand Daddy's dog-collar duties, had insisted even then that the engagement of a new mum was more her province than her father's.

Sean did, however, regret his crassness in not stopping to talk and apologize to Gran. In fact, inner calls for repentance were beginning to mount high at present: Katie and her 'definite possible' had not been addressed. There had been no time to see his son, and did moody Michael deliberately switch off his bedroom light last night as he drove up? And then there was Sammi. Could he really leave her funeral to a stranger? Finally, there was God. Exactly! Finally. At the end of everything else! To be sure, he had squeezed in his daily ration of psalms and prayers as any self-respecting cleric would. But it was stopgap stuff; no real stillness. No honest communication. Just his input, his views, his words, his readings. Empty praise, signifying nothing much.

'Don't bother me now,' he might as well have said. 'I'll get back to you when I can squeeze you in.' At moments like these, there was room for only one god in Sean Connaughton's life. And it wasn't God. Not when survival was at stake; not when he had to be fit enough to juggle his universes without dropping a single sphere. In survival! That was the mode. Or insanity!

'HELLO!' Winter's bark eventually rounded up the wandering flock of Sean's woolly thoughts. 'We're very sorry if we've been boring you, your eminence ... so, that's agreed then,' declared the news editor, 'we tell the police immediately we've finished with the contents of the killer's envelope' – a wicked smile anticipated beating even the TV boys – 'which should be about five minutes before our exclusive hits the streets.'

Turning to Connaughton he barked, 'Open up!'

'Isn't that my decision?' smiled Sean, playing for time. 'Won't be you standing before a judge charged with perverting the course of justice, will it?' The bristles on Winter's upper lip stood rigidly to attention and, accompanied by irrelevant adjectives, he exploded, 'This would never have happened if—'

An opening door aborted another dig at the enrolment of part-time amateurs. The editor's matronly secretary announced, 'A detective chief inspector and his nice lady sergeant say they have been invited to meet Mr Connaughton here.'

'Hope you didn't mind, gentlemen.' Sean tried to look serious. 'I gave them only my name, rank and number over the telephone this morning but they tortured me into submission.' Spencer and Hannigan entered and Sean pointed to the envelope. 'Over to you, chief.'

'Right, sergeant, quick as you can and don't mess it up.' Spencer sighed at the tediousness of delegation. Molly lamented her lost days off, donned regulation gossamer-thin rubber gloves and checklisted through the externals as though carrying out a post-mortem.

'No stamp, therefore hand-delivered ... thin, insubstantial envelope ... apparently not heat-rollered or sized, so fingerprints might be a problem ... also, standard-type available at any corner shop, so watermarks probably won't help beyond telling us the batch...'

'Sergeant?' Spencer tried to interrupt the flow but without success.

'... little content to envelope ... maybe only a single sheet ... outside, computer-generated print indicates good quality inkjet ... might get a make on the ink batch with the mass spectrometer—'

'Sergeant, let's not go all around the forensics,' the chief inspector broke in wearily. 'Just get on with it.'

In bold upper-case italics the address on the outside of the envelope read,

For the attention of...
SEAN CONNAUGHTON,
EDITORIAL,
THE ARGUS

and underneath,

Killer

'Letter bomb...?' the sergeant mused turning the envelope round and studiously ignoring her boss. 'Not really. Harmless enough.'

'You sure?' a rather nervous Henry Parrott asked.

'Yes, sir.' Molly was confident. 'Terrorists might be hi-tech these days but they still need just a tiny bit more bulk to mask timers and strips of explosives. But, just in case...' and she laid the envelope address down on the editor's table, took an artist's razor-bladed knife from a small kit of tools, 'we'll go in through the back.'

Several present, including the editor and chief inspector, took an unconscious half-step backwards while Winter and Connaughton moved forward for a good story.

Hannigan opened up a slit, half an inch in from the long edge of the envelope.

'This will also,' she murmured to nobody in particular, 'allow the lab boys to test the gummed ends for possible DNA material.'

She carefully reached in with tweezers and removed a folded piece of white A4. She fingertipped it open to reveal more print in a similar font and size.

'Whoever he is,' a now eager editor focused on the less-than-relevant, 'he likes his Century Schoolbook bold italics.'

'It doesn't have to be a "he", sir,' and Molly carried on to read the note out loud.

> ### SURVIVAL OF THE FITTEST?
> *He who lives by it shall die by it.*
> *Two already have.*
> *Two more to come, at least.*
> *– Halipegus*
> **P.S. Check for hyoscine in April 1st**
> **body, if in doubt.**

'Now, gentlemen, if you would allow us to get on with the important work instead of all these media theatricals.' Chief Inspector Spencer motioned his sergeant to plastic-bag the evidence.

'Perhaps you could give us your initial reactions, chief inspector?' the journalist in Connaughton asked.

'No comment,' said Spencer who then commented, 'it is far too early to make an assessment.'

'Fair enough, but would you say the killer is trying to say something to us?' Sean found that imbecile questions sometimes provoked replies from know-alls. Spencer refused to rise, and also remained dumb when Winter innocently asked whether the chief inspector could at least confirm that this was now a murder hunt rather than a suicide inquiry.

71

* * *

The editorial conference over, Connaughton sat drumming up inspiration with his fingertips below the keyboard space bar. The monitor remained grey-white and wordless, except for the patiently winking cursor.

The telephone rang. It was Katie using what she called 'her voice'. It was a quiet, softly feminine sound usually heard issuing from somebody of more than Kate's ten years, yet it sounded completely right for her. With this voice, Dad didn't play, for this was his real daughter.

'Have you and Gran-Gran had a row, Dad?'

'Not really, Katie. We just didn't get too much time to talk this morning.'

'She was crying before she came up with my brekkie' – and quite suddenly Kate's real voice crackled over – 'an' an-an's-een-eeing-umoddy, an' an-an's-owing-oo-eave-us, ad! 'U've-ot-oo-oo-umm-ing!'

Kate's physical voice was music to those who loved her, but she only used it in extremis, for it sounded like madness to her. Her natural voice had seemed fine before the road accident. She was beginning to put words together – 'Dada come' and 'milk all gone' being the most natural telegraphese to an already bossy little madam. She could echo nursery rhymes, and consonants were no problem, 'n' being the most used, as in the pouting 'No!' when she couldn't get her way. But then had come the accident, and something within had been mangled.

The first doctors had smiled reassuringly while hiding behind imprecise medical jargon. Sean had almost kissed a later consultant in gratitude for the relief that his much desired honesty brought. There was a candid confession that neither he nor his medical colleagues had a clue as to why Kate's speech had been damaged. After that, speech experts came and went. The vowels remained all present and correct, but somehow Kate's brain and lips just refused to co-operate with most consonants. At the wilful age of six, Kate had ruled therapy a dismal failure and promptly struck herself dumb, convinced that nobody would ever love a broken body with no pretty words.

That had remained the situation until two birthdays ago when Aunty Molly's present of a voice synthesizer had enticed Kate out of her self-woven cocoon of silence. Now, all the family agreed that she used it far too much, and it was only at times of high emotion – times when words were so important that they could not be trusted to artificial accents – when she yelled out in what she called her gabble-de-babble.

Dad automatically translated his daughter's noise: 'and Gran-Gran's been seeing somebody, and she's going to leave us, Dad! You've got to do something!'

8

Brian Mather's night had been unkind and much of him was hung over. His eyelids were at half mast, the insides like emery paper. During the early hours, revelling hooligans had twice tried to smash up his outside-broadcast van, and each time the hotel night porter had felt it his duty to rouse him.

'Tell Dr Henderson next time,' Mather had mumbled after the second vandal visitation.

'Oh, we couldn't possibly do that, sir!' The porter had stiffened. 'Our policy on our celebrated guests states quite categorically that—'

'Only kidding,' Mather smiled impishly. Fortunately, the damage was superficial, his unit having been allocated one of the armour-plated vans that had started to come on line soon after the right-wing youth riots.

In the grey morning, not only were his eyes protesting, but his stomach had come out in sympathy, sagging beneath last night's everything-in-oil feast. Many in his business might have drowned a Henderson-type in a bottle, if they didn't hit him with it first. Mather instead found solace by gorging his innards. And why not, on a BBC expense account? Not that he was teetotal. Being on location, the fare, of course, had to be washed down with the regulation evening intake of four pints or, for him, the equivalent in Johnny Walkers. This morning, a dehydrated tongue, as furred as his sound engineer's microphone cover, lolled with everything else.

Mather's self-esteem and spirit, not to be left out, drooped with the apathy of near-unemployment. While he was still permitted to direct the movement of cameras, it was, of course, only at the suggestion of Maestro Henderson.

There had been a time when he had thanked Dr Henderson for his 'kind suggestions', and then done exactly as his own tastes and style had directed. The ensuing seismic shock had been recorded in no less a place than the penthouse suite of the BBC's Langham Place, and Brian Mather had caught the full force of the returning tidal wave. It had left him with the distinct impression that it was not Henderson who would be swept away.

Mather now seethed in silence in the cool morning air. He had, as per instructions, set up a light mobile crew round the corner from WildWorld's main administrative entrance. Henderson, microphone in hand, overriding the soundman's muttered union threats, waited to pounce the moment Giles St John arrived.

Henderson loved doorstepping his victims. It demonstrated to his audience of millions how intrepid he was. While Mather accepted the technique for reaching the shy prima donnas of crime, he generally regarded it as a last resort. St John, in his humble opinion, which he had kept to himself, hardly qualified. This was merely a second approach. The day before, his office had politely informed their research assistant that Mr St John wished to consult others before commenting. That was all the excuse Henderson had needed. The safari boss was obviously a hostile witness, and doorstepping was the subpoena of trial by television. Henderson's beloved public jury must have their victim.

The doctor might be a pain in the annals of television, Mather thought as they waited, but nevertheless he had a certain morbid fascination with Henderson's cast-iron certainties. It was rare to find such self-assurance in a millennium that regarded words like 'absolute' and 'definite' as old-fashioned. And how did he find the audacity to practise the black and white science of the nineteenth century when quantum physics and chaos theory had left only multi-hues of grey?

As they watched the directors' parking bays on the lookout for St John's zebra-striped Land Rover, Mather had to admit to himself that Henderson was a man of great faith. True, he was somewhat blind and fundamentalist in his science, not unlike those old-time religionists, but he held it all together with a great evangelical zeal. On another continent and in another millennium, he would have made a powerful witchdoctor whose only god was nature and its potions.

Henderson had startled the whole location crew the other evening in the hotel bar while Mather was in the midst of musing on the simple beliefs and doubts he had carried round since Sunday school. They were somewhat buckled by the lone machine-gunner who had, hours before, sprayed home-time school children, killing and injuring at least a dozen. It was then that Henderson had roared, 'There is no God!'

The derision silenced the whole room.

'Look,' Henderson waved his arms, 'it's a con trick. A Big Bang. Evolution! That's what it's all about. Old Ma Nature preserving her best gene mutations while drowning her unwanted gene runts. Simple as that.'

'Really!' somebody in a hidden alcove had called. 'You tellin' me that those gunned-down kids and us are just pointless accidents? Surely we're more complicated than that. What about the eye? What about our consciences? How on earth could those have evolved?'

'Simple,' Henderson had beamed over his third Benedictine. 'They've all gently mutated over millions of years. There are no gods, nor rights and wrongs. Just a mechanical process – an algorithm!'

You could not talk to Henderson long before he would trot out his favourite word. 'An al-gor-ith-m,' he had intoned down his nose, tossing back his head and swilling it round like a wine taster appreciating a fine bouquet. 'Algorithm!' Then, the word taster seemed to realize that perhaps his audience hadn't evolved as well as he in the upstairs department of life.

'An algorithm is a foolproof, cannot-fail, recipe. Nobody guides it. It progresses to its brilliant end through tiny, smooth steps. And it always works!' He had ended on a rising exclamation, perhaps hoping for gasps of wonderment. When the swoons failed to materialize, he resorted to noise, trying to emboss the idea on his Neanderthal congregation.

'That's it!' he had cried out in triumph. 'Nature as we see her is the outcome of a simple, infallible recipe.'

Mather even now, waiting behind Henderson with the crew, relished the irritation that had flashed across Henderson's face when one of the lowly production lasses had quietly asked, 'Who invented the recipe? Where did the ingredients come from?'

Henderson, as though addressing a thoughtless child, had launched into an explanation about how clay crystals gradually increased in complexity until the process ended with amino acids, the building blocks of life – 'Of course!' he finished with a flourish.

The lowly assistant had then asked TV's Dr Nature to correct her biology, but wasn't it right that nobody had ever seen dead clay crystals produce life-giving material?

The bar had perked up at this point, and the crew had smiled in anticipation. Henderson had briefly seemed vulnerable.

'Of course, that's not the only theory about how life started,' Henderson had chuckled uneasily, sliding away from an awkward point. 'Oh, no. I mean, the most popular idea of all is still the stagnant primordial soup. Did you know that? The idea of the pond of chemicals as the earth cooled down and a shaft of lightning stirring it into life?' These last questions were asked as if he were addressing the elderly deaf. It was amazing how he could enrapture a television audience, yet be so inept, even offensive, on an individual basis.

'Now, there has been laboratory work done in this area where a few amino acids have successfully been produced in test-tube conditions. They even managed to create nine of the twenty carbon-based molecules that form life.'

He had now recovered his superior aplomb and was in full flow.

'And, of course, there is the brilliant concept of life originating in the ocean depths, where the earth's tectonic plates grate against each other. Here, fierce heat bubbles into being a positive abundance of the chemicals of which we are made.'

The Henderson arms and his dramatic delivery were now aimed at an audience rather than the individual. He had kept the bar room interested for a time. But one or two had turned away once the fun had finished.

Or so they had thought.

'Please forgive my ignorance, Dr Henderson.' It was the lowly assistant again and the attention of the bar had engaged once more in the remote hope that Henderson might meet his match. 'You're saying that this flash of lightning or underwater geyser, or whatever, produces the basic building blocks of life, these amino acids, many of which are extremely complex chemical assemblies? Is that what you're saying, doctor?'

Henderson had nodded. He looked genial, if a little wary.

'Okay, now, am I right in recalling that it takes at least a hundred of these amino acids, many of them of different varieties, to make up just one protein...?'

Henderson blinked behind steepled fingers.

'... and that a living or life-giving cell needs at least seventy or so of these intricate proteins for existence as we know it today? Am I still remembering right?'

The TV man's steepled hands had at this point exploded exaggeratedly into the air in one of his characteristic gestures and he had managed a 'Well...' before the assistant went on.

78

'... and not only does a living, life-giving cell need all this but it also requires a central office to run these protein machines on what we might call the cell's factory floor. Also, doesn't the acid of this office, the DNA, contain the whole blueprint of making the complete creature, whatever it is going to be?'

'Yes, but...'

Brian Mather, standing outside WildWorld, now remembered his pleasure at seeing the great television guru struggle under this gentle, insistent cross-examination. Especially as the lowly assistant stepped up a gear.

'... and, furthermore, is that DNA not folded into an incredible double helix of four highly developed chemicals? And doesn't the central office need another acid – RNA – to act as a factory messenger to tell the dozens of protein machines what to produce...?'

Henderson's mouth worked and his arms waved but he failed to get in. The production assistant was by now machine-gunning facts at the doctor.

'... and doesn't a cell need a skin of some sort to survive, plus food outside, plus a way of getting it in, plus a highly technical waste disposal system? After all this, hasn't it got to have some way of copying all this so that another living, life-giving cell can be made, and, Dr Henderson...'

(Here came a pause for effect.)

'... do you really think that all this can actually come about by accident? By lightning? By nature blundering around in some other mindless, mechanical way?'

And then had followed an odd silence.

Drinkers had looked at each other. Some had gazed, a little cockeyed, up at the bar ceiling. Was that a victory? Did it deserve applause, or what? Before a general consensus could be reached, Henderson had abruptly blustered back to life.

'This is stupid! Stupid! You're missing the whole point.' Henderson was plainly weary of having to defend himself before a jumped-up second-stringer from the pits of the BBC lowerarchy.

'You haven't understood a word I've said,' and the arms had pumped up and down to stress each word. 'It's simply the survival of the fittest, my dear child. Listen. I'll say it slowly. The algorithm, the recipe, produces slight changes in an organism. If one gene has an advantageous mutation, then it survives better than the others which don't have the advantage. Got it? The stronger genes go on and the others don't. In ... this ... way...' – again Henderson had slowed to imbecile pace – 'things change slowly, and great things happen.'

The television crew visibly slumped over their pint pots. That definitely was not victory. Good try. Another time perhaps. Noses went into beer glasses.

'Only, I just wondered, Dr Henderson,' and the noses bobbed back out, 'why you seemed so certain that there is no God?'

As if to add emphasis, the young assistant had stood up and walked towards Henderson. She was smiling patiently. She seemed almost to be tolerating the doctor, trying to help him gently through to some vital disclosure. Her quiet confidence generated intense curiosity in what she might now say.

'You see,' she looked up to the doctor, 'you don't seem too sure of where life has bubbled up from. You can't say how we got the recipe of life. Nor the ingredients. You don't even know how your recipe works. I just wondered what made you so absolutely sure that there is no Creator?'

She had smiled, wide-eyed. Enquiringly. There was silence. Henderson was looking into his glass.

'Why are you so certain, doctor, that there is no God when you have so many massive doubts?'

Still no reply. Henderson looked at the ceiling, his mouth without words, eyes rolling in search of an answer. The applause broke after a second with whoops and shouts.

Henderson's eyes, set in a reddening face, came back to focus on a point near the door. He rose to his full height and slowly declared, striving for a dignity that he just missed, 'You haven't an inkling. There are many fine and convincing concepts about how life started. In addition to the highly respectable theories I've already covered, there's panspermia—'

'Pan-what?' Mather remembered asking, and Henderson had looked down on him as though he doubted his ability to understand.

'It's to do with the sperm or seed of life being transported in cosmic debris from elsewhere in the universe—'

'From outer space?' blurted out a fortified Mather, 'You've lost your argument on Earth, so you now tell us that we come from little green bacteria on Mars. Seems easier to believe in a maker.'

'For you ex-Sunday school boys, maybe.' Henderson looked down his nose, and Mather exploded to his feet.

'Sneer away if you like!' Mather stood straight before him and snarled. 'You think we're an accident; just the end of a mindless, mechanical process in which there's no right and wrong. Tell me, Herr Doktor,' and Mather had been aware of shouting at this stage, 'was the gunning down of innocent schoolchildren just another accidental blip in your mindless scheme of things? Was there not one single right or wrong in the whole tragic episode?'

This time, there had been a different sort of quiet. Henderson had stared back, his face frozen into pure hatred. Eventually, and with a haughtiness, he stiffly walked out of the bar. Of course, when Mather had sobered up the following morning, Dr Henderson had insisted on an apology before the whole of the crew. Only after this would he consider setting off for the day's location. Mather had, of course, supplied it. The show must go on. Anyway, he doubted that he would have survived a second tidal wave from the BBC penthouse suite. He might have followed the lowly production assistant. Within twenty-four hours of the bar room debate, she had been transferred to an Antarctic crew filming the life cycle of emperor penguins.

* * *

Michael Connaughton huddled in the corner of the WildWorld stable he was paid to keep clean before and after school each day. He gently cradled in his lap the baby black buck that had been born during the night. The mother buck licked in attendance.

Michael would normally have been pleased at the privilege, but the sinews held his body taut and strained for want of heroin. His misery was such that not even a baby buck was able to lighten it. Michael hated the world. That included himself. Daft! Dumb! Half-witted! Simple and stupid! And what was it his English teacher used to say? 'A moronic retarded imbecile with the brain power of a dyslexic geriatric gnat on dope'! Such a way with words. His teacher could rant non-stop for ten whole minutes without repetition, trying, he claimed, to instil in his charges the relevance of their mother tongue.

Most in the class, though, still stuck to the four-letter words, and Michael Connaughton considered himself all of them rolled together. How idiotic could he be? Fancy forgetting what it was to be an addict! Imagine kidding himself that it was just going to be one last time! Now, he remembered why he took heroin: not primarily for the surge, but just to feel normal.

Mother buck listened as her part-time home help berated himself. The sounds were familiar. She had heard, if not understood, it all before. Michael again blamed himself for everything. His mother's death. His sister's wheelchair. His father's misery. His own boredom. Nobody understood him. Not even Aunt Molly, though she had tried. Not bad for a pig cop!

And here he was. A man! Well, virtually at thirteen. Tall and advanced for his age, with all the apparatus associated with manhood since coming out of his tenth year. Even the bus drivers had refused him half-fare, until he had begun to carry around his ID with his school books and heroin kit.

The 'blip boy' the papers had called him. Apparently, his five-month shoplifting, mugging and housebreaking spree had created a significant pinnacle in the graph of local juvenile crime. Aunt Molly had explained that, such had been the local pressure, organized by the two MPs at Houghton and Twistleton, they had had to set up a special juvenile task force just to track down him and his Druggies gang.

Since the court case last month, he had been, as his father had demanded, 'clean as a whistle and as honest as the day is long'.

'You're a vicar's son, for heaven's sake!'

But that was exactly the problem. Couldn't his father see that? Why did adults suddenly seem so stupid once you started to become one yourself? Michael recalled the day he had swapped from junior to high school, and his new mates were exchanging facts and figures in a bragging session. One girl, whom he had quite fancied, asked what his father did for a living.

'A plumber,' Michael had shot back. 'You know; mends U-bends and tampers with ballcocks.'

The following February, when the same girl fancied sending him a Valentine's card, she had sneaked a look at the school register for his address.

'How come you live at St Thomas's Vicarage if yer dad's a poncy plumber?' she had me-mowed in his face.

The school's tom-toms were drumming within seconds. Connaughton was one of those goody-two-shoes vicar's sons who hid a halo under his school cap.

The shame!

He felt as though he had peed in his pants in the middle of biology and everybody was sniggering behind his back.

Another four years of this! Impossible. Unbearable. Nobody should endure that torture. Something had to be done to prove that he was just as normal as everybody else. The first test had involved shoplifting. Then the Druggies had bet that 'nice church boys don't take trips'. They lost their bet. And he lost his freedom. Lost his innocence. Lost everything else. Next came truancy. Then burglary, and the rest.

And now, here he was again. Poised high on the slippery slope and starting to slide. Tuesday morning. Withdrawal symptoms. From drugs. Also from school. Truancy. Mother buck didn't ask any questions. Baby buck was infinitely more interesting than geometry. Later, he would stroll down the nearby WildWater tunnel and see if the sharks were in from the lakes.

* * *

'Go!' shouted Henderson, and he ran, fur-covered microphone outstretched, towards Giles St John who was stepping away from his parked Land Rover.

Henderson saw himself charging from the moral high ground, champion and defender of nature, against the enemy. He was ready, even yearning, for the side-effects of doorstepping – unready victims gibbering in panic with strange and unpredictable reactions. That, in Henderson's judgement, produced great television.

'Just one minute, Mr St John.' A pugnacious Henderson moved in, rolling cameraman as his shadow. 'We've been trying to interview you about this "killing for kicks" controversy at your safari park. Your office has barred our way. How can you possibly justify this slaughter of innocent animals as family entertainment?'

St John turned to face the onslaught and the microphone thrust into his face.

'Good morning, gentlemen,' he beamed brightly. 'Sorry you've had trouble. Do come on in and have coffee. Only too happy to have a good chat about things.'

'Cut!' smiled Mather.

St John then had to wait an hour for the crew to set lighting and sound and plan camera angles. The public might accept loss of quality when chasing reluctant interviewees; indeed, it often added to the realism. But indoor, set-piece television permitted only perfection.

While he waited, Giles pondered what he might say.

There would be no questions about the good news. Of course. No admiring queries of how he had rescued a hundred impoverished hill farmers on a score of moors in east Lancashire at the turn of the millennium. The farmers had been devastated by an outbreak of initials like BSE, CJD and the EU. Then there had been the withdrawal of government subsidies, scrapie in sheep, panic in meat markets, falling public confidence. The agricultural science that had made them was now inadequate to protect them. Once, it had taught them how to build better muscle and fibre on cheaper feed. Now, it couldn't prove that the end product was safe to eat. Of course it couldn't. Science could never give one hundred per cent certainties. Only probabilities. Contingencies. Possibilities. And that was never going to be good enough for a fickle public.

Sales had fallen. So too had morale. Suicides had risen, though not in Lancashire; not when St John had given them a stakeholder partnership in a modern safari with Millennium Fund aid; not when he had then offered most of them permanent, well-paid jobs with the added fascination of caring for exotic animals.

The real money, of course, had come from commerce; a partnership with a foreign water company cashing in on the perennial hosepipe bans and a British public tired of gardening with old bath water. The package had included Wild-Water – three new reservoirs, designed in the form of North America's Great Lakes. Two were fresh water and, thanks to improved salination technology, one sea water. All three met over a quarter-mile network of reinforced glass tunnels, affording close-ups of coral reef aliens and deep-sea monsters. A school of Great Whites were the main attraction, and feeding time for Jaws was big money.

A hotel-cum-shopping-cum-multi-cinema-cum-just-about-everything-else had completed a scheme that had not only saved Lancashire's farmers but rejuvenated a depressed and underdeveloped backwater of Britain. Of course, there would be no questions on all this. Good news was not news. There would be no pats on the back. Just accusations. Charges to answer about extending WildWorld into the northern reaches of Lancashire, again giving a life-saving package to the farmers, but also giving death sentences to some animals at the hands of big-game hunters.

It had been Crompton Stanley Richards' thesis after much research into the world's endangered species. Most remaining species, in fact. The Twistleton MP had begun the Wild-World thesis just a month after his wife's accident at St John's suggestion, primarily to keep his mind occupied, but also to provide a sane way of saving at least some of the dwindling number of wildlife species. Somehow, new money had to be raised and St John knew that Richards might have the answer.

Giles St John became aware of Henderson hovering, just before he pounced.

'Why are you and the local MP for Twistleton planning to kill these beautiful creatures for family fun?' Henderson asked as his cameras rolled.

'To keep some of these beautiful creatures alive.'

'You're not making sense. Lions, tigers, even elephants, gazelles. Shot to death! Surely, there won't be any of these left soon with people like you.'

'You almost got it right there, Dr Henderson, only it's the other way round. If there were not people like me, these beautiful creatures would all be dead within the next decade. The real wild world would be wiped out, and I suspect most of your viewers have come to realize that. The truth is that the world out there is too wild for these wild animals. Too many ivory poachers, millions of Orientals grinding up tiger bones for magic potions, others wanting aphrodisiacs from rhino horns. We've got to the stage when only humans can survive in the jungle nowadays, and—'

'Come on, Mr St John,' Henderson's look of sincerity was convincing, 'you're a businessman making a fast buck from the slaughter of these innocents. Isn't that nearer the truth?'

'Examine the WildWorld and WildWater finances any time. Most of the profits of our present set-up are being fed into this new venture. Unfortunately, it's not enough. The only way I can raise the remainder and give a home to these beautiful creatures is through a real-life safari. We are therefore allowing the equivalent of our annual cull to be done on a commercial basis. Safari hunters will be immediately on hand to ensure suffering is kept to a minimum.'

'It's killing for thrills!' Henderson accused bluntly. 'Crude slaughter for profit, and do you think we really should be encouraging that in a civilized world?'

St John paused and smiled. 'Dr Henderson, I'm afraid you have a quaint, rosy view of humanity. The sad truth is that you and I belong to the greediest species alive. We don't just kill for food, protection and clothing. You're right. We do kill for gain. For power. For thrills. For kudos. For ornaments on the study wall. We've annihilated most of the rainforests, killed off a million species, either directly or indirectly by grabbing their habitats. We've crippled whole ecosystems.'

Now St John had stopped smiling. 'Our stinking greed, Dr Henderson, has killed off the wild parts of this shrinking planet. The only realistic way of saving some of these creatures is to make that self-same greed work to their benefit. I won't enjoy seeing some of them killed, but I will be delighted at seeing some of them saved. Some even multiplying.

'The honest truth is this: the only way wildlife can survive today is to ration the time it comes into contact with the much wilder Homo sapiens.'

* * *

'Survival of the fittest,' mused Sean Connaughton.

A copy of the killer's note was clasped between plastic fingers attached to the side of his computer screen. The screen was still blank. The deadline getting closer.

Concentration did not sit easy with a conscience that judged him as a single parent without a single redeeming feature. But sacred deadlines respected no mere reporter nor his inability to care for a disabled daughter, an addicted son, a disillusioned mother-in-law, a rundown church, a reproachful God, and now an increasingly disgruntled news editor. Deadlines asked no questions about the fitness or otherwise of his family and church to survive.

Nor did they take into account another strange feeling: a loneliness that Sean had not felt for years; in fact, not since he had been single. It was a yearning for somebody to share the coping. A flesh and blood somebody. Amid everything, there was a quietly gnawing envy that almost made him laugh, if it hadn't been so sad. Ma Hannigan had found somebody and he had not.

It was the strangest, oddest feeling. Up to this point there had been Karen. Dead or alive, Karen had filled all there was. Increasingly, it was not enough. Perhaps the void had grown. Maybe the memory had shrunk.

His thoughts turned to her sister, Molly. He was conscious of himself smiling. Savouring.

Professionalism forced his wandering mind back to the screen and to the killer's note. But inspiration failed. The fingers pattered on. The screen remained blank.

9

'Gather round everybody.' Superintendent Charles Court motioned for stillness in the crowded Menagerie, as the enquiry room of Hoghton Police Station had been christened.

Both voice and actions held a quiet authority which naturally expected obedience, and both acted as an unseen control on the volume. Few words were wasted on welcomes. No team-talk preliminaries. No banter with those who had served in his special regional squads before, which was most of them.

'So far, we have what looks like two separate murders with the promise of two more victims at least. If this proves to be the case, I would say, ladies and gentlemen, that, at the most, we have one week's grace.'

Groans filled the Menagerie as most suspected what was coming.

'Sorry, folks,' shrugged Court. 'London's high-ups are already pressing for this to be transferred so that NCS can flex its muscles. Would I be right in assuming that we are not about to let them make us redundant?'

The reply was a loud chorus of 'yeses' harmonized with colourful expletives. The motley crew of regional crime squaddies, local CIDs and uniforms had been expecting, sooner rather than later, expansionist moves by the National Crime Squad. The FBI-like hybrid had been set up alongside the older National Criminal Intelligence Service (NCIS) in the nineties. It had started life as the fledgling of the British law and order industry, always pecking here and there to establish a higher status. Now, it had become a vulture, according to the lesser breeds on the lower county and divisional roosts. Not only had NCS netted many of the regional high flyers, but the squad had also left local forces struggling for a fair share of the seed cake. Hawkish politicians from both left and right, all fearful of losing support from an increasingly crime-besieged electorate, had carved out the biggest slice for the ascending NCS.

The National Crime Squad had, after all, been successful against the professional criminal classes, and was continually pushing to extend its jurisdiction into any crime that was not immediately and purely local. The appearance of a national religious figure on the list of victims, plus pressure from Canterbury, had raised the issue of NCS's involvement. Also, in the morning's television coverage, Hoghton's Member of Parliament and Privy Councillor, the Right Honourable Major Nicholas Paine ('in the neck', many added) had insisted that 'our great national force be immediately mobilized'.

He had harked back to the brutal thuggery that had put the wife of his neighbouring Twistleton MP in hospital for a year. Now they had multiple murderers on the doorstep, he had added.

'Once upon a time serial killers were only in the pages of fantasy. Now, they are in our children's playgrounds and family leisure parks. We find ourselves asking: Who's going to be next?'

Charles Court silenced the groans of the Menagerie as he paced between the desks and among upwards of fifty officers, most taking a quick sandwich lunch while their mouths were not otherwise occupied.

'Sergeant Johnson, let's get this education officer death nailed down for what it is. I want exhumation this afternoon and an autopsy report on my desk first thing tomorrow, with special reference to traces of hyoscine.' Court saw a protest forming on Johnson's face. 'Just make the impossible possible.'

'Hazeldene and co., you're on the bishop. Mayes, you and your team take the education officer's background. Usual stuff about lifestyle, relatives, friends, finances, work colleagues, enemies. Again, we need that as of an hour ago. Remember' – and his eyes swung in an arc to embrace all – 'we're looking for links between the two. Anything. No matter how trivial, I want it in the computer and SHERLOCK can tie up loose ends. Both victims were local top brass, moved in similar circles, possibly the same societies. Check a religious link. Anything. Okay?' He got responding nods and moved on.

'Inspector Crick,' he turned to SHERLOCK's minder with a wry look, 'is it too much to expect trouble-free access and retrieval this time?'

Ken Crick cringed remembering the recent teething troubles with the new fifth generation software. It had been so simple in the eighties with HOLMES (the Home Office Large Major Enquiry System). The nineties generation, the more sensibly named PNC2 – Police National Computer – made collation and detection a joy, and could deal with a phenomenal 125,000 queries a day and still get an answer in three seconds tops. But the bug that bit at the turn of the millennium had disastrously ended that. PNC3 and then 4 came in quick succession, invented by the founders of chaos theory, it was rumoured. Again, it was simply to appease law and order politicians, who were forever demanding more and more crackdowns on more and more crime. The likes of Inspector Crick were the puppets of trendy university criminologists who had – in desperation, he claimed – proposed bigger and better computers as part of the miracle that would cut crime. Crick privately thought that the money could have been better spent on studying solutions to the cause of crime: human nature. But then, perhaps that had been too simple for university types, and PNC5 had duly arrived on screen.

SHERLOCK was its perverse diminutive because it was, as one frustrated officer dryly observed, 'far from elementary and Sherlock Holmes it'll never be!'

'Jones,' and Crick breathed a sigh of relief as Court's attention moved away, 'how's SOC doing at WildWorld?' A series of ribald chuckles and half-jeers broke out, and Chief Inspector Francis Spencer, already half hidden beside a filing cabinet, shrank further into his niche.

'Difficult scenes of crime at both areas, sir,' Inspector Mark Jones replied. 'The elephant house where the education officer died was more than a month old and hopeless. Just going through the motions. Likewise in the lion's den. Half of Hoghton have driven through in the last twenty-four hours. Hopelessly contaminated. The approach path of the killer and his victim has been located, and the uniforms are combing it now. Some useful stuff already; odd strands of day-glo ginger hair, possibly from a wig. There's also a discarded syringe by the breach in the fence. We'll know more later.'

Court nodded and passed on. 'Harry Field, I need your forensics on this bizarre note. I want as much as possible, preferably the lot, before I leave tonight and—' A loud collective gasp interrupted his flow. 'Look, the NCS are breathing down your necks. Get to it! Give me all you can on the notepaper type, envelope, ink, fingerprints, everything. Right? Just get me a lead, and I'll recommend you for chief constable. One other thing, Harry, see what you can dig up on the killer's Halipegus signature.'

Court carried on allocating men and women to various parts of the investigation until virtually only Spencer and Hannigan remained free.

'Chief inspector, you're, of course, our local team so I need you feeding me any relevant background information. Particularly, I want you and Hannigan to double up on likely enemies of either of the victims. I understand the bishop especially had his detractors. You know the sort of thing: church people with axes to grind, members of the public, press cuttings, character and morals. Were either of them in relationships other than with their wives? Again, we're looking for links. Right! Let's go to it.'

* * *

Connaughton's feelings about his shortcomings as he studied the killer's note were more of remorse than repentance. 'Hypocrite!' he mumbled while awaiting an inspirational answer to one of his many telephone enquiries concerning the note.

Remorse, he recalled, was saying sorry but speeding on regardless. Repentance was slowing to a stop and changing direction, even doing a U-turn. In his momentary self-awareness, Connaughton knew he was not for turning. His will was not for tearing. He would remain intact, at least until he had solved the killer's puzzle and written his story; maybe even until he had enough to save his parish. Theologians might have argued over precisely which god ruled him at this present moment, but not Connaughton. He was too busy fending off the snapping demons of time and deadlines.

He desperately needed more facts. A solid hour of research by telephone and computer had been just the stuff to smother a nagging conscience. It left forty-five minutes before his deadline.

Some already contacted by Connaughton, had felt the killer's note had a neo-Nazi ring – only the fittest, the master race, living on. Others thought it came from the opposite political wing because of the question mark: those who lived by the selfish way would perish by it. One or two had mentioned Darwin's *The Origin of Species*, and only the fittest going on to reproduce successfully.

As to the 'why' of the killings, Sean had as many guesses as contacts. Maybe the killer was a madman who just made no sense at all; possibly a religious crank; someone who hated the town's leaders. One had asked if the signature could be an anagram which masked the killer's real identity. Connaughton had subsequently doodled with 'Halipegus' on his reporter's pad throughout the succeeding calls ... *Peg is a Huli. Pug has lie. Ugh, les pig.*

Connaughton reached the dregs of potential helpers, and quickly wrapped up his main story. He led on the killer's note and the education officer's death, and then merged in other reporters' copy from late press conferences given by WildWorld and the newly established county murder team. Chief sub Enty already had his boast for the front page – *Argus cracks two mystery deaths.* This was his exaggerated strapline over the main banner which read SERIAL KILLER AT LARGE? The question mark had been added by a cautious Henry Parrott who preferred truth to sensation. First, it was not yet fact that the killer's letter was bona fide, and secondly, killers did not apparently qualify for the 'serial' adjective until they had notched up at least three victims. He later changed Entwistle's inaccurate strapline boast to *'I've killed twice, two more will die'* – *Argus exclusive.*

Once the main story was safely filed, Connaughton, hoping for a sensible lead on Halipegus, rang church member Gladys Blackburn, who worked in Hoghton's reference library. It took her less than three minutes to discover eight obscure references on the Internet, and she fed what she considered the most helpful on to the telephone video screen alongside her own face.

<<Unknown HTML Tag>>114(3)3 Invertebrate Biology 114(3): 210c
2003 American Microscopical Society Inc.<<Unknown HTML Tag>>
Updated research on the effect of age on infectivity of cercariae of Halipegus occidualis (Digenea: Hemiuridae) to their second intermediate host.

'Thanks, Gladys.' Sean tried to sound grateful despite his continuing ignorance.

Gladys laughed. 'Something to do with worms from what I can make out,' her high-pitched voice trumpeted into his ear-piece. 'I'll try a few more search engines and get back to you.'

Why on earth should a killer want to identify himself with a worm? Sean had neither the time nor the inclination to fathom it. He simply reopened the story file and added a line on his new knowledge. He then rechecked his facts one final time. He had written the paragraphs on the killer's words so that they could stand alone, thereby allowing some imaginative sub-editor to pull them for a separate front page panel. They simply suggested that the killer might be criticizing a selfish world, maybe even one which had hit at him personally. Possibly, it was a macabre way of saying that a society which operated on a 'survival of the fittest' basis must have a question mark hanging over its own future. In defence of this argument, Sean had quoted an unnamed reputable expert on serial killers – actually Molly, whose master's thesis in Glasgow had dealt with comparisons and contrasts between different classes of murderers.

'If we're looking at serial killers,' Molly had briefed him over the videophone while awaiting the first meeting of the new regional crime squad, 'then they generally come in two types: one's in it for kicks, the other's into protest killings. Rarely both at the same time.' Sean had written furiously in a drowsy shorthand that was still not back up to speed.

'Reckon we can rule out the first,' Molly had drawled on. 'The kinky kicks killers don't usually leave protest notes. This cookie wants to make banner headlines.'

'What is he, some kind of maniac?' Sean had asked.

'Not black and white,' answered Molly. 'Some individual serial killers have mental disorders but, by and large, they tend to be a fairly sane lot, particularly the protest type.'

'Type? Can you describe it?'

'Not possible, technically.' Molly sounded confident on her subject. 'According to one US expert – we Yanks, God help us, lead the way in this field – protest killers come from all backgrounds: graduates, millionaires, owners of real estate and luxury homes, immigrants. Apparently one murderer used to campaign to save cuddly little seals and swerved to avoid turtles crossing the road. Another was a wildlife-lover who abducted eleven women and gave them electric shock treatment. Only three survived the ordeal of wires being attached to—'

'Fine, I get the picture.' Sean had cut short the gore with lunch approaching. Molly, however, insisted on adding a few more brush strokes.

'Your average serial killer is not your emotional murderer. I mean, most criminal deaths happen in the home, in a surge of passion. Our boy's different. He'll have suffered deprivation in some way or other, and over a long period. Maybe socially, but it usually involves personal loss of a highly prized thing or person. Maybe he didn't feel he belonged, or society refused to let him in. He was deprived of perhaps equality or esteem by his neighbours – like with your Hungerfords and Dunblanes a few years back. Or maybe he couldn't get on the same economic level as his peers.

'When something that our man wanted became irrevocably lost to him, at that point he began to look for what he would describe as justice, and what you and I would call revenge. In some way, Sean, our education officer and bishop, either directly or indirectly, deprived our killer of something that was precious, and they did it over a long period. If we ever find out what the victims took away, we'll have our killer.'

* * *

Kate Connaughton surfed through the latest batch of passport-size ladies tiled on her laptop screen. Each Internet entry was a full-colour 3D picture with a bar marked 'caption'. For some, it should have read 'prison number', thought

Kate. Many other prints seemed to have been frights spewed directly from ancient seaside while-you-wait booths. A few had obviously been computer-enhanced by a nerd with hiccups.

'Get me!' she thought. 'The beast criticizing the beauties.'

Not that she was unpleasant to look at. In fact, the mirror on her bedroom wall proclaimed her fair, if not the fairest of all. It's just that mirrors had no ears and so couldn't detect the real ugliness.

Kate balled a fist and banged the side of her head to disturb this unwanted thought trail. And anyway, she hadn't the time for such trivialities. She was fast running out of time. Even the latest 'definite possible' had been demoted after reading the caption. The woman's hobbies had included one-arm wrestling, thespian interests and Bangladeshi curries. Kate wondered if she only had one arm, and was equally hazy on the second pastime except that it sounded a bit rude. The third, however, was a definite no-no. Her new mother, whoever, would have to conform to good old British standards of bangers and mash and the weekly double-egg, bacon and chips. There were just not enough meals in a week to waste one on something called vindaloo. Gran-Gran would also never settle with her new husband if she thought they were being poisoned. Nor would Aunty Molly be happy; not she of the fierce bubble and squeak leftovers, fried to semi-burnt perfection on child-sitting evenings; not the creator of the angelic French toast nestling in soggy sugar.

On the whole, Kate was now rather glad that Dad had not managed to see her latest fancy. She promptly tagged her 'definitely impossible'.

'Another four weeks and two days to go before I drive down the aisle as a bridesmaid,' she thought, 'something's bound to flash on to the laptop in that time. Otherwise, it's back to last weekend's choice of Aunty Molly, and Dad will have to realize that this family has more than one vote.'

*   *   *

''ello, Mollee.'

A vaguely European voice echoed out of an unpleasant past. It had come from the doorway Sergeant Hannigan had just passed. She froze in mid-stride.

'Must be five, erm, no, maybe six years since north Wales.' Molly was by this time turning, reluctantly moulding the semblance of a smile with frosty face muscles. 'I hear you've made sergeant, yes?' the cold voice continued. 'Congratulations!'

'Jitka,' Molly nodded with a passably courteous smile.

'Aha, you forgets so soon,' the woman's laugh had no effect on her eyes, 'Jitka, with a soft J, like your American Y.' Molly, in fact, had not forgotten how the hard J intensely annoyed Jitka Lister.

'Sergeant Hannigan?' The voice came from behind her old rival.

'Yes, superintendent?'

'Good to see you know each other. Ms Lister is preparing a profile for us on the killer and I'd like you to give her a run-down on the local scene.'

'You put us on the victims' enemies, sir. We've quite a few still to track down, and—'

'Sergeant,' Charles Court was not an easy man to stall, 'now!'

Jitka Lister and Molly had once, in Glasgow, walked close: leading psychology tutor alongside star student. Now, they negotiated the narrow corridor stiffly and it forced them nearer to each other than either would have preferred. They both entered the extra space of the Menagerie with relief, and Molly mechanically ran through what they had so far collected. No more. No less. She was professional and cool and in no way anxious to repeat the farce of their last partnership in north Wales.

* * *

Michael's pains were snapping and gnawing.

The swimming nausea was back. The body of an addict cried out for another fix of normality. The stables had been haphazardly cleaned. All day in fact. Half a dozen times over, and they still looked unkempt. The baby buck had been nursed and cradled and nursed again; in fact, whenever Michael hadn't been raking or sweeping or swilling. Wild-World was closing and he was due home for tea, but food was the last thing he needed. So was company. They would spot his condition the moment he walked in.

So he got up to run, and wobbled out of the stables. Movement, at least, put a different pain in the body and it helped to mask the ones that were far worse. How fast could he run a hundred metres? Anything to distract his craving mind.

He had no money and Fritzy would want something this time. He'd fiddled with the WildWorld slot machines; even sized up the old man at the candy floss kiosk, ready for a quick cash grab and run. But he was known. They had told him it would be the juvenile hard labour camp next time he was caught, and his dad would be fined a thousand pounds. The camp he minded. What a stupid, idiotic fool. He once again rehearsed his litany of personal abuse. This time, he couldn't even remember the first part of what his English language teacher had called him.

He turned into a staff doorway and found himself gazing into the large eye of a conger eel. The side of its face lay against the reinforced glass in the main tunnel of WildWater. 'Now what was that before ... Oh yes, running.' And that was his problem. No concentration. Mind like a demented butterfly. 'Right. The hundred metres. Easy. About the distance to the first bend in the tunnel.' Before he could forget again, he released leg and lung muscles, lurching crookedly down the length of the illuminated cavern. He saw nothing: not the giant turtles and baby squid which, for some reason, darted in frightened patterns on the seawater side; nor on the freshwater side, the beautifully coloured giant koi carp. All he saw was the first bend of the glass tunnel. He eventually slammed into it.

'Who's there?' a vaguely familiar voice called in from the beginning of the tunnel.

Michael ignored the query, furious at the forgetful holes in his screeching mind. He hadn't timed himself. Never mind. He would try again. Keep his mind occupied. He crouched, half fell, into a sprinter's start looking at his wristwatch.

'Ready ... Steady...'

Lips moved, but sound for the last word failed to emerge. Michael had raised his head for 'Go', but legs also failed and his eyes bulged. He was looking at an arm. A human one, floating sleevelessly.

Its fingers curled inward on a hand that pointed upwards from whence it had descended. Its bloody and gnawed shoulder rested in the gravel on the salt-water side. Above and out of sight were sudden swirls and churnings. Michael's legs began to work on their own. He stumbled back along the tunnel and other body parts floated into view. And the water was not as clear as it had been a moment ago; a darker, violet hue was descending.

'NO-O-o-o-o!!' he screamed, and lost control of his bladder. He feared the crazy delusions of withdrawal had returned.

And then Michael saw the head. Not any old head. The last time he had seen this one had been on the portable television in his bedroom.

He wailed mournfully, now just a frightened little boy who had wet his pants, and he scrambled towards the outside voice. As he cleared the cavern, he was never more thankful to run straight into the arms of one of Dad's religious friends – Lionman Les.

10

Ma Hannigan's fourth morning coffee was at last warming a system that always preferred the last two-thirds of the day. It had been so ever since the heady hostess nights of Washington and St Augustine.

Now, only a headache lingered, and that had more to do with her grandson's ongoing absence than the time of day. Having risen with the sun, she now sat alone. Her eyes stared sightlessly out of the vicarage's panoramic kitchen window, oblivious to the first range of hills that marked the beginning of WildWorld. She feared for Michael's safety, and feared what Sean and Molly and the police might find.

The previous midnight, with eyes heavy after a long series of shocks, she had had no alternative but to excuse herself. Now, with a good six hours' sleep, her mind and body were more obedient. The first blow had come as she dusted Michael's room, and a small glint of the afternoon sun on metal had caught her eye at the foot of the bedside cabinet. It was the tip of a syringe needle.

'I'll be home in twenty minutes,' Sean had told her over the telephone from the *Argus* office.

Together, they had then waited for Michael's return from school. And they waited. Tea came and went, and suddenly, Molly was there with her chief inspector, asking to talk with Michael.

'We believe your son can assist us with our enquiries into a third death at WildWorld,' Spencer had begun.

On hearing the news of Nora's find and knowing of Michael's previous record, Spencer had immediately put out a call for him to be detained. A further message went to Superintendent Court, who had apparently then ordered an immediate round-up of every known drug-pusher within a ten-mile radius of the town. By late evening, she and Sean, and later an off-duty Molly, were all pacing and waiting, all avenues of enquiry having been exhausted. None of Michael's neighbourhood friends had seen him for a couple of days. His schoolmates said he had not been to any classes. He had, however, been seen by a couple of WildWorld keepers. Les Moore had called round late after police had finished taking his statement.

'I'm real sorry about your Mike.' Les had been on the verge of tears, blaming himself for not immediately helping Michael. 'It's just that he came out yellin'. He were tremblin' an' cryin', shoutin' that it weren't his fault. I asked 'im, what wasn't 'is fault, an' he sobbed summat about a body. Quick as a flash, I ran in 'tunnel to see if I could do owt. It were sickening! 'orrible! So, I ran through 'tunnel t' office and phoned t' police. By the time, I'd got back, your Mike was gone an'...' Les turned away and his voice trailed off as his face crinkled with emotion.

They tried hard to reassure Les, and even did what was normal for two churchmen. But prayers failed to deal with one nagging worry: Michael's reactions on discovering the various parts of David Henderson at WildWater. Sean and Gran had feared he might be suffering a flashback, after listening to Les's description of Michael's response. His reaction was startlingly similar to that Sunday seven years before, following the road accident and his mother's death. Then, it had been mid-afternoon before they found a tearstained six-year-old hiding in the bushes behind the church, sobbing, 'It wasn't my fault! Please! It wasn't my fault!'

A few minutes after Les had left, Molly had received news from a police task-group colleague to say that a pusher called Fritz had admitted that Michael had been begging for a fix earlier in the evening. Fritz had sworn that he hadn't supplied him.

Now on a sunny May Wednesday morning, Gran waited alone. There was little else to do. Upstairs, young Katie was unaffected by any trauma, save for the bedtime tears about her no longer having a Gran-Gran in a month's time. However, she had perked up on being told that she was not losing a grandma, but rather gaining a grandad.

Ma Hannigan wished she could sort out Michael as easily. Now, she simply prayed and waited.

* * *

'Thanks, Molly.' Sean turned and smiled as he stopped his black cab to let a group of zebras cross the tarmac. For a moment, his eyes left off searching for signs of Michael. 'I don't think I'd have made it last night without you.'

'Slightly over the top,' she thought, considering her contribution had consisted merely of listening, nodding at relevant places and holding him while he shook. The stupid man had the ridiculous notion that he was the worst father this world had ever produced. Sure, he might not have been the most attentive in recent days, but compared with the sorry domestic flotsam she had dealt with in her time, Sean Connaughton was an archangel in disguise.

After Ma had retired for the night, both had rested in reclining lounge chairs close to the telephone. But it too had rested. Soundlessly. They had dozed fitfully. At first light, both had been eager to be out and looking.

Molly might have spent a good part of her father's inheritance on Kate's disability needs, but she knew in honest moments that she more readily identified with Michael. It had been so ever since finding him in the bushes, crying with

103

that terrible blank and seemingly inconsolable lostness. A wailing without tears because he had used them all up. A six-year-old who had watched his mum and baby sister thrown into the air by a crazy car, and felt that he was to blame because he should have pulled them away in time. Molly's money had never been much use for Michael, and even experimental trips to the biggest toy shop in Twistleton had failed dismally.

Only her arms and her closeness had any calming effect. That, and a half-empty bottle of his mummy's Oil of Ulay, which was clutched to his young chest wherever he went. Every now and again, he would, with great care and some-times with a soundless sob, unscrew the top and breathe in the full rich aroma of his mother. Molly's heart had nearly broken a few days after the funeral when she had found Sean crying at the kitchen table. Michael was standing by him, slowly opening the bottle and then shoving it awkwardly into Daddy's face. All three had ended up huddled to each other on the floor by the sink cupboard.

Now Molly gazed at a departing zebra, and said, 'He'll be all right, Sean.' They both stared ahead knowing it was one of those empty, useless, pathetic things that one had to say in times like these. A vicar's phrase. An old wives' comfort.

'God willing,' Sean answered, and anger suddenly blazed up inside Molly.

'And where was your precious God when those Druggies hit on Michael in the first place? Where was he when I got shot and knifed? What was he doing when—'

She stopped as suddenly as she started. She was aware that it was not the time, and nor did Sean seem to be listen-ing. His eyes were fixed and lost in the green-gold quilt of far-off hills. She felt time tick in the silence and there was a long pause before Sean finally started the engine.

'He knows what he's doing.' Sean nodded and accelerated away with an uncharacteristic fierceness.

* * *

Congressman Joel Hannigan had turned out the local militia the time Molly and Karen had gone missing around West Palm Beach, Ma Hannigan remembered over her fifth cup of coffee. And they had been around the same age as Michael.

Even now, traces of that yawning ache could still be felt, reawakened by, and mingling with, the present fear. They – both Karen and Molly – had been so precious; so hard won from a harsh world. For years Nora had half accepted that they were merely on loan, and could be snatched back at a moment's notice.

'We waited so long for them,' she spoke out quietly towards the hills, and her mind was flying away over the years.

She and Joel had settled quickly in the damp back room behind the tiny carpenter's workshop in the downtown part of old St Augustine. Joel had acquired it after adding to his demob money a hefty bank loan. The town itself still had the feel of a pioneer frontier, despite it having been the first European settlement, dating back almost to Columbus. But now it was a pioneer mood of a modern kind. St Augustine was a town that had arrived and was ready for anything a new world of peace might bring. And Nora and Joel were part of it. Of course, children had been discussed and both had agreed that it would be irresponsible to bring babies into such a slum.

In any case, the business needed two pairs of hands, and could barely afford two mouths. They would wait. Wait for the promised post-war exodus to swell the flower state's meagre sprinkling of half a million souls, spread thinly from the Panhandle down to the Keys. And when the millions came, they would need furniture, and Joel was determined that his natural-wood look would share in that promised bonanza.

The dawn of a new decade had brought a property developer to their shack, promising an eight per cent clear profit margin if they could tool up in time to produce sufficient furniture for his rising block of flats in the new part of St Augustine. Two years, fifty more staff and three further contracts brought them to a new discussion about children in one of the new flats they had helped to furnish.

It was in 1953 that Nora had first miscarried. There was a second but then, after two years, along came David; beautiful and dark-eyed, with a hint of the Seminole that proudly lay in the branches of Joel's extensive family. The new Hannigan came with a ready-grown mop of jet-black curls, and Nora combed them every day for the five months that she had him.

One morning, he hadn't woken them up.

They went to his crib; a Noah's Ark of natural wood fashioned by Joel while awaiting the birth of his son and heir. David lay still and blue. Nobody had ever been able to tell them what had happened.

Nora found comfort in the psalms and hymns during the funeral at the First Episcopal Church, and Joel felt relieved that his wife was getting the kind of support that he was not able to provide. Nora had been 'chapel' back home, brought up on the long lusty Wesleyan hymns; and some weeks after the funeral, she made a fine addition to the choir. And in between hymns, she did the most natural thing in the world for a woman in her position. She prayed for another child. Her reward was another miscarriage... 'and God was deaf and cruel and...' And then it dawned on her what she was doing.

'You give me a child and I'll give you me.'

Nora saw herself as a mini human god bargaining with a bigger god who, on the whole, was just a larger version of Nora Hannigan; made in her image. He was somebody with whom you could strike a bargain, just as her husband did with those high-powered industrialist customers of his. But in that quiet morning of mourning, it was as though a voice inside her said, 'Nora, you give me you, and wait and see what I'll give you.'

Trust! Trust? But God wasn't for trusting. Surely, he was there to provide your needs. He was there as the cause of everything, the Maker of life, the one who might just possibly repair life when it went wrong. If he felt like it. If you caught him on one of his good days. Trust him? Now, there was a new thought. And she had tried it.

By 1957, both Joel and she thought they had trusted long enough and were more than happy to give the Lord a little help. They approached an adoption agency. Their age and success in business delighted the agency so much that they wrote to say the Hannigans had gone straight to the top of the waiting list. The evening the good news came, Joel and Nora relaxed and celebrated by making long and happy love – and Nora missed her next period. Then another. They hardly dared begin to hope. And a third. Not even when Karen lay in her arms did she fully rest. In fact, not until Molly had arrived two years later did Nora relax with a quiet prayer of thanks, before settling into her life of completeness.

Business had boomed with a Florida population multiplying into the millions. All came with their wallets and cheque books in search of modern sixties furnishings, and then later they had come with their electoral ticks to vote for a modern, forward-looking congressman to take them into their liberated age. And Joel had gone off to Washington.

But then had come that terrible day and night in '71 when the girls had gone missing. Every one of the old fears had flooded back. The militia had eventually found Karen and Molly huddled in a bus shelter miles from West Palm Beach, both none the worse for getting lost on the holiday hire bikes, both bursting with excitement about their adventure, completely unable to understand why their parents went on and on at them. After all, anybody could take a wrong turn, couldn't they?

And now another of her 'children' was lost.

Nora sat alone with her eyes on the hills. Trusting in the midst of doubts. It looked like there was to be no quick happy ending this time. Sean arrived home alone. Molly had gone in to work. There had been no sign of Michael.

* * *

'Hyoscine it was, sir,' Johnson answered Superintendent Court's first query of the morning conference. 'Quite a massive dose in the poor old education officer there was. Apparently, it was what Dr Crippen used about a hundred years ago to dispose of—'

'Haven't got time for the history tour, sergeant.' Court was curt. 'So that means we've got a serial killer on our hands. Just to complete the picture, Inspector Jones confirms the same substance in the syringe found where the killer cut his way in near the lions. Obviously, it's too early to tell about Henderson as yet. Mark?'

'Thanks, chief,' responded Inspector Jones, 'it's quite a common substance found naturally in deadly nightshade, belladonna, jimson weed and henbane, but for us the significant thing is that it is present in many forms of everyday anti-depressant drugs and even travel sickness pills. In large doses, it breaks down the brain's reasoning powers, which is why it was used as a "truth drug" in the form of scopolamine.'

The inspector was enjoying the attention of the Menagerie's eyes and ears, and he risked more despite what had just happened to Johnson.

'In milder forms, sir, it causes sensations of floating, which is why the local witches used henbane and felt as though they were flying on broomsticks. Even Shakespeare in *Hamlet* Act 1, Scene 5—'

'Where would we be without you?' the superintendent smiled patiently. 'Go on to the April Fool's Day death and fill us in on the details.'

'Like the bishop's death, it was a morning discovery,' Jones obliged. 'We surmise that Graham Paris – that's his name, by the way, sir, the education man's name, that is –

anyway, he was somehow manoeuvred into the elephant house around closing time on March 31st. Must have been then because the post-mortem showed he'd been dead for around fourteen hours when his remains were found by the keeper at eight the following morning. Apparently it was quite a mess. They'd taken delivery of a young male elephant the month before and it had gone rogue, chewing up a few car bumpers in the process. So they were keeping it behind a palisade of steel columns for retraining when our killer decided to introduce our Mr Paris to him. The ambulance lads had to use a scoop to get him on the stretcher.'

'Such a lovely turn of phrase,' Court nodded. 'Right, on to family background, enemies, etc....'

Inspectors Hazeldene and Mayes took turns to lay open the histories of both bishop and education officer, revealing to the macabre amusement of some that they were both members of the local branch of Lions Club International.

Hazeldene continued, 'A number of investigations are still going on but, in comparing notes with Chief Inspector Spencer and his sergeant—'

'Hey, Hannigan,' Crick jeered, 'that brother-in-law of yours fits the frame. My SHERLOCK tells me he's had it in for his lord bishop.'

'Good alibis, Ken,' Molly answered back. 'With an AIDS patient when the bishop was eaten and he was speaking at something called Spring Harvest around Easter when the first victim—'

'When you two have quite finished,' Hazeldene interrupted. 'We've come up with two long-standing public opponents of the bishop and both were linked potentially with the education officer's death, and neither had satisfactory alibis for the times of death.'

'If I may,' Francis Spencer interposed to quiet groans. 'As I covered these, perhaps it should be I who leads you on from here?'

Court said nothing. Just looked blankly.

'First is Nazeer Mohammed, one of Hoghton's Muslim imams. He's a fundamentalist Shi-ite rather than a more liberal Sunni. He's had arguments with Paris. Almost came to blows apparently when the education officer refused to help him campaign for special grant-aided schools for local Muslims. He also lambasted the bishop for implying that there was no God, or rather, Allah. He accused the bishop in the press of blasphemy because the bishop wanted all main religions to form a sort of coalition. He claimed that this was the same as saying that Islam was not the whole truth. As yet we haven't had time to consider a possible link with the television man.

'The second suspect actually works at WildWorld and was found at the scene of Henderson's death last night. As a member of staff, he would have known about access to the waters above the tunnel. As one of the keepers, he would also have had access to the type of meat chunks that were thrown into the water to entice the sharks from the lakes. He disliked the bishop intensely, attacking him in the local press on three occasions. So far, we're still trying to link him to the education officer. Finally, he was on duty at the times of all three deaths. He's a bit of a fundamentalist Christian, and I've had a brief word with Ms Lister and she's ticked him as a possible to fit her profile.

'He's the head lion keeper and his name is Les Moore. SHERLOCK has him down for burglary and grievous bodily harm. He's even got a GBH with intent on his record.'

11

_____

Sergeant Hannigan looked sideways at Chief Inspector Francis Spencer. He never ceased to amaze her.

'Sir,' she whispered up at him, 'we really are on the wrong track with Les Moore and—'

'Folks!' rallied Superintendent Court looking straight at Molly, 'Let's keep together on this. Harry, any forensics?'

'Zero, super.' Sergeant Harry Field dealt with simple sharp facts and worried not about impact. 'Nothing on the note and envelope beyond manufacturers' batch numbers and watermarks. Too general to identify point of sale. The killer's second note looks like the same story; and, anyway, that chief constable's job wasn't really my cup of tea, sir.'

'Right,' sighed Court, and with a slight flourish he withdrew a sheet of A4 white paper from a protective plastic folder. 'Ladies and gentlemen, last night's note.' Court nodded to a secretary who quickly circulated copies.

'By the way, Harry, anything on Halipegus?'

'A worm, sir. Odd little sod with a frantic lifestyle. Reminds me that I'm incredibly fortunate to be an overworked, underpaid detective sergeant in His Majesty's Service. Always somebody or something worse off than yourself. Apart from that, we're still investigating what it means.'

Court nodded, quiet for a second while he slotted the information into the right mental file.

111

'As for the new note,' he addressed the assembly, 'our killer is getting almost transparent in his riddles, and we seem to be getting a little closer to his point.'

The note read:

> *Teach a child that a shark*
> *evolved out of the same soup*
> *as himself, and you can't blame*
> *him for behaving like one.*
> *Three down. One to go.*
> *Then for the top man*
> *— Halipegus*

Court looked round wearily. 'I'm afraid the penultimate line and our friend's one hundred per cent mortality rate so far have now lifted the investigation out of our local hands. Exactly who the top man refers to we obviously have no idea as yet, but it means that the National Crime Squad get their wish. They took over as of midnight and we are now merely the local cogs in their national machinery.'

The collective groan mirrored his own sense of futility, and he went on,

'However, we still have the upper hand. The killer is local. So too are his victims and their backgrounds, save for Henderson. That means that it's our backyard, and we still have the best chance of catching him. Do that' – here Court paused for full effect – 'and the drinks are on me.'

Spirits lifted noticeably. Even smiles returned to one or two faces. Superintendent Charles Court might be a damn fine copper and an inspirational leader but he also had an uncanny genius for leaving his wallet at home, or in the office, or in the car, or in another suit, or anywhere else every time they stepped across the threshold of a pub. Team morale soared to hear such commitment from their chief.

'Jitka Lister,' Court waved an introductory arm towards her, 'is our forensic psychologist. For those who don't know,

NCS have sent her up from the central psycho unit in Staffordshire. So, over to you, Ms Lister. What or who are we looking for?'

Ms Lister was indeed known in a number of ways. Her sobriquet was Cracker, not solely because of some TV series that had been repeated ad nauseam every summer for the past decade, but also for her figure. It curved in places that policemen appreciated, even at fifty-five, when her peers had long ago resorted to hi-tech corsetry.

Some added an 's' because they thought she was crackers. In some cases, there did seem to be prima facie evidence. Ms Lister, for instance, was quite mad on publicity, as Inspector Jones could testify. He had once apprehended four youths following fine detective work into the murders of three Girl Guides on a camping trip. Ms Lister had been enlisted at the end simply to confirm that the arrested youths did indeed fit the profile for the crime, and to suggest certain lines of questioning. Following a successful trial, she was centrespread in two national tabloids. Both had somehow gained the impression that it was solely her profiles that had nailed the culprits. Jones had been relegated to a minor aide.

Sergeant Hannigan could have told them, had she felt inclined (which she did not), of the time Ms Lister convinced a Welsh murder enquiry team that a man being questioned for the sordid killing and rape of a young woman was '99.9 per cent guilty'. She had therefore suggested that she brief a female officer volunteer who could then befriend the man and wheedle a confession from him. She had promptly volunteered her former star pupil, Molly Hannigan, then serving in Rhyl.

Hannigan, in the space of one short meeting with the alleged murderer, had concluded that the suspect was '99.9 per cent innocent'. Against her better judgement, she had met the man on two subsequent occasions. When he later sued for police harassment, Ms Lister had extricated herself quite well, placing much of the blame on the ill-judged handling of the case by the operational officer. Meaning Molly.

'Thank you, superintendent.' Jitka Lister's wide smile took in each officer assembled. When needed, she could be charming and persuasive, still aware that men liked looking at her. She liked to be looked at.

She began with what seemed to be the facts. The serial killer was male because most were, and also because his victims, even though sedated, would still have required manhandling strength. She then expanded quickly and, as always happened when a subject more important than her English grabbed her, the staccato precision of her 'v's and 'w's was prone to inconsistency.

'We are dealing vith an uncomplicated, even elementary, personality. He probably has only a confused grasp of basic biology and chemistry, you know. I vould think, probably, he would be academically not bright enough to pass his school examinations. Yes? He is also impatient as well as simple. At first, he tries to be, er, yes, sophisticated with his first note but he is not subtle enough to maintain his er, what do you call it – yah, his charade. He cannot stop himself eventually blurting out his protest to the vorld. He is, if I understand his notes correctly, and I think I do, somebody who is against evolution.

'And now, here is my important point, and this is why I call him simple. This is why I say he is non-scientific man who is probably fundamentalist in his religion. A famous scientist vonce said, "It is absolutely safe to say that, if you meet somebody who claims not to believe in evolution, that person is ignorant, stupid or insane or wicked." Yah. You understand, yah?

'Evolution, as we all know very well now is, and has been for a very long time, simple incontrovertible fact. Our bishop was certainly an evolutionist, and the whole world of nature and television knows Henderson's "the fittest shall survive" slogan. The education officer, by his very job, vas responsible for a curriculum based solidly on evolutionary principle, yah?

'So, in essence, the profile I give you is of a man with obsessive tendencies. Somebody outside the mainstream culture. Probably a loner, a voice crying in the wilderness. He feels misunderstood and alienated from his neighbours. Probably in his late thirties, because this mentality takes time to develop, yet young enough to manhandle his victims. A simple man with simple tastes. A man who calls a spade a spade, as you say in Lancashire, yah? He is impatient to tell you why he vants these people dead.

'Also, not too simple a soul to be cunning enough to steal hyoscine from the safari vet's cabinet. Inspector Jones tells me that they have a New Age practitioner at WildWorld who calms his animals with these natural vegetable drugs. Hyoscine was one of them. Finally the killer, more than likely, is a fundamentalist Christian who thinks God is telling him to rid the world of those who teach evolution.'

It was Spencer who jumped in to claim the glory of voicing what was on most minds at this point.

'I'll have Leslie Moore brought in for questioning, shall I, sir?'

Hannigan bit her lip.

* * *

The bold banner proclaimed: 'OPENER: The Right Honourable Major Nicholas Paine, Member of Parliament for Hoghton'.

It had the strong, respectable ring of status, and Paine loved it. Of course, it had been even better in a previous Parliament when he could add Secretary of State for Education. Even so, he enjoyed the display of his full name and title wherever and whenever, especially as now on a gold and white banner announcing the official opening of the new Multiplex.

'A town within a town', the publicity boasted. It also claimed that you could live an entire life within Multiplex

115

and not want for anything. 'All you need from cradle to grave' was its boast.

In a few minutes, the banner would be lowered into the gaping silver blades of a giant pair of scissors. Then, as a trumpet voluntary reverberated on new plate-glass and crystal, Paine would reach out to activate the motor-powered blades to slice through the banner. At this point, he was to flourish his arms outward and upward. Cleverly concealed struts in the halves of the banner would then turn them into two wings. Simultaneously, hidden strips of material would fluff out to form a bird's body. The voluntary would then crescendo, the powered wings would begin to beat rhythmically and the phoenix would rise, by means of a powered cable.

It would be symbolic of the new Multiplex emerging upward and outward from the ashes of its bombed Arndale predecessor.

Paine's opening speech would then ring out with vision. '... no imbecile terrorist will ever triumph in this green and pleasant land as long as we British can draw breath. No bomber will ever conquer the spirit that has survived since 1066 and all that; not Ulster's political ragamuffins; not the inner-city drug barons; and certainly not the smug, self-righteous minority groups who now converse through bomb and bullet instead of civilized, cultured manners.'

The Rt. Hon. Major Paine mentally rehearsed his lines and walked with slow, majestic strides, mingling with crowds of potential voters. His right-hand researcher-cum-secretary hovered in attendance while his security men – a measly duo due to his reduced status, the struggling economy and the need to guard every other MP these days – had been banished to the podium wings. Protection officers with bulging biceps and guns just didn't go with pressing the flesh, kissing babies and wooing the odd fickle floater. The Major was cooing over his third mother and toddler when he felt a sharp pain in the left cheek of his well-upholstered backside.

A coo became a yelp, and the crowd around roared with laughter.

His brace of protection officers also relaxed, even smiling at the antics of a slapstick clown prodding the Major's posterior with a gaily striped, rolled-up parasol. The Major was the only one not laughing as he turned to look into sad eyes in rings of white paint. A comical orange wig crowned the giggling face of what he took to be one of the celebration clowns.

Furious indignation and punctured pride blended with sharp discomfort and he could hardly believe the audacity of the stupid clown who now danced and lurched before him. Only he was close enough to see a needle point, wet and glinting, protruding from the blunt end of the umbrella. Only he was close enough to hear the laughing words, 'Happy death day!'

'What? Humph! Eh?' Paine was nearing eruption. 'What the—'

'Happy death day, my dear Major. Only the fittest survive.' And with this, the clown turned and ambled away with a Charlie Chaplin swagger and a limp.

Paine's response was not immediate. Something in the slightly lopsided gait seemed somehow familiar. Sometime, somewhere he had seen it before. And the voice? But then a fresh surge of pain hit his posterior.

'Did you see that?' He turned and hissed at his secretary.

'You mean the clown?' the aide chuckled. 'Just a bit of fun, sir.' But then the secretary caught the MP's expression and, becoming alarmed, he rasped under his breath, 'Sir, please. The crowd's watching. Clowns prod. That's what clowns do. Please, laugh it off. Take it in good spirit. Pleeeease?' The pleading minion thought of votes that could be lost, not to mention his own job, in the forthcoming General Election.

* * *

117

Somebody had once remarked, in a warped literary moment, that the news editor of the *Argus* was to sympathy what hippopotami were to synchronized swimming. It came ungallantly to mind as Sean watched Frank Winter on the videophone monitor labour with unfamiliar and delicate sentiments.

'... and if there is anything I can, er ... do about your Michael's disappearance to, er...'

'Thanks, Frank.' Connaughton moved quickly to put him out of his misery. But then the uncharacteristic note played on.

'Of course, we realize with your son, er, things being like, well, you know, as they are, you'll need time to, er...'

'That's very nice of you, Frank. I really appreciate it.'

'Only...'

'Only what, Frank?'

'Well—' and there was a pause. 'There's a letter for you.'

'Fine, Frank. Perhaps you can redirect it, or maybe I'll pick it up in a couple of days.'

'Yes, but...' and Winter's dance with diplomacy came to a halt. 'Hell! Look, it seems important. It's one of those buff yellow envelopes with the green insignia of Parliament. There's no franking over the Commons stamp and it's been delivered by hand. It's obviously from some stuck-up high-up, and it's marked 'MOST URGENT: RE: SERIAL KILLER'.

At that moment, the vicarage front doorbell chimed.

'Frank,' Connaughton was terse, 'you open it. Feel free to put somebody else on to it. Now, if you'll excuse me...' and with that he flicked off the videophone.

'Sean,' Gran called through his study doorway, 'it's the bishop.'

The smiling warmth of Julia Durham framed in his study doorway was a vision. One glance at the concern edged around her smile was enough to tell him that her call was, unlike the news editor's, free from ulterior motive. She neither wanted an update, nor to talk religious shop. Not even to discuss the current rumour on the Church's grapevine: that the killer's 'top man' was the Archbishop of Canterbury himself. She simply wanted to be the pastor she was called to be: to tend to one of her hurting flock. And with affection and gentleness, she did it superbly well. She also brought news that the large diocesan network of drug-scene workers was on the lookout for Michael.

* * *

Frank Winter hated sympathy aimed at him and so he loathed directing it at others. Connaughton had had more than his fair share for this year so, two seething hours after his first call, he grabbed the telephone and again stabbed out Sean's number. This time no quarter was given.

'Connaughton, the letter's yours.' He swallowed the traces of meanness he felt at the edges of his conscience. 'The writer won't deal with anybody else and says he has valuable information about the killer's motives. He says that if our report on the psychological profile in our lunchtime edition is correct then the police have got it all wrong.'

'What's he writing to me for?' challenged Connaughton.

'Seems like you've got yourself a fan. He's been reading your stuff in the *Argus*. He thinks you'll understand.'

'Who?'

'He just happens to be our local hero of the moment, no less. Even awaiting a knighthood. It's our famous MP for Twistleton. Certainly worth an ear, unless it's just another gimmick on this blasted election trail.'

'Frank, I'm not coming in,' Sean said with a flat firmness. 'If you want to send it over, I'll see what I can do. No promises.'

'Lord, save me from amateurs!' he heard Frank mutter.

'How long have you been praying, Frank?' Sean asked innocently. The line went dead.

* * *

'You do not have to say anything. But it may harm your defence if you do not mention when questioned something which you later rely on in court. Anything you do say may be given in evidence. Do you understand that, Leslie Moore?' Chief Inspector Spencer asked.

'Anything ah say may be used?'

'That's right, Mr Moore.'

'God so loved t' world that he gave 'is one and only Son, that whoever believes in 'im shall not perish but 'ave eternal life.'

The startled reaction on Spencer's face forced Molly to stifle a chuckle.

'I beg your pardon,' blinked Francis Spencer. 'Mr Moore, erm, you do understand that you are being cautioned?'

''ave you written it down, chief inspector?'

'Written what down?'

''ave you written down what ah just said?' he grinned.

'Mr Moore—'

'Only, if you can't remember, it's what Jesus said an' it's reported in John's Gospel in chapter—'

'Leslie Moore,' the chief inspector was stern, and Molly felt far from stern. 'You have just been cautioned and we are taking you in to Hoghton Police Station for questioning about the death of the Right Rev. George Williams. We have reason to believe that you can help with our enquiries, and one last thing ... you are in deep, deep trouble and you should take this a little more seriously.'

'Oh, ah do,' smiled the detainee. 'If yer going to repeat everything ah say and use it as evidence, then I'll turn you int' finest evangelist Hoghton Magistrates' Courts 'as ever 'eard.'

* * *

'Good afternoon, Mr Connaughton.' It was the police. 'I'm just telephoning to say that your son was seen in Twistleton

120

earlier this morning in the cathedral grounds. Unfortunately, he vaulted over railings on to the boulevard and ran across the bus depot in the direction of the railway station. Before our officers could drive round, he had disappeared from view. But we are still looking. We thought you might like to know that at least he seems fit and well.'

'Thank you, officer,' Sean said and replaced the receiver.

12

'Sergeant Hannigan, enough!' Spencer was walking quickly ahead of her towards the interview room. Listening was not his immediate priority. His energy had been spent tracking down Les Moore who had inconveniently taken his wife for a day out to Blackpool. Now, he marched with purpose, heading for an interview that would convince his superiors, once and for all, that he was destined for higher things.

'Sir,' Hannigan tried again, 'he's hardly going to kill someone in his own lion's den, and make himself the prime suspect.'

Silence and a quickening of pace.

'Chief inspector, Moore was the first to suspect it was murder.' Still silence. 'He went out of his way to explain how the murderer got into his compound. Everything known about him and his beliefs suggests that he's not the type to—'

'Really?' Spencer stopped abruptly and Hannigan had to swerve to avoid him. 'You Americans!' It was a tone he usually reserved for something he'd stepped in. 'You come over here...' A dismissive toss of the head finished the sentence. 'Face the facts, Hannigan!' Spencer raised a splayed hand in her face, and began ticking off points on the fingers.

'This man disliked the second victim enough to send vitriolic letters about him to the press. He had easy access to each of the victims, plus the drug that was used to sedate them. As lion keeper, Moore had the necessary meat chunks to entice the sharks which finished off Henderson, and he also knew WildWorld back to front and precisely how to get his victims into just the right places. And further. He was on duty at the scene of the killings on all three occasions. He fits the psychological profile—'

'Only because Lister already knew about him,' Hannigan jeered desperately. 'I wouldn't put it past her to use him as her model. She's great in a lecture room but lousy when it comes to application out on the street.'

Spencer continued as though she hadn't spoken. 'Not only does Moore fit the profile precisely, but the man you're defending has a criminal record longer than my inside leg measurement,' and Spencer withdrew a sheet from the sheaf under his left arm, 'breaking and entering; drugs; taking and driving away for a car-snatch ring. There's one count of grievous bodily harm with intent, plus one GBH on its own.'

Spencer, opposition subdued, walked on to his destiny.

'Well, he's not killed many bishops,' Molly muttered in his wake.

* * *

'Aye-an-an,' Kate Connaughton abandoned her artificial aids and waved cheerily to Gran-Gran, ''ive un-al-o a iss-or-ee.'

Sean wondered as he drove away with Kate whether or not he should ask for the full story on just who 'un-al-o' was. Also, why Gran-Gran should take him a kiss from his daughter. The missing Michael, however, was more pressing.

They covered the distance to Twistleton in twenty minutes of unusual silence, and headed for the boulevard; such a pretentious name, Sean had always thought, for a bus terminus in the middle of an old Lancashire mill town. Equally ridiculous, of course, was coming to search for Michael there more than an hour after the police had rung. But it was better than pacing the vicarage.

'Everything okay back there?' Sean occasionally had visions of Kate's buggy breaking free from its anchorage straps to career around the back of the black cab.

'Why did he run off, Daddy?' Kate asked in her normal computer voice.

'Lots of reasons, Katie.'

'Was it drugs again?'

'Your ears are too big.'

'But why does he take them?'

'It's a long story.' Sean reinforced this answer adding, 'And you're here to look not talk.'

A wave of meanness lapped at the edge of his worries. He really should give her more. More time. More attention. Much more love. More, well – just more fathering. If nine-tenths of family fitness was the generous gift of time, he wondered how his own ever survived. And yet, against all odds, Kate was a survivor. Incredibly so! No mother. A part-time father. An eloping Gran-Gran. The voice of an imbecile. The useless drag of wasted legs. Trapped in her prison on wheels. Yet, amazingly, this free, bouncing, irrepressible personality refused to be contained for long.

'It was them Druggies again, wasn't it?' Sean smiled inwardly at her tenacity. Outwardly, he shot her a reproving look through the rear view mirror. Kate's stubby fingers punched her keyboard with the speed of thought.

'I'm looking! I'm looking! What's up, doc? Jeez! You kill me, man. What's a rabbit to do around here?' Kate ended by beaming her angelic 'Daddy-I'm-really-quite-lovely' smile into the rear view mirror.

Half a dozen slow streets later, Kate, back in her own computer voice, said quietly, 'It wasn't just the drugs. It was the crash that killed Mummy, wasn't it?'

It was more a statement, needing only the affirmation of silence. Of course, there was more, much more, in the intervening years of complications and puberty, but the kernel of truth was there. Their eyes held for a split second in

124

the mirror. After a moment, Kate added, 'Quiet little girls in computer land find out interesting things.'

'Quiet?' Sean arched an eyebrow, and Kate affected disdain and began to look for her brother.

* * *

Superintendent Court watched a miniature Commander Mark Green on his desk telescreen. He sat back and enjoyed the well-crafted diplomacy of the National Crime Squad boss, listening to a rather over-the-top southern apology for gatecrashing the northern investigation. Charles Court could no longer resist a rising temptation.

'You didn't manage to kick the macaroni cheese habit then?' he interrupted.

'And your jowls are not as svelte as they used to be either,' Green shot back immediately.

'We're on wide-angle lenses. Your excuse?'

'Lavish lunches with the top brass, old sweet.'

Green enjoyed this latest dig in a banter that bridged a generation of friendly rivalry since they were probationers together at Hendon Police College.

'Court, old fellow, that tatty red-brick university first was never going to take you far. Just shows the power of Oxbridge.' And Green smirked, fat-faced, into his sending camera.

'And a poor Oxford two-one at that,' Court corrected. 'You do realize that you would never have made commander in a proper police force?'

'Hah!' Green laughed, and the conversation swung to serious matters. 'Look, Charlie, you and I know this NCS expansion is more politics than police sense, especially with two hundred and fifty miles between the scenes of crime and those in charge, so we play this between you and me. Agreed?' Court nodded to camera.

'As a precaution, we've briefed existing security teams on

all leading personnel today. I've been updated by the overnight boys on the three murders so far. We are apparently expecting one more, a local one by the sound of it, then this "top man" thing. So, take me on from there.'

Court was now professional and rapid.

'We've checked out at least two dozen possible suspects, most of whom had good motives for doing away with one or two of the victims, but not all three. Most had good alibis, leaving two reasonable suspects. One a local Muslim leader and imam, but our profile has put him on the back burner. Also, there's no known link with the third victim and his alibis for the times of death check out. The second is an animal keeper at the scene of all three crimes. He's being questioned this evening.'

'Not bad for provincials,' smiled Green. 'Any minor things we can help you with?'

'We thought we'd better leave NCS to deal with the major stuff,' and Green smiled, wondering what Court had in mind. 'Halipegus! You got our latest faxes today?'

'Yes,' nodded Green. 'Just can't cope without us, can you?'

'Maybe we need a fresh mind, old boy,' mimicked Court with a smile. 'Perhaps an outsider's view. Nobody has so far made the link between worm and killer.'

'What do you make of this "top man" affair, Charlie?'

'Could simply be our mayor, except that would be moving down the social scale from a TV star and a bishop. After that, well, anything's possible. Top of the religious scene – Canterbury or York. Top of education or television and who's to say who those could be? Our best guess is political. This is a protest killer who wants to make a statement. Perhaps he's another crackpot after the PM or – heaven forbid after Horse Guards – another royal.'

'Good,' nodded Green. 'We're at one with you with that assessment – though, if it's royalty, there's no chance. Poor things are kept in strongrooms these days and they've even double-glazed the palace with armour-plated glass. It's easier now to get through the walls than the windows. And we've even taken a leaf out of the Pope's security book and got an armour-plated kingmobile for Trooping the Colour this weekend.' Commander Green was about to sign off when he added,

'By the way, Charlie, we've had your Paine on to us.'

'Serve you right,' laughed Court. 'Now you know what real policing is all about. I had him at lunchtime demanding we castrate some clown who had stabbed him. He then demanded an update on the serial killer, and stomped out once he knew I was only the monkey and you were the organ grinder.'

'Look, Charlie, he tells me he intends to raise the matter during PM's Question Time in the House tomorrow.' Green's face had become serious. 'He's also raising the release of a GBH prisoner who crippled a neighbouring MP's wife last year. The PM's got that covered, but we now hear that Paine is twinning this with the serial killings and a soundbite on the disintegration of law and order. He keeps asking, "who's going to be next?" Now that QT's back at twice a week, he stands every chance of being called, and the PM will need an update. Give me a buzz after lunch tomorrow, Charlie, unless something really useful comes up before. A signed confession from your safari chap would help.'

* * *

'This is an interview concerning the deaths of Graham Paris, George Williams and David Henderson. Present are myself, Chief Inspector Francis Spencer, together with...' he paused for others to authenticate themselves.

'Detective Sergeant Molly Hannigan.'

'Forensic psychologist Jitka Lister, and I'm observing.'

'Mr Moore?' Spencer paused expectantly. When nothing came, he added patiently, 'Give your name and address for the record, please.'

Still silence.

'Mr Moore?' Again Spencer waited. Patience broke and Spencer snapped out, 'The interviewee is Leslie Moore, of Thwaites Road, Twistleton. This is Wednesday, May 4th, at 18.30 hours. Mr Moore has waived his right to legal advice and has been officially cautioned. Would you please confirm that for the tape, Mr Moore ?'

A short pause grudgingly ended with a grunted 'Aye.'

'You seem to be in serious trouble.' Spencer rose from his chair and walked round the table to stand above his interviewee.

'So you say, inspector.'

'Chief inspector!' When Moore failed to respond, Spencer leaned over. 'You enjoy hurting those who get in your way, don't you, Mr Moore?'

'No.'

'Not what your record tells me. Rearranging people's features, breaking a couple of arms, a touch of the Stanley knife here and there. We've even got you down for mugging old ladies.'

'Twenty-odd years ago that,' growled Moore, and Molly wondered where the jolly Lionman Les had gone. This was the first time she had seen him without the ubiquitous cheeky smile, and a fleeting doubt came. Psychology had taught her that everybody was capable of murder, but optimism wanted to deny it in Les Moore's case.

'I don't do that sort of thing any more,' Moore added in a growl. 'I'm different.'

'Oh!' Chief Inspector Spencer rose up on tiptoe with his arms in the air and gave a little jig to emphasize his next words. 'That's right. A Jesus freak! Silly me for forgetting that. Not only that, but a born-again one. And, of course, nice little born-again Christians don't go around killing off bishops, normally, do they, Leslie?'

No reply.

'A vow of silence now, is it? I thought you were going to turn me into your Billy Graham mouthpiece—'

'Yer scared mi wife an' kids half to death with yer 'ouse search and bully-boy tactics.'

'Aww. So, we don't like it when it happens to us, do we? And just how many have you scared in a life of crime, eh Leslie?'

'My Mary told me on t' telephone that you'd left our place in a reet tip. Do it to me if tha must, but leave mi kids out o' it.' Les Moore stopped and Molly could see the outer signs of an inner struggle for control. She was about to intervene with a less threatening question, but Spencer sing-songed, 'Oh, Mr Moore, are we having a little trouble turning the other cheek this evening? Where's all this love and light and forgiveness you lot bang on about?'

'If I'm honest, inspector, just reet now I'd leave you to fry in hell. God loves you, but I'm finding it hard to, toneet. I dare say, it'll be different in t' morning. I'll say one thing, an' ah'll say it nobbut once. I've kilt nobody. Yer might just remember it were me who tried t' stop thee makin' a silly, blatherin' fool of thi'sen when yer kept gooin' on about suicide. And did yer listen? Did y'eck! It were like talking t' thick brick wall except tha were no echo back. Just a dense, pigheaded silence. Well, tha wouldn't listen to mi then, and you're no' about t' listen to me now. You've made up what yer call yer mind, an' there's not much point in us talkin' anymore, is there?'

Molly thought that summed up the matter rather succinctly, and she remained silent while Spencer's sarcasm slowly ground down to nothing. Her failure to assist with questioning was ignored by a chief inspector happy to take any glory that might be available. To Ms Lister, however, it was tantamount to a declaration of war. Non-co-operation was equivalent to desertion.

*　*　*

Sean Connaughton sat in his cab looking at the first star in the May twilight. Within, a seething anger at the rottenness of humanity was beginning to subside. There had been blazing resentment at those who profited from his own son's weakness, and this had mingled with resentment at a world that floated by without apparent regard for missing sons, drug barons and murderers. Now resentment was fading into realism. Sean knew himself to be just as selfish as those whom he judged. God only knew how to love this sinful world. He didn't.

The first star winked, and mundane perspectives returned. Kate was in bed. Ma Hannigan was out with her mystery man. Michael was still missing. Time to stop thinking. It hurt. Time to do something. He flicked on the in-car phone and punched the number of the Hon. Crompton Stanley Richards, MP for Twistleton. Apparently, not being a privy councillor like his Hoghton neighbour, Major Paine, poor Crompton Stanley qualified only as a plain 'Honourable'.

'Thank you for calling, I'm not here right now but...' Sean wondered whether to leave it. Hadn't he enough in his life at present? And then the recording tone was sounding.

'Oh, Sean Connaughton here, from the *Argus*. Just responding to your—' The receiver at the other end was lifted.

'Sorry about that, Mr Connaughton. I get so many calls these days and this is the only way I can survive when my secretary is away. I think I can give you a first-rate lead on your killer. Interested?'

Such a line would once have had Connaughton drooling over scoops and world exclusives, especially with the hundred or so national media hounds now sniffing around Hoghton. But now, a news tip, even this one, was merely a means to a viable parish. Missed priorities in the present hectic whirl made him doubt whether such means could ever be justified. Even for such an end.

'Mr Richards, you really need to go to the police. Why me?'

'I have a feeling you might understand, and according to your evening edition, the police seem to be heading in the wrong direction. I get the impression their ears will take in my words but their minds will not.'

'Mr Richards, I got the impression you had sent your letter before you had a chance to read today's editions.'

'Quite so, but I had my earlier sources, just as you do, Mr Connaughton.' This was getting a little bizarre, Sean thought. A lost Michael seemed far more important than an odd Mr Richards.

'I'm sure the police will listen and take note, especially in view of your status. If you still have misgivings, I can give you the number of a detective sergeant—'

'Your sister-in-law, I understand.' Sean was surprised at the MP's knowledge of his personal life. 'I will talk to you tomorrow morning, and she may come too if she wishes. I will be at the hospital between ten and noon – Curzon House, that is.'

With that the line went dead.

* * *

Jitka Lister was an iron lady to any who stood in her way. She turned on Molly Hannigan the moment they emerged from the interview room, her face red and blazing. Her star pupil was now an obstacle to Ms Lister's meteoric ascendancy. As such, Hannigan was to be bitterly resisted lest she threaten all that had been gained.

Born in post-war Prague, Jitka had arrived in England on her eighteenth birthday. She was a socialist, emerging from the heady liberal days of Alexander Dubček. She had cheered as he had taken on the mighty Russian bear, teasing it with his self-effacing smile.

'It vas terribly exciting reading all the newspapers each day,' she would often bubble when relating her youth during lectures. It was normally what one would share with friends, but Jitka had long ago chosen not to have any.

131

Jitka's first job in England had been in a Torquay convalescent home, living cheaply on baked beans while conjugating her English verbs between bedpans and incontinence pads. And then television had shown the tanks roaring back into her beloved home city. She knew that if she went back they would never let her out again. Both her parents were dead ('for which I would thank God, if there was one'). Her father had dealt with his three children as his hero Joseph Stalin had treated his satellites. Any liberal Dubček tendencies in his family were severely subdued. All had to obey. Without argument. No complaints were tolerated, not even those captured in facial expressions. Emotions were for inside. Behind your own Iron Curtain.

Her mother had died when she was fifteen, and a week after the funeral she had arrived home from school to find her clothes had vanished from her tiny wardrobe. She had eventually found them next to her father's in the master bedroom. Her mother's clothes had been tossed into the dustbin. Over tea, father had announced the new family sleeping arrangements, and all three children, even Jitka, remained outwardly passive. A year later, she sat on the sordid bed watching her father writhe in agony clutching his chest. Outwardly, she remained calm. Within, she smiled her vengeful smile of victory. She did not call the doctor until the heart attack had ended; until all was quiet, calm and quite dead.

In Devon, within weeks of the fall of Prague, Jitka had met Maurice Lister, a British soldier, and they had married by special licence within a month. It took less than twenty-four hours to discover she had married another Stalin. She left with his name and her British citizenship, and only after another year of bedpans did she eventually find the true love of her life – the long-dead and hence safe Sigmund Freud. Waves of gratitude had enveloped his memory and his subject as it began to explain all that was happening inside her. It had begun with the weekly psychoanalysis, and progressed via library books to workers' night classes and then battling on through university and even a postgraduate course. By that time, she had learned that Freud had long been debunked, and that the knowledgeable shrank from the quacks of analysis.

Psychology and her own struggle for survival had taught her one more valuable lesson: other human beings made excellent stepping stones. Life was turbulent, and others existed only to enable her to survive the cross-currents. Either she did. Or they did. It was a question of fitness. A matter of her will against theirs. The strongest made it.

Molly Hannigan, perhaps the nearest Jitka had ever got to a friend, would certainly not prove to be fitter than she. Rivals had to go. Losing was not an option.

'You think a silly Florida degree and a few scribbled notes on serial killers makes you a world authority all of a sudden?' Jitka spat in Molly's face. 'You wait until tomorrow. I interview, yah, and I want you anywhere but in that interview room. And if you continue in this way, I will make sure it won't be me who moves on. Yah? You understand?'

Molly gazed back. The demon that was Jitka slowly began to evaporate in such an undignified explosion. The anger of the previous half-dozen years since Rhyl began to be exorcised. Molly simply smiled sadly at the shell that remained, and Jitka saw it.

She turned and fled.

13

Cling-wrapped three-day-old remains of the weekend joint lay beside soggy listless lettuce at the rear of the fridge. Cuisine for the harassed twenty-first century working girl. Droning in the background was the dreary midweek telly that only the dissipation of countless digital channels could produce. Spinsterhood in an empty police flat!

Molly Hannigan felt that her warm Wednesday evening deserved more. Perhaps the distraction of friendly company. Maybe a cool Chardonnay and lemonade. On the way, a short motorway burst with the top off the XJS. A little pampering. Why not?

When she eventually arrived at St Thomas's Vicarage, she found Sean gazing into a dusk sky.

'Thunder, I wouldn't be surprised,' greeted her as she stepped out of her Jag, and quite suddenly she was eighteen and once again gazing at a dark and handsome journalist on the front porch in St Augustine in search of Florida's Lightning Alley. She giggled, thinking of those women's magazine short stories she used to devour, and faced an enquiring look from her brother-in-law.

'It's a sign you're cracking up,' Sean said with mock sternness.

'What is?'

'Laughing when there's no joke.'

She returned his gaze and thought of the time she had once looked up the old Book of Common Prayer to see if a woman could marry her sister's husband. It had taken her the best part of half an hour to fathom the prohibitions relating to her father's mother's husband and, had she had one, to her husband's mother's father. The only relevant ban was on marrying her sister's son, and she had felt that little Michael wouldn't be too disappointed about that. Her original laugh and then the short pause eventually raised a puzzled grin.

'And what little devil's got into you tonight, Ms Hannigan?'

'Oh, something and nothing. Is Ma in?'

'And I thought you had come to see me.'

'What on earth gave you that idea?' She feigned wide-eyed surprise. Sean had a sudden impulse to sweep her off her feet. What exactly he would do then he was uncertain. Perhaps put this minx across his knee and risk the consequent eruption against patronizing male chauvinism. Or, maybe, he should gently cradle her and smother that coy pout with a warm kiss? Now that would surprise her. The impulse certainly surprised him. Not its actual presence. That was not new. The shock tonight came from its intensity. While the heart savoured this strange new passion, the lips got on with safer, cooler matters.

'Ma's out with her mystery man and she's promised to make a complete confession tomorrow evening when our presence is formally requested for a fish and chip supper in his honour. Apparently, it's his favourite meal next to Bury black pudding. She wants you there.'

Molly's face darkened, and she shrugged. 'I don't know. There are – oh, things. Doubts.' She tried and failed to fit difficult feelings and thoughts into words that seemed too small. 'I saw him the other night briefly. Remember? When you needed a flying babysitting service?'

'Yes.'

'Well, he came back with them after an evening stroll, and I popped out to say hello. He kept going on about butchery and how glad he was to be retired now that the scares had torn the heart out of the meat trade—'

'So?'

'Well, I suppose he's not bad looking for an old codger but he looks his age, older than Ma's. What's more, he limps, and I think he's latched on to a cheap housekeeper and nurse for his last years. Then, of course, there's the money Dad left Ma...'

'Did anybody ever tell you, Molly,' Sean smiled softly, and tenderly brushed a stray hair from her upwardly turned forehead, 'that when your eyes sparkle with a slight glint of green anger, and the odd moonlight beam strikes your face at a certain angle, you look, how shall I say, like a frumpy, killjoy spinster daughter who won't let her mum enjoy her final fling.'

'And did anyone ever tell you, Sean Connaughton' – and the tone was rising and the hands clawing like the talons of a bird of prey and he began to back away with increasing speed – 'that you are the most obnoxious, irritating, repulsive...!!' He heard no more, for she lunged and he beat a retreat into the house, laughing and shouting back,

'Don't forget your car hood. There's a big anvil cloud developing over WildWorld.'

At least the horseplay stopped him making an ass of himself. It stampeded over unhelpful emotions. It also deflected both minds from killers, and wacky psychologists, and know-it-all policemen who knew nothing. It set aside dead bishops and, most of all, worries about Michael and his condition and whereabouts. She had not asked about her nephew on arrival, knowing that any news, had there been any, would have been reported immediately she arrived. Eventually, she got her chilled Chardonnay and they came back out to share the front-garden swing seat in a pleasant breeze. They gazed at the blue-blackness, relieved occasionally by the odd twinkle, and distant lightning over the horizon.

'You know, if it wasn't for that silly dog-collar of yours, you'd be almost human.'

'You say the nicest things, my dear.'

'Why?'

'What do you mean, why?'

'Why did you turn it round?'

'You know why.'

'I know the mechanics ... playing at holy ordinands at that Oak-something-or-other college in London. A bishop in fancy dress and pointy hat patting you on the head, and telling you to go and multiply the flock, or whatever. The mechanics I know, but you never told me the theory.'

'I tried once,' Sean smiled quietly, 'that night we huddled together by the kitchen cupboard. Remember, with Michael? We cried into the early hours. I started to tell you what I'd found and you told me I had to pull myself together, and keep a level head for the sake of Michael, and beware of doing stupid things under great emotional strain and—'

'Well...' she waved the Chardonnay arm, remembering it had not, perhaps, been the most tactful of comments, adding, 'You could have had anything but for these religious bits. Your own local paper, maybe even an editorship of one of the nationals today. You could even—'

'—have got myself the best job in the world!'

'Hah!' She looked belligerent, but with a tinge of humour. 'So? Go on. The theory?'

'Nope.'

'Playing hard to get, is it, your reverence? Get on with it and stop messing about!'

'There was once a merchant,' said Sean with an edge to his voice, 'who spent his life looking for fine pearls and when he found one of incredible value, he sold everything he had to possess it. And he showed it only to those he thought would appreciate it. And there was once a reporter who gathered news stories and then found the greatest scoop of a lifetime. He gave all the other stories away so that he might possess, and be possessed, by this one world exclusive, and—'

'—and you're not going to cast your precious pearls before swine! Is that what you're trying to tell me?'

'Such a shame when the swine looks like such a lovely pearl.'

'You really are the most chauvinistic, pigheaded, stubborn—'

'And you're not, I suppose?' Sean looked serious. 'You're given life. You take it. You tell the Giver to get lost. Remember Florida? You had a quick chat with him that time the knife went in. Didn't you?' She looked surprised because she had never shared that with anyone. Not even Sean.

'Only a fool ignores his Maker within inches of meeting him face to face. And you, Molly Hannigan, are no fool. And perhaps you even hammered out a bargain when the bullet hit. Nobody goes near death without developing at least a nodding acquaintance with the one who has power over it. Nothing makes this secular godless world crumble faster than a personal disaster.' Sean's voice was rising and quick towards the end.

'So?' Molly encouraged. 'Tell me.'

Sean snapped back fiercely, 'Someday! One day! Maybe! When you're serious.' His voice was rising all the time. 'Then I'll tell you the greatest story humanity's ever heard!'

It ended in sudden silence.

'Hey!' Molly looked shocked, and Sean turned away. 'Wow! Where did all that come from?' And there was silence for a while before Sean turned back. Their faces were illuminated only by the yellow light from a vicarage window.

'You mean a lot to me, Molly. I care where you're going, and where you'll end up. Sometimes, I care till it hurts.' She let the bristles relax. And looked long at his profile.

'What a big softie you really are, Sean Connaughton.' She leaned over and gave him a hug. The urge to respond was overpowering. Almost. Her features, produced by Anglo-Saxon genes influenced by Seminole darkness and the light Florida whiteness, enjoyed a delicate bath of moonlight. In fact, her face looked good in any light.

'By the way,' he pulled away, 'you and I have a date in the morning, and you'll need to square it with your super.'

* * *

Les Moore lay in his cell wondering why bunks had not improved much in twenty years. In search of distraction, his mind wandered back to his first ever bed, and to the time he discovered that normal kids ate more than one meal a day.

That had been the greatest day of his young life.

He had been told he was seven, but he hadn't been too sure what he was seven of. 'Years' was just a sound. They told him about the cycle of summer holidays and Christmas and birthdays, but he still didn't understand. 'Days' he had understood better. They began with the fear of waking and ended with the best that life could offer – sleep. In between was all about crying and pain and dried fat on cold chips.

And the parade of hurting uncles.

Sometimes there was only one. More often, they came in twos and threes. On big days they came in groups, dressed in weird flowing clothes, with their queer rituals and odd smells. It was better when there were other kids, and then he wasn't used as much. And then had come the day he had stood in a fancy room with lovely wood, and there were other men who wore white hair over their own hair, and the uncles were gone. Somebody said 'to prison for a very long time, and they'll never hurt you again!'

It was then that the greatest day of his life had begun.

He went to sleep, not on the floor, but on soft stuff on legs. He woke, and people called fosters gave him a bowl of crunchy stuff in white water, sprinkled with sweet white grains. But then had come disappointment. Only a piece of burnt bread and jam had followed. At least the cold chips had filled him. By midday, he had begun to think of running away, but then the woman brought him something called lunch. And he felt better. The man came in and there was another plateful; different from all the other foods. He couldn't eat it, nor the supper they gave him. And he thought again of running away. The ache of happiness within was too much. He reckoned he'd really have to pay in a big way for all this.

He wasn't wrong.

It started when his new dad left for a place called heaven, and it wasn't nice because his foster mum cried all the way along the streets as she took him to another home. The hurting had started again with the men who looked after him. That had gone on for years. And they did it in the juvenile centres as well. Even in the prisons.

One cell in particular he now remembered. He talked in desperation to Love. He was nineteen, and he wasn't too sure who Love was. He'd first heard about him when his foster mum had taken him to church. They had told him about a man who wanted little children to come to him. That sounded too much like a hurting uncle. They talked to 'Our Father', but he knew only too well what they were like. But then they talked about love and that sounded more hopeful. Love was getting four meals a day, each different from the one before. Love was not getting hurt. They kept telling him that somebody called God was love.

And this was the Love he talked to. 'Get me off on tomorrow's housebreaking charge,' was all he'd asked. And it happened. Amazingly! The judge, peering down at him in the dock, had said,

'Against my better judgement, Moore, I'm going to sentence you to three months' imprisonment, suspended for six months, and two years' probation.'

Now, two decades later in a Hoghton police cell, Les Moore remembered how well off he was. He remembered one extravagant gift after another: a good job, night school and education, a lovely wife. Then the kids – four girls. A life of love and being loved. Self-esteem and worth: enough to make the tone deaf break out in song.

The night-shift officer heard the baritone melodies and opened the connecting door a bit wider. It made a change from the usual cursing foulness. And fancy a serial killer singing hymns! This really would be something to tell his grandchildren one day.

* * *

'Good morning, Mr Connaughton.' It was the station sergeant at Hoghton. 'We're just ringing to check whether Michael has come home...'

'No, sergeant. Still nothing.'

'... only, somebody answering his description was seen on the main road between here and Twistleton in the early hours. Unfortunately, he made off over the fields when the patrol car pulled up.'

'Thank you, sergeant. We'll be in touch the moment he arrives home. We know you want him for questioning. Perhaps his story can also help Mr Moore.'

'Yes, sir.' But the flat voice did not sound hopeful.

* * *

Molly wedged herself not too uncomfortably on the cab's rear pop-down seat, slid the glass partition fully open and leaned forward towards Sean, bracing herself against the twists and turns of the country lane. 'Okay, shoot!'

'Meaning...?'

'My date!' She gave him a weary look through the rear-view mirror. 'And why on earth are we heading into the wilds?'

'Come on, copper, you've been around long enough to know our Stanley – local hero, poor-boy-made-good?' Sean's right eyebrow quirked upwards as he looked in the mirror. 'You tell me what you know and I'll fill in the blanks.'

Molly shrugged with slight irritation. 'Well, MP for Twistleton; bit of a tragic figure. Tends the bedside of comatose wife—'

'And that's where we're heading,' interrupted Sean. 'She's in this holding hospital out on the moors. Sorry. Go on.'

'Nope.' Molly's brow furrowed. 'Come on, Sean, this is going to take all day.'

'OK,' Sean sighed. 'It's been well over a year now since Sheila Richards was injured in Manchester's right-wing soccer riots after a European Championship qualifier at Old Trafford. His two youngsters died. The girl, aged about nine, was crushed against an alley wall and trampled to death by rampaging fans. His younger son ran out of the alley into the path of a passing juggernaut. Mum, understandably, flew at the ringleaders but was knocked flat with a crowbar and trampled underfoot. Richards went to her rescue and was also knocked for six. He came round to find his whole family had been virtually wiped out. The wife's been in a persistent vegetative state ever since.'

'Horrible!' Molly shifted her position. 'Nothing they can do?'

Sean ignored the obvious answer, adding, 'Richards wants the machines turned off, but they won't agree.'

'What's he like?'

'We did a full page on him in the *Argus* just before the accident, when he first came up for his knighthood. Orphaned quite early: father lost his life in some submarine accident in Old Trafford docks in the mid-fifties. Mother couldn't cope and went a bit loopy. The only thing they left him was his crazy name. I can't remember it all ... Crompton Carey Aston, something, something Chilton Cockburn, something, Mitten Stanley Richards. Dad was apparently mad on United and named his firstborn after the team which won that year's Cup. Actually, the last but one name was a Blackpool winger who Mrs Richards quite fancied—'

'Can we just stick to the point?' Molly said levelly.

'Well, Richards ended up in care and a succession of foster homes. All he got out of childhood, it seems, was a bagful of first-class exam results, an inferiority complex and a cardboard box in a siding at Piccadilly station. He managed university with the help of an old headmaster who'd spotted him begging one day, and completed some sort of science degree. With still nowhere to go, he stayed on for biology research work, then suddenly, for no known reason, threw away his test tubes and did a conversion course to law. He practised as a solicitor and rose to become one of the youngest stipendiary magistrates in London.'

'Not bad,' Molly nodded. 'So what then?'

'Our Stanley, being a bachelor boy, beavered away into the late hours researching for parliamentary committees. He eventually entered the Commons himself in the Thatcher era. He was said to have a "first-rate brain, second-rate personality and a third-rate telly rating". So he stuck to his first political loves – cold, analytical law and the Tory survival-of-the-fittest politics. He tolerated people only enough to get their vote; the perfect backroom boy for the Whips' Office. Much later, when he got married and they put him up for a European—'

'Whoa!' Molly put a restraining hand on Sean's shoulder and changed cheeks on the seat. 'Typical man, rushing over the important points. Go back to the marriage bit.'

Sean smiled into the mirror. 'Headline stuff at the time, it was. He always seemed such an old-before-his-time, stuffed political shirt. One of those born-and-bred bachelors. Then he astonished everybody by falling head over heels for the parliamentary researcher he'd worked with for ten years. Apparently, she was the only woman who had ever stayed long enough to crack through his defensive shyness.

'The *Argus* feature on his knighthood ended with him saying something about "ten years of bliss and a lifetime of heaven ahead". A week after the article, they were in Manchester shopping for new outfits for the investiture, when the soccer riots began.'

There was quiet for a mile or two.

Then Molly said, 'You were saying something about after his marriage when I interrupted.'

'Oh, they put him in charge of the Joint NATO-European Symposium on Germ and Genetic Warfare. Following Gulf War and suspected Balkan infringements of international agreements, it needed a chairman who knew his law and his biology and Richards was perfect. He's still quite a bigwig on the international scene, hence the knighthood, I guess.'

'Wasn't there some row about keeping deadly bugs alive? Was that his outfit?'

Sean nodded. 'His group was in charge of obsolete viral banks and the great debate was whether or not to rid the world once and for all of bugs like smallpox. Popular opinion was in favour, but the scientists wanted to keep every virus in case a later use was found for them.'

'Typical!' Molly burst out. 'I'll bet there weren't too many mothers on his stupid committee! Think of the kids. Imagine what would happen if ever the bugs escaped.'

'Well, it's not as black and white as—'

'Men always say things like that. I'm beginning to dislike this guy already.'

'Even killer bugs have their good points,' smiled Sean.

'Name one.'

'Well, apparently some viruses make perfect pack horses to carry repair kits into faulty genes. Kill all known viruses in stock now, and you may be ruining any chance of curing some genetic disease in the future. Anyway, Richards won with his argument, and every deadly virus known to humanity is now stored for whenever somebody finds a use for them.'

They watched the hills for a time as they followed a lane that twisted around and up and down the western slopes of the mid-Pennine moors.

'He's been in the news again recently,' Sean said as they spied Curzon House Holding Hospital nestling in the fold of

144

a valley. 'He kept on his biology as a hobby and had just done a thesis on saving wildlife from a wild world, or something like that. St John brought him into the safari park for the purpose. Seems Richards had ideas about channelling the greed of humanity into saving endangered species. I met him a couple of times, but he wasn't particularly forthcoming. Kept very much to himself. A bit morose.

'One other thing: there was a story about the release this week of the gang leader responsible for his wife's condition.'

'Already?' asked Molly incredulously.

''fraid so. They couldn't prove that the youths caused the children's deaths, and it was touch and go whether the video evidence was sufficient to convict them of beating up Mrs Richards. One was caught full-face by a community video camera and he got six years for grievous bodily harm with intent. Others, including the alleged gang leader and instigator, were mainly facing away from the camera, so they plea-bargained and admitted plain GBH with no intent. The maximum sentence for that is two years, but because they had pleaded guilty, the judge could only give them eighteen months. They got a third off for good behaviour and now they're due out. The story, of course, is that Mrs Richards is still serving her life sentence while they walk free.'

Sean turned into the hospital grounds and brightened up. 'There may be a happy ending. Looks like our local hero is at last going to get his knighthood. Rumour has it that there's something in the offing quite soon. Reckon he deserves it.'

* * *

The Member of Parliament for Hoghton was worried about the pain in his backside. Antiseptic ointment and a plaster had not helped as much as the major had hoped. He tenderly perched in his cubicle office deep in the bowels of Westminster, laptop on knees, crafting a question against hooligans who caused such suffering.

This would then be memorized in readiness for PM's Question Time. He had only once tried to smuggle in his question, written painstakingly on his shirt cuffs. Hardly had he adjusted his jacket sleeve before he was drowned out by derisory cries of 'Reading! Member reading!' He had subsequently dried up. Live, on BBC2! The embarrassment was such that it had dashed any lingering hopes of returning to the front benches.

Major Nicholas Paine's present problem was different. At most, his question could not exceed two hundred words, and only then if he spoke plainly and without hesitation. Within those small parameters he needed to do three things.

First, he must grab the House's ear and sympathy. He would do that with the serial killings plus the 'vicious attack' on his own person in broad daylight. Neither the weapon nor his assailant's make-up needed to be mentioned. Nor the precise anatomical site of the wound. Just the facts: viciously stabbed in public by a total stranger. He also needed to include the soundbite 'And who's going to be next?' *Newsnight* would love that.

Secondly, he needed a snappy sentence demanding that the nation be led back to absolute rights and wrongs.

The final part was the real headache; how to achieve such a goal?

How did one retain credibility in the corridors of power on such a taboo area? Dozens of reputations had floundered in these moral riptide waters. At all costs, he must avoid language like 'back to basics' and 'standing on the moral high ground'. These had started the slide of the last two governments. Awkward questions had been asked, like 'what are the basics?' and 'on whom or what should the grounds of morals be based?' Some had even wondered if ethics was a suitable subject for MPs who were perceived to be forever hopping in and out of each other's beds.

So, what was his solution to be? Teachers to ram home morality? No. Their unions would just get bitchy and insist it was the parents' job. Double the fines on parents with way-ward kids? Not a good vote catcher. And anyway, it was merely tampering with trimmings.

And which morality should be rammed home? That was the real question.

The good Major Paine had studied his Socrates, Plato and Aristotle and their classic hopes for reason and intellect, jus-tice and courage; their noble pleas for moderation and com-mon sense. It was all pure genius on paper but it somehow smudged and blotched when transcribed on to human souls. The ideas just didn't work when men and women wanted other men and women. They disintegrated when land or property was up for grabs. The Ulsterman bombed. The Bosnian butchered. Africans annihilated each other. Neigh-bours sued and schemed and screamed and scratched and modern-day Cains slew contemporary Abels.

And still the major searched for his solution on good and evil, and who decides.

The major also knew his philosophical radicals. Good equalled whatever brought the most happiness or the least suffering. But Paine was realist enough to know that greed always encouraged its own happiness, usually at the expense of others.

Paine toyed with a professor friend's suggestion that peo-ple wanted to be good because they liked to be good. They liked to be liked. This selfish desire to be good should be fos-tered. The major eventually concluded that the professor must have led a sheltered, middle-class existence and that ris-ing crime and disintegrating communities had failed to reach the cloisters of academia.

No! What Paine needed was something that made sense to Joe Public. And Paine had only two sentences left in his two hundred words.

What he certainly had to avoid was any recourse to the old way of keeping society glued together. There were few votes in trying to slot the Ten Commandments back in to society. The last six about loving one's neighbour might be useful, but the first four dealing with God were a total turn-off. The way the game of life was played today, nobody wanted an External Referee blowing the whistle on life's fouls. Everybody wanted their own whistle and their own personal version of the law book. All wanted to be their own referee. The old way might have kept the crime rate lower. It might have glued more families together. But only a foolish prophet would risk calling a nation to spiritual revival. One certainly could not do it in the mother of parliaments. And even if one could, he would not be the one to do it. Not the English way. 'Just not cricket, old boy.'

Teetering on his tender rear, he sneezed three times in quick succession, blew loudly into a tissue, and then poised expectantly over his laptop. Quiet and time. That was all that was needed.

He awaited the inspiration that had eluded the wisest of men since Cain.

14

Crompton Stanley Richards was a large man with a barrel chest and a shock of distinguished greying hair. He was good to look at but rarely to speak to. Relaxed he might be with old friends like St John, but hardly with strangers. He was slightly stilted in speech, could not abide trivia and he hated to stand on ceremony. When Hannigan and Connaughton entered the ward, he immediately ushered them into the ward lounge, and abruptly opened with a blunt accusation.

'You know you're holding the wrong man!'

Molly returned his expectant stare. The man could at least have had the humility to place a question mark at the end.

Until this frontal attack, she had almost warmed to him. She had observed him sitting tenderly stroking his wife's brow with a cool face-cloth, a tragedy surrounded by whirring cold technology. Sympathy glowed maternally as he rose to greet them. She almost offered a helping hand as he walked stiffly away from his bedside vigil. But then had come this overbearing prosecutorial manner. Perhaps he was overwrought. As if to show the way, Molly turned his statement into a question.

'You are going to prove that we're wrong, sir?' It would not have been professional to acknowledge that she considered he was right.

'What gives you such certainty, Mr Richards?' Sean added.
'Halipegus.'

'And that tells you what?' Molly was immediately interested despite herself.

'That your killer is not only a reasonably educated man but is also well versed in certain highly specialized areas of biology. Mr Moore, I believe, is not.' Richards smiled without humour. 'You still don't have much idea what Halipegus is, do you?'

A slight improvement, thought Molly. At least a hint of question mark had crept in.

'We know it's a worm,' she declared with confidence, 'and it appears to have strange habits.'

'That it?'

'Er, yes. But no doubt you're about to educate us?'

'Halipegus is a tiny worm which lives part of its fascinating life under the tongue of a frog. It has an amazing life cycle, and I believe your killer is challenging you to explain how it could have evolved.'

Molly felt excitement despite Richards' hauteur. 'So, we're looking for an intellectual crank. Is that it?' asked Molly.

'Intellectual? Possibly.' Richards was curt. 'Crank? Not necessarily.'

'But surely, no sane person denies evolution these days.' Now Molly was not bothering with question marks.

'If you don't mind my saying so, your education seems rather limited in this area.' The icy tone indicated that Richards didn't care whether Molly minded or not. 'Open-minded scientists have been re-evaluating Charles Darwin's fragile theory for the last thirty years. Darwin went on trial because many found him unconvincing. New ideas have bubbled up from the laboratory or computers, but evolution still remains a theory in grave crisis, even though the popular media treat it as fact. In recent—'

'Excuse me, sir,' Molly interrupted tartly. 'If you could keep to the point. Just why is a worm so important that our killer identifies himself with it?'

150

The MP snapped back, 'You would have to understand its life cycle to know that,' and his tone hinted that it might be beyond her ability.

Not all of Connaughton's pastoral skills were needed to detect a personality clash of gigantic proportions in the making.

'Perhaps,' he intervened diplomatically, 'you would be able to help us understand.'

'Halipegus,' the MP sighed, 'crawls from underneath the frog's tongue and climbs to the roof of the mouth where it blends in with the colour and all but disappears.' As Richards spoke he doodled on the back of a hospital snack menu. 'As a hermaphrodite it ejects its own fertilized eggs, which are then digested by the frog and excreted into the water.' Warmth began to soften Richards' tone and he seemed to be visualizing the wonder of his subject.

'Once in the water, the worms hatch into tiny tennis-ball like creatures, propelling themselves with beautiful wave motions of their long surface hairs, and they go on a seek-and-find mission for the ram's horn snail like this,' and he held up a doodle of a round spiralled shell. 'Of course, in real life these are no bigger than your smallest fingernail. Anyway, the tennis-ball creatures use tiny beaks to penetrate the snail's shell. Once inside, the balls explode into tiny worms and make a meal of the snail's liver.'

His audience grimaced.

'On reaching a certain size, the worms leave the snail and come to rest near the bottom of the pond where their tails sprout tiny fern-like tentacles to attract the attention of a passing water flea called a cyclops.'

The subject had generated a sparkle in Richards' eyes. 'Then, an absolutely astonishing thing happens. During this waiting period, it curls itself round and takes up residence in its own tail, and the moment a cyclops flea nibbles at the tail ferns, Halipegus launches itself with the force of a missile into the flea's mouth, through the intestinal walls, and into the body cavity.'

'Later, the cyclops, plus worm, becomes a fine meal for dragonfly larvae which then, in turn, are eaten by the frog. The moment it enters the frog, Halipegus pops out of its protective cyst and crawls up the gut in the opposite direction until it finds the tongue where it settles down to live and later lay its eggs.'

Richards smiled with satisfaction as he noted the attention of his audience.

'Incredible! Four different lives in four different hosts. And what your killer is telling you is that all this complexity stretches the imagination to such an extent that you can't believe it could possibly have evolved. He's saying that there must be a humorous designer somewhere who has arranged the whole thing for his own amusement.'

Sean searched the MP's face which had become more illuminated and animated as the explanation had progressed. 'You actually believe what the killer believes,' Sean said tentatively. 'Or, to put it back to front, you don't believe in evolution either.'

Richards laughed, not unpleasantly, and considered his visitors as though pleased that at least they had understood his explanation and were now moving the questions on.

'Oh, I believe in evolution if by that we mean that creatures adapt to their surroundings. I think your killer does too.'

'Then what's he killing all these people for?' Molly interrupted with the same prosecutorial tone that Richards had originally started with.

'Look, this sort of adaptation happens right before our eyes. Your dogs and cats, for example. This variation all happens through tiny gene mixes and some mutations. Scientists have genetically evolved fruit flies to live twice as long and even to change shape. They can turn some flies into subspecies so they no longer interbreed. Some have more wings than others, or extra legs where antennae should be. Now, that sort of small-scale evolution-adaptation is beyond doubt.' Richards paused for breath and emphasis.

'Species can change. But what we cannot do is to change a fruit fly into a non-fruit fly. We can't see how one of its off-shoots eventually evolved into the dog and another into the cat; and, if the *Argus* got the killer's note right, how humans and sharks can share similar parents way down the line of evolution. So, an increasing number of scientists are saying today that evolution through natural selection – the survival of the fittest – is only a small part of the answer. We're missing a huge part of how life came into existence and how it then developed.'

'Just a minute,' Molly intervened. 'Can we get back to killers and in particular, Les Moore. You're telling us that Moore would not have known about this worm, and for that reason he is not the killer?'

'Correct.'

'You knew about it!'

'But I obtained a first in biology, sergeant, and even then I had not come across Halipegus. I only met it during my postgraduate research into nematode worms, and even then it was not front-line material. I would imagine that Mr Moore is not in that category.'

'But Les Moore hates evolution,' pressed Molly. 'He would have loved to use something like Halipegus. How can you be so certain he didn't?'

'He doesn't have to. Fundamentalists like Les Moore have their own in-house examples of life's complexities.'

'For instance?' challenged Molly.

'If he was the killer he would have signed himself with one of maybe half a dozen other better known creatures with complicated lifestyles. Butterflies, perhaps. How could cater-pillars melt themselves down into a chemical soup and then recreate themselves into a crowning glory of the skies? Surely not an accident! Surely a design. If it's not the butterfly then the fundamentalists have their bombardier beetle.'

'Now, that rings a bell,' Sean interrupted with interest.

Molly summarized, 'So, the killer's saying that complicated

animals with complex lifestyles could not have evolved. Is that right?'

'This is all new to you, isn't it?' Richards' smile teased Connaughton, and Molly felt anger at being ignored.

'Not entirely,' Sean said defensively.

'You're a vicar and you've not bothered to sort out where you stand on this issue?' Richards sounded incredulous.

'When you two have quite finished...' Molly attempted to interrupt.

'I suppose...' Sean began slowly, '... I've always taken science at face value. Yes, I suppose I've always reckoned on evolution.' Sean was conscious that he must be sounding rather naïve, and had a growing urge to explain himself. 'I simply thought "great, that's the way it works", then got on with other things that seemed more important.'

'So you think everything evolved? Do you know about the bombardier beetle?'

'Excuse me!' coughed Molly

'There was some row about it recently, but...' and Sean shrugged as his memory failed.

Richards went into his animated mode again. 'This creature protects itself with rapid explosions from two swivelling rear-end turrets. It has two storage chambers in its abdomen, one holding hydrogen peroxide and the other hydroquinone. Pipes lead to a mixing chamber, and the percentage mix has to be just right. As the chemicals combine, an inhibitor is added to stop the beetle from blowing itself up, and—'

'If you've quite finished...!' Molly herself blew up.

'Sergeant!' Richards was clearly irritated, 'if I cannot explain my point in my own good time without police harassment, then this country is coming to a sorry state.' It was designed as a put-down, but Molly rose with iridescent fury.

'Sir,' and Sean could detect the constraint in her throat, 'you may be a Member of Parliament, but that counts for little when you have possible evidence that may help His Majesty's police officers in the execution of their duty,

154

especially when that comes to homicide, I mean murder.'

Richards pursed his lips, and nodded his head. Something seemed to click within and he smiled unexpectedly, 'Of course, you're quite right, sergeant. Please accept my apologies. I hope you feel that I have been of some help.'

'Quite frankly, sir, no!' Molly exclaimed, and Sean shot her a look almost pleading with her to take the olive branch. But all Molly wanted to do with such a branch was to take it and smash it across her opponent's smug face. 'What you have told us is merely background information. It will not help Les Moore's situation one little bit. And one thing further—'

'Yes, sergeant?'

'From my understanding, you asked Mr Connaughton to visit you before Les Moore was taken in for questioning. So, would you mind telling me why?'

Richards seemed to hesitate, as if momentarily caught off guard. 'I, er, I saw your brother-in-law at WildWorld once or twice and I enjoyed his articles in the *Argus*. He seemed to know what he was talking about and I thought I would like to tell him so. I couldn't go to him easily because of my wife so I asked him to visit me here.'

'And I appreciate your help, Mr Richards,' Sean interrupted. 'And I'm sure my news editor will be happy with this new angle, especially because half the media in the land have been speculating on the meaning of the notes and the signature.' His intervention did not work as he had hoped.

'You could have just written a fan letter.' Molly's chin jutted in defiance and Sean could not believe she was still pursuing Richards' motivation. She bulldozed on. 'If you had more information, you could have either written or phoned.'

Sean was preparing to bring Molly back to sense when Richards surprised them both.

'I wanted to know if I could trust you both.'

'Trust us?' queried Molly loudly.

'Yes,' smiled Richards, now at his warmest.

'And just exactly why do you need to know whether or not you can trust us?'

Richards beamed. Hannigan almost snarled, 'Just what are you playing at, Richards?'

'For heaven's sake, Molly,' Sean jumped in, 'Mr Richards is just trying to be helpful, and he does have a sick wife—'

'No!' snarled Molly. 'He's playing with us, Sean!'

'Well, now,' Richards smiled calmly. 'You'll just have to trust me for a start, won't you?'

Both he and Hannigan stared at each other; neither giving an inch.

'Enough!' Sean was emphatic. 'We're going.'

Molly clearly wanted to pursue the matter but Sean eventually completed speedy goodbyes and promises of prayer for Richards and his wife, and he guided a still reluctant Molly out into the long corridor of Curzon House. Within a few strides, she was thirty metres in front of him and walking fast.

'That infuriating, ignorant, insensitive pig of a chauvinist has not told us the half of it!' Molly's flow was beyond Sean's power to interrupt. 'I don't care what you say. You men are so easily taken in. He's up to no good. Poorly wife or not. There is something not right and I'm going to get to the—'

'Molly!' She turned to find herself fifty metres in front of Sean. 'Just listen to yourself, will you. Calm down.'

* * *

A seraphic smile of inspiration rested on Paine's face.

The gods had smiled. Smiled on him! He smiled back. He, of all humans! In all ages! He had become the Chosen One. The solution was there to slot into his question.

It made up for the headache, the runny nose and the limbs that had begun to stiffen. What a stupid time to catch a flu bug, he thought. And how quickly it had caught hold. But in true Dunkirk spirit, the parliamentary question must go on.

Not even a bug would stop him rising to his feet to take his turn on the Questions rota.

This must have been how Plato felt when Lady Inspiration soothed his fevered brow, or was that Aristotle – he could never quite remember. And that chap in the bath, as well: the Eureka fellow. Civilization had struggled five thousand years for the answer and now the golden finger of destiny had come to rest on Major Paine. When inspiration first struck, he was so overwhelmed that he observed a full ten seconds of humility. Not even a sneeze could shatter the proud moment.

At last, humanity had the basis for what was right and wrong. And he was to be the bearer. It was so simple, as indeed were all things of greatness. It was so elementary that it could be contained in a sentence. He had written it down with great care.

> *Would the Prime Minister agree with me that the everlasting see-sawing between anarchy and despotism will stop, and humanity will have self-generated freedom when, and only when, we bring ourselves to deal with the moral and political issues exactly as we now deal with scientific questions.*

That was it.

Beautiful in its simplicity.

Rights and wrongs to be determined in laboratory and clinical conditions. Cool. Logical. Original.

Well, perhaps, not quite original. Some of Paine's glow had faded when he remembered some dim and distant echo. He eventually found a similar quote in Huxley's *Science and Culture*. But who remembered Thomas Huxley these days?

A little more of the glow had faded when he wondered how to get man and wife to behave scientifically towards each other, especially if she ever found out about the other woman. He briefly wondered how factions in Northern

Ireland, Rwanda, Bosnia and the riot-torn East End of London would take to his test-tube approach to right and wrong. But surely these were all minor issues. And he couldn't have all the answers in one single question, could he?

He blew his nose and tottered out towards his golden future.

* * *

Les Moore was relieved to be out of his cell and in the much larger interview room. It also pleased him that Chief Inspector Francis Spencer was nowhere in sight, and that the rather pleasant Ms Lister was to be his companion. The previous evening, he had quite warmed to the psychologist who had sat without noise, occasionally smiling with encouragement.

Behind the smile was something that he had not been able to identify. He had, however, often seen it in others whom he had been called upon to help in the past. Of course, she wouldn't need his help. Not a professional like her.

'Leslie,' she began in a friendly, fresh voice, 'you don't mind me calling you that, do you?'

'Nope, but Les is best. What's your first name?' If surprised, she did not show it, and told him.

'As you can see, Les, this is not being taped and this is by no means a formal interview. I am simply here to try and break our deadlock and to show you that somebody is prepared to listen.' Her English was slow and careful, and she wanted to be sure that this man with his simple, uneducated ways understood her.

'Yer not married, are you, Jitka?' Again she took the personal query with outward calmness even though she involuntarily tensed whenever others trespassed. Her job was to invade gently, and counter-invasion was an occupational hazard. Still, it was an irritation.

'No, I'm single,' she lied, not wanting to explain about the half-forgotten soldier and the marriage which, to her knowledge, had never been dissolved.

'Why so uptight, Jitka,' and Les smiled. 'I used to be just like you when I were young. All precise and wound up like a clock spring. Sorry,' he went on, 'my Mary's always tellin' me ah gets carried away and goes a bit too far sometimes.'

'Yes, vell – well, we need to go on. Yes?' Jitka could spend hours in the lecture room telling others how to elicit what was needed in an interview. Occasionally, she wished it was as easy in practice. 'You were born and bred around here, I believe?'

'I'm a gnomer. Born above t' lamp-post in Twistleton. Everything above t' library lamp-post is old Twistleton, yer see. And the's an owd tradition 'round 'ere as to why Twistletonians are, on average, smaller than everyone else. They reckons as how the first women settlers kept gettin' caught by a frisky gnome what lived under t' bridge at 'top o't' village.' Les chuckled with the relish of his tale. 'But tha's no from round 'ere, lass. Russia or summat like it, I'll be bound. Am ah reet?'

'Almost. Tell me, Les, about your upbringing. What was your father like?' Ms Lister was now firmly back in control and getting down to the stock questions.

'A lady like you don't wanta know about that,' Les smiled.

'It would certainly help me to understand, and I am a very good listener.'

Les began with the greatest day of his young life – the day his palate was extended beyond cold chips – and he then filled in the events before and after. As he did so, he watched her watching him.

'You have had a tough life, Les,' she said sympathetically.

'So 'ave you,' he said quietly.

'And your wife?' Jitka sidestepped his comment, 'she is sensitive and sounds so lovely.'

'Yer won't mind me sayin' this, I 'ope,' Les said, 'but when I were tellin' thee about mi uncles and what they did to me, the muscle at t' top of your right cheek kept dancin' like.'

'Er, ve, er, we were talking about your wife, Mr Moore.'

'Ye've gone all formal agen, Jitka. I'm sorry. I didn't mean to intrude.'

'Of course you were not—'

'Only, sometimes,' Les carried on intruding, 'I gets this feeling within. Some super-spiritual types call it the inner Spirit prompting. To be honest, all ah knows, is that I start to get inklings about folks as I talk wi' 'em—'

'Meester Moore—'

'Well, yer see lass, I've got one about you.'

'Er, ve should be looking, erm, yah, we should be—'

'It's happened to you as well, hasn't it, lass?' And the voice was so gentle. 'The abuse I mean?' There was so much understanding in the voice that she almost burst out 'Yes!'

The iron curtain was rattled but not cast aside. She remained quiet. And the silence was deafening.

'Well, Jitka. The reason ah mentioned it is simple. I got help, yer see. Not human stuff, like. No. I were in prison and yet I 'ad another prison inside me and I prayed—'

'Er, thank you, Mr Moore.' Jitka rose abruptly.

She had lost what she needed for the interview to succeed. She could not afford to be interested in anything else. 'Well, perhaps, er, ve shall try later this afternoon. Yah? Thank you.'

And, once again striving for that professional briskness, she walked quickly from the room.

* * *

The start of the return journey from the holding hospital was quiet. Molly sat in the far rear corner of the cab and stared out, not seeing Lancashire's folding, rolling hills and moors. Sean slipped Handel's *Water Music* into the CD slot and before the opening bars he was making a series of calls.

There was no news of Michael, Ma Hannigan reported, and certainly no hints about tonight's guest. All would be revealed in due time. No, she did not think she was old enough to know better, and he still wasn't too old to get a clip round the ear.

Kate-a-la-royalty came on using the young King's voice declaring that Sean Connaughton's duty as a citizen was to provide his daughter with a new mother. If a grandma could turn up a new grandpa, surely it was not beyond the abilities of a reasonably handsome man in his prime to conjure up a new mother, and was he any nearer to making decisions on what had previously been discussed about Aunty Molly? Sean had quickly closed the cab's glass partition at that point, but a glance in the rear view mirror reassured Sean that his passenger was lost in a world of her own.

Sean reported his new findings to Bishop Julia, but she was more concerned about the alarm being felt by the top men in the Church of England, even though a suspect was being questioned. Sean promised to keep her informed.

Molly had then reached through to borrow the mobile and report her Halipegus findings to Superintendent Court, who said it confirmed what the London boys had just discovered in the British Museum Library. And yes, she was right, it did not make much difference to them holding Les Moore, though it might educate their questioning. She was then ordered to report in for a mid-afternoon session with Chief Inspector Spencer and Les Moore.

In reply to one of Molly's queries, Superintendent Court said that Ms Lister had reported good progress in her talk with Moore. She would be only too happy to brief the officers before their next formal taped interview. In fact she preferred to do this rather than again interview the prisoner herself.

On retrieving his receiver, Sean telephoned Hoghton Funeral Parlour to reply to a message left with Ma Hannigan. Yes, he would be free the following afternoon to take Sammi's cremation.

15

Superintendent Court waited for the telescreen to fill with Commander Green's bulk. He had still not briefed his superior, and the digital desk display showed 3.15, with Prime Minister's Question Time half over.

He had called frequently in the previous hour, aides each time apologizing for unavoidable delays; each time mouthing the stock request to 'give the commander a few minutes'.

On this occasion, he had been rerouted to parliamentary security where yet another aide, full of long explanations, put Commander Green's delay down to an irate radio listener throwing himself into the path of the PM's Daimler. The protester had been brandishing a pocket Dictaphone blaring out classic punk rock allegedly recorded on the refined Radio 3. He had yelled that the BBC 'wasn't fit to survive' after its latest evolution. All this, linked with the nation's top politician in the car, had caused an over-zealous NCS constable to encode for a full-scale alert.

'Sorry to keep you waiting, Charlie.' A breathless Green eventually appeared. 'I'm surrounded by incompetents.'

'Any time you want a transfer...' Court left the invitation hanging. 'We're still no nearer to a confession. We've moved a little on the note and there is – just a minute, commander.'

The superintendent's secretary had entered waving a

brown A4 envelope and blurting out, 'Sir, I'm sure you should see this now.'

It looked vaguely familiar despite having a see-through protective cover over it.

'Commander,' Court looked up, 'we have what appears to be a third note from our killer. We'll rush it over to forensics—'

'No time, Charlie. The PM's on his feet and I need something now. Paine's turn is coming up. Open it.'

Court carefully slid the packet out of the plastic, used his ivory-handled letter opener on the long side of the envelope and carefully withdrew a white sheet with fingertips.

'Well?' Green was impatient when Court did not immediately begin to read the contents. 'Charlie?'

'Commander...' Court again halted and expletives exploded from the London end. 'Now, Charlie! Now! Not next week!'

'Commander...' Court began, uncharacteristically sluggish, 'it claims that Major Paine has been infected with Kasai.'

Green stared, momentarily stunned; horrified at the consequences. A split second later reality rushed in, and then came irritation.

'Fake! Must be. Can't be true. Not in England,' Green rapped.

'Sorry, sir. Looks genuine.' An extra second of analysis made Court definite. 'Same Halipegus signature—'

'Everybody knows that by—'

'But nobody outside my team knows the typeface, design or paper quality. They're the same. And remember Paine's complaint about some sort of an attack at an opening ceremony yesterday?'

'And it definitely says it's Kasai?' Court nodded in reply. 'Crazy! There's nothing like that this side of Africa!'

'Sir,' Court was now formal and urgent, 'we have to go in. The major is sitting within a bench or two of the nation's top men. As I understand it, Question Time attracts upwards of

80 per cent of ministers and MPs. Ignore this and the media will have a field day if something is really wrong.'

Court was suddenly grateful to be a provincial superintendent full of easy, snap decisions, knowing that it would not be his career file going into the shredder if things went wrong. He knew full well the high attendance at Question Time, with MPs overflowing as usual into a cordoned-off section of the public gallery. He fleetingly wondered whether or not an officer could survive closing down Parliament by imposing tight military quarantine if it all turned out to be a hoax. And to do it on live television!

'We go in!' said Green.

Court wasted little time switching the videophone monitor over to television and flicking through channels to BBC2. He buzzed his secretary. 'Fax the note to Westminster, and then get any available members of the team into my office right now. Oh, by the way, somebody should stop Spencer interviewing Moore – no, I'll do that.' And he raced out of his office.

He was back within a minute, trailing a puffing chief inspector and Hannigan. His small monitor was surrounded by the Menagerie team.

'Nothing yet, sir,' Inspector Jones shouted over the Leader of the Opposition pounding his Despatch Box and in full flood.

'... and according to these figures, we give big tax rewards to those who stay unmarried, so will the Prime Minister, once and for all, come clean and tell us why his government still seems determined to crush the basic building blocks of society by...'

The rest was drowned out in a sudden hubbub at the sight of a uniformed commander emerging beside the Speaker's Chair. At the same time, police officers appeared at all doors, and a slightly raised but still dignified BBC voice commented, 'There seems to be some commotion. This really is quite out of the ordinary,' and the programme mixer flashed to a long view of the chamber, taking in both government and opposition benches flanking a bewigged Speaker who stooped towards Commander Green.

'The last time I can remember Question Time being interrupted like this' – the commentator's voice allowed a frisson of excitement to edge the measured tones – 'was when a former Minister of Transport grabbed the Mace and waved it in protest over his head.'

At this point the mixer began flicking between the various static cameras, each angle showing MPs and ministers turning to their neighbours, and some even rising to their feet to get a better view.

'Order! Order!' the Speaker demanded sternly. 'Ladies and gentlemen, please remain in your seats. Members WILL remember where they are!' The noise fell to a loud murmur.

'Thank you,' again the Speaker shouting. 'Please continue to be seated, except for the third row on the opposition side below the gangway. Would all of you, except the Right Honourable Member for Hoghton, please file out to stand on the floor of the House.'

Every eye locked on to the puzzled, bleary-eyed Major Paine, who was slumped slightly to one side. Those filing out tried to catch sight of him, causing some to bunch and crash into each other. Meanwhile, the BBC commentator was finding it hard to recover his sepulchral tones, as he informed the nation,

'This is perhaps the most extraordinary event we have witnessed in the House since television cameras were introduced twenty years ago. As yet, we have still not been told why the Speaker is ordering this bizarre evacuation of just one bench. We can obviously confirm that it is not one of the normal bomb scares, for all of us would have been evacuated according to my understanding of the Westminster Disaster Response Plan. Erm, George, can I bring you in at this stage? How do you read this highly unusual interruption?'

Political correspondent George Wallace was about to share his ignorance in however many words it would take to allow somebody to find out what was happening, when the Speaker mercifully saved him the trouble.

'Members, I have asked Commander Green of the National Crime Squad to take over directions for the next few moments.'

'On a point of order, Mr Speaker—' The thick cockney accent known to all in the House for a litany of inappropriate and irrelevant interventions, was immediately silenced.

'No points of order! The Honourable Member for Shoreditch will listen, as will the rest of us.'

'Thank you, Mr Speaker,' Green's commanding voice took over. 'Prime Minister, ladies and gentlemen, we are going to have to escort Major Paine from the chamber to an air ambulance that will transport him to the city isolation unit.' The major tried to rise but seemed either to lack the necessary co-ordination or the energy, and he thought better of it. Green continued.

'I stress that this is, at this stage, a precautionary measure and we ask you to remain calm, as I know you will.' Green nodded and two constables came to stand by Major Paine, though careful to remain a stride's distance away. 'We ask for a moment's patience while we await the arrival of an emergency unit which has already landed on the Commons helipad. Perhaps while we wait, those above and below Major Paine could vacate their seats and – ah! Here we are.'

Two medics, in yellow top-to-toe isolation suits and carrying a lightweight folded stretcher, emerged ponderously from beside the Speaker's Chair, scattering before them frontbench ministers and a plainly impatient and seething Prime Minister.

'As you may have guessed already, ladies and gentlemen, we understand that Major Paine has contracted a contagious viral infection. We apologize to you, major, that you should have to learn of it in this way. However, this interruption and speed is for your own good, and that of the whole House, as I am sure you will appreciate.'

The two spacemen-like figures had by now reached the wilting major who allowed himself to be manoeuvred on to the extended stretcher. As Paine was carried out, Green continued,

'As for the rest of you, I'm going to have to ask that you confine your movements to the precincts of the Commons for the immediate future. Should you try to leave, my officers, plus the extensive military personnel now assembling, have orders to detain you.' Five hundred voices of sudden protest produced the not abnormal Commons cacophony.

'Order!' called the Speaker, without discernible response. 'ORDER!' he screamed. 'Will members please come to order! Remember who you are and where you are. At this moment, the commander speaks with my authority and he will be heard. ORDER!'

The noise fell slightly. The commander continued with a raised voice.

'We will, of course, keep you fully informed—' and Green halted as Prime Minister James Baldwin rose to his feet. Complete silence now fell. The nation's leaders craved urgent leadership. Green wondered whether to obey the Speaker or continue to give way.

'Commander!' Baldwin was curt. 'My office. Now! With the Speaker's permission.' The PM stalked past without waiting for the Speaker's reply. Green eventually caught up with him along the corridors of power and Baldwin could contain himself no longer.

'What in blue blazes was that all about in there, commander? And why was I not consulted beforehand?'

'Sorry, sir.' Green was slightly breathless. 'The Speaker said it was his prerogative, and he was sure you would understand when you knew the full circumstances.'

'Well?' barked Baldwin as he swung round, arms straight down by his sides with hands balled in tight fists.

'We think it's Kasai, sir!'

The fists unfurled. The PM's mouth dropped for a moment. His eyes pierced into Green's trying to make sense of what he had just heard. His reply was subdued.

'In the House of Commons?' Baldwin's giggle was inappropriate but Green put it down to shock. Then, it was as though the Prime Minister realized that he was not behaving like one, and the old sternness reasserted its dominance.

'The disaster plan?' he snapped.

'Already activated, sir,' Green assured him. 'We'll be fully operational and up to speed within ten minutes.' They had reached the PM's office by this time.

'Kasai? Are you certain?'

'No—'

'NO!' blazed Baldwin. 'Then what the—'

'Almost certain,' cut in Green shouting. 'First tests will give us absolute certainty.'

'Convince me then. Just the main points at this stage.'

Green filled in the blanks missing from what the Prime Minister had already learned of the killings in preparation for Paine's expected question. He was finishing when a knock came and a private secretary entered.

'Excuse me, sir, but one of the commander's associates is asking to see him urgently.'

Green explained, 'I asked our forensic pathology inspector to join us, sir,' and the PM nodded. 'Thought he might be useful on the Kasai update.'

A middle-aged bespectacled man, bald-headed save for tufts of white above either ear, entered the room. Shades of all continents seemed to be written in his cosmopolitan features. A dash of Italian definitely, yet with African lips and piercing Scandinavian blue eyes. It was the oddest human concoction Baldwin had seen in a long time. The man bowed. The PM's eyes went to the ceiling and he snapped,

'Not necessary, er—' and he looked in Green's direction.

'Fundelly, sir, Inspector Mattabele Fundelly. He used to be with the Centre for Applied Microbiology and Research at Porton Down; joined us two years ago in forensics when organized crime began to launder money through lucrative medical research programmes, particularly in microbiology and genetics, cloning and so on.'

'Right, Fundelly.' The PM looked at his watch. 'A mutant from the Ebola virus. That much I know from the 2001 outbreak. What more do I need?'

'Well, er, ah, sir—'

'Look, man. I'm the PM. Wonder of wonders! Great to be in my company and all that rot. Now, let's take that as read. Cut the nerves and brief me quickly. Professionalism. Right!'

'Yes, sir.' Fundelly snapped to attention and launched himself at his subject.

'Ebola has kept up its appearing–disappearing act for thirty years since it first erupted on the Zairean river after which it was named. It had been dormant for a decade and then came the 2001 outbreak that you mentioned, sir, this time on the bigger Kasai River, that is in the western part of Zaire and—'

'Yes, yes, spare me the GCSE geography.'

'Well, the Ebola virus is shaped like a shepherd's crook, sir. It's curled at one end of a straight single thread of genetic code, and contains about eighteen thousand letters in all. But the Kasai type has a tiny mutation: an extra swirl in the crook and, of course, extra genetic letters. It is Ebola but much more virulent. Incubation for Ebola is between three and twenty-one days from first contact. The Kasai mutant is fully incubated in a much shorter time span, from thirty to forty-eight hours. Ebola hijacks the cells and forces them to follow its orders, producing an extra seven protein types, four of which are known to be extremely harmful. The Kasai version doubles the number of damaging proteins, which is why its potency is multiplied. Ebola's flu-like symptoms last days following incubation, but again this is reduced drastically to hours with Kasai, and then it follows the normal Ebola course. Massive internal haemorrhaging comes with the breakdown of tissue. Internal organs liquefy and the blood clots in the brain. It just seems that the jungle's killers keep getting more and more virulent from Lassa Fever, Rift Valley, then Machupo, Ebola, now—'

'Got that picture,' the PM flapped a hand, sensing deterioration into minor detail. 'Transmission! Tell me about that.'

'Yes, sir. Good and bad news, sir, on er, that, sir.' Fundelly took a deep breath to kill the plague of 'sirs', 'The good news is that the 2001 outbreak was so virulent that, though it killed a hundred, all were in one village and most of the victims were dead long before they had time to pass it on. Immediate and total quarantine can kill an outbreak stone dead. As far as our victim is concerned, we know for definite that he was infected at between nine and ten a.m. yesterday, when he opened the Multiplex, and that made him contagious potentially from the last hour or so onwards. Fortunately, by that time he was in the Commons, otherwise—'

'Fine. My imagination can work out that scenario. Now what's the bad news?'

'Oh, er, yes, well—'

'Come on, man,' Baldwin encouraged gently. 'You're doing well.'

'Well, as you know, sir, Ebola was transmitted through bodily fluids only. But it was never firmly established whether this was true of Kasai. There is a ninety per cent chance that it is transmitted only by bodily fluids—'

Baldwin broke in, 'And a ten per cent chance that it's airborne, and five hundred of the nation's top men and women, including most ministers of the crown and myself, have breathed in the virus.'

Commander Green wondered about himself too. Aloud he said, 'My team are the best, sir, and we'll ensure that you and the whole House get first-class attention from Harley Street, the Centre for Tropical Medicines as well as from the team already flying in from Porton Down. We're identifying medical personnel already in the House and they will be advised by the experts via landline.'

'Anything else before I report to the House?'

'Sir? Just one niggling thing.' Green raised a finger.

'Yes?'

'The fax of the killer's last note indicates that he is still going for the top man—'

'He's got me, hasn't he?' snapped Baldwin.

'The note states "Four down. Now for the Top Man."'

'So?'

Green lamely continued, 'Well, er, we are doubling your security once you get out and that goes for the nation's other top men.'

'Great!' and the way Baldwin said it indicated it was anything but that. 'At least whoever it is, he can't reach me or anybody in this House for, er, what, Fundelly? How long do we have to stay in this blasted place?'

'Certainly two days, sir, and by that time,' Fundelly now brightened noticeably, 'we will know for certain one way or the other, whether Kasai is airborne or not.'

'Fundelly, we're delighted to help you out.' The PM looked at him dryly.

* * *

Jitka Lister and Chief Inspector Spencer both let out involuntary protests of 'But you can't, sir!'

Court waved them away and looked around the assembled murder team. 'No arguments. I want Mr Moore out of this station within five minutes. Hannigan?'

'Sir?'

'Give Mr Moore the royal treatment. An apology, escorted to the discharge desk, superefficiency in returning his property and then use the unmarked Rover and chauffeur him back to his family.'

As Hannigan left quickly, Court turned back to the team. 'We have maybe three hours' grace while NCS deal with the London end. Then they will be flying up here in droves and we will be swamped. Crick, get SHERLOCK cranked up. Dig out again every question mark against every person we have interviewed so far, especially those with an axe to grind against any of the victims.

'Mayes, you took the background on the education officer. You and Crick pull me everything concerning that local Muslim imam you suspected, and double-check that alibi of his. We are now reduced to him as our one possible suspect. Hardly a prime one at that, but let's get to work.'

'Excuse me, sir,' Chief Inspector Spencer sounded a little peeved, 'That one was mine.'

'Fine. Link in with the others.' Court was impatient; this was no time for prima donnas.

'Inspector Jones, find that clown. I want every available tape from every community video camera and every town centre store and shop in Hoghton for Wednesday morning between nine and eleven. Especially get any media film of the reopening ceremony of the Multiplex. I also want an immediate appeal on television and local radio for any home-made videos of the event.

'Field and Hazeldene, you and your teams follow Inspector Jones's lead. I want the best full-face we have. And in the meantime, Crick, make sure SHERLOCK is free for full facial comparisons, enhancements and identifications with everybody we have interviewed and photographed on this case, and, of course, do a check against all the knowns on file.

'Remember, we have three hours breathing space. Then it will be mayhem. Mayes? Five minutes. Then start bringing me the imam stuff.'

* * *

'Les,' Molly aimed for nonchalance in her voice as she drove the Rover, 'what does "the greatest story humanity's ever heard" mean to you?'

'*Gone with the Wind*, the wife'd say.'

'No. I mean in your line. Your, er, you know?'

'Pass.' Les looked blank. 'Oh, you mean *Tarzan*, or how about *Jungle Book*?'

'I could quite easily do a U-turn and sling you right back in the slammer!'

'Honest!' Les laughed. 'I don't know what yer gettin' at.'

'Religious stuff!' exclaimed Molly.

'Should've said. It's the greatest romance ever told. The heart in the universe. God loves me.' As an afterthought, he added, 'Oh, and you as well.'

'So that's what that great lug of a brother-in-law of mine would mean when he talks of the greatest story?'

'Praps. Why's it so important, Molly?'

'No reason.'

'You! Say summat for no reason. Pull t'other leg, Molly. Yer keen on 'im, aren't you?'

Molly had not blushed for years and she felt the burning begin to creep across her cheeks. Les grinned wide and knowingly and she considered a subject change was overdue.

'What I am keen on is nailing a killer who puts people in with wild animals.'

'Count me out this time. Did your lot 'ave any luck with the clown?'

'What clown?'

'The one I told yer chief inspector about on the night the telly man died.'

'So, what about this clown?'

'Well, as far as I could see, there weren't many folks about with it being near closing time at WildWater. Perhaps one or two families, and then there were a couple of wardens in their Zebra Land Rover a few hundred metres away. But there was this clown, wig skew-whiff an' walking a bit fast, and rather awkward, for a funny man, if yer know what I mean. Ah reckons seeing as 'ow he were coming from near one of the staff entrances to WildWater, he might be worth 'aving a talk to. He must have seen more than me.'

'What was he like?'

'Well, clowns is all different, aren't they? He 'ad them big thighs, sort of stickin' out. A romper suit, sad face and bright orange hair.'

'Orange?'

'Aye.'

'Orange!' Molly squeezed her eyes tight trying to remember something.

'Would yer like me to drive?' Les asked nervously.

'Orange! Orange!' by which time Molly was open-eyed and striving for something in the dark recesses. 'Orange?'

They had just turned into terraced Thwaites Street, and Les's schoolkid neighbours were pointing at the big Rover. It was then that Molly suddenly recalled the hair strands found by the breach in WildWorld's outer fencing.

'Anything else?'

'No. Just past the next car'll do nicely,' said Les.

'No. I mean, what else about the clown?'

'Six foot, a large chest an 'e limped like mi Uncle Jack when he 'ad that bad hip. Always gettin' stiff he was when he sat down and then he 'ad trouble gettin' going. Some days he was fine but on others he were—'

'Voice? What did he sound like?'

'Didn't speak.'

'Which leg?'

'How d'yer mean?'

'The limp, Les, the limp!'

'Oh, it, er, the, yes – the left one.' Something was stirring at the back of Molly's mind. So much had happened...

'Anything else, Les, where did he go to?'

'Didn't see 'cos of your Mich—'

'Er, age?'

'Mid-fifties.'

'How can you be so sure?'

'Dunno,' Les shrugged. 'Must 'ave bin the bad hips, like mi uncle. He also 'ad greying hair, and he was thickset wi—'

'Hair! You saw his hair? How? You said he had a wig on?'

'I told you, it was on crooked. It was grey and silvery above t' ear on 'is limpin' side.'

An idea suddenly struck Molly.

On a human level it horrified her. In the professional part of her mind, the adrenaline surged, and that set off another electrochemical memory spark. Hadn't somebody joked about a clown giving Paine a pain in the bum?

'Les, I may want to call on you again.'

'Sure,' he said absently as he waved to a surprised and delighted wife at the kitchen window. He jumped out and grinned over his shoulder, 'Ten thirty any Sunday morning. We'll roll out the red carpet.'

16

Good evening. This is Petrona Harmsworth, and this is News at Five. Parliament is tonight under military quarantine following amazing and unprecedented scenes during Prime Minister's Question Time this afternoon when an MP was carried from the House of Commons believed to be suffering from a highly contagious virus. Nearly a million viewers witnessed the event live on television. Switchboards at the BBC and Parliament were jammed solid until a few minutes ago when Prime Minister James Baldwin broadcast live to the nation.

Sean, Gran-Gran and even Kate sat quietly in the black cab hanging on each word. Even the disappointment of once again finding no trace of Michael around Twistleton was momentarily forgotten as the Prime Minister's voice filled the cab. It was warm and reassuring.

Major Nicholas Paine, one of our most respected members, was taken ill this afternoon and doctors suspect an as-yet-unidentified but virulent strain of Asian flu. This should cause no alarm to members of the public as Major Paine had been in the

House of Commons all day and the contagious
stage of his illness did not develop until this after-
noon. As a precautionary measure, members of
both houses of Parliament and ancillary staff, plus
lobbyists, visitors and members of the media, have
chosen to remain within the precincts for the dura-
tion of the two-day incubation period. I wish to
record my gratitude to them, and also to the police
and army who have kindly agreed to set up a
quarantine zone to ensure members of the public
are, for their own safety, unable to enter the
restricted area. Of course, the security, running
and well-being of our nation continues under
normal government control and it is business as
usual.

Petrona Harmsworth's voice followed, cold and probing by
comparison.

The PM broadcast live simultaneously on televi-
sion and radio half an hour ago, and despite his
reassurances, there is still widespread concern.

Her cadence was sharp. Suspicious. The guardian of truth
standing against the purveyor of propaganda. She saw politics as a dance of many veils and herself as a reporter with
a sharp pair of scissors. No Westminster performer ever cast
aside a veil willingly, to her knowledge. Harmsworth
believed that you could have either truth or politics but sel-
dom both, especially when election fever raged. If ever a
politician smiled comfortably at the end of one of her inter-
rogations, she experienced loss. This particular evening, she
had a whole arsenal of questions waiting to be fired, but all
targets were hidden behind a wall of silence. She had to settle
for the grapevine.

News at Five tried to raise our own political corre-
spondents caught within the military cordon, but
their mobiles appear to be switched off. So, too,
are those of all ministers, Members of Parliament
and officials. The only line open for incoming calls
appears to be the Westminster Press Office, and
they have refused to answer specific questions
and instead offer transcriptions and video copies
of Mr Baldwin's statement.

Rumours of a government cover-up have
spread throughout the capital during the last hour;
even suggestions that there has been a military
coup. A parliamentary spokesman came to the
car park gates at the foot of Big Ben just before
we came on the air to specifically deny a coup
attempt, and has promised that the King will be
making a short statement at 6 p.m. tonight. We
shall be extending our programme to bring that to
you live, as it happens.

I'm joined now on the line by Martin Sanders in
Parliament Square, where a huge crowd is begin-
ning to gather, and also by Henry Walsall outside
Coppetts Wood Hospital in North London, where
we understand Major Paine is now being treated in
an isolation unit following his remarkable removal
from the House. First, to you Martin, and can you
tell us...

Sean switched off the radio, having arrived at the vicarage,
and disembarked Katie and her buggy from the back. They
both hurried in to join Gran-Gran already watching the television version.

* * *

Molly Hannigan rang Superintendent Court after accomplishing her Twistleton mission. 'That clown who attacked Major Paine?'

'Yes, Hannigan?'

'Les Moore said he saw one shortly before the WildWater body was found. He said he had mentioned it, but the officer didn't—'

'Got that, Hannigan.' Court's voice sounded weary. 'The chief inspector has just seen fit to report it in the light of the killer's last note and Paine's complaint. Did our Mr Moore get a close look?'

'Middle-aged to late years,' briefed Molly. 'Large with a barrel chest, limps on the left side, like somebody who has a bad hip. The clown also has grey-silvery hair beneath the wig.'

'Go back and let Moore know that we might need him.'

'Done that, sir. He's standing by.'

'Anything else?' Court waited for Hannigan's reply. 'Sergeant?'

'Er, sorry sir, must have gone through a bad reception spot. Didn't quite hear. I'll be back in the station shortly.' And she signed off.

She'd almost blurted out her new suspicions, but hunches needed facts before superintendents were told. Twice, she had dismissed the preposterous ideas from her mind since leaving Moore. But they kept returning. Perhaps Sean might be a good first sounding board. Maybe after Ma Hannigan's surprise do tonight.

*　*　*

'Order!' Deputy Speaker Virginia Latham banged her gavel. 'This may well be an impromptu and unscheduled emergency debate on our crisis but Standing Orders stand and the Honourable Member for Shoreditch will sit.'

'Madam Deputy Speaker,' shouted the Shoreditch MP,

'I think this House is being misled from the top downwards and I demand—'

'The member is stretching the patience of this House, and I must warn him that if he does not resume his seat and thereby acknowledge the authority of this chair—'

'I refuse to be silenced. I have every right to know what—'

'Officers of the court?' called Madam Deputy Speaker.

'... why can't we even call our families...?'

'Remove the Member for Shoreditch from this chamber but no further.'

'Government is a trust,' the Shoreditch MP began shouting out his favourite Henry Clay quote over the hubbub, 'and the officers are trustees...' He moved down an aisle away from the pursuing officers, '... and both trust and trustees are created for the benefit of the people, and...' – the officers caught up with him – '... and I'm one of the people and what's so secret...' The rest was muffled and his voice finally faded as the exit door swung to.

A knowing twinkle formed in the expression of Madam Deputy Speaker as she peered sternly over her reading glasses at an unruly and fearful shambles of MPs.

'And if anybody else seeks to have themselves expelled from Parliament's precincts through bad behaviour, let me assure them that, for at least the next two days, it won't work!'

* * *

Nora gathered up an armful of scrumpled paper. Her guest of honour and husband-to-be had insisted that the traditional fish and chips should be consumed in 'the only truly civilized Lancashire way', nestling in vinegar-sodden newspaper, and eaten with fingers. Thankfully, spoons and plates had been allowed for the prawn cocktail and chocolate fudge cake either side of the main course. But it was a small matter against the backdrop of missing teenagers on drugs, serial killers on safari and a nation in full-scale panic. Thankfully, the last issue had been eased at teatime with a heart-warming and reassuring address by the young King – 'bless his little cotton socks', she had clucked maternally at the time. He had calmly denied any coup while assuring the nation that all was well – except for a few coughs and colds in the Houses of Parliament.

At least there had been enough ice-breaker topics to ensure Nora's vital evening got under way. It was the encounter she had most feared: the meeting of her present family with the one who would be the centre of her future family. She needn't have worried. They had all loved him, even Molly who had arrived late due to mysterious 'ongoing investigations'. She was delighted to discover that her step-father-to-be was the twice-crowned black pudding king of Europe with enough put by not to need Nora's nest egg. In fact, he could probably buy out the whole Hannigan-Connaughton clan with his loose change. Except for the limp and a false lower leg, he was otherwise sound in body.

Any potentially embarrassing pauses were covered expertly by ComputaKate with one of her pre-programmed party pieces. There was even the chance for a family heart-to-heart on wedding bells, bows, bridesmaids and the calling of the banns. But then the vicarage telephone had rung, and Michael was immediately back in everybody's minds. Would the darkest shadow on the evening evaporate?

It had turned out instead to be that poor Mr Richards whose wife was still in that terrible coma. He was telephoning on his mobile from nearby and 'would it be possible to pop in and have a word?'

She almost had to force her son-in-law to do his Christian duty. She asked grandad-to-be to take up his granddaughter-to-be and tuck her in, while she cleared things up. And Sean and that nice Mr Richards could have a talk in the study. Ma Hannigan did not say what Molly should do, but was surprised when she too followed on into Sean's study.

Nora put the paper into the bin and started to wash up. With only the evening blackness at the kitchen window, her mind began to go on her favourite journey covering the last few weeks.

Nora Hannigan remembered that first afternoon. She knew him within seconds of seeing him limp into St Thomas's Autumn Club. That seventy-something memory, much more at home with the distant past, juggled hardly at all. Not with this special one.

Not with Joe Trezise.

His greying hair had confused her at first, and his frame was larger than she had remembered, or perhaps it was just the extra pounds of the in-between years. What was certainly the same was the pixie impishness, the old Cornish gnome genes still working their cheeky magic on a creased though still handsome face. He always had stood out in Lancashire, he and his family having emigrated from the foreign parts of the West Country. The south-west tin mines had closed down in the twenties, and he and almost his whole village had brought 'Little Cornwall' to Ramstwistle. They had been more than welcome on the shallow and cruel, fault-ridden faces of the local colliery. Not young Joe, of course. For he was 'nobbut a lad' at the time. He was, in fact, the boy next door, for 'Little Cornwall' had begun where the weaver's cottage of Nora's childhood ended.

At that first Autumn Club meeting, Nora had said nothing. Just watched him and waited with an unusual shyness. They even bumped shoulders at the next meeting while queuing for cups of tea during the whist drive interval. He had apologized, and she had smiled. Words might spoil. It felt good just to look, and to imagine, except that he would occasionally look in her direction and confusion would cover her. Silly, even girlish, in her mid-seventies. But certainly bearable.

By his third attendance she had established, through casual questioning of those who had already spoken to him, that he had recently moved back to Hoghton and lived on his own. There was no sign of a Mrs Trezise, and she began to wonder whether there ever had been one. Maybe he had been so broken-hearted that he had pined away in that butcher's shop belonging to his uncle on 't'other side o' Manchester', until the years covered the pain and he settled into the grumpiness of middle and then old age. There was, however, the odd thing wrong with that fantasy. Our Joe had 'made summat of 'imsen', for he was prosperous-looking and by far the best-dressed bloke in the Autumn Club. His shoes were always polished, possibly to make up for the contents of one being false. His sharply pressed flannels and his casual tops were certainly not from Ali's bargain stall on the local market. Top-drawer stuff, no less. And, if Joe was far from grumpy in dress, it extended even more to his manner. In fact, he was still a bit of a devil-may-care character. You could still imagine him running off to join up, telling the recruiting sergeant that he was a year or two older than he actually was.

Of course, not having said something the moment she recognized him, had made it progressively harder to explain her subsequent behaviour. She thought she could always resort to a little white lie. But then she remembered who she was: Ma Hannigan, blunt of nature with all the stature of a late congressman's wife. She was no longer that chit of a lass who had wept enough buckets to fill the old tin bath in the kitchen after Joe Tresize had left.

And so it was when Ma Hannigan came face to face with her long-lost first love in the progressive dominoes on the third afternoon. She chipped out, won the game, and said,

'Before I move on to the next table, Joe Trezise, I think you owe me an apology!'

'Sorry, lass,' he'd chuckled, 'did I put down the wrong bone?'

'It's not the bones on the table that worry me, so much as that thick one in your head. But then, yer never did 'ave much grey matter upstairs. Mostly thick stuff, especially when thee emigrated to Manchester an' ran off and left me.'

Joe stared back. His lower jaw went into free fall at the moment of recognition. But only for a second. A slow smile caught, and an imp climbed into the eyes.

'And no sooner had I left town than you, O faithless Nora Lumb, ran off with mi best mate and high-tailed it across yon ocean.' The domino board had almost toppled over as both rose to their feet and gave each other a hug that had kept the old dears' tongues wagging for days afterwards.

In their subsequent and frequent meetings, they had time-travelled in their stories. Hers first. Then his. Joe's went from a two-man butcher's to a one-man shop after his bachelor uncle had passed on to 'that great abattoir in the sky'. Young Joe had inherited the lot, and by the sixties, his cooked meats and black puddings were proclaimed on the sides of two dozen orange and brown daily delivery vans around the north-west. By the eighties, he had a string of burger bars. The nineties brought a welcome buy-out just before the big food scares, and rather more than a nice nest egg for his retirement. Crime and traffic chaos in Manchester had eventually merged with a yen to see the dear old place, and the prodigal had returned.

The more Nora saw of him, the more she thought it was time to kill the fatted calf and make him feel really at home. Especially as there never had been a Mrs Trezise.

'Now, young Nora Lumb,' Joe's voice brought her mind racing back over the intervening sixty years and back into the vicarage kitchen, 'I've got you all to myself.'

'You just behave, Joseph Tresize, or you'll have a wet dish-cloth round the back of your neck.' Difficult to imagine such words spoken in tenderness. But Nora managed it.

Suddenly, raised voices were heard from the study, and they wondered what could be keeping Sean and Molly. Perhaps that poor Mrs Richards had finally died.

While they finished off the pots, she feared for Michael's return. It haunted always the recesses of her mind. Would he be back home and fit and well enough in time to give her away? Sean would do the marrying, so it would have to be the other man of the house.

She would have given much to be on his arm right now.

17

It was not long after his eleventh birthday that Michael Connaughton decided his dad was stupid. For one thing, his father actually expected to be obeyed. He was like something left over from the twentieth century. A joke. Few of the others had fathers, but they certainly had mothers and none of the gang listened to them, nor to the variety of uncles who came and went. So, why should he?

And anyway, what could his dad do? Hit him? Not a chance. He'd be done for child abuse, just like Fritzy's uncle had been. Nobody could touch you these days. The law said so. And if he came on too hard, well he'd go and get himself caught and earn his dad a thousand-pound fine.

Now, two years beyond that birthday, as he lay in the dark straw tenderly cradling the black buck Bambi after sneaking back into WildWorld, Michael knew even more.

Teachers were stupid as well.

His body shivered with the relief of a fresh fix, but his mind wallowed in malice. It made a refreshing change to deflect his anger away from his own shortcomings for a while. He smiled, remembering what they had done to the science master who kept screaming 'silly goose' at those who talked in class. It had taken months of carefully planned aggravation and teasing, knowing that there was nothing the teacher could do except hand out lines or detention.

Eventually, they'd triumphed. 'Silly Goose' had dissolved into tears and eventually hit one of them. Well, not actually hit, but he'd grabbed Chas Mitchell's arm. And that was enough. They had him. The whole class had jumped up and punched the air. Victory had been sweet.

After that, it had got boring. The adults took over their job, and turned 'Silly Goose' into a gibbering wreck. And the adults did it with even greater planning, and over a much longer period. Suspension. Then the court case. The governors' disciplinary hearing. Finally, the sack. Much later, Michael had heard that the science teacher had gone silly himself in some sort of mental home. They wouldn't have been that cruel. They had just wanted to put some fun into school. But then adults were stupid. Teachers were ditto. Parents were less than nothing.

Somebody had talked about parent power in schools. He'd never seen any. Pupil power, more like. Parents especially had no power at home, and that was doubly so in split families, the Druggies had reckoned. You could play one off against the other. Last Christmas, they'd had a league to see who could manipulate the biggest and best presents out of their keepers.

'For parents read pathetic,' Fritzy had jeered.

'But why?' he asked baby buck aloud, smiling crookedly in a warm haze of heroin. He stared into the buck's enormous brown eyes, and chanted,

> Adults make the rules.
> Adults are mostly parents.
> So why make rules
> that stop them being parents?

Michael stroked the long tapered nose. 'Parents with no power to be parents, baby buck. Kids couldn't have planned it better themselves,' and he grinned stupidly in the blackness of the stables, and strange shapes began to swim in dim shadows.

'And do you know what, little fluffy-scruffy buck?' His voice began to blur. 'Theys daren't even tell us whatsh right and wrong. Ooooh no. That would be judg-sh-mental. Now, there's a big word, baby buck.' Michael rubbed his nose in the soft nape of the buck's neck. Suddenly tears were rolling down his cheeks.

'Idiot parents!' he screamed aloud. He drooled, and snuggled back into the soft hair. 'You won't be bad, little buckie, will you, 'cos your mummy won't let you. And your mummy buck doesn't explain ... Hic! Jusht gives you a kick when you're in danger. Your mummy'sh a good mummy because she doesn't know what elshe to do but be your mummy. Our mummies and daddies forgot...' The voice trailed off as logic swam away.

The baby buck wriggled as Michael bayed like a stricken animal, and cried and laughed and giggled and wailed – a lost little boy despite his budding manhood, and the neck of the buck was wet, and it struggled to get free, and Michael clung on so that Mother Buck butted Michael's bent head so hard he had to let go.

'Why? Why? Whysh is the world so stupid?' he yelled into the blackness, and Mother Buck took her baby into care.

'Good Mother Buck,' Michael sobbed as he produced a small plastic bag of white powder. Then another, and another. The hands shook, not in anticipation of the drug, but with a sudden intense desire for an end. The shaking subsided, and the hands became calm and decisive, and he opened up each packet.

Appetite, desire, satisfaction. It was the gang's vicious circle. All driven. Some by drugs, yet others could take it or leave it. A lot wanted sex, but he preferred heroin. Some of them just fed their faces, caring little for drugs. Some were queer, but they all were, one way or the other. The gang girls came on chemist raids only for make-up and smells. Stupid when they could have any trip they wanted. Some just took the bottles of meths, and others pinched money to buy a different kind of alcohol. All driven by appetites and desires.

And now just one desire to be satisfied. Thirteen years were enough. The syringe sucked up the massive overdose. No need for his belt this time. And he plunged.

'Bye-bye, baby buckie ... buckie ... buckie ... buck ... bu ... b...'

* * *

'Come to see if you can still trust us?' Molly smiled mockingly as she followed Crompton Stanley Richards into Sean's study.

'Enough!' Sean turned on her sharply. Sarcasm was hardly the best greeting at a vicarage door. He turned to Richards. 'Good to see you're safe and well. Terrible thing in the House today.'

'Yes. Hospital needs kept me up here today, otherwise—'

'Very convenient.' Molly almost jeered.

They both looked at her as though they had not quite heard correctly.

'Molly, perhaps Mr Richards needs a word alone,' Sean said, even though the MP appeared much lighter and brighter than before. 'Perhaps Ma could do with some help with the dishes.'

'No need to leave on my behalf, Molly,' smiled the MP. 'In fact I'd like you in on this, if you have the time.'

'So kind of you, Mr Richards,' came the tart reply. 'And it is Detective Sergeant Hannigan to you. I noticed this morning that you had difficulty getting going when we left your wife's bedside to go to the lounge.'

The MP laughed, the first time either of them had seen such a response from him. Sean was about to intervene but Molly went on, 'And you hardly seem to be limping at all tonight?' There was a split second's hesitation.

'Kind of you to notice, sergeant, but it's nothing. It comes and it goes. A lot depends on the weather.'

'A hip thing, would it be, sir?'

'Molly?' Sean wondered what she was doing; where she was going.

'It's all right, vicar,' nodded Richards. 'Arthritis, actually, and they've told me to grin and bear it. If I take it easy, I'm fine. If there is a lot of walking or activity, it tends to wear me down. New joint, they say, eventually.'

'The left, I see.'

'Yes.'

'Molly, what do you think you're doing?'

'My job!' she snapped. 'And part of the job this afternoon, Mr Richards, was to look into your background. Would you care to tell me about the row your safari partner was having with David Henderson on the day before the remains of his body were found in WildWater? Apparently, the doctor was preparing to brand you both as ecological terrorists in his next nature series—'

'Molly, that's enough.' There was a curt finality in her brother-in-law's voice. 'You are out of line and you're also out of my study. This is not an interrogation centre, and this is a visitor to a vicarage whose wife is ill. Enough is enough.'

'And I'm investigating three murders and...' Molly trailed off, suddenly wondering whether she was going too far too early.

'Really, Mr Connaughton, I don't mind.' Richards was soothing. 'Though perhaps, sergeant, we should continue this later. Could be quite an interesting session. But please, what I have to say bears on the killer's motive. And you both need to hear it.'

Molly gave the men a blank stare, swung on her heels and walked off to a corner of the study.

'Quite a woman,' murmured Richards.

'A pain in the neck!' Connaughton did not murmur. 'Now, Mr Richards, what can I do for you?'

'It's more what I can do for you, Sean. Do you mind first names? My friends usually stick with Stan.' Connaughton nodded and smiled with an encouragement he did not feel.

'I see your story on the killer's signature got a good showing. Pity it didn't make the front page, what with Westminster and all the excitement. Anyway, I wanted you to understand a bit more about our subject this morning. It's not only for the killer's motives, but also so that you can read more clearly what I believe is on the killer's mind. And, by the way, I was glad to hear on the radio coming here that Mr Moore is no longer suspected. I suppose his release came as a result of the new death more than anything I had said?'

'Yes, it was, Stan. Look, don't feel the need to bother. No doubt, one day I'll get round to evolution and all that.'

'Could I then make an unusual request?'

'Yes.'

'Would you take it on trust that in the near future it will become important for you to understand this subject?'

'I don't see how,' Sean replied.

'That's why I'm asking you to trust me.'

Sean was not so much bothered about trust as about how to suggest a more appropriate time. It was now obvious there was no pastoral crisis. The front of Sean's mind was concerned for Ma Hannigan's truncated evening while the back was busy worrying about son Michael. In between, there was not much space left for extras. He was about to suggest they compare diaries when Stan Richards added, 'This really is a matter of life and death, and a killer is still at large, and I do believe that you will need this background sooner rather than later.'

An expectant pause.

Had this been somebody else, Sean would have put his foot down firmly. But this was an MP. A European leader. A knight in waiting.

'Right, Stan, but could we keep it short?'

'Fine,' and Richards hurried on. 'Tell me what you know of evolution.'

'Just my old GCE biology plus odd additions.'

'Fire away,' and the glow of this morning was back in his eyes.

'Well, it's one of those theories that's graduated into fact, even though I suppose it isn't. There are variations within a given species.' Richards gave a reassuring nod.

'You get environmental changes, such as colder climates and the struggle for food. Some in a species may be better able to cope. They therefore survive longer to have more offspring. Those that inherit the advantageous variation will continue to thrive better than those that do not. The advantageous variation will start to take over and become the norm. In this way, over time, a species changes.'

'Not bad,' Richards nodded gently, 'and eventually these changes could continue until they were sufficient to bring about a sub-species and even a new species altogether. Sorry, Sean. Go on.'

'Well, we're told that new species crop up in this process of competition and selection because the fittest survive. The swiftest rabbits live to breed another day. The moth with a peppered surface survives in soot-peppered industrial England far better than the plain variety because its camouflaged wings deceive the birds. The longer livers will obviously begin to outnumber the shorter livers, those less able to cope with environmental change. Given enough time, they will, so say the experts, mutate into a superior race of rabbit, moth or whatever.'

'Very good,' beamed a nodding Richards, thoroughly enjoying himself, 'except that your moth illustration was proved wrong a few years back. The theory suggests that this process of selection has happened over three billion years or so, ever since life itself first burst forth by some means or other. Sorry, sorry, there I go again. Carry on.'

'Well, that's it really.'

'What's your understanding of how life, we, you and I, came to be?'

A book clattered to the floor, and Molly called out, 'Don't mind me!' And they didn't.

'Oh, well.' Sean paused to crystallize the fuzzy areas of his education. 'Once we had a cell complicated enough to reproduce itself – sorry, I'm a bit hazy about how we get to the cell stage – each new generation faced possible mistakes as the genetic code was copied. Then there was the pressure of natural selection so that, over the generations, the cells or creatures began to change slowly, or sometimes in little jumps.

'I never could remember what was supposed to develop into what, but from this first start branched the whole bush of life as we know it today. Millions of massive whales at the end of one branch, billions of human beings as twigs on another, and goodness knows how many zillions of insects. That's about it. The survival of the fittest, the most selfish and strongest cell or gene or species winning out and exerting its influence. Happy with that?'

'The main elements are there.' It sounded like he had scored a C plus. What did the man want at ten o'clock in the evening?

'So,' and Richards steepled his fingers, 'what about us Homo sapiens?'

'Just basics,' shrugged Sean. 'Apes with a more upright posture and a larger brain survived more readily than those that stayed on all fours. The advanced apes had hands free for tools, and the bigger cerebral cortex could design them and use them.'

'Fine!' That was a B plus. 'Now, as we noted this morning,' and Richards suddenly sounded like a schoolmaster, 'we know adaptation takes place within a species. We've no problem with that, and I suppose this bug in the House of Commons is an example of how a flu virus can mutate into something stronger from year to year and—'

'Bugs!' Molly suddenly said out loud. Richards and Sean turned to her in surprise. 'Of course,' she mused, 'I'd forgotten.'

She strolled to the middle of the study to take over the floor. 'What are you, now? Europe's leading luminary on little nasties that make our lives a misery? Is my brother-in-law informant right?' It was rhetorical. 'So, professor or chairman, or whatever you are, you'll know just what sort of germ we're dealing with in Parliament, won't you?'

'Sorry, my dear.' The patronizing tone so grated with Molly and there was a hint in Richards' face that he knew it. 'Asian, or something. That's all Mr Baldwin and the television people seemed to know. Nor am I likely to know more. Our European group is policy. Not practical. We get to know the details three months down the line when the professionals submit reports to my committee.'

Sean knew so well the look that Molly returned – 'Try again, sunshine, you don't kid me for a second'. He wished he could have pulled a few files from her brain to read just what was going on in there. His sister-in-law swung away back to her book.

'So, Sean,' Richards carried on, 'evolution or adaptation takes place within a species and we used the more domestic example this morning: the various stages and changes between, say, the original wolf and today's terrier or even a dachshund. Right? So, if evolution happens on the much bigger scale between kinds of creatures, what should we expect to find when we dig up fossils?'

Sean, feeling somewhat patronized at this stage, offered, 'Bones?'

'Come on, man. Think! If one kind has turned into another; if fish led to amphibian, reptile into bird and so on—?'

'The in-between stages, you mean. Those that were neither reptile nor bird, or whatever?'

'Right. How many fossil examples would you expect to find if there were thousands and thousands of tiny mutations and changes in between the various kinds of creatures?

'Thousands and thousands?'

'Correct!' Richards granted a straight A plus. 'Charles Darwin wrote in *The Origin of Species* that this was the weakest part of his argument on evolution, but only because not many fossils had been found by the mid-1800s. He claimed that within a few years we would have plenty of fossil evidence.'

'Wasn't he right?' Sean countered. 'I mean there's that bird-reptile, the archaeopteryx. There's the lungfish. Wasn't there a dinosaur that had rudimentary wing flaps, even one with a chicken-like wishbone?'

'About a couple of dozen!'

'What? A couple of dozen what?'

'They've got around twenty or so fossils which some claim are in-between stages. There should be hundreds of thousands. But all they've got is a handful. And every one of those can be placed in normal phyla or classes of animals today.

'The fossil record contradicts gradual change. First, creatures appear in the fossil record looking about the same as when they disappear. Secondly, they all appear fully formed without any sign that they evolved. And they all appear in the same fossil band. Let me quote you one expert,' and Richards took out a notebook, flipped over a few pages and began to read,

> the single greatest problem which the fossil record poses for Darwinism, is the Cambrian explosion of around 600 million years ago. Nearly all the animal phyla appear in the rocks of this period, without a trace of the evolutionary ancestors that Darwinists require.

'Here's another expert on fossils...

> it is as though they were just planted there, without any evolutionary history.

'And another...

*the fossil record does not convincingly document a
single transition from one species to another.*

'Not that these palaeontologists dismiss evolution. They
wrote all this trying to disprove Darwin's idea of gradual
change. They put forward the idea that creatures changed by
little leaps. Punctuated equilibrium, they called it. Some even
suggested "big leaps" such as the first bird hatching out of
the reptile's egg. Of course, scientists laughed saying that this
involved such enormously complex changes. For instance,
all the tissues and organs would have to change in a million
ways at the same time. That was so improbable that one
might as well believe in miracles and a Creator.

'So, most scientists have begun to look at the conservative
"little leaps" idea, but even they cannot adequately fill in the
very real gaps we face when envisaging how major groups
of plants and animals change. If evolution has occurred,
whether by gradualism or by a hopscotch of little leaps, there
must still be countless intermediate forms between known
species, or between classes or phyla. There simply aren't any
which can claim this without great controversy.'

Richards flicked through his notes again.

'One expert describes the extreme rarity of transitional
forms in the fossil record as "the trade secret of palaeontologists". Another reveals, "we palaeontologists have said that
the history of life supports the story of gradual adaptive
change, all the while really knowing that it does not".'

Molly suddenly gatecrashed their tête-à-tête.

'Will you two listen to what you're saying? Only a tiny
minority of creatures ever get fossilized, and many intermediate stages are soft tissue, so there are bound to be
few fossils.'

'Good point,' Richards agreed. 'But come on, sergeant.
Let's be realistic. Wouldn't you think that with thousands of
palaeontologists digging in hundreds of sites all over the
world and doing so for a hundred and fifty years, they might

by now have come up with just one missing link that wasn't controversial? Just one?'

Molly's chin jutted. 'You're unbelievable! Charles Darwin and evolution have been one of the main philosophical planks on which our twenty-first century is built. And you're now telling us that the whole of Western civilization has been totally wrong for the last hundred and fifty years, and you're the only one that's right? Have I got that correct?'

The sarcasm flowed freely, but Richards merely shrugged. He was quiet for a moment then added,

'There was a time when I was on my own, doing postgraduate work in the then new molecular biology. I got so fed up with crying in the wilderness that I ducked out. My molecular research work wasn't being published, simply because it contradicted the gradualist evolutionary beliefs of science. So I gave up, and turned to law.

'Today, it's different. Hundreds of scientists are now questioning Darwin and even new ideas developed from his work. The feeling among honest scientists is that our Third Millennium demands a fresh start with a brand new theory.'

'And why should we believe you?' Molly persisted. 'Why should we rewrite the whole of modern science on your say-so?'

'Remember you're a detective, sergeant. Bring that skill to science. Work it out. Test the ideas. Don't take them just because a venerable old man like Darwin said them.

'Also, remember the golden rule: science only makes progress by climbing on the backs of its mistakes. We save lives today, because medical science learned through past mistakes with patients. Same with philosophy. The last century of progress, wars, cold wars and beliefs was largely based on three great thinkers – Sigmund Freud, Karl Marx and Charles Darwin. Marx and his communism are all but dead. Freud is old hat and well past his sell-by date. Now, many are saying it's Darwin's funeral. Also, remember: science and philosophy have been more wrong than right.

Yesterday's science is today's superstition.'

'A prophet, no less,' and Molly's mocking laugh was hard. 'Come to tell us to repent of our Western ways.' She disdainfully swung back to her bookshelves. Sean saw pressure building in Richards and was about to suggest a cup of coffee, when the MP blew.

'Well, Ms Hannigan, so I'm wrong or presumptuous to question the planks of Western civilization. Well, don't you think somebody should? People who rob me of my family, hooligans who tear up children and society, serial killers, rapists, murderers, the crime rate soaring, nobody knowing what's right and wrong anymore, drug barons and addicts and your own nephew in—' Richards suddenly trailed off. 'Sorry. I, er, sorry. I heard of your difficulties. I didn't mean to...'

Richards seemed to shrink smaller into his stammering apology. Molly's face was a puzzle. Her eyes blinked rapidly and the pupils darted here and there as though trying to fasten on some elusive idea.

'It's late,' Sean said. 'I really think we should call it a night.'

'No! I have some questions,' Molly insisted. Richards looked at his host and Molly.

'I am sorry about your son, Sean. I shouldn't have said that. Please let me go on with our chat.'

Sean suddenly felt tired. 'Another time, Mr Richards. Perhaps. Now, if you'll excuse us...' and he walked out towards the front door.

As Richards drove off, Sean turned on his sister-in-law.

'What the devil was all that about in there, Molly? What's got into you?'

'Open your eyes, Sean. He's our serial killer!'

18

Serial killers, and especially Molly's preposterous suspicion, were still lodged firmly in Sean's mental pending tray as the kettle boiled for a nightcap of black coffee.

Such mental dexterity was needed in vicar-ing. Shutting off was vital. The job was all about the person you were with at any given time. Personal problems and those of others all had to be filed away so that the person of the moment got the pinpoint focus of attention. Of course, the mental pending tray often overflowed, giving some clerics the perennial appearance of absent-mindedness. It was not that they were so heavenly minded as to be no earthly use. It was more to do with being surrounded by mountain ranges of problems, each needing to be moved with more faith and concentration than any single human possessed.

As he poured the hot water, Sean hoped that Nora and Joe had, if belatedly, received from him what was needed; not only as the vicar who would marry them, but also as the dutiful son-in-law. At least, Nora seemed to have trotted off to bed quite happily.

But not Molly. She was still around and prowling somewhere. Nor Sean, who felt the need to unwind. A sweet mug of the black stuff, and a half-hour stroll with the Lord in the midnight cool of the garden would allow a hectic day to settle.

'Mine with two sugars, please.' Molly popped her head round the kitchen door and smiled with the nearest she had in her repertoire to angelic sweetness. 'He's our man!'

'Later, Lord.'

'What was that?'

'One cuppa coming up,' and he flicked the kettle back on.

'Richards. It's him!' Molly burst out. 'You must know it!'

'No, I don't.'

'It's all there.' Molly spread her hands. 'The television people were out to get Richards and Giles St John. They were set to crucify WildWorld's latest kill-for-thrills venture on national television, and Richards had every reason to enjoy seeing Henderson chewed up by the sharks.'

'And the bishop? Where does he come in, and are you also going after St John as an accomplice and—'

'One thing at a time.' She smiled, took the coffee he offered and waltzed it round the kitchen table. 'Let me paint you my picture.'

'Yes Constable.'

Molly groaned at the pun, then went on. 'Richards fits the description. We now know that a man of Richards' general size, age, weight and hair colour was seen shortly after Henderson's body bits floated into view.'

Sean shook his head. 'There must be thousands like Richards in north-east Lancashire alone, and just because he had something against—'

Molly jumped in. 'I've only sketched the skeleton as yet, my dear vicar. Drink your coffee and pay attention.'

She sipped from her own mug smugly. Sometimes Sean could hug her. At other times, he could cheerfully strangle her. At the moment, it was touch and go which urge was the stronger.

'Next,' continued Molly, 'he knew all about the bug – oh! You don't know about that, do you? You're still thinking Asian flu. Well, Paine has Kasai, and that's got to be in the domain of our Mr Richards.'

Sean was lost for a response as he absorbed the news. Finally, his mind ticked on to other considerations. 'So why is he trying to kill Paine?'

'Maybe Paine was planning to campaign against his WildWorld plan in Parliament; or they're jealous competitors at Westminster; or money, power—'

'You're guessing. And what of the education officer, and the bishop, and the top man, whoever that turns out to be?'

'Okay, try this trio. One, Richards knows about Halipegus. Two, he was more bothered than normal about an innocent man in jail. Three, why is he being so weird about us and trust? What's he up to that's so special?'

Sean followed the numbers. 'One, Halipegus just happens to be his thing. Two, he doesn't want innocent people to suffer. Three, I haven't the foggiest idea why he's so bothered about us.'

'Aha!' Molly cried as though she had hit the bull's-eye. 'Now add this: he's had access to WildWorld – keys, codes, everything – while doing his thesis on wild animals. He'd know exactly how to get the animals to eat up those not on his Christmas card list—'

'Molly, you've told your boss about this?'

She smiled nervously, pulled her face crooked and scratched her head rigorously. Sean interpreted that as 'not yet'.

'Heard the one about the man who cut the legs off a flea?'

Molly stopped scratching and stared imperiously. 'You have a point?'

'Well, having cut off its legs he ordered it to jump. When it didn't, he concluded that fleas hear through their legs.'

'Rubbish! I'm not jumping to wrong conclusions.'

'You're also doing exactly what you once accused me of doing.'

'How so?'

'You once said that I believed pie-in-the-sky nonsense about there being a God. I then spent half an hour detailing a dozen decent reasons for accepting that there was a God, half of which you had trouble criticizing, then, at the end of it, you still accused me of being too irrational and intuitive.'

'Well...'

'And now, Molly Hannigan, you have the audacity to believe that Richards is the serial killer merely because one of the four victims didn't like him; he knew the area where they were killed; he's acting a bit funny towards us; he fits some vague description that all men his age fit. Oh, yes, and he knows a bit about worms. Have I missed anything out?'

'He limps,' she offered limply.

'Against all this, Richards is a highly respected Member of Parliament. He would already be a knight of the realm but for tragic circumstances. He has an impeccable record of service and dedication to his King and country and there's not one blemish on a record that has turned him into a local hero. Of course he's our serial killer. Why didn't I think of it?'

Molly's chin was jutting again. 'One thing I didn't mention. It's in here,' and she plunged a forefinger into her stomach. 'I feel it. I know it, and I'm going for it.'

* * *

James Baldwin had been awake since light dawned over a lazy Thames. He now watched the river drifting by on the other side of the floor-to-ceiling window of his emergency bedroom. His wakefulness had more to do with army-issue mattresses and rough blankets than his eagerness to confront an ill-tempered House of ministers and members. He had been wondering for half an hour what the collective noun might be for politicians. A grizzly of MPs, perhaps. A grouch! A cantankerHouse? Whatever, he knew it was not going to be a pleasant day, not when they had all planned long weekends on pre-General Election hustings.

'Sorry, sir,' whispered Commander Green, 'I couldn't help but notice you were awake. Here's your morning coffee and the update you requested for first thing.' A sheet of paper was proffered.

'Read it.' The PM took the coffee.

'Well, they're making good progress with the imam suspect. We already knew he had written acrimonious letters to the local press about the first victim whom he considered a "suitable casualty of Jihad", er, that means—'

'Holy War, Green. Do try and remember I've been around a bit.'

'Of course, sir. The education officer was suitable for Holy War attrition because he refused Muslim children their own aided school. The bishop qualified because he denied the existence of Allah and proposed that all religions should be merged into one. Now, there's a new development, Prime Minister. Mohammed Ahmed had complained to the BBC about the third victim.'

The PM looked up from his coffee, wanting more details.

'He had criticized Henderson's thirty-part *World of Life* series as propaganda which totally ignored God and encouraged people to worship rainforests, whales, endangered species – "anything but a Creator". He apparently believed Henderson was a Darwinist preaching that all creatures of evolution, "from flatworms to Homo sapiens", were equal. Different in degree, but not in kind. He declared Jihad against Henderson for preaching that life on earth was just "a television wonderworld" with no meaning. It had no origins. It was simply a beautiful accident going nowhere. Then a new—'

'Go back to Jihad, Green. Do we know the extent of Ahmed's version of Holy War?'

'It's the total line, sir. Economic and political pressure involving subversion and propaganda. Invasion of non-Muslim cultures with their so-called truth. Then the ultimate conversion of all to the Muslim way. Even armed conflict in certain circumstances. On the other hand, Ahmed has told our Lancashire people that it does not involve individual killings. The Koran, he says, orders them to obey the laws of the land in which they live. But that could be just a front.'

'Anything else?'

'We also think we have him linked to Paine, but it is a bit difficult to keep a straight face on this one—'

'Try,' Baldwin said dryly.

'Yes. Well, it appears that some toilets in Hoghton's council houses faced Mecca, and Ahmed had waged a sort of "change the loos" campaign during which he tried to enlist Paine's help.' Green smirked.

'Do I laugh at you rolling up a trouser leg and baring half your chest in your silly lodge rituals?'

'Yes, er, sorry, sir. The major apparently took the matter too lightly and they ended up having a blazing row in the Saturday morning surgery. The major also would not back the campaign for Muslim schools. By the way, one good thing has emerged for you, sir.'

'And that is?'

'If this is our killer, then it looks like you are safe, sir. You are apparently one of his heroes and he regards you—'

'Try not to sound so surprised, Green. One or two of our ethnic friends have been known to vote for me.'

The commander smiled and carried on, 'Ahmed is, however, not at all enamoured of his own national religious top man here in London. Too Sunni; too wishy-washy, apparently. We've given him twenty-four-hour protection, in case there are accomplices.'

'Speak up a bit,' the PM shouted over the sound of his electric shaver.

'Just one more thing: Interpol say he was in Paris in 1970 when the Ayatollah Khomeini declared Holy War while plotting to overthrow the Shah. He did a spell in the United States working against what they called the Great Satan. In his younger days – Ahmed's in his mid-fifties, by the way, and he fits the general build and description – he is on record as urging Pakistan to use the Islamic nuclear bomb as part of

Jihad. Otherwise, he seems a nice quiet and polite gentleman, according to our Lancashire lads.'

'What about the Kasai?'

'No connections so far, but it's conceivable that one or more of the workers at a germ holding centre might just be a fellow sympathizer.'

James Baldwin finished dressing and was now ready for whatever the day would bring. His secretary was first.

'Two quick decisions needed, sir. Tomorrow morning's Trooping the Colour and the King's birthday celebrations. Obviously, nobody can go from here, and the palace and the Ministry of Defence are wondering what is the best course of action. The King is also fitting in a quick investiture at the palace before the trooping. Not a big affair. Appears somebody missed out on the last couple of ceremonies. They want to know your thoughts, sir.'

'They're on. No argument!' Baldwin was firm. 'No terrorist, no serial killer is going to bring this country to a standstill. We will fight them on any front they choose, and they will lose every time. Get one of the communication boys to tart that up a bit and put it out as a press statement. Now send in the first grouch of MPs.'

* * *

Shards of glass remained suspended in stubborn putty at the top of the long window of Hoghton Police Station's Menagerie. The remainder of the pane was shattered in a thousand pieces across the floor, the furniture and the clothing of the assembled investigators.

Superintendent Court's quick check of personnel revealed only a few cuts and abrasions but, whatever the injuries, he would have pressed on regardless. A fast-acting killer was still seeking his *crème de la crème* victim, the PM was regularly chewing his ear, via Commander Green's mouth, and a gang of NCS detectives despatched overnight to the north awaited attention. Finally, there was a houseful of MPs all demanding swift action.

The broken window was the only one overlooking the street where the Asian protesters had gathered, so Court, having despatched officers to prevent the launch of further missiles, pressed on with the briefing.

'Spencer, you were saying before you were so rudely interrupted...?' and the chief inspector was caught in indecision. He didn't know whether to beam in the limelight or sulk at the disrespectful use of his surname without title. Spencer chose the middle road: lightly morose.

'Ahmed obviously still claims he was elsewhere,' Spencer began. 'He has alibis for at least three of the murders but, with these ethnics, sir, they could just be covering for him.'

Crick interrupted mainly because he couldn't stomach Spencer's pomposity, nor his racism.

'SHERLOCK says our Asian gentleman sees everything in revolutionary terms. The Western economic and technological revolution is bad because it has produced "a decadent and evil society". The Islamic Revolution is good because it's "back to the traditions, values and aims of the Prophet Mohammed". The Western materialism of the Great Satan – America – is particularly evil. Apparently, Britain only qualifies as a "minor Satan", because of its small political and economic interference within the Gulf area.'

Spencer tried to restore himself as the focus of attention. 'I'm surprised he can even tolerate living in this intolerable country and—'

'Well,' Crick took the floor back, 'this is what bothered our security boys when he first came. They originally thought that he was sent as an *Ensan en Hari* – a suicide man! He was also down on record as approvingly quoting "the man who dies without having taken part in a raid or without having made the decision to do so, dies a hypocrite".

'Jihad, says Ahmed, is *Fard ala'l-Kifaya*, a duty for all sane, male adult and free Muslims who must rally to the

Muslim army when it assembles for Holy War. They're called to wage Jihad until all perform the *salak* ritual prayers and all pay the *zakat* alms tax.'

Spencer tried again. 'We're working on the premise that the clown outfit and the make-up were used because Ahmed's quite famous in these parts, and he would have been easily recognized.'

'Video-wise,' Inspector Jones jumped in with his related subject, 'we've got one or two shots which catch our man from the rear or side. Those in profile are also too far away and fuzzy, though we're trying for enhancement. On one or two shots, it's almost as though he knows where the community cameras are. He seems to be shading his face as he turns in front of them. Obviously local and in the know about—'

'Mark,' Court interrupted, 'work with Hannigan on this. Hear that, sergeant?'

'Yes, sir,' Molly responded from the back of the room.

'Apparently, Les Moore's been telling her that he got a good view of a clown just before Henderson was discovered. How far have you got with the tapes, Mark?'

'Trouble these days, with so many security cameras, we have too many tapes. Even with the latest Mandrake face-matching software we're still only about halfway through.'

'Seeta?' Court turned to his most recent recruit, save for the overnight invasion of the London NCS team. 'What's your reading of the situation, inside and out?'

Detective Sergeant Seeta Sandhu had officially been brought in to assist Jitka Lister. Unofficially, after Ms Lister's misreading of Les Moore, Seeta was her replacement. She was a psychology graduate fast-tracking through the provincials and marked out for eventual high rank. She was efficient and ready for the question.

'We have a tiny fraction of the area's sixty thousand Asians outside the station, and they are mainly the young hot-headed Shi-ites. Ahmed's not really one of the local Muslims. He's a foreigner and not from any of the villages and towns from which the majority originate. He represents only one of the forty-odd mosques, and his extreme views are by no means typical. As far as Lancashire Muslims are concerned, he is a voice crying in the wilderness, except for some of the young who think he should be an ayatollah. I don't think the community protest will grow much bigger, so long as Ahmed is seen to be treated fairly.'

'And inside, sergeant? What's your reading of our man, and has he got an axe to grind on evolution?'

'Difficult, sir. Most Muslims are not too bothered about evolution, rather like most Christians. In Islamic terms, there are three levels of texts in the Koran. Creation comes in the middle order, according to which people are encouraged to keep thinking about these matters without any need for rigid beliefs. Quite frankly, superintendent, I'm having difficulty seeing Ahmed as our killer on this score. All his previous concerns have been of a political or sociological nature.'

'What about his alibis? Would local people cover for him?'

'That's my other problem, sir. Muslims in north-east Lancashire are law-abiding people, even when they disagree. For example, some do want their own aided schools, but they all want to pursue it through the political arena. The last thing they need are hotheads trying to ruin community relationships. I think we have to treat his alibis seriously, sir. I think they stand up.'

'Superintendent?' It was Hannigan. 'Would you consider an alternative suspect at this time?'

Every head in the room turned in her direction. In the silence, you could even hear a foot grate on the dull glistening carpet of glass splinters.

'You have the floor, Hannigan.'

'Perhaps in your office, sir?'

'Come on, sergeant, shyness doesn't become you, and we haven't got time for it either. Spit it out, lass!'

19

'It looks like malaria.' Dr Maurice Johnstone, head of the high-security isolation unit at Coppetts Wood Hospital, was testing his students. 'Why isn't it, Raymonds?'

Trainee Raymonds, over from the States on six months' placement, peered at the perspiring, jerking body of Major Nicholas Paine through the double-layered balloon and considered putting his hands through the glove holes to feel for a pulse – anything to win time for inspiration. And then, mercifully, a hint surfaced.

'Er, cyclical, sir?'

'I'm asking you.'

'Well, that's it, Dr Johnstone. Malaria is cyclical, going up and down, but Kasai stays up and keeps on going up.'

'We spend a fortune on you, Raymonds, and that's all you can manage? Anybody?'

The mechanical drone of fellow Yank Jessica Akmond seemed at home in cold clinical surroundings. 'You get all the signs of Ebola but in a much shorter period, sir ... high fever, aches in joints, stiffness, irritability, though it must be said that this particular patient has been irritable ever since he came in. Classical diarrhoea began after midnight, vomiting has now reached the compulsive stage, and the eyes have begun to secrete bodily fluids. Nose and mouth will follow also towards the end, which shouldn't be long now.'

'Good,' nodded Johnstone. 'Raymonds, at least tell us what's happening inside.'

'Haemorrhaging, sir.' He sounded excited, and was then unstoppable. 'It turns you into the ultimate haemophiliac, and thins the blood to such an extent that it seeps out everywhere, especially when the compulsive vomiting puts everything under pressure. You could say that the patient basically retches himself to death. The brain starts haemorrhaging and you go psycho, and then lose touch with reality. If the Kasai pattern is followed, you're dead within two hours.'

'Psycho? Retching himself to death? Ultimate haemophiliac? Raymonds, could you try and remember that you are training to be a scientist. A doctor. Not a tabloid hack? Akmond, treatment?'

'I've got that as well, sir,' Raymonds came bubbling back. 'Well?'

'Oh, thank you, sir.' Raymonds was relieved at the chance to redeem himself. 'Starting first with Ebola as the comparison, every three hours you blast the patient with heavy doses of his own blood platelet plasma, which causes the blood to coagulate, to thicken, and that gives him a bit more respite. Over the next three hours, the Ebola kills off all that, and then you zap him again, and again and again. You're not curing him because everything you put in, the Ebola kills. Now, with Kasai, if you can catch the patient early enough, you might just get enough blood out to extract enough platelets, but it needs to go in continually and it's just a hopeless and losing battle.'

'Not bad, Raymonds. We shall yet send you Stateward to save the world, so long as you don't zap or blast too many patients. Now, a bit more on treatment, and you'll need to take notes: there was one possibility with Kasai with the 2001 outbreak. One patient survived for two weeks, and we thought – well, what did we think, Akmond?'

'Probably the same as Ebola, sir. In the Zairean outbreak at Kikwit in the nineties, one of the doctors survived and they used his blood with eight victims. One was in a coma already and died. The other seven recovered within an hour.'

'An hour!' Raymonds gasped.

'Incredible, but true,' nodded Dr Johnstone. 'Of course, Western doctors are still unsure. It happened in Zaire, with no clinical trials and no controls to test it against. Even so, the Atlanta Centre for Disease Control plus our tropical disease centre on Merseyside has freeze-dried and stored the blood with the alleged antibodies in case of future outbreaks. In fact we tried a couple of packs with Paine shortly before midnight but without improvement. The extra swirl in the Kasai crook obviously didn't fit the antibody.'

Doctor and students stood looking through the blood-spattered isolation balloon around the bed. The victim was bleeding from practically every pore. His half-open eyes were filling with blood. The skin was torn in several places where the major had tried to massage his aches and pains.

They were turning to move away when their subject abruptly arched upwards, caught in a massive seizure. Blood and virus sprayed in all directions on the inside walls of the billowing balloon, so that the medics gradually began to lose sight of their patient. Just as quickly as it had started, it ended. A warning red light flashed and the heart monitor's beeping deteriorated into a mournful monotone.

Dr Johnstone shook his head, raised his hand to a panel, and flicked off all the life-monitoring systems.

* * *

Dew drenched Michael Connaughton's clothes. His shivers grew so violent that he was shaken back into the cold world he had tried to flee. He struggled to rise but slumped forward and gave up to the grass what felt like the whole of his innards.

Through the slits of half-open eyes, he found himself at the rear of the stables, resting on the edge of a small ravine, and he moaned with self-pity. His present plight bore no comparison to the cosseted comfort of his own home, with Gran and Aunt Molly to love him; even his dad, who kept kicking him to do something with his life. 'Good Daddy Buck,' he groaned.

His mind swam in the befuddled after-haze of heroin, and he screamed 'Daddy Buck!' again and burst into tears. His frame racked until the ducts in his eyes were dry, and something like soberness descended, and he came to a conclusion.

'I know what I'll do,' he sniffled. 'I'll go home.'

He raised himself to his hands and knees, and then knees only, but as he straightened, the grass swam and the ravine became a wave and suddenly he was plummeting into it, and under, over and rolling.

Blackness fell in on him. Then nothing.

* * *

Five days!

It seemed like five years since he had stood by Sammi's intensive-care bed at Hoghton Royal Infirmary. Now, several more deaths later, Connaughton stood beside her coffin. A congregation of six – half from the undertaker's firm and half from St Thomas's pastoral team – looked lost in the mushroom cream crematorium chapel draped with purple. There were no relatives.

Sammi's coffin was adorned with a single red rose. Sean intensely disliked funeral flowers. Radiant poetry they may have been in soil, but a dying waste when laid on fake funeral oak. Sean had once estimated that floral tributes at one of his more luxurious despatches could have fed and clothed a hundred street kids for a year in the Tanzanian orphanage his church helped to fund. The economy of a single rose ordered for Sammi spoke of the poetry of salvation. A blood-coloured triumph coaxed from choking weeds and tearing thorns. It signalled hope. New life.

'The best is yet to come,' Sammi had often said. 'It can't be any worse than what has been.' A simple faith. A childlike one that would take her into the arms of a safe eternity and justice. And that she badly needed. In addition to AIDS, Sammi had been hopelessly twisted by use and abuse for others' satisfaction. And the abusers had been her model. And so it had seemed natural for her to mould herself to use and abuse, especially with those weaker than herself. But then had come a different time and another model, encountered in the refuge of a prison chapel. A model who had provided power to turn; to repent. She had blossomed in being forgiven, but could never quite learn to forgive herself.

And that, in the end, hastened her end. The 'just one last time' drug she took to forget went through a needle which, from rust of habit, she had forgotten to sterilize.

Little of this, of course, featured in Sean's funeral address, for the confessional of counselling was for his ears only. He dwelt instead on what was for the world's abusers a terror – the final Judgement Seat. For the Sammi-like victims of this world, it represented vindication. Before this seat, the justice that Sammi badly needed would be seen to be done. For here, those who had torn her would stand. And there was a hell.

If there was not, God would indeed be the very devil himself. Sean committed Sammi to the God who invented justice. The God who balanced the scales of eternity.

* * *

Molly Hannigan concluded her presentation in the Menagerie, 'At the very least, we make Richards a priority. There are too many questions, and I would feel happier with answers.'

Chief Inspector Spencer cleared his throat and Molly feared the worst.

'I can't imagine why such a notable dignitary should wish to indulge in serial killing...' Hannigan felt like strangling

213

him, '... but we have to take seriously Detective Sergeant Sandhu's profile on Ahmed and his alibis. I think we should give it a go, sir. After all, we have nothing to lose.' Now, Molly could have kissed him, despite his pomposity and the strong suspicion that he was covering himself with an each-way bet.

Court was quiet, assessing the previously unconsidered. He was observing Hannigan from a different perspective, 'Not just a pretty sergeant, then', and was grateful his thoughts couldn't be read by the politically correct police.

'Indirectly then,' he finally decided. 'No face-to-face stuff today. Just background info and as many answers as you can get. If it still stands up this time tomorrow, we all go in together. All weekend leave is cancelled.'

The moans were more for show than from conviction. Each knew that the eyes of a nation were now on them. Morale had climbed since they realized that Parliament and the Prime Minister were relying on them to provide quick answers.

'Hannigan, use Crick and SHERLOCK as much as you want, and I can give you two DCs, Blake and Farnsworth, but no more. Our priority is still the video search. Have you thought out which way you want to go?'

'I know exactly what I need, sir,' and Molly was rushing now with elation and the desire to start before Court changed his mind. 'First, Richards' whereabouts at the time of the killings. We need to check his parliamentary schedule, also his hospital visits. They have the usual security signing-in book for fire drill and insurance.

'We ask around regarding motivation. He certainly had cause to dislike Henderson but, if he is our killer, there has to be something bigger that unites all the victims to Richards. We need to recheck his accessibility to WildWorld and the drugs, and also to the Kasai bug through his chairmanship of this Euro germ and genetic group. We'll feed a good photo of him into SHERLOCK in readiness for comparisons with any tape shots that turn up.'

'Take three DCs, then,' Court recanted. 'Let's see ... Michaels, as well.'

* * *

Q. C. Bocker strutted away from the lodge at Kirkham Open Prison. Each freshly released inmate was expected to make his own way back to civilization, and that suited him.

He would continue to stroll away to the main road, and then exercise his new freedom: left to the sea, and maybe the bright lights of Blackpool, or right to Manchester where he had reigned supreme with his gang. Of such was liberty. The only choice allowed him for the last year he had used to complete a science degree foundation course. Ironically, on the outside, he had never had the freedom to do such a thing.

He expected no welcome party. The old Bentley parked up on the prison access lane as it bent right to the main road would not be for him. It was only as he drew alongside that he realized his mistake.

On the back bench seat, and with the rear window rolled down, sat a sad-faced clown. The shotgun he held pointed to the newly freed man's midriff. The voice was as grave as the judge who sent him down.

'Quentin Charles Bocker, you drive.'

The clown cocked both barrels of the gun, and 'QC' immediately forgot the hated use of his first names. He glanced back hoping for help, but Kirkham had already forgotten him. Bocker opened the driver's door, slid behind the wheel and followed instructions.

Few words passed between them beyond terse directions and the occasional QC query about their intended destination. Within twenty minutes, they were both sitting in the still Bentley, parked by the large commercial complex at the foot of Blackpool Tower. Trams protested and grated against their metal constraints behind them while ahead, high tide brought sewage and brown waves licking at the promenade wall.

'Roll up your sleeve.' The shotgun came to lodge under Bocker's right ear. 'You probably know the drill better than I.' The muzzle dissuaded QC from protesting too vigorously and in any case, it was somewhat difficult to get a word in edgeways. His abductor was quoting poetry.

> Upon my secure hour, thy uncle stole,
> With juice of cursed hebenon in a vial,
> And in the porches of mine ears did pour
> The leprous distilment...

Quote over, the clown, careless of precision, used his free hand to plunge the syringe into the bare arm.

'Fear not, Mr Bocker, that you will suffer the fate of Hamlet's father.' Richards waved an empty syringe in his prisoner's face. 'No leprous distilment this henbane, this hebenon. Merely a watered-down version. The truth of scopolamine. Relax. Simply answer my questions. Then, you go free to get your seaside kiss-me-quick hat.'

Already the drug was soothing Bocker back into old soft leather.

'Your crime?'

'GBH.'

'On whom?'

'Some Sheila; some high-up's wife.'

'Why do it?'

'She was giving us grief, man. We weren't to blame for her stupid kids getting killed.'

'Did I ask about the children?'

'No. But it weren't our fault!' And there was agitation behind the drowsiness.

'Whose was it then?'

'Not us!' and it was expelled like a curse.

'Bothers you, does it?'

And the scream that replied caused a seagull to lift off the Bentley's bonnet. Bocker emitted a short sob. The clown continued the interrogation.

'You like life?'

'It's a better pain than jail.'

'How so?'

'You choose the punishment on the outside. You give it if you're strong. You get it when you're weak.'

'And you?'

'I give it.'

'And right and wrong?'

'No such thing!' QC gave a cynic's laugh.

'Then it's not wrong to kill kids?'

'Listen, mister!' Bocker said warningly. 'We didn't kill 'em!'

'As good as.' Richards' voice was still level. 'So, was it wrong?'

'What's it to you, anyway?'

'Was it wrong, Mr Bocker?'

'Stop it! Stop it! Yer doin' mi head in!' and Bocker seemed to lose control. 'I dunno. Maybe. Right? Wrong? Who's to say? This is wrong!' And Bocker suddenly jabbed a finger at the gun muzzle by his ear. 'Yeah, man. This is wrong, man. This is dead wrong—'

'And the two children, Mr Bocker?' Richards pressed the muzzle harder into Bocker's neck. 'My two children, Mr Bocker?'

A sharp intake of fear paralysed QC.

'Get out.'

And Bocker could not move.

'Get out and walk!' and the gun prodded the nape of his neck. Still no movement. The barrels clipped the ear painfully, and Bocker yelped and forced his sluggish limbs to obey. The nerves of his back were suddenly alive with expectancy. He took a short step. Then two more, quicker ones. Then stopped. Should he run? Where could he hide? He heard the click of a door opening behind. A shuffle of feet! Another door banged closed. He froze in a cringe, and waited.

217

The impact, when it came, hit Bocker with a greater force than he could ever have imagined. It came not from hot metal but from three quiet, halting words that seemed to explode in his head.

'I – forgive – you!'

Bocker retched, grasped his stomach and sobbed. The sound was masked by a terrible lost howl coming from behind. This in turn merged into the sound of the Bentley reversing away at high speed.

20

Committee Room 15 was redesignated the emergency Commons Isolation Unit. By Friday lunch, its oak furnishings and gold-embossed green leather chairs were for the exclusive and enforced service of nineteen patients, all intensely irritated. Each insisted endlessly that they could not possibly have the Major's flu bug. Their colds, coughs and assorted bronchial complaints had been with them long before any possible contact with Paine.

Fosdyke and Carradice, both in general practice before winning their seats, together with Parker who had been something in microbiology at Porton Down, had been press-ganged into crewing the room. All knew of Paine's true condition. All were staffing the room under the collected wisdom of outside specialists. Each was adamant that their charges did not need to know about Kasai.

Especially the latest.

The Hon. Member for Shoreditch had made the mistake of sneezing twice in rapid succession in the crowded terrace tea rooms overlooking the Thames. One moment he was in a political scrum, plotting with others how to escape to their constituencies. The next, before his second sneeze had expired, he had yards of space for as far as he could exhale in every direction. Co-conspirators had deftly leapt for distance, handkerchiefs rampant. Three smog-masked whips, revelling in their bring-out-your-dead roles, had quickly frog-marched the Shoreditch MP, shouting and spluttering, up Italian marble stairs, along the dark oak committee room corridor, and into Room 15.

It was shortly after this that the Kasai rumour had hit the tea rooms.

From whence it came, nobody was sure. But, within thirty minutes, the Commons was again doing what came naturally: holding yet another emergency enquiry. This time it was on the most serious of all parliamentary crimes: Misleading the House. With the deadly topic transcending political loyalties, the Prime Minister subsequently faced a huge majority demanding his personal answer to the charge.

Articulate though Baldwin was, emotions and close proximity to earth's deadliest known virus won the day. Rational thought departed. Members could not accept the necessity for a deliberate lie to the House, and it mattered not that television cameras had been live during Question Time and that the truth would have caused national panic. They rejected outright the PM's assurance that he had planned to give the House the full facts once security needs had been served.

At one point, the ferocity of the House implied that members would have been happy with nothing less than the speedy return of beheading at the Tower of London. A vote of no confidence in his government was carried with a lynch-mob majority, mainly because most knew it meant little. If Kasai was present, they'd all be dead soon. If it wasn't, then cooler and calmer heads and political self-interest would later prevail. Censure could easily be redrafted into praise for strong leadership that had contained a nightmare scenario. But not for the moment. James Baldwin was on notice to quit. He would be obliged to seek audience with the King, as early as the present crisis allowed, to inform him that the government could no longer command the trust of the House.

All this, of course, remained on the outside of Committee Room 15.

* * *

The acting Bishop of Hoghton telephoned Sean Connaughton in the middle of a *News at One* dedicated to the crisis in Parliament. A tanned announcer was using her most righteous nuance to condemn the total news blackout in a free democratic country.

Bishop Julia's voice was refreshingly real and honest. First, the good news. Michael Connaughton, according to a diocesan youth worker, had called in at Twistleton Youth Centre the previous evening. He had looked fit and well. The bad news revealed that he had been after drugs, and a greater quantity than usual. He had eventually succeeded in scoring heavily. One extra snippet of gossip revealed that Michael had talked of returning that night to Hoghton. Sean agreed with the bishop that a fresh check on his local haunts might prove useful.

Before signing off, he brought her up to date with events. She hesitantly reminded him that the future of his parish was still on the agenda. Delicately but firmly, she reminded him that parish amalgamation plans still needed to be addressed. However, all would wait until after the present crisis and certainly until after Michael was safely home.

Ma Hannigan had come in halfway through the conversation. She had jotted down a list of haunts to visit before Sean flicked off the videophone. WildWorld came first.

* * *

Molly sat in a humming Menagerie in mid-afternoon. Her eyes were open but there was no outsight. All neurones were on overload in search of insight.

Why would a Member of Parliament want the town's education officer dead? And on April Fool's Day? Was that significant or just a red herring? Why wait a whole month, and then produce three more victims on three successive days?

Questions were vital. Ask the wrong ones and you ended up in a cul-de-sac at a false destination. Fail to ask the right ones and there was no hope of progress. This stage of detection was Molly's pet hate, but also the source of her highest highs. The figuring followed by the finale. And the triumph. And, yes, if she was honest, the kudos. But that was still far off.

What could possibly link the disparate victims? What was the motivation? How did Richards' explosive tirade against the world's woes in Sean's study fit in? Did Richards have the means plus opportunities?

The means were being investigated by Detective Constables Michaels and Blake. While Michaels was looking at Richards' access to the working end of his European germ and genetic group, Blake was checking Richards' research work at WildWorld and possible access to the safari vet's hyoscine. He was also reading up how easy it would have been for Richards to have distilled his own supply of hyoscine from henbane, belladonna or jimson weed. Farnsworth was detecting the opportunities that Richards had had to carry out the crimes, checking on both hospital and parliamentary attendance records.

Hannigan had spent the morning investigating the killer's motivation. This was beyond delegation, especially since Richards had moved it into her personal domain. Why was it so important for both Sean and herself to understand him? What were his survival of the fittest lectures all about?

The seemingly endless round of calls, both over the telephone and in person, included relatives of the victims, friends, work associates – all had had to be re-questioned with antennae alert for links to Richards. Molly had spent a full hour with Giles St John interrogating him about Henderson. She had finally concluded that, if the television programme was the cause of the deaths, then Giles St John should also be in the frame. It was, after all, his territory where the killings took place, and he had just as much an axe to grind as had Richards. Hannigan even went to the point of asking St John where he was at the times of the death events. His alibis were impeccable. But so what? It didn't stop him being an accomplice.

Added to the professional questions were the personal ones, especially those raised in meeting Sean just a few minutes before. He was leaving the police station as she returned. The line of his shoulders drooped as he brought Molly up to date on Michael, explaining that he had just requested extra police help for a fresh search of WildWorld.

She had reached out to give him what she had naturally offered dozens of times before – a sisterly hug.

The oddest thing had then happened. Or had it? Even now she couldn't dismiss an element of hopeful imagination, but there was something different. There was a more than usual warmth in the response. Even enthusiasm. Nor was it just the clinging one might associate with the need for comfort. In fact, the gentle hands on her back reminded her more of a lover than a brother; a caress more than comfort. And when a sisterly hug should have been concluded, Sean had held on. Just a fraction longer than necessary.

It was then – still in the embrace – that she had looked up; in confusion, in hope, she couldn't honestly say. But their lips came to within an inch of each other.

She had read about hearts missing beats. Every self-respecting heroine of every short story in every romance monthly she had ever read knew what happened to hearts when lovers' lips brushed or eyes met across crowded rooms. Now, she had her own personal testimony of what it felt like. It suddenly seemed ludicrous that she had lived so long without experiencing one fully fledged missed heartbeat through romance.

And then, appallingly, heartlessly, he had stepped away. Let go! Just like that! It was such a surprise! Missing heartbeats was one thing; missing one's footing and almost flopping down on the police station steps was embarrassing. She had looked hastily around to see if any of her colleagues had witnessed the same. The world seemed oblivious.

Suddenly, so too had Sean.

'Right,' he had said, cool as a brother-in-law, 'Better get on.'

* * *

By late Friday afternoon, Superintendent Court had all but given up on the videotape search when Mark Jones popped his head round the door.

'We've got a reasonably clear profile of the clown, sir.'

The sweet news had the superintendent hurrying with excitement down the corridor to one of the two viewing rooms. Jones added more information as they went.

'Strangest thing ... the clown seems to have checked camera locations and angles to within a few degrees. The shot we've got is of him standing with his back towards a camera after jabbing Paine. He's pouring a small phial of what must have been petrol over the tip of his clown's umbrella. Looks like he knew exactly what dangerous stuff he was playing with. Then, cool as anything, he fires it with a lighter, and as it burns, he looks round and up to the camera on top of its high stand. And the sad face just grins. He almost winks at us at one stage. Weird, it is!'

'Have you done any comparisons yet?'

'We've ruled out Ahmed, sir. No way his ears are the same unless they are heavily camouflaged with stage make-up. There are two distinct types of lobe on the human pinnae, depending on which alleles are dominant in your genetic make—'

'English, Jones.'

'Well, some lobe bottoms join straight to the side of the head and others curl upwards to form a rounded lobe before joining the head. Our clown is curled, and Ahmed is straight.'

'What about Hannigan's MP?'

'The ear lobes are right, sir, and there is a reasonable correlation between eyes, nose and mouth. Structurally, there are similarities but we're not comparing like with like. The photo of Richards which was fed into SHERLOCK was full face. Comparisons with a profile, and a tilted one at that, can only be approximate. What we can say is that Richards is not ruled out. We've got a few more tapes left, but we're not expecting much from them...' Inspector Jones seemed to hesitate as he finished.

'There's more?' encouraged Court.

'Maybe nothing,' shrugged Jones, 'but we got most of our community cameras through a Single Regeneration Budget government scheme in the mid-nineties. If memory serves me right, local MPs, including Richards, helped plan and launch the scheme.'

* * *

The final teatime edition of the *Hoghton Evening Argus* led with the release of the local imam and easing of racial tensions.

Its inside leader opened with 'Days of Trouble', and dwelt on racial street protests, serial killers, drug barons and 'a society acting like the residents of WildWorld'. It suggested that 'Parliament might productively use its incarceration to solve the law and order issues once and for all'. It forecast that the victors in the forthcoming General Election would be whichever party did just that.

'Even economic worries are running second to fears of lawlessness,' ran the leader. 'What does it profit the voter if he has wealth but is terrified to own it?'

A side panel down the front page teased the reader with extraordinary rumours behind the closure of Parliament, and enticed the reader to turn to Page Two for 'the full facts'. There, every imaginable cause was laid out in coloured panels. There were no facts.

Across on Page Three, the lead story was headlined '*"Armed clown kidnapped me" – Ex-Con.*' The story ran:

A newly-released prisoner staggered into a Lancashire seaside police station this morning claiming that he had been kidnapped by a clown and forced to drive at gunpoint to Blackpool Tower.

Quentin Charles Bocker alleged that his assailant had also injected him with drugs.

Mr Bocker told police that he had been ordered into a car at gunpoint on being released from Kirkham Open Prison, where he had been serving time for grievous bodily harm on the wife of a Lancashire MP, who is still in a coma more than a year after the attack.

Mr Bocker was invited to make a statement, but on being asked to describe his abductor, the former prisoner said to the desk sergeant, 'The clown forgave me.'

A police spokesman told the Argus, *'The man then began crying, ran out of the station and has not been seen since. We are anxious to trace Mr Bocker so that he can help us further with today's incident and other matters.*

* * *

Molly Hannigan drove towards the vicarage in the early evening. Her sluggish mind had wearied of moving blocks of facts from one perspective to another. Her eyes had tired of SHERLOCK's monitor, and her ears rang with reports. She was also anxious for news of her nephew.

All good and legitimate reasons for her destination; all perfectly explainable. But not the whole truth. Then again, she thought to herself, she had given up admitting the whole truth where the vicarage and its chief occupant was concerned. Not easy for somebody who liked to be honest with herself.

The reports that had wearied her had been on Richards' means and opportunity. Michaels had reported that Richards' Euro germs could not be removed without the highest possible clearance and even then not without full scientific supervision. However, 'highest possible' did include the chairman, who himself was an accredited scientist.

Between Blake and herself, it had been established that Richards not only had full access to WildWorld for his research, but still retained skeleton master keys. Also, the codes to the vet's laboratories had not been changed since his research.

Farnsworth, on the other hand, had little of help. Certainly the hospital held records of all relatives who came and went, plus relevant times of arrival and departure. As the Irish charge nurse had assured them, '... for sure, don't the relatives themselves fill in the attendance book.'

Farnsworth had mimicked, 'To be sure and begorrah, there was nothing sure at all, at all, about that system. Richards could have put down any times he liked.'

And parliamentary attendance records were proving somewhat difficult to obtain, for the relevant office was within the inaccessible isolated enclave.

Molly depressed the superdrive button below the gear lever of the XJS and took off along the Hoghton bypass, way beyond the speed limit, in an attempt to blow away the cobwebs.

21

Sean, on rare occasions, could have enough of the women in his vicarage. Molly was now being particularly difficult.

'I give in!' Sean grunted in resignation. 'Yes, all right, maybe Richards is worth a closer look. Anything for a quiet life and a peaceful Friday evening.'

'Your trouble is,' huffed Ma Hannigan, 'you're a man and you can't help it.' Sean simply smiled blandly.

'No. Face it,' challenged Ma, saddling a favourite high horse, 'you fellas need a bomb under you. I've just waited sixty years for one old flame to make a move, though I've had one good fella and I'm not complaining. Now, here's poor Molly, surrounded by thick male detectives with the intuition of soggy mashed potatoes. Heaven knows how Sherlock Holmes managed it! Must 'ave been a woman in a deerstalker.'

Sean tried again. 'Look—'

'Yer talking tripe, vicar,' said a gummy Gran, her teeth having already retired for the night. 'Take that time after our Karen: you were faffing about for weeks, demanding that God move the earth. And there was his earth and the rest of creation staring you in the face all the time. And even then it took a thunderbolt to make up your mind!'

'I'm converted. I give in. Richards is our killer! Great—'

'Thunderbolt!' interrupted Molly. 'What thunderbolt?'

Gran galloped on, 'That's why there's more women in the pews, you know. Full-blooded, women's intuition. That and the fact that they've got more courage in their little fingers than men have got in their whole bodies. You fellas are so lily-livered that you can't afford to be seen at work worshipping any god but yourselves—'

'What thunderbolt?' Molly tried again.

'—and Molly's got a chief inspector who can't tell suicide from murder, a superintendent who pussyfoots around clear evidence, and then there's you.' Ma Hannigan prodded a finger at her son-in-law. 'You actually need a murderer to visit you twice, wave his blood-soaked victims around your study and virtually shout "Yah-boo, I did it!"'

'At him, Ma! At him!' Molly encouraged. 'Now, tell me about the thunderbolt.'

'You'd better watch it!' Sean looked past Molly and prodded his own finger towards his mother-in-law.

'And what can thou do, O puny little man!' Ma Hannigan peered over her reading glasses.

Sean produced his best imitation of Kate's Mafioso voice, 'I make-a your life-a difficult, old woman.' He attempted a sinister Italian snigger. 'I geta somebody to stand up anda give-a justa cause why you shouldn't geta married. Right?'

'Stick to the day job,' Ma Hannigan grimaced, then changed the subject. 'Did you catch the *Argus* tonight, Molly?'

'No. Will somebody tell me about this thunderbolt?'

'What about the *Argus*?' asked Sean.

'A clown kidnapped that hooligan who turned that nice Mr Richards' wife into a vegetable.'

Molly swapped thunderbolts.

'Where is it?'

'What?'

'The paper.'

'Under the cushion on the settee.' Ma could never cope with untidy bits lying about.

The Connaughton dog was unceremoniously evicted. Within minutes, Molly was telephoning Blackpool police for the full details. They had nothing more than in the news item. She replaced the receiver and turned thoughtfully.

'Let me use you both for a second,' and her eyes peered through and beyond them. 'The clown was Richards. Right! Got to be, considering Les Moore's clown at WildWorld and then the one at the Multiplex opening. But, if so, why let Bocker escape? Or did he escape? This killer's been so professional. Every death, every move, has been thought out precisely—'

'Even, it seems, to the point of seeing whether he could trust us for some reason,' Sean added.

'Praise be!' Ma Hannigan could not stop herself. 'The man really does believe!'

'So,' Molly continued to put sounds to her thoughts, 'our killer lets off the man who all but wiped out his family, yet he kills bishops and MPs. Why? Why meet Bocker in the first place?'

'Forgiveness?' Sean offered. 'Didn't the paper say—'

'Rubbish!' dismissed Molly, 'You don't forgive people who've as good as killed your kids!' Then there was silence as Molly's brain ticked around the next step. Her audience, pleasantly tired after the evening's verbal fencing, wondered if there was a next step.

'Richards is mopping up unresolved issues!' Molly suddenly said. 'No. No. That's not it. There's more ... something I'm missing, something obvious.'

'I would have said,' Sean bravely ventured another idea, 'that you kill when your nearest and dearest are threatened or taken, but even that doesn't make sense if Richards let Bocker go and—'

'And his victims were somehow responsible for his family deaths!' Molly shouted triumphantly. 'Sean Connaughton, you're brilliant!' And she was halfway to the door before Sean caught up with her thinking.

'Now, hang on, Molly, I wasn't going to say that.'

'But it's obvious!'

'No, Molly. Not necessarily. Think it through. An MP's family are killed or injured by hooligans on the rampage. The MP smacks the wrist of one of those responsible but then goes and kills an education officer, a bishop, a television star and a Member of Parliament. Where's the sense in that?'

'What are you?' Molly asked Sean.

'Pardon?'

'Who are you?'

'A father? Reporter? Vicar? What do you mean, who am I?'

'You're a man! Isn't he Ma?' and Molly laughed. On her way out she shouted over her shoulder, 'I've got a date with SHERLOCK! Don't wait up.'

* * *

Crompton Stanley Richards knelt by his prostrate wife in the cone of light produced by the angle-arm wall lamp above her bed.

'Nearly over, my love.'

Irish charge nurse Bridget O'Hanlon passed just beyond in the shadows of a darkened ward and smiled at the scene. It was so good to see Mr Richards at last coming to terms with his tragedy. In recent weeks, he had begun to smile; to interact with others; even to thank nurses and auxiliaries instead of grunting and criticizing them. Some younger nurses had asked to be relieved after only a few days tending his wife. Bridget had remained, knowing what stirred and tormented him.

She drew from thirty years of handling the bereaved – for that was how she saw those who mourned the living dead. The person whom they knew had departed leaving only what gradually grew into an alien other.

This, though, had not been true of Richards. He had treated his wife as if she were merely a sleeping beauty awaiting the kiss of some medical magic: this, despite all the negative tests; despite a string of consultants with their second, third and countless other equally pessimistic opinions.

She knew, of course, that he blamed himself. Bridget had seen it written in every accent of his body language; in every sag in his face. The grunts and anger had not been aimed at her, but at himself. He blamed his slowness in not saving his children; for allowing himself to fall into unconsciousness; for not being there for his Sheila: as though he had had a choice in the matter.

Sister O'Hanlon had seen many crack wide open under the pressure of such imagined guilt. Some had gone mad. Others had been eaten away by an inner psychological cancer until there was little remaining save a mercifully unfeeling shell. One or two had even taken to drink or drugs, anything to kill the pain and shame. The shame of not being there when needed.

The scene in the cone of light was for Bridget O'Hanlon truly a blessing, 'To be sure and no mistake!' she sighed. Such a pity, though, that he had stayed so long tonight. Morning, actually! While there was never a time limit imposed on immediate family, it would surely be good for himself to be on his way soon.

Perhaps she would give him another few minutes.

* * *

SHERLOCK was next to useless. Male by name. Probably built by one too.

All the questions Molly asked needed an opinion for an answer and SHERLOCK did not stoop to such unscientific irrelevancies. The mega-mind gloried in facts alone, but you could only get at those if you knew how to feed in the right question.

SHERLOCK could have written an encyclopaedia on Quentin Charles Bocker, his habits, habitats and associates.

Molly could fill a library with the printouts on each of the victims, together with their families and known affiliates and contacts. But, always, there were irritating gaps, and no way to fill them without going elsewhere. At 3.30 in the morning, and without Superintendent Court's express permission to conduct a face-to-face interview, there was no way forward.

Except perhaps one. Eventually she steeled herself for it. She flicked on the telephone and punched in a number.

'Sean?' A grunt answered.

'It's me. I'm really, really sorry—'

'Is it Michael?' More grunting.

'Oh, Sean. Sorry. I didn't think. No. No. Still no news.'

'What then!' He meant to sound short.

'Sean, you know me. I wouldn't do this unless it was absolutely vital.'

'Molly, I know you and...' Sean seemed to think better of finishing the sleep-sodden thought. 'Yes, Molly?'

'I need your bishop's private home number, Sean.'

'You've finally flipped, haven't you?' he groaned. 'You ring me at ... whatever time it is, and...'

'It's a matter of life and death,' Molly pleaded. 'In five hours I've got to convince the team that we're on the right track, and I desperately need to establish a link between at least one of the victims and the MP, and Bocker's the key—'

'So?'

'So, I figure that the dead bishop would have kept a record of his contacts and correspondence. It would be simple to put his computer engine into search mode for Bocker, or something similar.'

'Molly, you just can't go ringing bishops at this time. She's having a tough time right now, not unlike some vicars I know.'

'Please.'

'No.'

'Pretty please!' A strangled sigh followed.

'One condition.'

'Yes. What's that?'

'You leave it till at least nine a.m.'

'Six a.m.!'

'Eight-thirty!'

'Eight?'

'Done. And I'll be checking up on you! The number's 493-5306.'

* * *

It was 8.30 when Molly awoke in the spare police cell – with only thirty minutes to go before the team meeting and her big chance in front of Court. She cursed herself. By the time she had raced upstairs and swilled her face with cold water and raised Bishop Julia another four precious minutes had gone. The bishop said she would be only too happy to instigate the search, and would call back.

Molly meanwhile busied herself jotting down the main points of her report. That completed, she made various checks.

First, she called Richards' home; not to confront him, but simply to establish his present whereabouts. After one minute, she concluded that he was not at home. Next, the hospital.

'Hello, Evergreen Ward, Sister O'Hanlon speaking.'

'Detective Sergeant Molly Hannigan at Hoghton Police Station. I wonder if you could tell me if Mr Richards is visiting his wife at present, or is expected to do so this morning?'

There was a long pause.

'Hello, are you there, sister?'

'I'm, er, yes, sorry, but we're not able to give information over the telephone.'

'Has something happened? You seemed to pause, and—'

'I am so sorry. Look, I'm just about to go off duty and I know you will understand if I'm not able to help—'

'Sister O'Hanlon,' and Molly's voice toughened. 'This is police business and—'

'And how do I know who you really are?' The sister's voice was haughty.

Molly paused. She was not going to win this way.

'Sister, forgive me. I'm going to put the receiver down. Would you be good enough to ring Hoghton Police Station and ask for me. We promise not to keep you long. The number's in the book, so you can be certain that you are ringing us.'

Two minutes later, they were again introducing themselves.

'Sergeant, I'm afraid I have some rather sad news. Mr Richards left the ward in the early hours, and shortly afterwards his wife's heart stopped beating. We did all that we could, but I'm afraid that we were not able to resuscitate her.'

'And Mr Richards?' Molly asked quietly.

'Well, we tried to reach him at home first, and then, when we got no answer, we were going to ring the police to ask for the motorway patrol to look out for him. In the end, we decided that we would leave it until after nine and then try and get a message left for him at Buckingham Palace.'

'Where?' Molly's incredulous question came out hoarsely.

'Oh, of course, he was after keeping the investiture quiet because this was the third time—'

'Oh my God!' gasped Molly. 'The top man!'

22

Molly sprinted the length of the corridor and burst into the Menagerie and the disgruntled hubbub of the early Saturday shift.

'Superintendent!'

Court, frowning with irritation, swung away from his conversation with Inspector Jones, set to remind a detective sergeant of the niceties of rank and etiquette. His subordinate's expression reduced his reaction to a raised eyebrow.

'It IS Richards, sir!' Detective Sergeant Hannigan could be impressively formidable, displaying a quiet but fierce professionalism, 'and he is due any minute to meet the Top Man – the King – at Buckingham Palace.' She added, more a command than a question, 'Can somebody raise NCS while I explain?'

'Do it!' Court snapped at Jones.

'The means he definitely had, sir. Access to every murder site, and also to the hyoscine, plus being one of the very rare people who could even get near the Kasai bug. He obviously had the scientific knowhow to use it. We still have problems with opportunity and availability to commit the crimes but nothing so far rules him out. We know already that he fits the description of the killer clown and compares well with the video shot. We now have two new things, the last one just now.

'First, we believe he kidnapped the man responsible for his wife's condition yesterday morning—'

'We'd already seen that possibility.' Court was unimpressed.

'—and I'm waiting right now for confirmation of a link between him and one of the victims.' Court raised the eyebrow again. 'I believe that, given more time, we could establish links with all the victims and Bocker and the MP's family. I'm expecting a call any minute now but—'

'The commander's on the line, sir,' Jones interrupted.

'Ask him to wait.' Court needed more, though he was impressed about access to Kasai. Molly took a long deep breath for the last stage.

'The MP's wife has been in a coma for more than a year, and we know that persistent vegetative states can, and do, go on for years. We also know Richards has appealed in the past for the machines to be turned off to allow nature to take its course. So, he stays until the early hours of this morning and then, within a short time of him leaving, his wife's heart stops. The hospital say it was totally unexpected. Why should it happen now, sir, all of a sudden?' Molly paused before the final thrust.

'I believe that he has settled his wife's future because he knew his own from today onwards would be uncertain. And that has something to do with what he is planning this morning at the palace.'

'Is that it?'

'Yes, sir.' Molly was confident, though she now wished that she had finished on the Kasai note.

Court snatched the telephone receiver from Jones.

'Commander, do you have any way of finding out if there is an investiture, or something like that, at Buckingham—' Court's flow was interrupted, and he listened. 'Oh...! Yes ... Do you know what time...? No. No ... just give me one minute, commander?'

He turned to Hannigan and there was a deathly hush

across the room, save for a telephone ringing in one corner. Jones went to answer it.

Court studied the far wall, hating to be ruled by events, illogically yearning for a different timescape, and a chance to confront the MP in his own good time rather than have a knight frog-marched from the King's presence.

'Hannigan, one piece of hard linking evidence...' Court's face was creased with stress, and he held out a hand, palm open, towards her. Molly stood rooted to the floor. Face frozen. Mind kaleidoscoping across a hundred facts.

'Hannigan, is it a bishop you're waiting for?'

'Thank you, God!' Molly ran to the telephone and listened. Receiver still in hand, she shouted, 'That's it, sir. Bishop Williams wrote a court reference for Bocker when he was facing GBH on Richards' wife. Bocker had been one of his youth leaders in one of his churches when he was a vicar.'

'Commander.' Court was short. 'Stop Richards before he gets to the King. We think he's our serial killer.'

The receiver went dead and Court held it in mid-air, staring at it.

'If you are wrong, Hannigan, you'll have a new boss by lunchtime.'

'If I'm right, sir, God save the King!'

* * *

The Honourable Crompton Stanley Richards had arrived in London in his old Bentley shortly after six o'clock on a bright and fresh May morning. He had driven into the grounds of St Thomas's Hospital, gaining access with an old pass he had retained in the glove compartment from some event long gone and forgotten. He had parked at the far end overlooking the Thames. In his rear view and wing mirrors he could see three aspects of Archbishop's Park and Lambeth Palace.

He sat watching the flow of the great river, occasionally glancing across to Victoria Tower Gardens and the Houses of Parliament. Pleasure steamers were beginning to emerge from overnight moorings in readiness to ply a brisk Saturday morning trade, and he could see signs of life across in the terraced tea rooms of the Commons. He tried to imagine what it must have been like to have been imprisoned for thirty-six hours with his fellow Members of Parliament, and shivered.

He then checked the invitation from the Lord Chamberlain's Office, the Central Chancery of the Orders of Knighthood. It requested that he arrive by hire car or carriage at 8.30 a.m. He was required to present his party at the main gates where he would be directed to the Grand Entrance in the Quadrangle.

The writer expressed the King's anticipated pleasure at giving the accolade to Mr Richards, following the unavoidable disappointments of missing the general investitures in the previous July, December and February. Further, the King hoped that Mrs Richards was comfortable. The secretary also begged Mr Richards' patience for the pioneer mood of the event. Not only was the investiture to be necessarily brief, but there were many innovations following the recent reorganization of the monarchy. Not least of all was this year's new Trooping date, advanced by a month for practical and military requirements. For this reason, most personnel would be otherwise engaged and his investiture would be quite a modest occasion. The secretary hoped that this would be acceptable.

Richards had informed the secretary in his reply that he preferred it that way, and expected nothing more.

And so, at precisely 8.10 a.m., Richards took from the boot of his car a small suitcase containing his new robes of knighthood. He left the hospital grounds and hailed a taxi on Lambeth Palace Road.

He would have liked to have gone past the Florence Nightingale Museum and then left over Westminster Bridge.

It would have been good to travel one last time through the heart of government, going beyond Big Ben and right into Whitehall and passing between Downing Street and his own office in the Norman Shaw Building. He would have saluted the Ministry of Defence and Horse Guards before going left under Admiralty Arch and up the Mall by St James's Park to the gold-tipped gates of Buckingham Palace. Of course, that was impossible while Horse Guards awaited its sovereign and the Trooping, and so he had to be content with Lambeth Bridge and the Horseferry Road.

Alf the taxi driver, with his broad Jamaican humour, made up for what Richards regarded as the back-street approach. A. L. F. turned out to be an acronym for African Ladinos Fernandez, the name bestowed on him by a culturally correct mother determined that he should not forget his roots. He apparently hailed from black African Iberian stock in the sixteenth century, and a tribe called the Ladinos who had been transported from Spain to Peru. Moma Fernandez swore on the family Bible that Great-Great-etc.-Grandma Conchita had married the grandson of the great Spanish explorer Fernandez before all their offspring emigrated to the West Indies.

As traffic slowed them, they marvelled together at the Rolling Stones and Sir Mick Jagger, sixty-odd going on twenty-one, still able to pull a hundred thousand at Hyde Park. They shook their heads and tut-tutted about the thief who had stolen Alf's mountain bike the day before by chopping down the fifteen-foot tree to which it was chained. They both deplored the 'sad sign of the times' that caused Alf to speak to his passengers via an intercom from his bullet-proof cab.

They were quiet while the policeman at the main entrance to Buckingham Palace checked Richards' credentials, and telephoned ahead the announcement of his arrival.

The cabby abruptly pulled away the protective glass division between them and chuckled, 'Hey man, if I couldn't

240

trust the likes of you, see'n' as how yer going to see the young King, and all.'

The police officer saluted, then waved them towards the left arch to take them through into the inner Quadrangle.

'And you might tell the young King from me, that there are too many out 'ere that think they're above his law. What we need is a law that's above everybody.' Alf looked in his mirror for a response and saw Richards writing. 'Oh man, are you going to make me famous?'

Richards looked up from his notebook and smiled as they drew up to the Grand Entrance.

'Call it your tip, Alf. It's a registration number and a note verifying ownership.' He stepped out of the cab and lobbed over the keys to his Bentley. 'You'll find it in the hospital grounds near where you picked me up. Give it a good home, Alf.' He smiled at the large mouth that was temporarily lost for words but had found the biggest grin in London.

Brigadier Horace St James welcomed the knight-to-be with fitting gravity. He added a slight smile to suggest that, majestic as this occasion and its surroundings might be, it was also an event involving real live human beings. As senior Gentleman Usher in his final season at sixty-nine years of age, he was relaxed enough to know that even practised MPs needed to be put at their ease on such daunting occasions; even those who had visited in the past, as he knew to be true in this instance.

He gently touched Richards' arm and led him between the impressive French patinated and gilt bronze candelabra which guarded the Entree, and then on to an archway of a less glorious material.

'Sorry, Mr Richards!' The brigadier shrugged and waved the MP towards the electronic security scanner. 'That's fine, sir. Perhaps you'll let me have your case for the X-ray. It was installed after the Trooping tragedy. As you probably know, we've even had to replace many of the more vulnerable windows with polycarbonate. You just never know these days.' The brigadier shook a weary head.

Richards cleared security without trouble and stepped into the Grand Hall he affectionately remembered from previous visits. Here, he himself had occasionally mingled with foreign guests to help make them feel at ease. He had always loved how Nash had retained the low proportions of welcoming warmth and then – modestly for an architect – had lowered the central floor area to shift the focus away from its own glory and on to the people. Now, of course, without the people, one could only stand and gaze afresh at the Corinthian columns of white Carrara marble, some with gilded bronze capitals.

'We were truly concerned about your wife,' the brigadier smiled and took Richards left towards the Grand Staircase.

'You are kind,' smiled the MP. 'Our situation has improved immeasurably and the future is now full of hope.'

'I am delighted to hear,' beamed the brigadier, much more at home with happy talk.

'Which way do you prefer?' he asked as they reached the landing of the Great Staircase. They paused as did everybody, surrounded by a significant fraction of the nation's artistic assets. All were cast in shadow by the sumptuous and magnificently sweeping balustrade of gilt bronze embellished with rich Grecian foliage. 'Personally, I always choose the right arm of the staircase, for the light catches Cellini's *Perseus and Medusa*, almost bringing it to life.'

Richards hesitated, wondering whether or not the brigadier knew it was only a copy. Suddenly, his eyes stung and filled, and he reached for the balustrade seeing only a vivid picture of his Sheila dancing with gypsy abandon around the real Cellini in the Loggia dei Lanzi in Florence. It had been their honeymoon.

Even now, with months to practise his mourning, stupid and irrational emotions would surge up to catch him unawares and unprepared. Even now, when he knew he was going to see her again very soon.

'Are you all right, Mr Richards?'

'Yes.' He took out a handkerchief and wiped his eyes. 'Yes, of course, Brigadier St James,' he laughed. 'Merely a touch of the May hay fever. We'll go your way.'

Richards felt quite sorry for the old chap. The brigadier had probably been using that line in his welcoming piece for the last twenty years, without once drawing tears. They eventually arrived in the Green Room, and a page was on hand to take Richards' suitcase and assist with the black velvet robes of his coming knighthood.

'Oh, dear.' The brigadier pointed to Richards' robe. 'You must have caught it.' The brigadier took hold of the material. 'No, by Jove! Somebody's cut this with a razor or something. Workmen! I'd play merry hell with whoever's responsible, Mr Richards.'

'Oh! Yes, indeed.' Richards was aware that his voice was too high.

'Let me see if our page can find a needle and thread.'

'No. Really,' laughed Richards. 'It is but a small cut. Please don't trouble. See,' and he swung the robe over his shoulder, 'you don't notice it really.'

The brigadier nodded, shrugged and decided to press on.

'Well, let's run through the order, Mr Richards.' The brigadier became brisk. 'We will enter the Throne Room in a few minutes and take our places in the middle, well in front of the proscenium arch, which obviously you'll know well from past visits. Before you, and towards the dais and the throne chairs, will be the investiture stool. His Majesty will enter from the Picture Gallery door to the left, escorted by five Yeomen of the Guard.' An apologetic smile broke across the officer's face. 'As you might have guessed, the Lord Chamberlain, who takes charge of these investitures, is otherwise unavoidably detained in Parliament today, so his place will be taken by one of his representatives.

'There will be senior members of the household bearing the investiture sword and insignia, the Secretary of the Central Chancery and probably one or two secretaries and aides plus His Majesty's bodyguard. Of course, in the good old days, the guard did not enter and we had two splendid Gurkha Orderly Officers, but defence cuts...' A resigned shrug finished off the sentence.

'Incidentally, the King prefers to use his grandfather's Scots Guards sword. Quite light and still as sharp as any battle weapon. However, not to worry. We haven't lost anybody as yet.'

Richards had only half listened up to this point, having researched this information for himself. The other half of his mind soaked up the extraordinary ceiling designs of complex domes and concave and convex covings giving the room a tentlike Mogul feel. Falling from the ceiling, and framed by glittering gilt lattice pattern pilasters, were the rich green silk wall hangings he admired so much. He had fallen so in love with this Green Room on his first ever visit, that he had created a miniature version in his own study. Of course, it could never compare; rather like trying to reproduce a Pavarotti aria with his bathroom baritone.

'I understand,' began Richards, forcing himself to pay attention, 'that the yeomen stand to the rear of the King, then the various staff to his left and the Lord Chamberlain – or rather, now, his stand-in – will be to His Majesty's right.'

'Very good,' nodded the brigadier. 'I see you've done your homework. The King will take up his position standing before the throne dais – he never sits at such events – and the Lord Chamberlain's representative will announce your name, your achievements and service, and the reason why you are being honoured. You advance to the stool, one, two, three' – he took two steps and did a pretend kneel on the third count – 'then pat pat'– he mimed the sword dubbing – 'Will that be any problem?'

'Not at all.'

'Hope you didn't mind me asking, only you seemed to be limping a little, and, if the kneeling is difficult we have other ways of—'

'Really, just a stiff joint,' smiled Richards coldly and hurried to change the subject. 'So, after the sword, I assume the King simply says "Arise, Sir—"'

'Oh dear, Mr Richards,' chuckled the brigadier, 'perhaps only nine out of ten. I'm afraid you are confusing us with Hollywood. No. His Majesty will first tap you on the right shoulder. Then, after you feel the left tap, you rise to your feet and go forwards to the left. His Majesty will take your insignia and, let me see, yes, I think it's a sash according to your order of knighthood; so, he will lift this over your head, shake your hand and probably have a few words before departing for the Trooping.'

He glanced at his watch. 'Come, I think we had better take our place in the Throne Room.'

They entered and stood waiting for the King.

* * *

'Stupid boy!' Sean cursed out loud, not for the first time. He grasped the steering wheel hard. 'Please keep him safe!' he silently blessed for the millionth time.

'Why?' he screamed through his open side window. A disinterested audience of elephants wallowed in a nearby mud hollow. He half sobbed, half chuckled seeing an elephant cow pull her wayward recent-born from a boggy bank.

'Stubborn, headstrong nippers!' Sean began to scan the grounds through binoculars while his mind searched out a refuge from the guilt he felt.

Not for the first time, he wondered if there could ever be a free world without pain and evil. Was a world possible in which kids never ran away; never abused or got abused? It was hard to imagine a world in which earthquakes never happened and planes never crashed. Fancy a planet where, with each danger, a supergod swooped to save, or quench or catch; a world in which nobody could do anything wrong, and nothing could go wrong. Such a world was so far

245

removed from reality that it was unimaginable. How could you give freedom, yet withdraw the choice to take drugs, or abscond, or even to worry your family half to death?

Long before Michael's court case, and shortly after Michael had first escaped the apron strings, Sean had fleetingly entertained other restraints. An after-school lock in! Early curfews. He had once visited an old people's home and realized how easy it would be to turn Michael into an obedient and compliant son. Geriatrics drugged! Why not a sedative-controlled offspring? Easily led; little will power; no energy to rebel. Switch them off with a pill. At least it would keep Michael away from the other drugs. Ludicrous and horribly attractive! Wonderfully obedient children but, of course, they'd never mature; never fulfil their human potential. But they would be safe. Safe as robots.

Grotesque! Of course. Child abuse in practice. The pain of free will was immeasurably better than the programmed perfection of a zombie. Of course he couldn't do it to Michael. It wasn't how he had been designed. Not even the Chief Designer had drugged his creatures. He'd taken the risk. The pain. Free will given out of free love.

The in-car phone now raised him from his deep questions.

'Hello. Sean Connaughton here.'

'It's Molly. Can you come to Hoghton Police Station right now.'

'Michael?'

'No.'

'So?'

'It's the MP Richards. He's holding the King hostage. Says he won't negotiate with anyone except you.'

23

Sean listened for five minutes without comment as he drove the cab at cheetah speed out of WildWorld. Eventually, Molly finished her update.

'So now we know what he was preparing us for,' said Sean. 'And you, Molly? What about you? He's asked for you as well, of course?'

There was no response, and Sean assumed he had hit a reception blind spot after turning out of WildWorld on to the Hoghton road. But then...

'I can hear you breathing, Molly.' And the sounds were now growing louder and more frequent. 'Molly? Come on, stop messing about.' The breaths grew in intensity and speed, and then began to break up into gasps.

'Molly!' Within seconds her breathing was at a rate that caused a dozen imagined fears to crowd in on him.

'For God's sake, what's happening to—?' He stopped short as understanding burst upon him. He could have kicked himself.

'Okay! Easy, love.' Sean breathed calmly into the mouth-piece as if to inspire Molly to the same. Quietly he added, 'Strong, steady breaths ... I'm with you ... slow it down ... deep, deep breaths.'

Most of the time, Molly's hidden terror was dormant, capped by a mountain of will power. Even Sean had only glimpsed it rarely. She had emigrated across an ocean to escape a fear, but every now and then it threatened to overwhelm. Now it was on the verge of taking over.

Before Sean's questions had ignited the inner panic, Molly had been her usual efficient self. She had outlined the bishop–Bocker court link, and then how a search of court computer records had revealed a similar connection with the education officer, who had once been Bocker's headmaster. Crick had meanwhile tried out a new 3D facial recognition package on SHERLOCK to identify the clown positively as Richards.

She told him how eyewitnesses had described Richards rising from the Investiture Stool to relieve a surprised young monarch of his sword, and then how he had swivelled the King round to bring the blade squarely across the royal Adam's apple. The Yeomen of the Guard had jumped forward brandishing halberds, and the poor brigadier had tangled and tripped in his ceremonial regalia. The bodyguard had assumed the regulation crouch, feet apart with both hands stretched out ahead grasping his Smith and Wesson automatic. He had ordered the new knight to step away from behind the King and relinquish the sword.

Richards, with a chilling, cold flatness, had replied slowly, 'You have killed my family. I have nothing more of importance to lose. One shot might nick my cheek, if you miss the King...' and his last sentence had been paced and precise, 'Put - the - gun - down - now - and - your - King - lives.'

There had been a stand-off. No two witnesses had afterwards agreed on its duration. Then, the old brigadier, still crumpled on the floor, had broken. 'For God's sake man, drop it!'

Still nothing had happened.

There was a sudden exhalation of the air which the guard had held in to steady his aim. Hesitantly, reluctantly, he had lowered the gun to the floor, and stepped back. Richards had quickly ordered two yeomen to push the King's throne chair behind the red velvet backdrop of the dais. Others were forced to drag the spare thrones, chairs and tables into a barricade in front of the curtain. At this point, the palace alarm had sounded as the video security man belatedly noticed what was going on, and Richards had exchanged the sword for the bodyguard's gun and cleared the room.

The King had then been placed on his own throne chair and enveloped with the folds of the twenty-foot-high reredos velvet drapes. After what had seemed like a brief struggle behind the curtain, during which nobody had dared enter the Throne Room, Richards emerged with a cord tied to his left wrist, apparently a strip of velvet sliced away from his own robes.

'The other end is tied to the hair-trigger of the automatic,' Richards had shouted. 'The gun is attached to the King's person.'

It was at this point in Molly's narrative that Sean had interrupted with his idiotic query as to whether the killer wanted her. Thankfully, the breathing was now becoming more regular; much deeper. He continued to be quietly comforting into the receiver.

'Yes...!' Molly eventually hissed and Sean could feel the constriction in the voice. 'Yes, he has asked for me. And there's no way ... there's absolutely NO WAY—'

'Easy, Molly. Nobody is going—'

'Sean...' and the breathing was laboured but now stronger, '... not the NCS, not a king's life, not you; nothing will drag me in there, and that's final.' Small wavelets of hysteria again began to lap at the edges of her voice. 'They can sack me, scream coward in my face but nothing will change my—'

'Hey, hey, steady, Molly, steady.' But this merely unleashed the full rush, punctuated by gasps and sobs.

'I gave up sunshine every day in Florida for mist over Lancashire ... I threw away twice my present salary ... and swapped my beautiful beach condominium for a terraced-house flat, and I did all that to stop pieces of metal being shot or plunged into my body and—'

'It's okay, Molly, I'm—'

'Did you know...' stress caused a half giggle, half sob to explode inappropriately, '... I had to have therapy after I was stabbed? Therapy! Me! Just to pick up a knife and butter my bread—' another sob echoed in Sean's ear, 'and ... and ... you expect me to walk into a hostage situation with a killer wielding three foot of steel and a Smith and Wesson that can blow a hole in your body bigger than a fist?'

'No, I don't—'

'So, if you think I'm going anywhere near that—'

'Molly!' Sean shouted. 'No! I don't want you in there.'

'You don't?' She took a massive gulp.

'That's the last thing you're going to do!' Sean's voice had taken on a proprietorial, commanding note. The instinct to protect that which was precious took over.

'Believe me, Molly, there's no way I'll allow you to go in there.'

'No way?'

'No way!'

'Why?' Her breathing rate had suddenly slowed.

'Because I want to keep you safe!'

'You want to keep me safe?' She seemed to be having trouble making sense of the words.

'Molly, I care for you and there is no way that I would let you come with me into such a dangerous situation.' There was a pause and silence except for the breathing, which was now almost normal.

'Molly?'

'YOU ... let me...?'

'Molly, you're right.' Sean was firm, though puzzled by her change of tone. 'I'm just saying you are right and—'

'You ... LET ME ... come with you?'

'Molly, I was only ... Molly, hel— Hello, Molly?' Sean found that he was talking to himself.

* * *

250

Superintendent Marcus Brown feared that his status as leading hostage negotiator with the National Crime Squad might come under some scrutiny if matters did not improve soon.

The pressure on each word and decision had never been greater. For a start, sixty million pairs of eyes were now on him, courtesy of live, channel-to-channel television. A still photograph of him in his younger days, before the worry-lines had developed, was being regularly flashed across the nation's four-foot-square wall televisions. Saturday afternoon sports coverage had been drastically curtailed, and some outside broadcast units had been redirected from London's Premier League clubs to supplement the crews already on location for the fiasco that had been this morning's Trooping the Colour.

The Trooping presenters, Brown thought, must have felt rather foolish. There were the brave stirring brass and skirling pipes. The screens were filled with military glory, and rank on rank of red and gold Guards, and they had to announce that the sovereign was unavoidably detained due to a heavy cold. A minor royal had agreed to step in to represent His Majesty at the last minute.

Most of the media had soon begun to ignore the pageantry and the marching waves of black bearskins. Instead they had tuned in to the rumours raging across air and telephone waves, and through street crowds. The King, the grapevine unanimously declared, was the latest victim of the dreaded Asian flu, and Buckingham Palace itself was under military quarantine. What other explanation could there be for the sudden arrival of massed troops in combat gear from both road and air? Was it not a repeat of what had already happened down the road on the other side of Parliament Square? To head off what was rapidly becoming a Whitehall farce, it was eventually announced on special noon bulletins that the King was held hostage by a gunman in Buckingham Palace, and would the nation unite together in prayer for his safety.

Marcus Brown was, of course, familiar with Establishment lies, all told within the safety of the Official Secrets Act behind its comforting thirty-year gag. His own lies, his stock in trade as he saw them, were on a less grand scale, but just as vital. He was a skilled negotiator whose primary task was to promise the world yet give nothing. Prevarication and procrastination were his main tools. Certainly, nothing had been given to Richards during the first two hours concerning his one and only demand 'to negotiate only through the Rev. Sean Connaughton and Detective Sergeant Molly Hannigan'.

Brown had rationally argued that it was impossible to transport the people mentioned from Lancashire in time to make any difference and, besides, the two people concerned were in the midst of a family crisis and were therefore not available. After Richards' initial demand, Brown had found himself talking to himself. There was no response to his genial, chatty explanations.

Two things had changed Brown's mind about what he would, and would not, give to the hostage taker. The central chandelier of cut glass and gilt bronze which dominated the space beneath the high ceiling of the Throne Room had tingled and swayed as a Smith and Wesson bullet passed through it. Richards had stepped behind the dais curtain hiding the King and fired one round. It had happened at Brown's fourth bid to explain why only he would be negotiating.

A different and more persuasive bullet came moments later via the videophone from no less than the Prime Minister himself.

'Get the confounded pair here, and quick!' Baldwin had exploded.

Brown was staggered at being countermanded by, of all people, an incarcerated politician who was a kilometre away from the front-line action. How was he supposed to do his job effectively? And soon he was to be further handicapped by two rank amateurs.

In addition to all of this, he had a gung-ho colonel to contend with. The colonel's SAS contingent were pushing a hair-brained plan to invade on four fronts. They wanted to blast their way through the armour-plated windows from the Quadrangle balcony. While the killer's attention was thus caught, three other teams of crack shots would race in from opposing directions – from the Green Room, the Picture Gallery and the hidden service door just to the left of the barricade thrones.

Could they guarantee to shoot Richards stone dead?

'No problem.' The colonel was smug.

Could they shoot Richards and ensure that he remained upright so that the cord betwixt wrist and trigger was kept loose? The colonel had at last hesitated, and then, mercifully, agreed to return to his war-room drawing board. Another bright spark had come up with the idea that a bullet from his unit's top marksman could sever the cord. He was, however, not quite as confident that such a pressure break on the cord would not do the killer's job for him.

There were one or two other minor snags. Nobody knew whether or not the King was still alive behind the curtain. The whole incident had been observed via the Throne Room security cameras, but Richards had spent a long time behind the curtain with the King, and there seemed to have been a struggle during which one shape fell to the floor. The cameras now showed only the tips of the royal shoes peeping out from the drapes before the throne chair. Ominously, there had been no other movement, except for an occasional view of the killer behind the barricades.

'Hello, Mr Richards?'

Superintendent Brown wiped perspiration from his balding dome as he sat in a specially set up control area in the Picture Gallery below Rembrandt's *Agatha Bas*. As he waited for a reply, again he studied the intricate detail of Agatha's white lace shawl-collar and the curled cuff turnovers. She had watched him passively to begin with. Now, he could read other things in the eyes. Pity, for one thing. Brown decided on a new tack.

'Mr Richards, or perhaps I should say Sir Crompton.' Still nothing. 'Yes, well, we have some news for you. Would you like to hear it?'

Again nothing.

'Mr Richards.' The 'Sir' approach was dropped. Knights, after all, did not usually hold their sovereigns at gunpoint. 'Your people are en route, travelling in the Lancashire police jet helicopter. They've just passed over Birmingham, but I'm afraid ETA will be five minutes past your deadline. They will then have to be brought from the gardens, and that will make their arrival with you at ten minutes past two.'

Still no reply. He looked up into eyes that now mocked him.

'Well now, Ms Bas, and what would you do?'

* * *

The helicopter, slowing for its final approach, flew towards the Mall and both Molly and Sean watched a distant lopsided butterfly materialize out of Hyde, Green and St James's parks together with the extensive palace gardens.

Their headphones crackled and Ma Hannigan came through to report that somebody had spotted Michael late the previous evening wandering around WildWorld, and that the search had been stepped up.

'Connaughton,' Frank Winter's belligerence burst in, 'just looking after your mother-in-law. Remember that you're our man in there. Over.'

'Frank, you make me feel so wanted. Over and out!'

'Not so fast, Daddy,' Ma Hannigan had called back.

'Go ahead,' Sean replied with a puzzled expression.

'It's little ole me.'

It was Kate's normal computer voice. 'Save the King, Daddy. For ME! And then, when you've done it, give him a hug from me. Tell him to wait for me, and not marry any of these soppy Sloane women. Tell him he's my definite possible.'

'... over and out,' Gran-Gran concluded.

Sean looked across at Molly. The bit of her face he could see in the frame of her helmet looked ashen. He reached round and gave her an encouraging hug. She responded. He enjoyed her warmth and felt oddly guilty that he should have pleasure while she suffered. The embrace lasted until the wheels touched down on a famous garden often graced by the national great and good. The back passenger door flew open.

'Come this way, please, and keep low,' an NCS officer shouted.

They crouched and raced across the palace gardens and on to the brown-grey-white gravel of the main path before running up the steps to the long, wide rear patio.

'Follow me, please,' the officer was still shouting as the helicopter lifted and sped off. Once inside a long red-carpeted hallway, Sergeant James Francis introduced himself and gave them a geographical briefing.

'We're in the rear wing, furthest away from the Mall, and this is the Marble Hall. Directly above us is the Picture Gallery where we have set up our centre of operations. Next door to the gallery is where Richards and His Majesty are. Just take a moment to catch your breath and take your bearings while I do a radio check to see if we can go up.'

Plain furred scagliola walls were backdrops to marble statues and busts setting off portraits of a young and even pretty Queen Victoria and her handsome consort Prince Albert. Within thirty seconds, the sergeant was leading them along the hall.

'We're going via the Minister's Staircase,' the sergeant smiled with the satisfaction of imparting secret knowledge. 'Mr Baldwin himself climbs these stairs for his weekly audience.'

They reached a landing and Francis pointed left. 'That door leads to a service staircase, and through to the King's private wing. One spur leads directly to a hidden door which lets out into the Throne Room to the left of the dais. When you go in, you can just make out the fine line of the surrounding door jamb. Of course, there's no handle on the Throne Room side but, rest assured, in case of emergency, an SAS team are there. They're your nearest support, probably no more than two yards away from the barricade through the door.'

They entered the Picture Gallery control room with its tables and monitors, and small pockets of assault troops perched alert and attentive at the two double doors leading into the Throne Room. Beneath them were large sheets of polythene, protecting the house-size Indian carpet of white and gold from their boots and battlefield dress. Sean wondered what use camouflage uniforms were amidst such plushness.

Molly, on the other hand, deliberately distracted herself with the grandeur, and found herself gazing up at Rembrandt's *Christ and Magdalene at the Tomb*.

What must it be like to have a Messiah come and wipe your life beautifully clean and empower you with new life? All she had had since learning of Richards' demands was the normal mental steel trapdoor that most humans use to batten down inner torments. That and bloody-mindedness! Defiance against Sean's chauvinistic bravado provided an initial shield of defence. The distractions of preparations and the flight down had helped. Now, there was only the splendour on which to focus. Anything, other than that Picture Gallery door and what was beyond! She caught sight of Canaletto's *Piazzetto in Venice* and smiled at memories of the summer holidays before last. Sergeant Francis's last briefing act was to introduce the newcomers to negotiator Brown who was able to tell them remarkably little.

'Truth to tell,' he shrugged, 'it's been a monologue. We've tried to raise some info on the man, just to try and guess which way he would jump. Most of those who know him are locked up in Westminster, and whatever I could tell you about him, you probably already know. Anything else will be guesswork, and you may as well try your own guesses as mine. At least you seem to have a relationship with him already.'

'What happens between us and you once we're in?' asked Sean.

'Just talk in a normal voice,' replied Brown. 'We've more directional microphones around the Throne Room than troops and officers, and that's a lot. We'll speak to you through speakers at the door openings. We need to know two things. How the King is. He hasn't moved since first thing, not even the toes of his shoes. We're getting worried. Then we need to know Richards' demands. We have to warn you that we will give him nothing if we can possibly avoid it. Any questions? Right, just one last thing, take these with you.'

An SAS officer gave them each a protective bulletproof apron and Molly grabbed hers with gratitude.

'Inside, in a hidden pocket half way up in the left edge, is one of these on a spring release,' and the SAS man held up a small knife which opened up like an old-fashioned cut-throat razor. Molly's face hardened. 'In the other edge, is one of our new slim Smith and Wesson two-two specials, again spring loaded for easy release, and it works like this.'

The SAS officer concluded his demonstration with pride and promptly received Molly's jacket full in the face as she swung round and marched away down the Picture Gallery.

'Give me a minute,' Sean called back over his shoulder as he followed her. He caught up as she entered the East Gallery. She slumped on a gilded lyre-backed chair that looked too delicate even for Molly.

'Sean, I feel so, so stupid.' She gripped the chair's edges. 'God, what a mess!'

'Tell him some more!' The words blurted out of Sean.

'Pardon?' Molly looked wide-eyed.

'Prayer, Molly! You started, so why not finish. God knows it's a mess. Tell him some more.'

Then she laughed. Not mocking. It was a gentle, hopeless sort of sound.

'What?' shrugged Connaughton uncomfortably.

'You're unbelievable, Connaughton!'

'What? How do you mean?'

'You really do make a lousy vicar!'

Sean sat on his haunches looking at the floor.

'How come you preach a twenty-minute sermon with verve and confidence, but stammer and stutter on the rare occasions you get religious with me?'

Sean shrugged.

'Come to think of it, why do you always avoid the subject when you're with me?' She arched an eyebrow, and felt better talking instead of thinking. 'How is it that every time I ask you about him, you push me away? You've done it umpteen times since I came over from Florida. You've done it twice, no, three times in the last couple of days alone. Last night there was that thunderbolt thing—'

'Well, I er, I just thought...' Sean breathed out heavily.

'You wanna say one of your prayers, don't you?' Molly saw him squirm with some inner turmoil. 'Well, I've tried everything else. It can't hurt.'

Sean smiled with relief. He kept it short and simple, about a King of Kings who overruled even in earthly throne rooms. He asked for help. She added the Amen.

'I'll take the flak jacket but nothing else,' Molly said curtly as they walked back into the Picture Gallery. Sean took his, complete with lethal accessories.

'Good luck,' Brown said as they stepped over the threshold. Connaughton hoped he had more than that.

'Far enough!' shouted out Richards, as they entered the Throne Room. 'Jackets off and empty your pockets on the floor where I can see.'

Molly looked across to Sean, and chuckled.

24

'Sorry, Prime Minister,' Fosdyke apologized through a half-inch gap at the ajar door of Committee Room 15, 'three-thirty is the absolute earliest moment we can vacate Parliament. That is the best medical opinion we have.'

James Baldwin turned away to Commander Green fuming, 'Absolutely incredible. I'm running a nation, and here I am, cap in hand, asking a jumped-up pipsqueak of an MP when I can leave the room!' And turning back to Room 15, 'Do you have any concept of what is happening out here in the real world?'

'Do you?' the hidden voice of the Shoreditch MP chimed in unhelpfully.

'Look, Fosdyke, I don't want to pull rank but—'

'It is not a question of that, sir.' A prim Fosdyke straightened up before his Prime Minister. 'All of us in here would be delighted to leave right now. We still only need paper tissues and a few cough drops. Wherever this bug is, it's certainly not on this side of the door and you all sound in remarkably rude health.'

'Far too rude!' whispered Green, who had borne the brunt of MPs' simmering anger, and seemed about to endure more again as another member elbowed his way towards him.

The PM pressed on regardless. 'Are you then up to date with what's happening at the palace?'

'Yes, sir. We've had lunchtime editions—'

'Rags!' Baldwin snarled.

'Quite, sir, and we all think it is absolutely scurrilous what they've dared to print,' fawned Fosdyke, despite the PM's earlier nastiness. 'I think it is safe to say, sir, that regardless of party persuasions, we unanimously deplore the tabloids' treatment of the whole issue.'

'Almost unanimously!' Shoreditch again.

The so-called tabloids were in fact the much respected new *London Millennium Gazette* and the *Evening Standard*. Spurred on by ever more alarmist rumours, they too had joined the media lynch-mob demanding immediate scapegoats. The Prime Minister and his Cabinet were the prime candidates. One influential columnist had asked, 'How can we expect James Baldwin to maintain national security and our individual safety if he cannot even look after himself, his own House and his King?'

The *Gazette* leader demanded the dissolution of Parliament and added, 'Let an immediate General Election deliver, once and for all, the great British public's damning verdict on this administration of shambles.'

Fosdyke sympathized with the PM and Baldwin again tried to solicit an earlier release time.

'Sorry, sir, but they won't hear of anything less than the full forty-eight hours to ensure no more bugs have developed.'

'Sir,' Green tried to interrupt but Baldwin was too focused.

'Who the hell's in charge of this decision?'

'The military, sir,' replied a crestfallen Fosdyke who saw his hopes of any future junior ministry post dwindling. 'It's their doctors who have been advising us from the outside and it is their deadline.'

'Excuse me, Prime Minister.' Commander Green dared to touch Baldwin's arm in urgency.

'What now, Green?'

'An NCS man is in your office with a message from the palace, sir.'

'Quick with it, man!'

'Well, er...'

'Come on, spit it out!'

'The killer, it seems, now wants you.'

Baldwin walked quickly away from Committee Room 15 and the echoing raucous laughter of the Hon. Member for Shoreditch, leaving Green to battle through a wake of disgruntled parliamentarians. By the time he caught up, NCS emissary Sergeant James Francis was facing the full wrath.

'... and all your bungling team got in nearly five hours was just three useless sentences, while the whole country sits and waits and prays for His Majesty. You now have the audacity to inform me that a lowly insignificant MP and killer has deigned to grant me an audience in the Throne Room? How very—'

'Sir.' Commander Green coughed, and gave Baldwin a look to suggest, respectfully, that this was not helping. Baldwin broke away with a final aside. 'What sort of incompetent have we got as a killer, anyway? Surely Richards, of all people, should know I can't leave here yet.'

'He claims you can, sir,' Sergeant Francis said. 'And I'm afraid it looks like you've all been stuck here for nothing.'

'What!' snapped Baldwin.

'Well, er...'

'Spit it out, man! What exactly do you mean by that?'

'Richards says there's a report in his desk over in the Norman Shaw Building. He says the Kasai research team sent it to him as chairman of his germ group a few weeks ago. It concludes that Kasai is transmitted like its parent Ebola – only through bodily fluids.'

An immediate surge of swear words, applause and cheers rippled and grew to a crescendo along corridors that had never felt so powerless. Meanwhile, James Baldwin stood motionless, his face still full of thunder.

'Will nobody rid me of this turbulent pest?' It sounded rather unoriginal and over-dramatic, as though the speaker was bidding for inclusion in some future thesaurus of famous quotations.

'We're checking the report now, sir,' Francis added, 'but it looks like you are free to go to the palace, if you choose.'

Baldwin inflated with indignation at a mere sergeant advising him, and Green quickly jumped in. 'That will be all, Francis.' He turned to Baldwin. 'Of course, sir, with respect, our advice will be that you cannot allow yourself to be placed in such a situation. Our Superintendent Brown on the scene knows this already.'

'Then why messenger Francis?'

'Well, it was, er ... Brown thought you would want to know, after having overturned his last decision about bringing in the vicar and sergeant. It seems—'

'So, you think I shouldn't go to the palace?' The Prime Minister was not so much asking Green as talking out loud, mainly to himself. 'And if I don't go, they'll brand me a traitor for not going to the King's rescue, and I'll be accused of high treason.'

'Excuse me, sir,' Green interrupted, 'of course there would be no question of that. None whatsoever, sir.'

'Oooh!' the PM mocked Green. 'Tell me more.'

'Sir, with the exception of certain strict liability offences such as bald tyres and letting your cow escape on the highway—'

'You wouldn't be trying to make a point, by any chance, would you?'

'I'm simply trying to say that a conviction under our law is only possible if it can be established that a defendant has *mens rea* – that is a guilty mind – and has done the *actus rea*, the guilty act. Now, in your case—'

'Green,' Baldwin smiled without amusement, 'do they actually give you lessons in this?'

'Well, a refusal to assist the King in his predicament is neither *mens rea* nor *actus rea*, so no offence has been com—'

'Enough!' Exasperation burst forth. 'How can one of my

leading NCS commanders be so obtuse?' The PM expelled a rush of air. 'It's the people who will judge me, you silly old fool – not a court of law. I'm going to announce a General Election any day now, and, pray tell me, how can I go to the country as the Prime Minister who left his King to the mercy of a serial killer? Just what do you think the opposition will do with that, commander? And do you think the voters will accept that I'm a great guy simply because I didn't have a guilty mind?'

* * *

The cord on Richards' wrist pulled dangerously taut as he jumped to his feet and swivelled to face Molly as she entered the Throne Room.

'Is he coming?'

'Not another thing!' Molly said quietly.

'What's that supposed to mean?'

'You get nothing until I have checked His Majesty. Nothing. That is the deal. Take it or leave it.'

Sean, who sat on one of the barricade thrones, noticed the defiant Hannigan chin jutting out. Up to this point, she had been meek, even compliant. She had been overawed by her surroundings; by the King of England behind the curtain, his life partly in her hands. There had also been fear of the sword Richards wielded in his right hand. So far, she had been Richards' obedient messenger, for he seemed to prefer this rather than shouting out his directives.

'More dignified,' he had said. Sean wondered if there could be anything less dignified than the circumstances they were now in.

'I'll leave it then!' Richards' jaw muscles pulled tight, the outward sign of inward stubbornness.

What Richards chose to leave were the replies not only from the Prime Minister but also from the BBC. Molly had taken out a demand that the PM appear with Richards on live television after the Saturday sports results at 5 p.m. Richards had reckoned that more households than not would be tuned in at that time. Had he but understood his full impact, he would have realized that the only houses not switched on were empty. Most channels had cleared their schedules, opting for live coverage. Others, having lost their outside sports broadcast units, were showing old films interrupted by frequent news flashes. Richards had also insisted that the BBC give warnings that there would be a 5 p.m. live broadcast from the Throne Room, and wanted proof that his orders were being carried out.

Richards motioned with the sword for Molly to return behind the barricade.

'You're an evil bastard!' Molly spat out and remained where she was, halfway between the dais and the Picture Gallery exit.

'Poor orphan I may be, my dear Molly,' mocked Richards, 'but hardly illegitimate. And as for being evil, what on earth makes you think that?'

'The killings, for one thing!' Her voice was hard. 'Not exactly good, is it? And frightening people half to death, not to mention attacking your King.'

'And tell me, Molly, why do you think that this is wrong?'

'Don't be so stupid. You know very well why.'

'Do I, Molly? Do I really? Why is it evil to kill people and take the King hostage?'

'Mr Richards, you—'

'Not you, vicar!' Richards flicked the sword under Connaughton's throat and Molly gave an involuntary cry. 'Not your argument, old son. I'm conversing with your sister-in-law.'

Sean rose from the barricade throne, and looked at Richards on the level. 'You wouldn't.'

They looked unblinking at each other.

'In pushing this,' Richards' voice was quiet and menacing, 'I trust that your prayers are prayed, vicar.'

'You couldn't do it.' Connaughton's muscles were rigid. 'Not your style, Richards. You have to get animals to do your killing—'

'Sean, for God's sake!' Molly hissed.

'... or pick on defenceless MPs and jab them when they can't hit back, or verbally attack defenceless women while you bravely hold a military sword. Cowardly is hardly the best word but it will have to do for now. Quite honestly, Richards, you disappoint—'

Sean stopped, not initially from any pain, but mainly due to the flash of the sword. As he refocused, he noticed the redness of the tip. Only then did he feel a wetness trickle down his chin. He raised a hand to explore his cheek and it came away red.

'Evil!' screamed Molly and advanced to the dais and to the point of the sword now coming over the barricade.

'No! Sergeant,' Richards grinned. 'Not another step.'

All action froze. Save for Molly. Slowly, she leaned forward until the point of the sword rested against her bosom.

'Just a piece of metal,' she said quietly, but the voice trembled unmistakably.

'No, Molly. Go back. Please.' Sean reached out with a free hand and caught her arm. He pulled backwards, then shouted, 'Out there – I'm all right, do you hear me, superintendent? Nothing rash now. Let's just keep calm,' and he sank on to a barricade throne as the sting spread across his face.

'What a sensible suggestion,' smiled Richards. 'Now, Molly, back to business while we await our illustrious Mr Baldwin, who, I am sure, will not feel able to resist my invitation. Oh, one more thing: worry not about His Majesty. He is quite well. In fact, far better than you. He sleeps like a babe.'

Brown's voice came through the speakers. 'What have you done to him?' 'Really, superintendent,' a weary-sounding Richards frowned, 'would you please keep out of our private conversations. Now, as I was saying, my dear Molly, our young friend knows nothing of what is transpiring here. I felt that he had enough problems of state already to be bothered with my mere trifles, so I gave him a gentle mixture of hyoscine and a tranquillizer. I topped him up while you were on our errand.'

'He has been behind the drapes,' Sean contributed.

'How?' challenged Molly. 'It's not possible. You couldn't have got needles and drugs through security.'

'Yes, that was a problem,' Richards smiled smugly, 'so I brought in two full plastic syringes three weeks ago. We were welcoming European ministers and officials, and I had to bring some equipment and displays for a talk on our genetic committee work. It was easy to slip along here and fix them under the throne. I'm glad the royal cleaners are as inefficient as mine. Now, can we stop worrying about the King and make progress?'

Molly gave him a look of utter disgust.

'So, why am I evil?'

'Don't be so stup—'

'No, Molly.' Richards waved the sword. 'You've already used that line. I'm not stupid and I want you to tell me why killing people is evil.'

'Everybody knows it's wrong to kill.'

'Everybody? Hitler when he gassed millions? He thought he was doing the world a favour. What about Herod when he put out a contract on all babies? What about us when we kill three million unborn babies every year? Or the thousands of old folk we put down last year with our unofficial brand of euthanasia? And what of those who killed my two children? They didn't think they were particularly evil.'

Molly thought it best to humour a killer. 'What I'm saying is that, in general,' she talked slowly, trying for a patience and calm logic that she didn't feel, 'the vast majority of people say it is wrong. It doesn't make sense to go round killing each other. It's not the best way society works.' The measured statements were more for her own inner calm. The touch of steel earlier was her act of bravado, but now the nerves of her flesh crawled, and she wanted to keep Richards manageable.

'A bit of Pythagoras there, Molly, methinks. Not bad for a sergeant. Our Mr P. said that the brain was mightier than the feelings. Therefore, better education would stop people bumping each other off. Wrong, wasn't he Molly? And anyway, why should some people, even the majority, decide what is right and wrong? The question is, Molly: who decides what's right and wrong?'

Molly was silent, and worried for Sean.

Richards remembered him. 'Vicar, for goodness sake stop bleeding on the fleur-de-lis.' He motioned towards the Picture Gallery. 'Go and get yourself seen to.'

Sean hesitated.

'I'm fine, Sean.' She squeezed his arm fondly and winced at the long, shallow gash from chin to ear. 'At present, our killer appears to want to slaughter normal logic more than me.'

'You can thank me if you wish.' Richards looked wide-eyed and expectant towards Molly as he nodded in the direction of the departing Sean. 'Perhaps not then. You were trying to tell me why it was evil to kill people.'

'Because...' and Molly had to force herself to think. 'Because it would make life horrible and fearful.'

'You mean it makes life nice if we don't butcher each other? A touch of hedonism there, old girl. Whatever brings pleasure is right, and whatever makes people unhappy is wrong. But who decides what brings the greatest happiness? Maybe killing MPs and TV gurus will. Who knows?'

'QUIET!' roared Molly, throwing caution aside. 'Do you realize what evil you're doing right now – to millions in the nation, to the King, to me, to—'

'And do you realize what that nation, that King and you have done to me!' Richards' voice was equally loud, but cracking with high emotion, and Molly shuddered as a glint of madness crept into his face.

'All I got was a long stupid name after some equally inane soccer team. The rest I had to fight and scrape for, and then, when I had made it, when I could stand on my little mountain and survey all the others, then they came along and bulldozed it out of existence.'

The MP's voice suddenly cracked wide open. 'I had everything!' he sobbed. 'Can't you see?' He was fighting to hold himself together. 'You should especially, Molly Hannigan – hard on the outside, tough as old boots, while on the inside yearning for something tender, something to love, somebody to love you.'

Molly, not for the first time, wanted to demand how this man knew so much about her and Sean. But the moment was shattered as Richards screamed across the Throne Room, arms in the air, sword aloft. Naked, blatant madness was now etched in every line of the killer's face. Molly saw the cord go taut and cringed, waiting for hot metal to explode into the King. Instead, there came a crashing of steel on old hard wood, and Richards brought the military sabre broadside down on top of a barricade throne chair just by her face. She screamed and jumped backwards.

'I found her!' Richards cried out, then sobbed. 'She was mine. Ten years I'd looked at her. Hoping. Daring to wonder. Keeping my distance because I thought she could never ever love anybody like me. And suddenly, she was looking back, and, Molly, oh Molly...' and the voice broke and tears were trickling down his cheeks, 'Molly, she was smiling, she was smiling at me.'

He slumped to his knees, down on to the edge of a chair, and stayed there, head bowed. Molly was caught between sudden sympathy at his loss, and amazement that the gun had not exploded. Why had it not gone off when the cord went taut? Maybe she should rush him. But then, maybe, the cord just pulled the wrong way. Maybe she—

'Know what I mean, sergeant?'

Suddenly the old fierce Richards was back up and

thrusting the sword out to Molly. 'Life on your own. All alone. Bachelor sounds better than spinster, but they're both the same. Some are born to it. Maybe you are, Molly Hannigan. I certainly wasn't. And then I had my lovely Sheila and two of the loveliest babes you could ever imagine. And all I asked of you,' and Richards, voice hardening, thrust the sword forward with each emphasis, 'was one simple question – who decides what is evil?'

Richards glared, daring, challenging, demanding, and shouted, 'Who!?'

'Thou shalt not kill!' screamed back Molly.

'WHO?' Richards still demanded.

Molly thrust out her last hope, 'GOD!' and Richards burst into laughter – long, triumphant, uncontrolled, almost hysterical laughter, and out of it he shouted.

'Took you long enough, Molly Hannigan!'

He looked up beyond the ceiling. 'Lord! It took her long enough!'

25

A television screen twice the size of a suitcase and half as slim was pushed by hidden hands from the Picture Gallery, and propped against the inside jamb of the Throne Room door. A moment later, it flickered into the dark colours of a giant gorilla in a steel cage, and Molly felt an instant rapport with the beast.

We interrupt our film and return you to our news desk for the latest update on the palace crisis. We shall return to King Kong *shortly.*

The screen faded and the face of top BBC newscaster Jeffrey Surtees emerged against a blue background with 'News Flash' picked out in gold behind and to one side of his head.

A few moments ago at three-thirty, the Prime Minister, Mr James Baldwin, announced that he was to enter the Throne Room in Buckingham Palace to talk face to face with the MP who is still holding the King at gunpoint. Mr Baldwin is to insist on one condition: that he be accepted as hostage in exchange for the release of His Majesty. The Prime Minister has further agreed to take part in a live broadcast at 5 p.m. The MP, Crompton

Stanley Richards, who represents Twistleton and is on several national and European committees, is wanted by the police for questioning concerning the deaths of four leading citizens. They also want to talk to him about the unexpected death of his wife in the early hours of this morning from a drugs overdose. When the broadcast goes ahead, we shall bring you live coverage.

This ends our bulletin, and ongoing live coverage of the palace crisis continues as usual on BBC's twenty-four hour News Channel Seven. We now return you to our Saturday afternoon matinee film.

* * *

Commander Green smiled with satisfaction as *King Kong* replaced Surtees on his videophone monitor. He was at last beginning to feel in control.

BBC producer Chevron Chase glided gracefully into his picture. 'Of course, dear commander, your primitive teensy-weensy screen won't have done my glorious creation full justice.'

'No, but it's marvellous what we can do with technology,' smiled Green at the offending apparatus.

'Oh! Ghastly word!' Chevron feigned shock. 'Art, my dear man. Pure art. Technology's merely the tool. Now, mon commander, we do hope that we here at Shepherd's Bush news desk have made your absolutely dreadful chore just that tiny bit easier.'

'Looked no different from the real thing.' Green felt obliged to pamper the artistic temperament. 'Did you manage to mock up a couple of spare newscasts, just in case Richards wants to view other channels?'

'Not the slightest grief!' Chevron infused each sentence with drama, whether or not it was required. 'ITV and

271

Channels Five to Ten, plus Sky, and ourselves have all set up little dummy studios with the *crème de la crème* of our off-duty newscasters. We are all linking into a special mixing van outside dear old Buck House. Worry not. We can beam in and out anything that takes your fancy. Rest assured, there's no way our naughty Mr Richards will go out live.'

* * *

The sound had been turned down but *King Kong* rolled on, and Molly Hannigan watched upturned faces emitting silent screams. A beam of sympathy lit up her emotions. Next, giant hands parted iron bars as though they were tinfoil, and the terrified faces turned and fled. She wished she could follow. Kong charged out into New York nightlife, and Molly suddenly smiled.

Fleetingly, her memory transported her to a pew, sitting beside Ma with Kate and her buggy in the aisle: a rare church appearance, especially for Sean's first sermon at St Thomas's. *King Kong* had loomed large then.

'They took away their god,' Sean had thundered from the pulpit, 'and tore the heart out of that tribal society.' Even now she could remember the words from perhaps the only religious message that had ever made sense. Sean had said that Kong's kidnappers symbolized the money-grabbing greed of Western materialism, adding, 'Now the West is doing the same thing to itself. It's killed off God. It's wrenched the heart out of its history and culture. No God, no purpose. No purpose, no point to life. So why bother? Why not eat, drink, cheat, steal, lie, kill, and try to be merry, for tomorrow we die!'

The picture suddenly flickered and died, and as anonymous hands withdrew the large screen, Sean stepped past and into the Throne Room. A wide strip of plaster, a little too pink against a four o'clock shadow, adorned his cheek, and several wires dangled from his hands.

'Far enough,' called Richards. 'Explain.'

'The King's doctors are outside.' Sean held up the multi-coloured leads. 'They ask for these to be attached.'

Richards considered the proposition, a chess player pondering the scheming. Eventually, he nodded. 'But I'll do it.'

'Not really that easy, Stan.' Sean was slow and casual. He'd had instructions to report back on exactly how the gun was fixed to the King's person. 'They've given me a diagram and spent several minutes demonstrating—'

'Sean,' Richards smiled patiently, 'national politicians don't reach their mid-fifties without having had at least half a dozen electrocardiograms. Emery and dissolvent to clear the skin, stick-on terminals etc. etc.—'

'All the same—'

'Drape the leads over that throne!' Richards' voice barked. 'Pass me the diagram.'

He waved the sword towards the Quadrangle balcony windows, and in a gentler tone added, 'You and Hannigan make yourselves comfortable over there on the floor.

'You out there,' he called to Brown and company, 'one wrong move while I'm behind the curtain and...' It seemed unnecessary to finish the sentence.

Sean sat down in front of a bored-looking SAS trooper, with only the thick glass between them. He gave the soldier an understanding smile; feeling for him as he entered his sixth hour in an uncomfortable crouch. Molly sat opposite, her fingers tracing the bronze mount of a Chinese porcelain jardinière.

'How does it feel?' she asked, looking at the plaster on his cheek.

'I'll live. You?'

'Better than I thought I'd be. The anger helps.'

'Brown gave me some news while I was out.'

'Like what?'

'Your lads turned over Richards' place as we flew down. They found you and me pinned up all over one study wall.

Seems he not only took a liking to my press reports, but he also had fairly comprehensive biogs on both of us. They also found a file in his computer itemizing everything from the day he introduced the education officer to the rogue elephant to the plan to end his wife's life.'

Molly shivered slightly. 'Quite a little swot, our Mr Richards. No wonder he knew so much about us.'

They were quiet. Both stared out beyond the Quadrangle and at the rear of the famous royal rooms and balcony that in turn overlooked the Mall. Everywhere were soldiers in battle fatigues. All had guns. Some peered down their sights. Sean hoped it was only out of habit.

'So,' began Molly slowly, 'why do you always dodge the issue?'

Sean stared back and his only reply was a furrowed brow. Molly shook her head, which eventually elicited from him, 'What do you mean?'

A deliberately dumb act, she thought, but encouraged, 'I've asked you dozens of times.'

Connaughton smiled, catching her drift. 'And every time you've turned it into a joke.'

'Not always! Not always! Just a false front. Come on. Be honest. Why do you never trust me with your vicar talk? There's got to be more to it than me joking.'

He said nothing more and continued inspecting the troops. 'There is, isn't there?'

Sean smiled at her and again turned as though one section of the troops was of particular note. 'It's difficult to explain.'

'Try,' encouraged Molly. Silence followed.

'Okay,' Molly spoke quietly as Sean continued to inspect the troops. 'Let me hazard a guess—'

'No.' He turned to face her, and she saw from his expression that he had come to a sudden decision. She waited.

'I want you to believe. I want you to have what I've had for the last few years. An inner peace, a joy – but I don't want you to believe to please me, Molly.'

'Why not?'

'It's important to me.'

'Why?'

Silence.

'Why is it important to you, Sean, that I believe?'

'Because it is.'

'So, why?' This time she refused to let go.

'Because we're given free will to choose, and if I put undue pressure on you, then—'

'And that's the only reason?'

'Yes!' Sean sounded emphatic.

'Certain?'

'Absolutely!'

'And vicars never lie!'

'Never!'

They both gazed out into the Quadrangle, and silence was observed. Molly's face grew taut with a strange disappointment.

'Well, hardly ever...' Sean turned back to face her, his expression set so seriously. Molly felt the frustration fade in his surprisingly warm attention.

'There was one small thing I missed out...' Still she stayed silent. '... neither of us know what will happen from this moment on. To you. To me. I need you to know that, erm—' His voice appeared be breaking down. She desperately wanted to reach over and drag more words out of him, words, in fact, not unlike those that gently and quietly came next.

'Molly, I love you.'

* * *

Superintendent Brown came to a decision. 'This news stays on this side of the door.'

Commander Green disagreed. 'He has a right to know, and it might give them a lift.'

'No!' Brown was emphatic. 'It will lift Connaughton right out of that room to demand a helicopter back to Lancashire.'

'Trust him,' Green pleaded. 'For heaven's sake man, it's his son, after all.'

Brown paused again. Green was his superior but not in negotiations. He was captain to Green's commodore and the helm was always in Brown's hands. 'Colour co-ordinated!' some trying wit had called it, with a play on their surnames.

'Mr Richards.' Negotiator Brown swung away from Green. 'We have an important message for Sean concerning his son. Would you allow him to come out?'

Connaughton did not wait for Richards' permission but got to his feet and left, with Molly still reeling from his last words.

As he emerged, Brown gave him a confident smile. 'You'll be delighted to know that he's safe and well in hospital, Mr Connaughton.'

'Hospital? Why? What's happened to—?'

'Just a check-up. Your boy's in fine fettle and looking forward to your return home.' Sean, his emotions already in turmoil, stifled the sudden tears of relief.

'I'll be right in a moment.' He swung away, and then went towards the Throne Room. 'Thank you,' he called over his shoulder. 'Molly will want to know,' and he disappeared inside.

'You're supposed to lie to the terrorist, not the hostages,' Green snarled and swung away in disgust.

* * *

'Mr Richards?' Sean approached the dais with Molly in tow. 'Look, we're needed back home, and quite honestly we are having a bit of difficulty understanding just why exactly you need us here—'

'My witnesses,' Richards broke in. 'That's what you are! Whatever happens here, you are guarantees that the truth will not remain buried. That, and one other duty.'

'Which is?' Molly challenged.

'Later, my dear. Later.'

'Stan,' Sean tried friendliness, 'we're hardly in a two-bit bent republic. You hardly need objective witnesses. This is Britain. We don't bend the truth.'

'Try not to lose that, my friend,' Richards smiled sadly.

'What?'

'Never mind. Are you ready for your last lesson?'

'On what?' asked Molly.

'Survival of the fittest,' and Richards, noting their expressions, quickly added, 'You wouldn't deny the condemned man his last wish, now would you?'

'Don't you believe it, Richards.' Molly was hard. 'You'll have at least thirty years in a cell to make your last will and testament.'

Richards looked long at Molly. 'Somehow, I don't think so.' The tepid smile involved only his lips.

'We said that evolution was in crisis because it could not account for the extraordinary complexity of many animals, like Halipegus or the bombardier beetle—'

'Look,' Sean interjected, 'this is bizarre! You hold the King and country to ransom and suddenly you start lecturing us on worms and beetles—'

'Patience, my friend,' purred Richards. 'Patience. This is, after all, why we are here; why four people are already dead – five if you include my wife, and yes, if you want to know, I did arrange for her to be put out of her misery. What you are about to learn is the reason for a king being unconscious behind these drapes and why another person will die tonight.'

Richards let the ensuing silence have its impact. He enjoyed the attentive expressions that he had suddenly conjured.

'There was a second reason why evolution is in crisis, Sean?'

'Pardon?' Sean shook himself.

'And that is...?'

'Oh, er, missing links or something.'

'Go on.'

Sean gave a resigned sigh. There seemed no alternative but to humour the killer. Sean rallied his mind. 'You claim there should be hundreds of thousands of links in the fossil record if one kind of animal has turned into another kind.'

'Now another step.' Richards was the schoolmaster once again. 'Towards the end of the seventies, I was researching into the still newish field of molecular biology. Thanks to the advances of modern biochemistry, it had become possible to compare not just the visible features of organisms but also their molecules. We could peer into the incredible proteins and nucleic acids, and we could compare them with each other.'

Again the glow was back on Richards' face and he was wading into his element once again, giving urging looks to both Sean and Molly to keep up.

'For example, we could look at the long chains of, say, five hundred amino acids which make up a protein such as haemoglobin. This is found in a great number of species and so we can easily compare the haemoglobin of one species with the haemoglobin of another. If, say, fifty of the amino acid places or types are different compared to another, we can then say that there is a ten per cent difference. See what I mean?'

Richards' eyes were piercing, suddenly demanding they understand.

'Surely you can see that, once armed with this new technique, we thought we could succeed where the palaeontologist had failed. We could find the missing links or intermediary forms at the level of molecules.'

At this moment, it was as though a light went out in his eyes. He continued flatly, 'We began to discover that the amino acid sequences pointed not to Darwin's gradual evolution, but rather to set types and species. There were no clear intermediate forms. No obvious links in between species.

'I tried to publish my findings in scientific journals and they were rejected. The editors said they contradicted evolution, and were therefore deemed unscientific and consequently unlikely to advance useful knowledge.'

Richards let out an exasperated gasp.

'Do you know the biggest problem with the living sciences today?' Molly and Sean felt obliged to shake their heads. 'They're stuck in a cul-de-sac and there is no way out until they realize it. I took the easy way out. I changed to the law. No way could I stomach spending the rest of my life with people wearing blinkers.'

'My heart bleeds for you.' Molly turned on the sarcasm.

'Bless you, my child,' smiled Richards. 'There are a dozen other good reasons to question evolution. In the end, when all the questions have answers, I might be wrong. I'm not narrow-minded or bigoted. I just want the truth. It may turn out to be right in the end, though not until scientists have the courage to examine the crisis honestly. And that means admitting that they might just possibly be wrong.

'They have to admit that competition and natural selection is just not powerful enough to produce creatures of such complexity. There is still a power or cause that they have failed to locate.'

Richards looked pointedly at Sean. 'You may, after all, be right. It may be the way a great God has chosen to create and make life and all its incredible variety. If he has, he has hidden the missing links very well.

'Evolution, or rather adaptation, has certainly happened on the small scale within cats and dogs and the like, but there is no crystal-clear evidence for large-scale evolution, and by that, I mean the links between life and non-life, between plants and animals or between fish, amphibians, reptiles, birds and mammals. And, to be honest, it scares me when I look at the motives of some atheist scientists today. They sound like blind-faith fundamentalists trying to prove that everything has simply popped into existence without a creator.

'Science has gone about as far as it can go down this cul-de-sac and the scientists are too scared to turn round and begin looking elsewhere. They are like the flat-earthers of old, hanging on to an outmoded theory. They remind me of those who crucified Galileo. It was obvious that the earth could not be the centre of the universe. There were just too many anomalies with the old theory, but only Galileo had the courage to return along the cul-de-sac and find a new way; a new model.'

Richards slumped down.

'Mr Richards?' Brown's voice came through the speakers. 'We hate to interrupt your flow, but the Prime Minister has arrived.'

'Send him in.'

'Not as easy as that, I'm afraid,' Brown said. 'He's willing to come in as soon as you release His Majesty, as we announced on television. A life for a life, Mr Richards.'

'Not a chance,' smiled Richards pulling the cord at his wrist taut. 'And listen out there: you do as I say. Remember, I've nothing to lose. I want Baldwin in here. No deals. I want that television crew with their lights at the Picture Gallery door. Also give them your mobile videophone. And I want it all now! Is that clear?'

26

'Always were a bit of an odd one, Richards,' growled the Prime Minister as he came to a halt before the dais. A television crew, lights blazing, camera rolling, queued behind him, one assistant with the mobile videophone and miniature camera nestling in his arms. 'Right, let's get on with it.'

Sean and Molly both recognized in their shared looks that the famous Baldwin bluntness and hostage negotiation might not quite go together.

'Grumpy as usual, James.' Richards smiled affably and beckoned with the sabre. 'Come and rest your weary limbs. I've really felt quite guilty about locking you up in that madhouse for so long.'

Baldwin ignored the offer of a throne and instead nodded curtly to Sean and Molly, 'Be over soon.' Turning back to Richards and striving for full command of the situation, 'Everything's ready. There's one minute to live transmission on all channels, and we're already live on Channel Seven.'

Richards erupted in laughter. Molly and Sean again saw the cord tighten, even to the point of rippling the drapes.

'Nice try, James, old boy,' Richards chuckled. 'You there!' He beckoned the TV crew assistant. 'Plug in the videophone. There's a couple of sockets near the hidden door to the left of the dais. Put the unit on the barricade. Then go.'

Richards turned back to Baldwin. 'You forget, James, I have played this game almost as long as you have. I've been in the same House when we stood four-square against terrorism. We'll never give in to blackmail, we all chorused. Do you really expect me to believe that we are now on the air?'

Baldwin seemed momentarily deflated. Reflation came with indignation, 'Then why the devil all this nonsense about TV crews and broadcasts and—'

'The wrong foot, old man,' said Richards quietly. 'I needed you on it. Now get that crew out of here.'

The retreating cameras, sound and lighting began to concertina into each other. The Picture Gallery door eventually closed on a shambles of wires and humans, and Richards switched on the videophone and beckoned Sean over to punch in a number. It was written on the back of his sword hand.

'Bonjour, France Inter?' A pasted-on receptionist's smile accompanied the greeting from an attractive brunette.

'Bonjour. Je suis Crompton Stanley Richards, Membre du Parlement Britannique.' He stopped to survey the Throne Room as if to ensure everything was in place.

'C'est moi qui à présent detiens en otage le roi d'Angleterre au palais de Buckingham. Je voudrais parler au réalisateur du journal de dix-huit heures que vous diffusez actuellement. Dites-lui que je peux lui accorder immédiatement en direct un entretien en exclusivité mondiale.'

Baldwin was looking back towards the Picture Gallery exit with a thunderous expression on his face while slashing his thumb across his throat.

Sean watched mystified, and turned to Molly. 'Surely they can't cut off a French broadcast, can they?'

Molly shrugged in ignorance. 'Did you catch what he wants?'

'Something about offering them an exclusive for their six o'clock news ... they're an hour ahead.'

Sean saw a figure appear on the monitor. The producer, he guessed. Richards once again began to speak rapidly in

French. Suddenly the screen blurred, then sizzled and finally disintegrated into static. The cord attached to Richards' wrist went taut and so too did his voice. In English, and with slow deliberateness, he said, 'You have ten seconds to unscramble your interference ... nine—'

'Stop this madness now, man!' barked the PM.

'Seven, six—'

'This is the wrong way,' cried Connaughton.

'Four—'

Molly screamed, 'No!'

'Two, one ... Thank you!' The producer had reappeared on the monitor. 'Hello, Sorry about that, we seem to have had a bit of interference.'

A few more words of French were spoken then Richards added in English, 'I shall speak in my own language, and I will assume that you have already briefed your listeners as to my identity and the present situation. Finally, you may have five minutes to sell this broadcast live to any British television or radio channel you wish.'

The four conscious occupants of the Throne Room stared at each other. Waiting.

'This is pre—!' Baldwin's explosion was quenched.

'Not another syllable!' Richards' arm held the ribbon taut.

Five minutes seemed like five hours. Sean at last saw the producer signal. Richards began with a steady authority,

As you listen to this broadcast from the Throne Room of Buckingham Palace, the King of England and his Prime Minister are my prisoners. They serve a nominal sentence as the figureheads of a society that robbed me of my family—

At this, Baldwin authoritatively stepped forward and said 'No—'

The rest was cut off. The broadside of Richards' sword smashed down on the crown of the PM's head, sending him crashing to the floor. Richards carried on as though nothing had happened.

> *A young man and his gang beat the life out of my wife and caused the deaths of my two children. I met this Quentin Charles Bocker two days ago on his release from prison. He had served his sentence. Not a great one, but then again, neither was his responsibility. I forgave him.*
>
> *The real responsibility lay with those who made him; those who fashioned him in their own image; those who taught him that survival was only for the fittest. These people I also met, and, in the absence of justice, I sentenced them to live by their own code. None of them, it would appear, was fit enough to survive.*
>
> *Mr Bocker's teacher, a certain Graham Paris, taught him that he was the product of a mindless, purposeless, mechanical process. His body was merely an armed struggle between selfish genes, each only existing to reproduce itself. A television guru explained in beautiful Technicolor how Mr Bocker had evolved from the jungle and ocean depths. Bocker's vicar – our late, great doubting bishop – taught him that he must be his own divine spark, for there was nothing beyond man. No creator to begin with. No eternal judge to end matters. No eternal consequences. And presiding over all this godless mess was the then Minister for Education, our late Major Paine.*
>
> *Between them, they taught young Quentin Charles that he was an accident of nature. He was a sophisticated electrically driven, chemically powered ape evolved from nowhere and with nowhere*

to go. Some encouraged him to be nice to others, but failed to show him why, or how, and by what power. Why should an electric ape love anybody but itself? Why should a survivor of a race of fitness give a fellow contestant an advantage over himself?

My family has not survived this teaching. Will yours? Will you?

'Hah!' Prime Minister Baldwin erupted as he struggled back to his feet. 'The danger's not out there in society! I'm looking at it right now!'

Sean and Molly cringed, fearing the worst.

Richards still looked into the sending camera. His early political career might have been blighted by shifty television eyes. Now, he remained calm, unblinking, with a patient smile playing at the corner of his mouth. The overall effect made Baldwin sound like an immature and petulant schoolboy.

To continue ... a year is a long time in politics, especially at the bedside of a loved one. Time and space to think. The ethics of our cities have exercised us since Plato, and still we have not learned. We still abuse kids. We still go to war. We commit genocide with machetes in Africa and do it with computers in Bosnia and Kosovo. Our crime rates climb and our solutions dwindle. We cry out to get back to basic rules. But somebody's lost the rule book.

Up to this point, it seemed to Sean that Richards had been following a pre-programmed sermon. But now, the eyes seemed to glaze over, almost as though he had forgotten his worldwide audience.

I sat by that bedside and thought of what or who caused my beloved Sheila to be. I thought of my children's bodies lying in the roadway. Crushed. Jokes of cruel nature? Accidents? Unfit to survive? I doubted it. It demanded too much blind faith to believe they were only aimless accidents. I gazed at a sparkling universe at night. A beautiful design? If so, what a great designer. But also what an incredible intelligence must have provided our intelligence to understand such things. And who made humans worship, whether in churches, soccer temples, or just before the bathroom mirror? I looked inside at the 'ought'. Bocker knew that he ought not to have wiped out my family. And I want to know who put the 'ought', the conscience, within him and us?

Would a bundle of selfish genes do all that? Can we even trust a bundle of mindless, senseless, purposeless selfish genes to come up with anything but selfishness? Do we really think that the Cause and Intelligence behind the world is an irrelevance in our lives? Can we really survive without his input; his right and wrong and his commandments? Can we play the game of life without the Eternal External Referee and his rules? And as we see what is happening now as we progressively forget the old rules, what will happen in the next generation when nobody is around who even remembers these rules?

Richards halted. He gazed into the sending camera, one eyebrow cocked, as if waiting for an answer. He then reached across and quietly flicked off the videophone.

'Sermon over?' snarled Baldwin.

'One of your predecessors tried to get back to basics and society laughed at him. Another came after claiming the moral high ground until his colleagues' corruption and cronyism caused subsidence. Fancy your chances, James?'

The Prime Minister's face was granite. Politician first and foremost, his mind tripped over a thousand calculations as to how this broadcast would affect voters. What of his interruptions? How would he be judged for his inability to stop the broadcast? And the young King's safety! Would the pundits tear him into tiny pieces or would there be sufficient left to present to an electorate? At this moment, he thought not.

'Come here.' Richards pointed to Baldwin with the sword.

There was hesitation, and the arm with the cord attached began to rise. The Prime Minister suddenly considered that he might have a slim political chance if he brought the King out alive. And maybe, just maybe, if he could get close enough to Richards, there would be a chance of an heroic, vote-winning end to this farce. And it was only a sword. What was a slash or two if a landslide victory was the prize?

Baldwin advanced round the barricade, and stopped at the point of the sword. Richards eased the cord from the wrist with his teeth, and allowed it to drop into his sword hand. The freed hand reached behind his back and withdrew a Smith and Wesson automatic pistol from the belt of his dress trousers.

'Where the hell did that come from?' cried Baldwin, and turning towards the Picture Gallery door, he yelled, 'Brown, you're dead when this is over. There's nothing on the end of that stupid cord.' And he stopped as though realizing he had made a rather obvious point. 'What a crazy, idiotic shambles!'

Richards dropped the useless cord and the sword. He stepped up to the Prime Minister's turned back and lodged the warm muzzle of the automatic under the lobe of Baldwin's right ear. His left arm snaked around his neck.

'Stan!' Connaughton called out, 'Please, for mercy's sake, don't do this. For your sake, for the sake of the God you've just been talking about, please, this is not the way—'

'That's the second time you've said that, Sean. You're repeating yourself. So this is not the way, is it?'

'Fire that gun, mister, and you won't do another thing,' Molly said quietly.

'Oh, very American, my dear. Tell me, Sean, why this is not the right way?'

'For a start, Stan, vengeance is not yours. It doesn't belong to you. Do that and you're just as guilty as the society you accuse. Killing ... fulfilling your own desires—'

'Wrong, Connaughton!' Richards retorted, suddenly angry. 'Six months ago I decided to end it all. I had the hyoscine, a massive dose from WildWorld, and Sheila and I were quietly going to pass away into whatever the next life held. That was my desire, Sean, and nothing else. Then I thought of all the young Bockers of this world, and I thought that maybe society might listen. Trouble is, before you can catch this mad, mad world's attention, you've somehow got to stop it. At this moment, I think it's going about as slow as it possibly can. Wouldn't you agree? If it doesn't hear now—'

'It's still not good enough, Stan.' Sean was urgent. 'No matter what you say, your actions are as bad as everybody else.'

'True!'

'So,' Sean gathered himself for his main appeal, 'if you believe there's a somebody in charge, why don't you trust him to make things right in his own good time.'

Richards laughed derisively, and Baldwin seemed to be on the point of wilting. 'You're a fine one to talk about trusting, Your Reverence.'

'What's that supposed to mean?'

'Can you honestly, hand on heart, say that you trust God with everything?'

Sean hesitated. What was Richards getting at?

'I try to trust. Yes. Yes, I do trust.'

Richards smiled. It was a cold smile of satisfaction. It was the smile of a hunter looking down on his captured prey.

'Even with your parish, my dear vicar?'

Connaughton's mouth hung open.

'Can't trust him with that, can we?' taunted Richards. 'Can't practise what we preach, dear reverend Father. Won't trust him to provide.' A mocking hollow laugh rang across the Throne Room, drowning a massive sob that belched from Baldwin.

'Get out of that one.' Molly looked up at Sean with wide-eyed innocence.

Connaughton's mouth still hung at half mast. A question echoed and ricocheted round his head, 'O God! What have I done?'

'But Stan...' the mouth began to work as the mind sought for half a defence, 'I had a godless bishop who was on the point of closing the church down, and if I hadn't taken another job—'

'So you trusted yourself,' smiled Richards.

'No! I mean—'

'Your church or God's?' Richards' voice started level but began to rise. 'If it's the latter, why won't you trust him with its future instead of slaving for some stupid newspaper on your days off?'

The voice had now risen in emotion. 'Don't you realize that yours is the greatest job in the world? Look at Baldwin here,' and Richards tapped the PM's temple with the gun, 'he's just the furniture remover; hopelessly shifting around bits of society trying to make it work better.

'You, on the other hand, are the master builder, or at least you work for him. And between you, you have power to change society because through you the lives of its members can be changed.'

At this point, Richards' voice hardened for an accusation. 'You are supposed to go and teach people a different way, and instead you spend your time reporting bad news for a local rag? Maybe if you and your clerical kind had done your job better in the past, I might not be stood here now. I might still be enjoying my family.' Richards was almost shouting at the end.

'Stan, I see your point,' Connaughton said without conviction, adding wearily, 'but that doesn't give you the excuse to blow away a Prime Minister.'

'Maybe. Maybe not. Shall I give myself up now, Sean? Is that what you would like?'

'Yes, Stan.' And Baldwin also nodded his head vigorously. 'I promise that I will do everything in my power to ensure your safety with as fair a trial as possible.'

'Thank you, Sean, but I don't think so. You see I'm not going to aid and abet a corrupt society in its injustice.'

'But the British system of justice is—'

'Sssh!' Richards quieted Sean, and shifted Baldwin in his arm grip. 'Listen. I've taken four lives. Five including my wife's. That amounts to a living hell for several families. They're the sad victims in all this. I've taken breadwinners. Wives have lost husbands and children their fathers and grandfathers. I've brought Parliament to its knees and held a king to ransom. And do you know what this silly nation will now do to me?

'It will smack me across the hand. They've even repealed hanging for treason. This soppy society will put me in a comfortable room with en suite facilities, a television in one corner and a desk in the other. Prison warders, inmates and social workers will treat me with awe and boast to their grandchildren that they were with the King Taker and Serial Killer. Sunday columnists will write erudite articles about me while others will make a fortune from analysing my mind. Then, after a few years, they will let me out, to become a television chat show celebrity and write my own story. Maybe even do a film or two.

'Tell me, Sean, do you think that will be justice? Considering all the lives I have taken or crippled?' Richards shook his head. 'No, my dear son. This society, for once, is going to have to let justice be done. It's going to have to execute me. By firing squad.'

The room was still as the occupants took this in.

'Stan, please think—'

'Sean, you wanted to know the real reason why you're here. This is it. You're chaplain to the condemned man. Me!' Sean and Molly stared at the sagging PM and a killer.

A killer resolute that he be killed.

'Pray for me, chaplain?' Richards asked.

Killer and hostage were framed incongruously in the cream, gold and gilt proscenium arch of the Throne Room: a crazy drama with a barricade of thrones for a backdrop. Somewhere, off stage and behind the dishevelled drapes, was an unconscious king.

Sean sank to his knees and was silent. Was there a prayer for such a situation? In the silence, something simple began to form. It dealt with the odour of death that pervaded the room, of a God who had loved them enough to have experienced it himself on a rugged cross on a hill. It spoke of the odour becoming an aroma in a resurrection, the scent of an everlasting love.

'Dear Lord Jesus, forgive this man his sins,' Connaughton continued, 'even for the deaths at his hands. Forgive me my sins, and especially my lack of trust. Forgive each one of us for putting our own petty desires before you and each other; for playing at being our own gods. And even if this man goes through with his threat, please receive his soul into your loving and just hands—'

'Amen,' said Richards. 'So be it.'

Sean looked up.

'Both of you,' Richards gestured with a nod of his head, 'over by the Green Room door.'

Sean stood, took Molly's arm and slowly, reluctantly, knowing what might happen when they reached it, they moved. A cry escaped from the Prime Minister as he was thrust away and towards them. All three looked back at Richards. Alone. His gun still pointed towards Baldwin. Slowly, he began to turn towards the Picture Gallery door.

'Armed police! Armed police! Drop the gun, Richards.

Now!' Green's voice was loud and clear. Richards continued to turn.

'Last time!' snapped Green. 'Drop the gun!'

Richards had almost finished his turn when the explosion of weapons came from the two Picture Gallery doors. Molly recoiled and screamed, burying her face in Sean's chest. Everything etched itself in slow motion on Sean's mind. Richards lifted backwards into the air, the gun looped up to the low-slung chandeliers, and the MP's body danced and twitched in a lower arched flight. It was probably lifeless before it landed with a sickening thud at the foot of the proscenium arch before a Quadrangle window. It lay bloody and discarded, like an unwanted rag doll.

NCS officers, troops and SAS poured in from every aperture. Sean and Molly and even the Prime Minister were momentarily forgotten. The dais drapes were flung back to reveal a cord tied to a knob on the royal throne. Two empty shoes lay before the vacant throne, and the young King slept on his back with a peaceful smile on his face.

'Come on you two.' It was Sergeant Francis. 'Commander Green has ordered the fastest helicopter in our fleet for you and it's waiting on the lawn outside.'

'Thanks, sergeant,' smiled Sean, 'Perhaps another few minutes while we make sure the King is all right. I have a message for him from a very important person.'

'Er, I'm sorry, sir.' Francis could hardly look at them. 'I'm afraid our superintendent wasn't entirely honest with you before. They did find your son but he's taken a massive overdose and is suffering from exposure. He's also sustained a head injury, and is in a coma. They still don't really know how bad he is.'

27

'Now, Sean, my good mate,' Frank Winter sounded comical when he tried to be anything but Frank Winter, 'let's not make this hard, shall we?' Nice and chummy he was not, and never would be. Nevertheless, for Sean and Molly, listening on the helicopter's headphones, it was almost a welcome distraction from the troubles ahead, and those behind.

'The decision's made, Frank,' stressed Sean. 'I quit. You'll have the written version tomorrow.'

'But why?' whined Winter. 'Why all of a sudden when you've got the greatest story of the year, nay the decade? Do you have any idea what you could make from world rights alone with the inside story on the Throne Room? After you've done right by us, that is! Think it out, man. Think of St Thomas's. You could keep a cathedral going hawking this story round the globe. Imagine what the Yanks would pay! And that's just for starters. Why this crazy change of heart all of a sudden?'

'Mysterious ways, Frank. Mysterious ways,' teased Sean. 'Guidance comes through strange people. Even serial killers. I'm off home to look after my family, my church and be quiet to see what the future holds.'

'Just a short piece?' the news editor's voice wheedled yet again.

'Frank, give it up, will you? You've said it yourself: can't serve two masters. Let's just say I saw the light.'

'Or one of those palace chandeliers fell on your head!'

'At least you might get your full-time reporter, Frank. Look on the bright side. No more amateur Holy Joes messing up your schedules, and you can swear to your heart's content. However, my dear child, should you ever find yourself in spiritual need—'

'Connaughton,' Winter at last exploded into his natural self, 'if I hear you've signed up for one of those Sunday tabloids for some six-figure obscenity, so help me, I'll—'

'And bless you too, my child,' Sean chuckled. 'Tell you what, Frank, for old times' sake, give me a day with the family then send round one of your lads for an exclusive interview. How's that?'

'That's Birmingham to your right,' called the pilot, as Frank Winter signed off to write his own story, no doubt entitled 'Our man saves the King' if Enty got his hands on it.

The pilot added, 'Another thirty minutes with this wind should have us beyond Manchester and nearly home. By the way, Hoghton Infirmary have okayed a drop-off in their grounds.'

He switched off his connection to leave Sean and Molly in their own private sound loop. Sean fidgeted. Occasionally he craned to look over the pilot's shoulder, not content with side views. Molly noticed his white impatient knuckles as he gripped the pilot's seat. The silence ended abruptly.

'Until he was born, I'd never really looked at life...' Sean stopped mid-sentence and Molly looked across expecting him to expand. '... Well, not seriously—' The rest caught in his throat, and Molly reached out to him. 'I don't know what I'll do if...' Connaughton wiped the back of his hand roughly under his nose. 'I held in my palm this tiny five-pound bundle with enormous brown eyes. Karen had spent that whole first hour bonding. That was the in thing in those days. Then it was my turn, and I sat there for the next hour doing nothing else while Karen slept, and the nurses fussed and buzzed, wanting to take Michael and do things with him. And I wouldn't let them. They got so angry at one point until I eventually...' Sean took a massive intake of breath in a big effort to keep control.

Molly just held him. The helicopter's quiet drone beyond the headphones filled an otherwise comfortable silence.

'Then, we were together by another bedside. Little Katie's, after the accident. Michael was trying to hold me this time.' Sean tried to laugh but it came out as a gasp. 'Still young enough to hug his dad. And Michael had sobbed and sobbed until I thought he'd burst open. He couldn't ... no ... he wouldn't let go of the idea that, somehow, little tyke that he was, he should have saved them; and I just wanted to take a sponge and wipe out the inside of his mind, erase all the past and start again. But you can't, though. You can't ... can you...?'

And again there was silence, and not much more for Molly to do than support him.

'... And then the thunderbolt came.'

Molly was suddenly interested. 'Go on.'

'Yeah,' he gave her a reproachful look, 'sorry about last night.' This time a chuckle came. 'I knew you were dying to know.'

She waited.

'I'd always reckoned that if there was somebody behind all this universe, he didn't much like me. I was brought up with a monster god who dangled me over the pit of hell. He was my parents' bogeyman, the one they used to frighten me into goodness. And it worked. I grew up thinking that I would go straight to hell the moment I died. You only had to look at the opposite sex and, well, you can imagine the rest...

'My bombshell from above came by that bedside with Kate swathed in bandages and Michael holding me. You know you get those disclosure moments – glimpses that set you free. Suddenly life changes colour.

'I suddenly saw it and it was beautiful. This God had made me in his image. Right? Therefore, as a father, I am fashioned after the heavenly one. I loved my kids until it hurt. So, as I sat by that bedside, I wanted it to be me suffering, not little Katie. Same with Michael now. And here was the beauty: if I, as a mere copy, loved my children so much, how much more must the original heavenly parent love me?

'That was it. The truth just exploded through me. One minute I was bound for hell. The next, heaven. Not because I'd changed. But my picture of God had. I remember grabbing the Gideon Bible beside Kate's bed and there it was, on every page. Page after page after page. A father waiting with open arms for his prodigal son to come home; the disciples being taught to pray "Our Father". The greatest romance in the universe – God actually loves me!

'The secret of life was no secret after all: just a Father, with tears in his eyes, weeping over his disobedient children. Not all that much different from me now. Suddenly, Molly, I could read the mind of God; think his thoughts; walk in his footsteps. I could see his love and his yearning. It was written in my flesh and blood relationship with Michael and Kate, and I understood how I could have a relationship with God.

'Best of all, Molly, he could even do what I couldn't do for Michael. He could come inside and wipe everything clean. A fresh start. All this was on offer. I simply had to stop being my own god, and give him the role.' Sean turned and tilted his head and raised an eyebrow. The combination was a question: Do you see?

And Molly smiled. Struggling to see.

'Thanks,' she said.

'For what?'

'For taking the risk. For treating me as though I was worth the risk of being laughed at.'

They sat comfortable in each other's presence.

'Before, Molly?'

'Yes?'

'In the Throne Room. You never responded.'

'Did I have to?'

Sean nodded, an anxious look across his face.

'You really are thick, Sean Connaughton. I've loved you from the moment you stepped on to our veranda in St Augustine hunting a different kind of thunderbolt.'

For a moment they both failed to react. Suddenly they were into the unexplored. Gone was the safety of duelling; the jousting; the jocularity. In its place was something much more precious; more dangerous; less controllable, even volatile. The eyes of each softly acknowledged the change, and it seemed more than appropriate to celebrate in the manner of all lovers. Sean crooked a finger under Molly's chin and lifted her face to his. Their lips brushed together, gently savouring. He cupped her face in his hands, as well as crash helmets allowed, and kissed her. For a blessed brief moment nobody but themselves existed; cocooned together, hurling out of the darkness that had engulfed them for so long, and on into blazing sunlight. Flying free; no ties; no consequences; no down-to-earth practicalities; nothing but the passion of this blazing moment; that and the frightening desire to lock out the world and stretch it into eternity.

The earphones crackled unromantically, 'Hospital to your left. ETA less than two minutes.' Reluctantly, they disentangled themselves and stretched to look over the pilot's shoulder.

Before the wheels touched down, they could see Kate and her buggy making good headway along a path, leaving Ma Hannigan and her Joe Tresize waddling and limping and laughing behind.

Laughing!?

The door swung open and they ran to meet Kate, and a fair impression of a Dr Kildare voice boomed out, 'He's opened his eyes! Michael's opened his eyes!'

'What a mess!' Ma Hannigan said as she spied her son-in-law's plastered face.

297

'Thanks very much!' said Sean, and then there were tears and hugging.

'It's good news, then?' he asked.

Ma Hannigan was rooting for a handkerchief to wipe her eyes, and Joe answered, 'We're not out of the woods yet, but the doctor has said it's a hopeful sign. We can go straight in to see him.'

'Did you see him, Daddy?' Kate's normal computer voice sounded. 'Did you tell the King that he's my definite possible and that he should wait for me to grow up? Did you, Daddy?'

Sean looked helpless.

'I tell you what, Kate,' Molly answered, 'we can talk about this later. Come on, I'll race you to Michael's bed.'

At the ward, the sister stopped them. 'You have to prepare yourselves. He's a bit the worse for wear. Cuts and bruises and a bandage like a turban over the top of his head. We have no idea yet how much damage, if any, has been caused. We certainly know there has been some swelling of the brain but time is still on our side.'

'But he did open his eyes this afternoon,' encouraged Ma Hannigan, 'and that was good, wasn't it sister?' She nodded, though not with enthusiasm.

They walked or wheeled in quietly and sat or stood and watched. Michael lay still, save for the rising and lowering of his chest. Sean thought of Sammi, and the rising, falling sheets. He did what all parents did by the side of a sick child's bed. He prayed. Hard.

'Gran-Gran still wants to look after us and bring Uncle Joe back to stay with us,' Kate's computer voice suddenly piped up. 'Isn't that great, Daddy?'

Sean looked inquiringly across at Nora and Joe who were suddenly confused. Nora's face flamed red, and then a glint came into her eye. 'One of these days, Katherine Connaughton, your ears and that voice machine of yours are going to be chopped off. You'll listen at doors just once too often. Sean, I'm sorry—'

'His eyelids moved!' Molly gasped.

'Michael? Hello, Michael. It's Dad.'

His son groaned. His body slowly arched upwards and his face contorted. He let out a piercing scream, and shot up into a crouched sitting position, hugging his stomach.

'Please leave!' called one of the two nurses who came running from their station to either side of the bed.

The curtains were hastily pulled round, excluding all five visitors. Gran and Joe made Kate drive away and followed. Sean and Molly were left at the ward entrance, holding each other for comfort. More nurses arrived and others left. A struggle was waged behind the curtains; Michael's gasps and cries were mingled with nursing orders and occasional soothing words. Two doctors arrived from different directions within seconds of each other and disappeared beyond the curtains. The five minutes it took for peace to return seemed to Sean and Molly as long as the flight home. A short time later, the curtains were drawn away, and one of the doctors came over to Sean and Molly.

'I don't know how much you've been told,' his face was serious, 'but I'm afraid we still have nothing definite for you. We are pretty certain that he took a massive overdose, though it looks as though he collapsed before injecting the full dose. They found some still in a syringe some distance from the body. To be honest, we're surprised that he's still with us. We also suspect brain damage from the ravine fall at WildWorld—'

'What's just happened now?' Molly interrupted.

'Well, he's certainly coming out of the coma, but at the same time withdrawal is hitting the system—'

'It looked like the cramps he had last time he came off,' agreed Sean. 'Is he on Britlofex?'

'No.' The doctor shook his head slowly. 'We can't consider detoxification until we know your son's true condition. Just methadone. At least it will relieve cramps and other symptoms.'

'So, what now?' asked Molly.

'Waiting, I'm afraid. Just waiting. Shouldn't be too long now that he's out of the coma. We'll see what brain damage there is and take it from there. Sorry.' The doctor ran out of words, gave a sympathetic hunch of his shoulders and walked off. Gran and Joe and Kate returned, and the bedside vigil began all over again.

It was now obvious that Michael was just under the surface of consciousness. He twisted restlessly and occasionally his face twitched with some unidentified distant pain. One eye abruptly sprang open then closed. And then both eyelids tried to tilt upwards. The pupils looked glazed and unseeing and his lips were moving, striving...

'You ... erm ... Mummy Buck ... er...' and the eyes closed and a silly grin dragged his mouth lopsided. Sean looked anxiously at Molly, then at a nurse who had come to join them.

'Mummy Buck!' Michael's voice came louder and clearer. He giggled and dribbled. 'Kick me!'

'What do you make of it?' Sean asked anxiously.

Michael began a rambling mumble, 'Mummy Bucks are good mummies ... kick 'em Mummy ... show who's boss...'

'Words are a good sign,' nodded the nurse. 'Is he making any sense?'

'No,' said Sean, and looked round to the others who shook their heads. 'Could it be, er, brain damage?'

Michael giggled again, raised a hand to wipe his mouth, and opened his left eye. There was a wicked squint as he looked at his dad.

''allo, Mummy Buck!'

Before Sean could reply the nurse began answering his question. 'We generally find that with brain swelling, there can be hallucinations and—'

'Stupid! You calling me stupid?' Michael's other eye was now open, and a grin began to spread across his face. Suddenly, everybody was smiling and laughing and Kate did

300

her mechanical 'whoop' that sounded like a flotilla being welcomed into harbour.

The eyes cringed and closed at the noise and Sean pulled the sound switch on Kate's buggy.

'What was all that rubbish about a Mummy Buck?' Sean tried tentatively.

'If you behave yourself and be a good dad,' Michael formed the words slowly but with a wicked smile, 'I might tell you one day.'

'Cheeky young monkey!'

Michael winced as he tried to prop himself up on his elbow and Molly and Gran lunged forward to plump up his pillows.

'Anything happening?' Michael lay back tired, though his face looked less drawn, and not as grey. 'Same old boring stuff, I suppose.' They had only told half the story when the ward sister came over.

'Excuse me, Mr Connaughton, you're wanted on the videophone.'

'Not now, sister. Could you tell whoever it is that I won't be available for some time to come.'

'I'd rather not, if you don't mind.'

'Sister, please!'

'Take my word for it, Mr Connaughton,' and the sister smiled knowingly, 'this is a call you should take.' Sean reluctantly gave in and followed.

Ma Hannigan and Joe continued the telling. Kate, fingers dancing along her keyboard, rolled to where Molly was standing at the foot of the bed.

She pressed 'send' and Shirley Temple said, ''course, it would be good if I had a mum of my own as well as a Gran-Gran.' She was learning to put on a lot of appropriate facial expressions to suit the voices, and Molly said it looked good. 'But what about the vacancy, Aunty Molly? I'm running out of definite possibles. None of them can burn bubble and squeak like you.'

'Then, my dear Kate, pray for a miracle.'

'Does it really work for new mums?'

'You can only try.' Aunt Molly smiled, then looked round, wondering where Sean had vanished to. She eventually spied him through the side window of the ward office, behind the nurses' station. He was just putting down the receiver.

He quickly emerged with an enquiring smile. 'Anybody fancy a trip to London?'

'All right!' grinned Michael wearily.

'"en?' asked Kate, ignoring her computer.

'Maybe next week when Michael's fit to travel.'

'What? All of us?' asked Nora.

'Everybody. We're invited for lunch.'

'Who with?' asked Joe.

'Katie, choose your best voice, and break out your prettiest dress. You've got a date with your definite possible.'